The Duchess of Wrexe

Hugh Walpole

THE DUCHESS OF WREXE

HER DECLINE AND DEATH

A ROMANTIC COMMENTARY

BY HUGH WALPOLE

Author of "Fortitude," etc.

NEW YORK
GEORGE H. DORAN COMPANY

TO
MY MOTHER
A SMALL EXPRESSION OF GRATITUDE
BEYOND WORDS

"And we'll have fires out of the Grand Duke's Wood."*Letter to Maria Gisborne*

THE RISING CITY: I

THE DUCHESS OF WREXE

NOTE: This is an age of Trilogies and Sequels. The title at the beginning of this book, "The Rising City: I," may lead nervous readers to fear yet another attempt in that extended and discursive direction.

To reassure them I wish to emphasize this point—that The Duchess of Wrexe *is entirely a novel complete and independent in itself. It is grouped, with the two stories that will follow it, under the heading of "The Rising City" because the three novels will be connected in place, in idea, and in sequence of time. Also certain of the same characters will appear in all three books. But the novels are not intended as sequels of one another, nor is "The Rising City" a Trilogy. —H. W.*

CONTENTS

BOOK I. THE DUCHESS

BOOK II: RACHEL

BOOK III: RODDY

BOOK I
THE DUCHESS

CHAPTER I
FELIX BRUN, DR. CHRISTOPHER, RACHEL BEAMINSTER—THEY ARE
SURVEYED BY THE PORTRAIT.

I

Felix Brun, perched like a little bird, on the steps of the Rede Art Gallery,
gazed up and down Bond Street, with his sharp eyes for someone to whom
he might show Yale Ross's portrait of the Duchess of Wrexe. The afternoon
was warm, the date May of the year 1898, and the occasion was the Young
Portrait Painters' first show with Ross's "Duchess" as its principal attraction.

Brun was thrilled with excitement, with emotion, and he must have his
audience. There must be somebody to whom he might talk, to whom he
might explain exactly why this occasion was of so stirring an importance.

His eyes lighted with satisfaction. Coming towards him was a tall, gaunt
man with a bronzed face, loose ill-fitting clothes, a stride that had little of the
town about it. This was Arkwright, the explorer, a man who had been lost in
African jungles during the last five years, the very creature for Brun's
purposes.

Here was someone who, knowing nothing about Art, would listen all the
more readily to Brun's pronouncement upon it, a homely simple soul, fitted
for the killing of lions and tigers, but pliable as wax in the hands of a master
of civilization like Brun. At the same time Arkwright was no fool; a
psychologist in his way, he had written two books about the East that had
aroused considerable interest.

No fool, Arkwright.... He would be able to appreciate Brun's subtleties and
perhaps add some of his own.

He had, however, been away from England for so long a time that anything
that Brun had to tell him about the London world would be pleasantly fresh
and stimulating.

Brun, round and neat, and a citizen of the world from the crown of his head
to the top of his shining toes, tapped Arkwright on his shoulder:

1

"Hallo! Brun. How are you? It is good to see you! Haven't seen a soul I know for the last ever so long."

"Good—good. Excellent. Come along in here."

"In there? Pictures? What's the use of me looking at pictures?"

"We can talk in here. I'll tell you all the news. Besides, there's something that even you will appreciate."

"Well?" Arkwright laughed good-humouredly and moved towards the door. "What is it?"

"The Duchess," Brun answered him. "Yale Ross's portrait of the Duchess of Wrexe. At last," he triumphantly cried, "at last we've got her!"

II

The Duchess had a small corner wall for her own individual possession. The thin glowing May sunlight fell about her and the dull gold of her frame received it and gave it back with a rich solemnity as though it had said, "You have been gay and unrestrained enough with all those crowds, but here, let me tell you, is something that requires a very different attitude."

The Duchess received the colour and the sunlight, but made no response. She sat, leaning forward a little, bending with one of her dry wrinkled hands over a black ebony cane, a high carved chair supporting and surrounding her. She seemed, herself, to be carved there, stone, marble, anything lifeless save for her eyes, the tense clutch of her fingers about the cane, and the dull but brooding gleam that a large jade pendant, the only colour against the black of her dress, flung at the observer. Her mouth was a thin hard line, her nose small but sharp, her colour so white that it seemed to cut into the paper, and the skin drawn so tightly over her bones that a breath, a sigh, might snap it.

Her little body was, one might suppose, shrivelled with age, with the business and pleasure of the world, with the pursuit of some great ambition or prize, with the battle, unceasing and unyielding, over some weakness or softness.

Indomitable, remorseless, unhumorous, proud, the pose of the body was absolutely, one felt, the justest possible.

2

The Duchess of Wrexe

On either side of the chair were two white and green Chinese dragons, grotesque with open mouths and large flat feet; a hanging tapestry of dull gold filled in the background.

Out upon these dull colours the little body, with the white face, the shining eyes, the clenched hand, was flung, poised, sustained by its very force and will.

Nothing in the world could be so fierce as that determined absence of ferocity, nothing so energetic as that negation of all energy, nothing so proud as that contemptuous rejection of all that had to do with pride.

It was as though she had said: "They shall see nothing of me, these people. I will give them nothing" ... and then the green jade on her bosom had betrayed her.

Maliciously the dragons grinned behind her back.

III

Arkwright, as he watched, was conscious suddenly of an overwhelming curiosity. He had in earlier days seen her portrait, and always it had been interesting, suggestive, provocative; but now, as he stood there, he was aware that something quite definite, something uncomfortably disconcerting had occurred; life absurdly seemed to warn him that he must prepare for some new development.

The Duchess had, he was aware, taken notice of him for the first time.

Little Felix Brun watched Arkwright with interest. They were, at that moment, the only persons in the room, and it was as though they had begged for a private interview and had been granted it. The other portraits of the exhibition had vanished into the mild May afternoon.

"She doesn't like us," Brun said, laughing. "She'd turn the dragons on to us if she could."

"It's wonderful." Arkwright moved back a little. "Young Ross has done it this time. No other portrait has ever given one the least idea of her. She must be that."

Brun stood regarding her. "There'll never be anything like her again. As far as your England is concerned she's the very, very last, and when she goes a heap of things will go with her. There'll be other Principalities and Powers, but never that Power."

"She's asked us to come," said Arkwright, "or, at any rate, asked me. I wonder what she wants."

"She's only asked you," said Brun, "to tell you how she hates you. And doesn't she, my word!"

There were voices behind him; Brun turned, and Arkwright heard him exclaim beneath his breath. Then in a moment the little man was received with: "Why, Mr. Brun! How fortunate! We've come to see my mother's portrait."

Arkwright caught these words, and knew that the lady standing there must be Lady Adela Beaminster, the Duchess's only daughter. He had never seen Lady Adela before, but it amused him now that she should resemble so exactly the figure that he had imagined — it showed, after all, that one could take the world's verdict about these things.

The world's verdict about Lady Adela was that she was dull, but important, bearing her tall dried body as a kind of flag for the right people to range themselves behind her — and range themselves they did. Standing now, with Felix Brun in front of her demanding a display of graciousness, she extended her patronage. Thin, with her sharp nose and tight mouth, she was like an exclamation mark that had left off exclaiming, and it was only her ability to be gracious, and the sense that she conveyed of having any number of rights and possessions to stand for, that gave her claim to attention.

Her black hat was harsh, her hair iron-grey, her eyes cold with lack of intelligence. Arkwright thought her unpleasant.

Standing a little behind her was a tall thin girl who was obviously determined to be as ungracious as a protest against her companion's amiability should require. The girl's thinness was accentuated by her rather tightly clinging white dress, and beneath her long black gloves her hands moved a little awkwardly, as though she were not quite sure what she should do with them. A large black hat overshadowed her face, but Arkwright could see that her eyes, large and dark, were more beautiful than anything else about her. Her nose was too thin, her mouth too large, her face too white and pinched.

Her body as she stood there was graceful, but not yet disciplined, so that she made movements and then checked them, giving the impression that she wished to do a number of things, but was uncertain of the correctness of any of them.

She was of foreign blood Arkwright decided — much too black and white for England. But it was her expression that demanded his attention. As she watched Felix Brun talking to Lady Adela, she seemed to be longing to express the contempt that she felt for both of them, and yet to have behind that desire a pathetic hesitation as to whether she had a right to be contemptuous of anyone.

It was the pathos, Arkwright decided, that one ultimately felt concerning her. She looked lonely, she looked frightened, and she looked "in the devil of a temper." Her black eyes would be beautiful, whether they were filled with tears or with anger, and it seemed that they must very often be filled with both. "I wouldn't like to have the handling of her," thought Arkwright, and then instantly after, "I'd like to take away some of that loneliness."

"She'll have a fine old time," he thought, "if she isn't too sensitive."

Lady Adela had now moved forward with Brun to look at the picture, but the girl did not move with them. She did not look at the portrait nor did she appear to take any interest in the other pictures. She stood there, making, every now and again, little nervous movements with her black gloves.

Arkwright moved about the gallery by himself a little, and he was conscious that the girl's large black eyes followed him. He fancied, as, for an instant he glanced back, that the Duchess from her high wall leaned forward on her cane just a little further, so that she might force the girl to give her attention. "That girl's got plenty of spirit," thought Arkwright, "I'd like to see a battle between her and the old lady. It would be tooth and nail."

Then once again the door opened — there was again an addition to the company. Arkwright was, at that moment, facing the girl, and as he heard the sharp closing of the door he saw in her eyes the welcome that the new-comer had received.

She was transformed. The pallor of her face was now flooded with colour, and she seemed almost beautiful as the hostility left her, and her mouth curved in a smile of so immense a relief that it emphasized indeed her earlier burden. Her whole body expressed the intensity of her pleasure; her awkwardness had departed; she was suddenly in possession of herself.

Arkwright's gaze went past her to the door. The man who stood there was greeting the girl with a smile that had in it both surprise and intimacy, as though they were the two oldest friends in the world, and yet he was astonished to see her there. The man was large, roughly built, with big limbs and a face that, without being good-looking, beamed kindness and good-nature. His eyes and mouth were sensitive and less ragged than the rest of him, his nose the plainest thing about him, was square and too large for his mouth. His hair was white, although he looked between forty and fifty years of age. His dress was correct, but he obviously did not give his clothes more consideration than the feelings of his friends required of him. Ruddy of face, with his white hair and large limbs and smiling good-humour, he was pleasant to look upon, and Arkwright did not wonder at the girl's welcome; he would be, precisely, the kind of friend that she would need—benevolent, understanding, strong.

They greeted one another, and then they moved forward and spoke to Lady Adela and Brun.

Arkwright watched them. There they all were, gathered together under the sharp eyes of the Duchess, and she seemed, so Arkwright fancied, to hold them with her gaze. Little Brun was neater than ever, and Lady Adela drier than ever by the side of the stranger. They talked; they were discussing the picture—their eyes travelled up to it, and for an instant there was silence as though they were all charging it with their challenge or surrender, as the case might be. The girl's eyes moved up to it with a sudden sharpened, thinning of the face that brought back the gleam of hostility that it had worn before. Then her eyes fell, and, with a smile, they sought her friend.

Arkwright did not know any reason for his interest, but he watched them breathlessly, and the sense that he had had, on first entering the room, of being on the verge of some new experience, deepened with him.

Brun was apparently suddenly conscious that he had left his friend alone long enough, for he detached himself from the group, shook hands with Lady Adela and the girl, bowed stiffly to the man and joined Arkwright.

"Seen enough?" he said.

"Yes," said Arkwright.

They went out together.

IV

The Duchess of Wrexe

Felix Brun and Arkwright were not intimate friends. No one was intimate with Brun, and the little man came and disappeared, was there and was not there, was absent for a year, and then back again as though he had been away a week, was, indeed, simply a succession of explanatory footnotes to the social history of Europe.

It was for the social history of Europe that he lived, for the eager penetrating gaze into this capital and that, something suddenly noted, some case examined and dismissed. Life is discovered most accurately by those who learn to watch for its accidents rather than its intentions, and it was always the things that occurred by change that gave Brun his discoveries. He was a cosmopolitan of a multitude of acquaintances, no friends, no occupation, an enthusiasm only for cynical and pessimistic observation, invaluable as a commentator, useless as a human being.

When, as was now the case, some chance meeting had assisted his theories his neat little body shone like a celluloid ball. If, having made his discovery, he might also have his audience to whom he might declare it, then his very fingers quivered with the excitement of it. His hands, white and thin and tapering, waved now. His eyes were on fire. As they walked up Bond Street one might have imagined air-bladders at his armpits, Mercury's wings at his heels. The quiet evening air was charged with him.

"Well," said Arkwright, smiling and looking down at his companion. "Who are they all?"

"Lady Adela Beaminster, Rachel Beaminster, Christopher——"

"Christopher?"

"Dr. Christopher, the Harley Street man. He's the Duchess' doctor, has been for years. The girl was the Duchess' granddaughter—Lady Adela's niece."

"Well?"

"The girl's coming out in three days' time. They're giving a ball in Portland Place for her. Nobody knows much about her. She's been educated abroad, and always kept very close when she's here. I shouldn't think the old Duchess loves her much. She loved the girl's father, but he married a Russian actress, bolted to Russia with her, and the old lady never forgave him. He and the actress were both killed in a Petersburg fire, and the child was sent home—only tiny then——"

7

"Ah! that explains the foreign air she had. She didn't look as though she loved her aunt very much either."

"No—don't suppose she does. But that's not it—that's not it."

They had arrived now at the top of Bond Street, and they paused for a moment to allow the Oxford Street traffic to sweep past them.

It was an hour of stir and clatter—hansoms, carts, lumbering omnibuses, bicycles, all were hurled along as though by some impatient hand, and the evening light crept higher and higher along the walls of the street, leaving grey-purple shadows beneath it.

They crossed over, and were instantly in a dim, golden, voiceless square. It was as though a door had been closed.

Brun still held Arkwright's arm. "Now we can talk—no noise. Francis Breton has come back."

To Arkwright this name, unfortunately, conveyed nothing.

"You don't know?" Brun was disappointed.

"Never heard of him."

"Fancy that. World of wonders; what have you been doing with your time? He is the Duchess's grandson, son of the beautiful, the wonderful Iris Beaminster, who eloped with Kit Breton thirty years ago. I believe the old Duchess pursued her relentlessly until the end. They were married only a few years and then Iris Breton committed suicide. Kit Breton beat her and was always drunk; an absolute rascal. There was one boy, and he wandered about Europe with his father until he was twenty or so. Then Kit Breton died, and the boy came home. Revenge on his grandmother was his one idea. He was taken up by her enemies, of whom she always had a goodly store, and they might have made something out of him, if he hadn't developed his father's habits and finally been mixed up in some gambling scandal, and forced to leave the country.

"You can imagine what all this was to the Beaminsters—the great immaculate Beaminsters—you can picture the Duchess.... He went and saw her once ... but that's another story. Well, abroad he went, and abroad he stayed—just now, coming out of the Gallery, I saw him——"

The Duchess of Wrexe

"You are sure?"

"Positive. There could be no mistake. He's just the same, a trifle tireder, a trifle lower down—but the same, oh yes."

It was when Brun was most excited that he was unmistakably the foreigner. Now little exclamations that escaped him revealed him. As a rule in England he was more English than the English.

They had left the square and were passing up Harley Street. The houses wore their accustomed air of profitable secrecy. The doors, the windows, the brass knockers, the white and chastened steps were so discreet that Sunday morning was the only time in the week when they were really comfortable and at home. In every muffled hall there was lying in wait a muffled man-servant, beyond every muffled man-servant there was a muffled waiting-room with muffled illustrated papers: only the tinkling, at long intervals, of some sharp little bell from some inner secrecy would pierce that horrible discretion. Upon both men that shining succession of little brass plates produced its solemnity.

Arkwright was nevertheless interested by Brun's discoveries. He was accompanied, as they talked, by that picture of the thin, dark girl moving restlessly her long, gloved hands. He could see now that look that she had flung at the picture.... Oh! she was interesting!

"But tell me, Brun," he said, "you go on so fast. As I understand you there are these two, Breton and the girl, both of them the result of tragedies.... Do they know one another, do you suppose?"

"No. The girl was only a small child when Breton was in England, and you can be sure that she was carefully kept out of his way. But now that he's back ... now that he's back!"

"It's the girl that interests me!" said Arkwright.

"Oh! the girl!" Brun was almost contemptuous. "There you go—English sentiment—missing all the time the great thing, the splendid thing."

"Explain," Arkwright said, laughing; "I know you won't be happy until you have."

"Why—it's the Duchess, the Duchess, the Duchess all the time. She's the centre of the picture; she is the picture. She's the subject."

Arkwright said nothing. Brun tossed his hands in the air.

"Oh—you English! No wonder you're centuries behind everything—you miss the very things under your nose. There's the Duchess, sitting there—a great figure as she has been these sixty years, but a figure hidden, veiled. There she has been for the last thirty years, shut up in that great house, wrapped about and concealed. Nobody knows what the matter was—I don't know. I should think Christopher's the only man who can tell. At any rate, thirty years ago she retired altogether from the world, and sees only the fewest of people. But all the ceremony goes on, dressing up, receiving, and the influence she has! She was powerful enough before she disappeared, but since! Why, there's no pie she hasn't her finger in: politics, society, revolution, life, death; nothing goes on without her knowledge, her approval, her disapproval——"

"Her family, poor dears!"

"Oh; they love it—at any rate, the ones who are left do. The rebels are the younger generation. Society in England, my dear Arkwright, is dissolved into three divisions—the Autocrats, the Aristocrats, and the Democrats. I take my hat off to the Aristocrats—the Chichesters, the Medleys, the Darrants, the Weddons. All those quiet, decorous people, poor as mice many of them, standing aside altogether from any movements or war-cries of the day, living in their quiet little houses, or their empty big ones, clever some of them, charitable all of them, but never asserting their position or estimating it. They never look about them and see where they are. They've no need to. They're just there.

"The Democrats are quite a new development—not much of them at present—the Ruddards, the Denisons, the Oaks—but we shall hear a lot of them in the future, I'm sure. They'll sacrifice anything for cleverness; they must be amused; life must be entertaining. They embrace everybody: actors, Americans, writers; they're quite clever, mind you, and it's all perfectly genuine. They're not snobs—they say, 'Here are our lands and our titles. You're common and vulgar, but you've got brains—you're amusing and we're well born—let's make an exchange. Life must be fun for us, so we'll have anyone with money or talent.'

"Then, last of all, the Autocrats—the Beaminsters, the Gutterils, the Ministers. I'm using Autocrat in its broadest sense, but that's just what they are. You must have your quarterings, and you must look down on those who haven't. But, more than that, everything must be preserved, and

10

continual ceremonies, dignities, chastities, restraints, pomps, and circumstances. Above all, no one must be admitted within the company who is not of the noblest, the stupidest, the narrowest.

"The Beaminsters are the bodyguard of this little army, and the Duchess is their general. There, behind her shut doors, she keeps it all going; an American like Mrs. Bronson, a democrat like George Lent, she spoils their games here, there, everywhere. So far all has been well. But at last there are enemies within her gates—that girl, Breton. Now, at last, for the first time in her life, she must look out."

He paused. They had reached Portland Place. To right and left of them the broad road was golden in the sun—dark trees guarded one end of it, bronzed roofs the other.

Two carriages stood like sentinels at the upper end.

Brun raised his hand as though he would invoke the spirit of it. "There, Arkwright, there's your subject. The Duchess, tiny, indomitable, brooding over this place. This square of London round the Circus, your prostituted street, this splendour, Harley Street, Morris Square with its respectability, Ferris Street with its boarding-houses, over them all the Duchess is ruling. There's not one of them, I dare fancy, that is not conscious of her existence, not one of them that will not see life differently when she is gone. Meanwhile, she'll fight for her Autocrats to the last breath, and she's got a battle in front of her that will take her all her time. And when she goes the Autocrats will go with her, the Beaminsters as Beaminsters will be done for; life here round the Circus will never be the same again. There's a new city rising, Arkwright, and the new citizens may forget, the Aristocrats may compromise with the Democrats, but they'll turn out the Autocrats. A lot of good things will go with them—good old things—but a lot of fine new things will come in."

As they passed out of Portland Place the wooden-legged crossing-sweeper touched his hat to them.

"Will he come in?" said Arkwright, laughing.

"Perhaps," said Brun gravely.

Arkwright shook his head. "You can talk, Brun, you can say a lot. But it's artificial the whole of it. Your subject, as you call it, is in the air. We're realists nowadays, you know."

11

Brun's flat stared at them with its hideous red brick and ugly shapelessness. No romance for Dent Street; the glittering expanse of Portland Place was gone.

"You can't be a realist only, if you're to do the Duchess properly," said Brun. "There's more than that wanted."

CHAPTER II
RACHEL

"My dear thing, it all comes back, as everything always does, simply to personal pluck. It's only a question, no matter when or where, of having enough." — Henry James.

I

No. 104 Portland Place was the house where the Duchess of Wrexe had lived now for sixty years. On the left as you go towards the park it had an air that no other house in the Place had ever been able to catch. There were certain buildings, Nos. 31, 26, 42, for instance, that were obviously doing their little best to present a successful imitation, but they were left a long, a very long way behind. The interesting thing would be to know whether No. 104 had had that wonderful "note" sixty years ago, when the Duchess came to it. Probably not; it was, beyond question, her presence that had thus given it its distinction. Its grim facade, without her, would not so strangely have hinted at beauties and wonders and glories within, nor would the windows have gleamed so finely, nor the great hall-door have symbolized such rich dark depths.

Here the temple of the Beaminsters, here, therefore, the shrine of all that is best and finest in English aristocracy. It was indeed the largest house in Portland Place, and most of the houses there were large, but, across that blank austere front more was written than mere size. It was Age at its most scornful, but observant Age, an Age that could compare one period with another, an Age that had not forgotten the things that belonged to its Youth.

There was very little, up and down Portland Place, at morning, at midday, at night, that the house did not perceive. Those high, broad, shining windows were not as other windows—there was assertion in their very bland stupidity.

Within the house was dark and cold, with high square rooms, wide stone staircase, and a curious capacity for clutching any boisterous or seedy humanity on the very threshold and strangling it.

From the hall the great stone staircase was the feature. It struck a chill, at once, into the heart of the visitor so vast was it, so cold and white, so uncompromising, so scornful of other less solid staircases. Very ancient, too—went back a long, long way and would last, just like that, for ever!

What people it must have known, what scenes, what catastrophes encountered! About it, on either side, the hall vanished into blackness; here a

13

gleaming portrait, there some antlers, here again an eighteenth-century gentleman with a full wig and the Beaminster nose and comfortable contempt in his eyes ... and, around and about it all, silence; no sound from any part of the house penetrated here.

Up the stone staircase, passages, doors, more family portraits, more staircase, more passages, more doors and, somewhere, in some hidden solemnity, the ticking of a clock, so lonely in all that silence that every now and again it would catch its breath with a little whir, as though it wondered whether it really could go on in the teeth of so contemptuous an indifference.

Rachel Beaminster's sitting-room overlooked Portland Place, and caught the sun on lucky days for quite a time. It was small, square of shape, like a box with a high window, a tiny fireplace, an arm-chair, and a squat table with a bright blue cloth.

Always during the two years that had been devoted to "finishing" in Munich she had had that little room, cosy, compact, before her. Now did it seem a little shabby, the carpet and tablecloth and curtains a little faded; it yet had its cosiness, there in the heart of the great waste and desert that the house presented to her.

The little silver clock on the mantelpiece had struck five: she had come back with Aunt Adela from the picture gallery, and, hearing voices in the Long Drawing-room (the voices said, "My dear Adela, we just came...." "Adela dear, how well...."), she slipped up the stairs and secured her own refuge, and rang for tea to be brought to her there.

She wanted to think: she wanted to lie in the arm-chair there with the window a little open and the evening air coming from the park across Portland Place curiously scented like the sea.

As she lay back in her chair her body seemed fragile, and, almost, in its abandonment, exhausted. Under the black eyes her cheeks and neck were very white, and her black hair gave it all the intensest setting.

She was tired, horribly tired, and she wondered, vaguely, as she lay there how she was ever to manage this life that, in three days' time, she must take up and carry, a life that offered, perhaps, a little freedom, a little release, but so many, so many terrors.

The Duchess of Wrexe

As her gaze took in the little room—its grey paper, a photograph of Uncle John, a book-case with poets, some miscellaneous and untidy-looking novels, and a number of little red Carlyles, a china cockatoo with an impertinent stare, a copy of Furze's "Ride," and a water-colour of red Munich roofs signed "Mary," a tiny writing-table with one old yellow photograph of a sad dark woman in a silver frame—these things were, it seemed the only friendly things she knew. Outside this room there was her grandmother, the house, London, the world—more and more horrible as the circles grew wider and wider.

At the mere thought of the things that she must, in three days' time, face, her heart began to beat so that she could scarcely breathe, and, with that beating, came the iron determination that no one should ever know.

She could not remember a time when these two emotions had not come together. She saw, as though it had happened only an hour ago, a tiny child in a black frock stumbling across endless deserts of carpet towards someone who looked older and more curious than anything one could have conceived possible. Someone sitting in a high carved chair, someone leaning on a stick, with two terrifying great dragons behind her.

The child was seized with such a panic that her breath came in little pumping gasps, her legs quivered and trembled, her mouth was open, her eyes like saucers. And then, suddenly, after what had seemed a century of time, there came the thin trembling voice: "Why, the child's an idiot!"

Since that awful day Rachel had determined that "no one should ever know." There had come to her, at that moment, the knowledge that round every corner there might lurk dragons and a witch. Sometimes they were there, sometimes they were not, but always there was the terror before the corner was turned.

Life for Rachel during those early years was one long determination to meet bravely that half-hour, from six to half-past. Every evening at five minutes before six down the long passages she would be led, then would come the short pause before the dark door, a pause when the beating of the child's heart seemed the only sound in the vast house; then the knock, someone's voice "Come in," then the slow opening of the door, the revelation of the strange dim room with the old mirrors, the purple carpet, the china dragons, and grandmother in the high carved chair. There was always, in the hottest weather, a fire burning, always Dorchester, a large ugly woman, behind the chair, always the cockatoo see-sawing on a golden perch and crying out every now and again with shrill, hostile cries. And then, in the centre of this, grandmother, with her terrible hands, her terrible nose, her terrible eyes, and, most terrible of all, her voice.

Rachel would sit upright on her chair, and very often nothing would be said throughout the half-hour. Sometimes Dorchester would ask questions, such as: "And what has Miss Rachel been doing to-day?" "Did Miss Rachel enjoy her walk in the park this afternoon?" "Has Miss Rachel enjoyed her lessons to-day?" Sometimes, and these were the terrible occasions, her grandmother would speak: "Well, have you been a good little girl?" or "Tell me what you have been doing, child."

At the sound of that voice the room would flood with terror: the child would still, by an effort of will, her body. She could feel now, from all that distance of years, the discipline that it had needed to steady her little black legs that dangled from her chair. She learnt, in time, to control herself so that she could give long answers in a grave, reserved tone.

The old lady never moved as she spoke, only bent forward and stared at her, as though she would see whether it were the truth that she were speaking.

As the days passed and Rachel grew older it was around this half-hour that the house ranged itself. The things in it—the rooms, the passages, the stairs, the high, cold schoolroom with its shining maps and large frigid table, the tapestry room, long and dark and mysterious with strange beasts and horsemen waving in the dusk, the white drawing-room so delicate and fragile that the furniture seemed to be all holding its breath as though a little motion in the air would dissipate it, the vast dining-room with the great hanging candelabra, and the family portraits and the stone fireplace—all these things existed only that that terrible half-hour might fling its shadow about the day.

The child was much alone; she had governesses, a music master, a drawing master, but from these persons, however friendly they might be, she held aloof. She told them nothing of her thoughts. She had behind her her very early years that were now to her like a dream; she did not know that it had ever really existed, that picture of snow and some dark kind figure that was always beside her protecting her, and in the air always a noise of bells. As she grew older that picture was not dimmed in the vision of it, but only she doubted its authenticity. Nevertheless, the memory provided a standard and before that standard these governesses were compelled to yield.

There were, of course, her uncles and her aunt. Aunt Adela was more immediately concerned in the duty of her niece's progress than any other, but as a duty she always, from the first, represented it. From that first morning, when she had given her cold dry cheek to the little girl to kiss until now, three days before Rachel's freedom, she had made no suggestion nor provocation of affection. "It is a business, my dear niece," she seemed to say, "that, for the sake of our family, we must go through. Let us be honest and deny all foolish sentiment."

To this Rachel was only too ready to agree. She did not like her Aunt Adela. Aunt Adela resembled a dry, wintry tree, a tree whose branches cracked and snapped, a tree that gave no hope of any spring. Rachel always saw Aunt Adela as an ugly necessity; she was not a thing of terror, but merely something unpleasant, something frigid and of a lukewarm hostility.

Then there were the uncles—Uncle Vincent, Uncle John, and Uncle Richard.

Uncle Vincent, the Duke, was over sixty now and very like his mother, withered and sharp and shrivelled, but he was without her terror, being merely dapper and insignificant, and his sleek hair (there was only a little of it very carefully spread out) and his white spats were the most prominent things about him. He was fond, Rachel gathered, of his racing and his club and his meals, and he was unmarried.

Uncle Richard had been twice Prime Minister and was a widower. He lived in a beautiful house in Grosvenor Street, and collected wine and fans and first editions. He was always very kind to Rachel, and she liked his tall thin figure, bent a little, with his high white forehead, gold-rimmed pince-nez on the Beaminster nose, and beautiful long white hands. She went to have tea with him sometimes, and this was an hour of freedom and delight, because he talked to her about the Elizabethans and Homer, and, when she was older, Nietzsche and Kant. She liked the warm rooms, with their thick curtains and soft carpets and rows and rows of gleaming glittering books, and he always had tea in such beautiful china and the silver teapot shone like a mirror. But she never felt that she was of the same value to him as a first edition would be, and he talked to her of the Elizabethans for their sake, and not for hers.

Lastly, there was Uncle John, and her heart was divided between Uncle John and Dr. Christopher. Uncle John was a dear. He was round and fat, with snow-white hair that had waves in it, and his face resembled that of a very, very good-natured pig. His nose was not in the least a Beaminster nose, being round and snub and his eyes beamed kindliness. Rachel, although she had always loved him, had long learnt to place no reliance upon him. His aim in life was to make it as comfortable, as free from all vulgar squabble and dispute, as pleasant for everyone everywhere as it could possibly be. He was a Beaminster in so far as he thought the Beaminsters were a splendid and ancient family, and that there was no other family to which a man might count himself so fortunate to belong. But he was kind and pleasant about the rest of the world. He would like everyone to have a good time, and it was vaguely a puzzle to him that it should be so arranged that life should have any difficulties—it would be so much easier if everything were pleasant. When, however, difficulties did arise they must at all costs be dismissed. There had been no time in his life when he had not been in love with some woman or other, but the hazards and difficulties of marriage had always frightened him too much.

He was not entirely selfish, for he thought a great deal about the wishes and comforts of other people, but unpleasantness frightened him, like a rabbit, into his hole. He lived the life of the "Compleat Bachelor" at 93 Portland Place, having a multitude of friends of both sexes, spending hours in his clubs with some of them, week-ends in country houses with others of them, and months in delightful places abroad with one or two of them.

He was very popular, always smiling and good-natured, and cared more for Rachel than for anyone else in the world ... but even for Rachel he would not risk discomfort.

There they all were, then.

Gradually they had emerged, for her, out of the mists and shadows, arranging themselves about her as possible protections against that horrible half-hour of hers. She soon found that, in that, at any rate, they would, none of them, be of use to her except Uncle John. Uncle Vincent did not count at all. Uncle Richard only counted as china or pictures counted.

Uncle John could not count as a very strong defence, it was true, but he was fond of her; he showed it in a thousand ways, and although he might never actually stand up for her, yet he would always be there to comfort her.

Not that she wanted comfort. From a very early age indeed she resolutely flung from her all props and sympathies and sentiments. She hated the house, she hated the loneliness, most of all she hated grandmother ... but she would go through with it, and no one should know that she suffered.

II
Then, when she was seventeen, came Munich.

18

On the day that she first heard that she was to go to Germany to be "finished" the flashing thought that came to her was that, for a time at any rate, the "half-hour" would be suspended. Standing there thinking of the days passing without the shadow of that interview about them was like emerging from some black and screaming, banging, shouting tunnel into the clear serenity of a shining landscape. Two years might count for her escape, and perhaps, on her return, she would be old enough for her grandmother to have lost her terrors — perhaps....

Meanwhile, that Germany, with its music and forests and toys and fairies, danced before her. Her two years in it gave her all that she had expected; it gave her Wagner and Mozart and Beethoven, it gave her Goethe and Heine, Jean Paul and Heyse, Hauptmann and Mörike, it gave her a perception of life that admitted physical and spiritual emotions on precisely the same level, so that a sausage and the Unfinished Symphony gave you the same ecstatic crawl down your spine and did not, for an instant, object to sharing that honour.

Munich also gave her the experience and revelations of May Eversley.

There were some twenty or thirty girls who were, with Rachel, under the finishing care of Frau Bebel, but Rachel held herself apart from them all. She could not herself have explained why she did so. It was partly because she felt that she had nothing, whether experience or discovery, to give to them, partly because they seemed already so happy and comfortable amongst themselves that they had surely no need of her, and partly because she feared that from some person or some place, suddenly round the corner there would spring the terror again. She could even fancy that her grandmother, watching her, had placed horrors behind curtains, closed doors, grimed and shuttered windows. — "If you think, my dear," she might perhaps be saying, "that you've escaped by this year or two in Germany, you're mightily mistaken. — Back to me you're coming."

But May Eversley was different from the other girls. She was different because she saw things without a muddle, knew what she wanted, knew what she disliked, knew what was delightful, knew what was intolerable.

To Rachel this clear-cut decision was more enviable than any other quality that one could have. At this stage of her experience it was the assent, so it seemed to her, that could give life its intensest value. "Sit down and see, without any exaggeration or false colouring, what you've got. Take away, ruthlessly, anything that you imagine that you've got but haven't. See what you want. Take away ruthlessly everything that you imagine that you would like to have but are not confident of securing. See what's happened to you in the past. Take away ruthlessly any sentimental repentances or sloppy regrets, but learn quite resolutely from your ugly mistakes."

Rachel's world had hitherto been limited very largely to the schoolroom in Portland Place, the park and Beaminster House, the country place-in-chief (three others, one in Leicestershire, one in Northumberland, one in Norfolk), but even within this limited country the terrific importance of those rules was driven in upon her.

She felt that her grandmother was clear-headed, but, no, none of the others—not Aunt Adela, nor the uncles, nor any of the governesses. She was allowed to meet one or two little boys and girls of her own age. She walked with them in the park, played with them at Beaminster House, had tea with them occasionally, but they were, none of them, clear-headed.

She was not priggish about this discovery of hers. She did not despise other people because their definite rules did not seem to them of importance. She did not talk about these things.

To see facts very steadily without blinking was impelled upon her by the necessity for courage. It was the only weapon wherewith to fight her grandmother. "Now," she might say to herself, "this half-hour of yours. Is it so bad? What definitely do you fear about it? Is it the knock at the door? Is it the crossing the room? Is it answering questions?"

So challenged her terror did fall, a little, away from her, ashamed at its inadequate cause. So she went to face every peril—"Is the danger really so bad? What exactly is it?..."

May Eversley was thin and spare, small with sharp features, pince-nez, hair brushed sternly back, and every inch of her body trained to the purpose that it was meant to fulfil. She rang her sentences on the air like coin on a plate. Meanwhile, as she explained to Rachel, she had been fighting since she was five. Her mother, Lady Eversley, was the widow of Tom Eversley, now happily deceased, once the most dissolute scamp in Europe. He had died leaving nothing but debts behind him. Since then his widow and his daughter had lived in three little rooms above a public house off Shepherd's Market, and the widow had battled to keep up the gayest of appearances. May had been, at a very early age, introduced to the struggle. "My silver mug and rattle were pawned to get a dress for mother to go to a drawing-room in. I shouldn't be here now if it weren't for an uncle, and it's the last thing he'll do for us. So back I go in two year's time—to do my damnedest."

Of course she was clear-headed — she had to be.

"There are only two sorts of people," she said to Rachel. "Like soup — thick and clear — the Clear ones get on and the Thick don't."

May obviously liked Rachel, but was amused by her. Nobody, it seemed to May, showed so nakedly her emotions as Rachel, and yet, also, nobody could produce, more suddenly, the closest of reserves. May, to whom the world had been, since she was six, a measured plain of contest, marvelled at the poignancy of Rachel's contact with it. "If she's going to be hurt as easily as this by everything, how on earth is she going to get through?"

Then, as the Munich days passed, May found, to her own delight, Rachel's keen sense of humour. Munich afforded enough food for it, and finally one discovered that Rachel smiled more readily than she trembled, but she hid her smile because, as yet, she was not sure of it.

"All she wants," May Eversley concluded, "is to be told things."

Nobody in the world could be better adapted to give out these revelations. London, to May Eversley, was an open book; moreover, the most stormy of battle-fields on which the combatants fought, were wounded, were slain, were gloriously victorious.

She told Rachel a great deal — a great deal about people, a great deal about sets and parties, a great deal about likes and dislikes. She had on her side one burning curiosity to know about Rachel's Duchess. "Is she as terrible, so tremendous as people say? Has she such a brain even now? Old Lady Grandon, who was a great friend when they were both girls, says that she wasn't clever then a bit — rather stupid and shy — but you never know. Jealousy on old Grandon's part, I expect. They say she's wonderful still."

Questions of taste never worried May Eversley, and it did not worry her now that Rachel might dislike so penetrating an inquisition. But at least May got nothing for her trouble. Rachel told her nothing.

May's final word was, "You care too much about it all — care whether it's going to hurt, whether it's going to be frightening or not. My advice to you is, just dash in, snatch what you can, and dash out again. It doesn't matter a hair-pin what anyone says. Everyone says everything in London, and nobody minds. They've all got the shortest memories."

Rachel, sitting now in her little room and thinking of Munich wondered how completely her own discovery of London would coincide with May's. May's idea of it was certainly not Aunt Adela's. Aunt Adela, Rachel thought, was far too dried and brittle to risk any sharp contact with anything. None of her uncles, she further reflected, liked sharp contacts, and yet, how continually grandmother provided them!

How comfortable all of them — Aunt Adela and the uncles — would be without their mother, and yet how proud they were of having her! For herself, Rachel faced her approaching deliverance with a tightening of all the muscles of her body. "I won't care. It shall be as May says — and there are sure to be some comfortable people about, some people who want to make it pleasant for one."

Then there was a tap at the door and Uncle John came in. Uncle John often came in about half-past five. It was a convenient time for him to come, but also, perhaps, he recognized that that approaching half-hour that Rachel was to have with his mother demanded, beforehand, some kind of easy, amiable prologue.

To-day, however, there was more in his comfortable smiling countenance than merely paying a visit warranted. He stood for a moment at the door looking over at her, rather fat but not very, his white hair, his pearl pin, his white spats all gleaming, a rosiness and a cleanliness always about him so that he seemed, at any moment of the day, to have come straight from his tub, having jumped, in his eagerness to see you, into his beautiful clothes, and hurried, all in a glow, to get to you.

"They're all chattering downstairs — chattering like anything. There's Roddy Seddon, old Lady Carloes and Crewner and some young ass Crewner's brought with him and your Uncle Dick looking bored and your Aunt Adela looking nothing at all — and so out of it I came."

He came over and sat on the broad, fat arm of her chair and looked out, in his contented, amiable way, over the light, salmon-coloured and pale, that now had persuaded Portland Place into silence. His eyes seemed to say: "Now this is how I like things — all pink and quiet and comfortable."

Rachel leant a little against his shoulder, and put her hand on his knee —

"You've had tea down there?"

"Yes, thank you — all I wanted. What have you been doing all the afternoon?"

He put his own hand down upon hers.

"Oh! Aunt Adela and I went to look at grandmother's portrait."

"Well?"

"It's as clever as it can be. To anyone who doesn't know her, it's the most wonderful likeness. It's what grandmother would like herself."

He caught the note in her voice that threatened the pink security of Portland Place. He held her hand a little tighter.

"In what way?"

"Oh, it's got the dragons and the tapestry and the purple carpet. All the coloured things that grandmother like so much and that help her so. Why, imagine her for a second in an ordinary room, in an old arm-chair with a worn-out carpet and everlastings on the mantelpiece; what would she do? The young man, whoever he is, has helped her all he can."

Rachel felt his grasp of her hand slacken a little.

"Yes, I know it's wrong of me to talk like that. But it's all so sham. It's like someone in one of those absurd fantastic novels that people write nowadays when half the characters are out of Dickens only put into a real background. I'm frightened of grandmother—you know I always have been—but sometimes I wonder whether——"

She paused.

"Whether there's anything really to be frightened of. And yet the relief when I can get off this half-hour every evening—the relief even now when I'm even grown up—oh! it's absurd!"

"Well, my dear, you're coming out, you're going to break away from all of us—you'll have your own life now to make what you like of."

"Yes, that's all very well. But I've been brought up all wrong. Most girls begin to come out when they're about ten and go on, more and more, until, when the time actually comes, well, there's simply nothing in it. I've never known anyone intimately except May, and now at the thought of crowds and crowds of people, at one moment I'd like to fly into a convent somewhere, and at the next I want to go and be rude to the lot of them—to get in quickly you know, lest they should be rude to me first."

Now that she had begun, it came out in a flood. "Oh! I shall make such a mess of it all. What on earth am I to talk about to these people? What do they want with me or I with them? What have I ever to say to anybody except you and Dr. Chris, and even with you I'm as cross as possible most of the time. Grandmother always thought me a complete fool, and so I suppose I am. If people aren't kind I can't say a word, and if they are I say far too much and blush afterwards for all the nonsense I've poured out. It doesn't matter with you and Dr. Chris because you know me, but the others! And always behind me there'd be grandmother! She knows I'm going to be a failure, and she wants me to be—but just to prove to her, just to prove!"

She jumped up, and standing in front of the window, met, furiously, a hostile world. Her hands were clenched, her face white, her eyes desperate.

"—Just to prove I'll be a success—I'll marry the most magnificent husband, I'll be the most magnificent person—I'll bring it off——"

Suddenly her agitation was gone—she was laughing, looking down on her uncle half humorously, half tenderly.

"Just because I love you and Dr. Chris, I'll do my best not to shame you. I'll be the most decorous and amiable of Beaminsters.—No one shall have a word to say——"

She bent down, put her arms round his neck, and kissed him. Then she sat down on the edge of the arm-chair with her hands clasped over his knee. Uncle John would not have loved her so dearly had he not been, on so many occasions, frightened of her. She was often hostile in the most curious way— so militant that he could only console himself by thinking that her mother had been Russian, and from Russia one might expect anything. And then, in a moment, the hostility would break into a tenderness, an affection that touched him to the heart and made the tears come into his eyes. But for one who loved comfort above everything Rachel was an agitating person.

Now as he felt the pressure of her hands on his knees, he knew that he would do anything, anything for her.

"That's all right, Rachel dear," was all that he could say. "You hold on to me and Christopher. We'll see you through."

24

The little silver clock struck six. She got up from the chair and smiled down at him. "If I hadn't got you and Dr. Chris—well—I just don't know what would happen to me."

Meanwhile Uncle John had remembered what it was that he had come to say. His expression was now one of puzzled distress as though he wondered how people could be so provoking and inconsiderate.

He looked up at her. "By the way," he said, "it's doubtful whether mother will see you this evening. You'd better go and ask, but I expect——"

"What's happened?"

"I may as well tell you. You're bound to hear sooner or later. Your cousin Francis is back in London. He's written a most insulting letter to your grandmother. It's upset her very much."

"Cousin Frank?"

"Yes. He's living apparently quite near here—in some cheap rooms."

May Eversley had, long before, supplied Rachel with all details as to that family scandal.

Rachel now only said: "Well, I'll go and see whether she would like me to come."

For a moment she hesitated, then turned back and flung her arms again about her uncle's neck.

"Whatever happens, Uncle John, whatever happens, we'll stick together."

"Whatever happens," he repeated, "we'll stick together."

His eyes, as they followed her, were full of tenderness—but behind the tenderness there lurked a shadow of alarm.

CHAPTER III
LADY ADELA
"At first it seemed a little speck,
And then it seemed a mist;
It moved and moved, and took at last
A certain shape, I wist."
The Ancient Mariner.

I

Lady Adela had returned from that visit to her mother's portrait with a confused mind. She was not used to confused minds and resented them; whenever so great an infliction came upon her she solved the confusion by dismissing it, by leaving her mind a blank until it should take upon itself to be clear again. To obtain that blank an interval of reflection was necessary, and now, to-day, that had been impossible. On returning, she had been instantly confronted by a number of people who required to be given tea and conversation, and no time had been allowed her in which she might resolve that her mind should be cleared.

Her confusion was that the portrait of her mother was precisely like, a most brilliant affair, and yet wasn't like in the least. Further than that, in some completely muddled way, it was in the back of her mind that her mother, suddenly, this afternoon, presented herself to her as not entirely living up to the portrait, as being less sharp, less terrible, less magnificent. Horror lest she should in any way be doubting her mother's terror and magnificence — both proved every day of the week — lay, like a dark cloud, at the back of her confusion.

She could not, however, extract anything definite from the little cluster of discomforts; old Lady Carloes and Lord Crewner, a young thing that Lord Crewner had brought with him, and her brother Richard were all waiting for tea, and floods of conversation instantly covered Lady Adela's poor mind and drowned it.

The Long Drawing-room, where they now were, was long and narrow, with two large open fireplaces, a great deal of old furniture rather faded and very handsome, silver that gleamed against the dark wall-paper, one big portrait of the Duchess, painted by Sargent twenty years ago, and high windows shut off now by heavy dark green curtains.

The Duchess, it was understood, did not approve of electric light and the house therefore disdained it. Parts of the room were lighted by candles placed in heavy old silver candlesticks. Round the fireplace at the farther end of the light shone and glittered; there the tea-tables stood, and round about them the company was gathered.

The rest of the room, hung in dark shadow, stretched into black depths, lit only now and again by the gleam of silver or glass as the light of the more distant fire flashed and fell.

The voices, the clatter of the tea-things, these sounds seemed to be echoed by the darker depths of the farther stretches of the room.

Lady Carlos was eighty, extremely vigorous, and believed in bright colours. She was dressed now in purple, and wore a hat with a large white feather. Her figure was bunched into a kind of bundle, so that her waist was too near her bosom and her bosom too near her chin and her chin too near her forehead.

It was as though some spiteful person had pressed all of her too closely together. But this very shapelessness added to her undoubted amiability; her face was fat and smiling, her hair white and untidy, and she maintained her dignity in spite of her figure. Nobody knew anything with certainty as to her income, but she was charitable, and ran a little house in Charles Street with a great deal of ceremony and hospitality. Her husband had long been dead and her two daughters had long been married, so that she was happy and independent. Many people considered her tiresome because her curiosity was insatiable and her discretion open to question, yet she was a staunch Beaminster adherent, an old friend of the Duchess, and saw both this world and the next in the proper Beaminster light.

Lady Adela depended on her a good deal, at certain times: she had forseen that the old lady would come to-day; she had heard of course of Frank Breton's arrival in town, she would demand every detail; Lady Adela knew that the account that she gave to Lady Carloes would be the account that the town would receive.

By the fire Lord Richard, Lord Crewner and the nondescript young man were talking together. Lady Adela caught fragments. "But of course Dilchester is incautious—when was he anything else? What these fellows need——"

That was her brother.

And then Lord Crewner, who believed that the windows of White's and Brook's were the only courts of Ultimate Judgment. "That's all very well, Beaminster, but I assure you, they were saying last night at the club ——"

As far as all that was concerned Lady Adela flung it aside. She must attend to Lady Carloes, she must give to her the version of Frank Breton's arrival that her mother would wish her to give. But what was that version? And was her mother really to be depended upon?

At so terrible a flash of disloyalty Lady Adela coloured. —Why were things so difficult this afternoon? And why had she ever gone to that picture-gallery?

Lady Carloes had, however, not yet arrived at Frank Breton. She never paid a visit anywhere without tabulating carefully in her mind the things that she must know before leaving the house. Her theory was that she was really very old indeed, and couldn't possibly live much longer, and that no moment therefore must be wasted. The more news that she could give and receive before her ultimate departure, the more value would her life have in retrospect.

She never went definitely into the exact worth that all the gossip that she collected might have for anybody or anything; as with any other collection it was pursuit rather than acquisition that fired the blood. At the back of her old mind was a perfect lumber-room of muddle and confusion—dusty gossip, cobwebs of scandal, windows thick with grime and tightly closed. There was no time left now to do anything to that. Meanwhile every day something was purchased or exchanged; muddle there might be, but, thank God, nobody knew it.

"You must be very busy about the ball, my dear."

"Yes—it means a great deal of work. It's so long since we've had anything here, but Norris is invaluable. You don't find servants like that nowadays."

"No, my dear, you don't. But, of course, it will go off splendidly. We're all so anxious that Rachel shall have a good time. It's the least we can do for your mother."

At the mention of Rachel Lady Adela's thoughts straightened for a second; that was where the confusion lay. It had been Rachel's attitude to the portrait that had caused Lady Adela's own momentary disloyalty. Of course Rachel hated her grandmother. Lady Adela made a little sound with her fingers, a sound like the clicking of needles.

"As far as Rachel is concerned nobody can tell possibly how she's going to take it all. I don't pretend to understand her."

Lady Carloes found this interesting—she bent forward a little. "We're all greatly excited about her. You've kept her away from all of us and one hears such different accounts of her. And of course her success is most important—as things are just now."

Lady Adela answered, "I can tell you nothing. She isn't in the least like any of us, and I don't suppose for a moment that she'll listen to anybody. She made a friend of May Eversley in Munich, and I don't think that was the best thing for her. But you know—I've talked about this to you before."

Not only had Lady Adela talked; all of them had done so. In the Beaminster camp this appearance that Rachel was about to make was of the last importance. There were enemies, redoubtable enemies, in the field. Rachel Beaminster's bow to the world was for the very reason that all the world was watching, a responsibility for them all.

But there were many rumours. Rachel was not to be relied upon—she hated her grandmother, she was strange and foreign and morose. Lady Carloes was not happy about it, and Lady Adela's attitude now was anything but reassuring.

John Beaminster came in. Lady Carloes liked him because he was good-tempered and injudicious. He told her a number of things that nobody else ever told her, and he had so simple a mind that extracting news from it was as easy as taking plums from a pudding. He did not come over to them at once, but stood laughing with Lord Crewner and his brother. He would come, however, in a moment, so Lady Carloes made a last hurried plunge at her friend.

"What's this I hear, my dear, about Frank Breton?"

"Yes, it's perfectly true. He's come back, and has taken rooms quite near here. He wrote to mother——"

Lady Carloes took this in with a gulp of delight. "My dear Adela! What did he say?"

"Oh! a very rude letter. He told mother that he knew that she would like him to be near at hand and that they ought to let bygones be bygones, and that he was sure that she would be glad to hear that he was a reformed character. Of course he hates all of us."

"What will you all do?"

"Oh! Nothing, of course. We gave him up long ago. By a tiresome coincidence he's taken rooms in the same house as my secretary, Miss Rand. I would send her away if she weren't simply invaluable. But it gives him a kind of a link with us."

"Monty Carfax saw him yesterday. He's lost his left arm, Monty says, and looks more of an adventurer than ever. So tiresome for your mother, my dear."

Then, as Lord John began to break away from the group at the fireplace and move towards them — —

"Roddy Seddon told me he might look in this afternoon.... Your mother's so devoted to him. He seems to understand her so well."

The two ladies faced one another. Their eyes crossed. Lady Carloes murmured, "Such a splendid fellow!" then, as Lord John's cheerful laugh broke upon them — —

"Isn't Rachel coming down?" she asked.

II

Lady Adela left her brother and Lady Carloes together and crossed over to the group at the fireplace. Of all her brothers, she liked Richard best. He seemed to her to be precisely all that a Beaminster should be: she liked his appearance—his fine domed forehead, his grey hair, his long rather melancholy face, his austere and orderly figure.

He had to perfection that reserve, that kind benignancy that a Beaminster ought to have; whenever Lady Adela questioned the foundations upon which the stability of her life depended he reassured her. Without saying anything at all, he gravely comforted her. That is what a Beaminster ought to do.

She knew, as she saw him standing there by the fire, that he would never doubt his mother. To him she would always be splendid and magnificent, and with what determination would he expel from him any base attacks on that loyalty! Lady Adela thought that power to expel resolutely and firmly everything that attacked the settled assurance of one's mind the finest thing in the world.

Lord Crewner was a thin, handsome man of any age at all over forty and under sixty. He was polished and brushed and scrubbed to such an extent that he looked like an advertisement of some fine old English firm that produced, at great cost and with wonderful completeness, Fine old English gentlemen. He believed in not thinking about things very much, because thinking let in Radicals and diseases and the poor, and made one uncomfortable. He loved the London that he knew, a London bounded by Sloane Square, the Marble Arch, Trafalgar Square and Westminster.

He was a bachelor, but might have married Lady Adela had the Duchess not refused to hear of Lady Adela leaving her; he adored the Duchess, although he was scarcely ever allowed to see her because he bored her. He always lowered his voice a little when talking to women, and heightened it a little when talking to men; to his valet he spoke in the voice that Nature had given him.

Lady Adela was reassured as she came towards them. Although she did not especially desire to marry Lord Crewner, the thought that he might, had affairs been differently arranged, have asked her, placed him, in her eyes, apart from other men. At any rate these two were comfortable to her, and, for a moment, she was able to dismiss Rachel and Frank Breton from her mind.

They talked easily beside the fireplace. The voices of Lady Carloes and Lord John, the pleasant murmur of the fire, the ticking clocks, all helped that lazy swaying of time and space about one, that happy reassurance that as the world had been so would it continue ever to be, and that the old emotions and the old experiences and the old opinions would always hold their own against all invasion and decay.

Lord Richard talked of Chippendale and some wonderful Lowestoft, Lord Crewner talked of Madeira and Lady Masters' new house; Lady Adela listened and was soothed.

Upon them all broke a voice:

"Sir Roderick Seddon, my lady."

There stood in the doorway the freshest, the most beaming of young men. He was tall and broad; his face was of a red-brick colour, and his dark London clothes, although they were well cut and handsome enough, were obviously only worn to please a necessary convention. His hair was light brown and cut close to his head, and his body had the healthy sturdiness of someone whose every muscle was in proper training.

He came forward to the group at the fireplace with the walk of a man accustomed to space and air and freedom; his smiling face was so genial and good-humoured that the whole room seemed to break away a little from its decorous and shining propriety. They were all pleased to see him. Lady Carloes and Lord John came over and joined the group, and they stood all about him talking and laughing.

Roddy Seddon was the only young man whom the Duchess permitted, and people said that that was because he was the only young man who had never shown any fear of her. The knowledge of this fact gave him in Lady Adela's eyes a curious interest. She beheld him always rather as she would have beheld anyone who had learnt an abstruse language that no one else had ever mastered or some traveller who was reputed to have said or done the most extraordinary things in some savage country. How could he? What talisman had he discovered that protected him? And then, swiftly on that, came the curious thought that she herself was glad that she had her terror, that she was proud, in some strange, inverted way, that any Beaminster could have the effect upon anyone that her mother had upon her.

But Roddy Seddon had another especial interest for her, for it was Roddy, all the Beaminsters had decided, who was to marry Rachel. Roddy was, in every way, the right person; not very wealthy, perhaps, but he had one nice place in Sussex, and Rachel would not, herself, be a pauper.

Roddy would never let the Beaminsters down; he hated all these new invaders as strongly as any Beaminster could. He hated this mixing of the classes, this perpetual urging of the working man to think.

"Lots of our fellows," Lady Adela had heard him say, "get along without thinkin'—why not the other fellers?"

She felt now that a conversation with Roddy would complete the soothing process that Lord Crewner and her brother had begun. He would finally reassure her.

She had no difficulty in securing him. Lady Carloes sat by the fire and talked to Lord Crewner, and the nondescript, and the two brothers departed.

When Roddy had drunk his tea, she led him away to the farther part of the long dim room, and there by that more distant fireplace the two of them sat, shadowy against the leaping light, their faces and their hands white and sharp and definite.

"Who else is dinin' on Thursday?"

She gave him names. "The Prince and Princess are coming, you know, but they aren't alarming. They've been often to see mother when they've been over here before. They're getting old enough now to be comfortable. He dances like anything still."

"I always like dinin' in the place you're dancin' at. You don't get that shivery feeling comin' up the stairs and puttin' your gloves on. You're one up on the others if you've been dinin'."

Lady Adela looked at him, and sighed a little impatiently. He was incredibly young and might, after all, let them down.

He was thirty now, but he looked not a day more than nineteen, and he always talked and behaved as though he were still in his last year at Eton. She opposed him, in her mind's eye, to that figure of Frank Breton that had been before her all day. How could a mere boy stand up against a scoundrel like that?

Moreover, she had heard stories about Roddy. Women had terrible power over him, she had been told, and then, with a glance at him, sighed again at the thought that her own time had gone by for having power over anybody, even Lord Crewner.

Well, after all, her mother knew the boy better than anyone did and her mother loved him—better than everyone else put together her mother loved him.

"How's Rachel takin' it?"

"How does Rachel take anything? She never says anything, and one never knows. She seems to have no curiosity, or eagerness."

"I was talkin' to May Eversley about her the other night. May says she'll be splendid."

"I don't like May Eversley"—Lady Adela nervously moved her hands on her lap. "I wish Rachel hadn't made such friends with her in Munich."

"Oh, May's all right." Roddy's blue eyes were smiling. "Took her down to Hurlingham yesterday and we had no end of a time."

It was a pity, Lady Adela reflected, that Roddy was so absolutely on his own.

His mother had died at his birth, and his father had been dead for five years now, and here it seemed to Lady Adela a curious coincidence that both Rachel and Roddy were orphans—and both so young.

She leant forward towards him—

"You can do a lot for Rachel, Roddy. You can help her to understand her grandmother, you can reconcile her to all of us."

"Oh! I say," Roddy laughed. "Perhaps she won't have anythin' to say to me, you know. My seein' your mother so often is quite enough——"

"No. She likes cheerful people—Dr. Christopher and John. You're in the same line of country, Roddy. She doesn't like me, and I haven't got the things in me to draw affection out of her. I'm not that kind of woman."

As a rule Lady Adela betrayed no emotion of any kind, but now, this afternoon, both to Lady Carloes and Roddy she had made some vague, indefinite appeal. Perhaps the news of Breton's arrival had alarmed her, perhaps her visit to the gallery with Rachel had really disturbed her. She seemed to beg for assistance.

Roddy analysed neither his own emotions nor those of his friends, but, this afternoon, Lady Adela did appear to him a little more human than before. He was suddenly sorry for her.

"Rachel'll be all right," he assured her. "Wait a bit. By the way, I met that little feller Brun yesterday—said he was comin' on Thursday. He's wild about your mother's picture——"

"Yes—we saw him at the gallery this afternoon. Rachel and I were there."

"Rachel! What did she think of it?"

"Seemed to take no interest in it at all. We were there only a few minutes —
—"

Silence fell between them, a silence filled with meaning. Lady Adela had
intended to speak about Breton—now, suddenly, she could say nothing. The
mention of the picture-gallery had brought back all her earlier discomfort—
she saw the picture, the eyes, the nose, the mouth, the white pinched cheeks.
Then she saw the great bedroom upstairs, the high white bed, the little
shrivelled figure.

Had Rachel pointed this contrast? Had Breton? Was it something that Roddy
had discovered already, something that had made his courage so easy for
him? What, what was going to be done with her if she were no longer
afraid? Why, on that terror, on that trembling service, were built the
foundations of all her life. How could she face that picture that the world
had of a splendid, historic, dominating figure if she herself saw only a sick,
miserable old woman tumbling to pieces, passing to decay?

The minutes had passed, and she had said nothing. Roddy must be
wondering at her silence. To her relief Lady Carloes came towards her to say
good-bye.

Roddy's eyes were puzzled. For what had she carried him off if she had
nothing to say to him?

III

When they were all gone she went up to her mother. Before the door she
paused. The house was very still, and her heart was furiously beating.

She opened the door, and at the sight of the room was instantly reassured.

Dorchester met her. "Her Grace went to bed early to-night. But she will see
you, my lady."

Lady Adela stepped softly to the farther door. All was well. About her,
around her, within her, was that same splendid terror, that same knowledge
that she was approaching some great presence that had been with her all her
life — —

35

As she opened the bedroom door and saw the high white bed she knew that her mother was more magnificent, more wonderful than any painted picture could possibly make her.

CHAPTER IV
THE POOL
I

On that same afternoon in another part of the house Miss Rand, Lady
Adela's secretary, finished her work for the day, and prepared to go home.

It was about a quarter-past six, and the May evening was sending through
the windows its pale glow suggesting soft blue skies and fading lights. Miss
Rand's room told you at once everything about Miss Rand. For efficiency
and neatness, for discipline and restraint, it could not be beaten. Miss Rand
herself was all these things, efficient and neat, disciplined and restrained.

Her room had against one white and shining wall a black and shining
typewriter. Against another wall was a table, and on this table were so many
contrivances for keeping letters and papers decent and docketed that it
made every other table the observer could remember seem untidy and
littered. There was nothing in the room superfluous or unnecessary, and
even some carnations in a green bowl near the window looked as though
they were numbered and ticketed.

Miss Rand was a little woman who appeared thirty-five when she was busy,
and twenty-five when someone was pleasant to her. When she was at work
the broad dark belt that she wore at her waist was her most characteristic
feature. Then, in keeping with this, was her dark hair, beautiful hair perhaps
if it had been allowed some freedom, but now ordered and sternly
disciplined; she wore no ornaments, and about her there was nothing out of
place nor extravagant.

Her face was full of light and colour and her eyes were beautiful, but no one
considered them: it was impossible to look beyond that stern shining belt —
one felt that Miss Rand herself would resent appreciation.

From ten o'clock in the morning until five o'clock in the evening the huge
Portland Place house absorbed her energies. She saw it sometimes in her
dreams, as a great unwieldy machine kept in place by her hand, but leaping,
did she leave it for an instant, trembling, soaring, carrying destruction with
it into the heart of the city.

Meanwhile her hand was upon it. From Norris the butler, from Dorchester
the guardian of the Duchess's apartments, down to the smallest, most
insignificant kitchen-maid, Miss Rand knew them all. There was, of course,
Mrs. Newton, the most splendid and elevating of housekeepers, but when
matters below stairs went beyond her control Miss Rand could always

arrange them. There was nothing, absolutely nothing, that, in the way of managing her fellow-creatures, Miss Rand could not do.

But it was because Miss Rand never occurred to any single creature in the Portland Place house as a sentient breathing human being that she succeeded as she did. She had no prejudices, no angers, no rebellions, no rejoicings. She was the little engine at the heart of the house that sent everything into motion. "One can't imagine her eating her meals, Mrs. Newton," Mr. Norris once said. "And as to her sleeping like you or me——"

To see her now as she put the final touches to her room before leaving it, arranging a paper here and a paper there, going to the bookshelf and pushing back a book that jutted in front of the others, setting a chair against the wall, placing the blotting-pad exactly in the middle of the table, finally taking her hat and coat and putting them on with the same careful and almost automatic distinction—this sufficiently revealed her. She seemed, as she looked for the last time about the room with her bright eyes, like some sharp little bird, perched on a window-sill, looking beyond closed windows for new adventure.

It was one of the striking points in her that her eyes always seemed to be searching for some disorder in some place outside her immediate vision.

She closed the door behind her. As she stepped into the passage someone was coming down the staircase to her right, and looking up she saw that it was Rachel Beaminster. Rachel was on her way from her grandmother's room, and before she saw Miss Rand standing there, waiting to let her pass, her face was grave and, in that half-light, strangely white. Then, as she saw Miss Rand, she smiled—

"Good evening, Miss Rand."

"Good evening, Miss Beaminster."

"I'm afraid that this ball is giving you a lot of trouble."

"I think that everything is arranged now, Miss Beaminster. I hope that it will be a great success."

Rachel sighed and then laughed.

"Don't I wish the whole stupid thing was over. And I expect you do too!"

Miss Rand smiled a very little. "It's good for the servants," she said. "They're always happy when they're really busy."

For a moment they stood there smiling. It occurred to Rachel that Miss Rand must be rather nice. She had never thought of her before as anything but Aunt Adela's secretary.

"Good night, Miss Rand."

"Good night, Miss Beaminster."

II

In Portland Place Miss Rand drew a little breath and paused. So many times during the last five years had she walked from Portland Place to Saxton Square, and from Saxton Square to Portland Place, that the streets and houses encountered by her had become individual, alive, always offering to her some fresh adventure or romance. Portland Place itself was no bad beginning, with its high white colour, its air, and its dark mysterious park hovering at the edge of it.

If one had not known, Miss Rand thought, one might have supposed that just beyond it lay the sea, so fresh and full of breezes was the air. The light was yellow now and the houses black and sharp against the faint sky. In another half-hour the lamps would be lit.

It was pleasant and fitting that the end of Portland Place should be guarded by the Round Church and the Queen's Hall. "Leave that calm and chaste society behind you," those places said, "but before you plunge into the wicked careless world (that is Oxford Circus) choose from us. Here you have religion or music, both if you will, but here at any rate we are, the very best of our kind."

The Queen's Hall looked shabby in the evening light, but Miss Rand liked that; it heightened her sense of the splendour within—Beethoven and Wagner and Brahms needed no illumination—it was your musical comedy demanded that.

Miss Rand liked good music.

Then there was the Polytechnic with wonderful offers in the windows enticing you to see Rome for eleven guineas, and Paris for three, and there was a hat shop with three glorious hats wickedly dangling on poles, and there was a pastry-cook's, a tobacconist's, and a theatre agency: all this variety paving the way between music and religion and the whirling, tossing, heaving melodrama of Oxford Circus.

Miss Rand loved Oxford Circus. It was like the sea in that it was never from one moment to another the same. Miss Rand knew the way that it had of piling the melodrama up and up, faster and faster, wilder and wilder, bursting into a frantio climax and then sinking back, for hours perhaps, into comparative silence. She knew all its moods, from its broom and milkman mood in the early morning, to its soiled and slinking mood somewhere between midnight and one o'clock.

Just now it was getting ready for the evening. Up Regent Street the cabs and buses were straining, the flower women with their baskets were bunched in splashes of colour against the distant outline of the Round Church. Out of every door people were pouring, and in the middle of the Circus three of the four lines of traffic were turned suddenly into something sleepy and indifferent by the hand of a policeman. For an instant the restless movement seemed to be crystallized—the hansoms, the bicycles, the omnibuses, the carts were all held, then at a sign the flow and interflow had begun once more; life was hurled in and hurled out again, stirred and tossed and turned, as though some giant cook were up in the heavens busy over a giant pudding.

And the light faded and the lamps came out, and Miss Rand, walking through two streets that were as dark and secret as though they were spying on the Circus and were going to give all its secrets away very shortly, passed into Saxton Square.

To-night Miss Rand had more to think about than Oxford Circus. She was tired after all the work that there had been during the last few days, and she always noticed that it was when she was tired that she was ready to imagine things. She had been imagining things all day and had found it really difficult to keep steadily to her proper work, but out and beyond her imaginations there was, before her, this definite, tremendous fact—namely, that she would find, this evening, on entering her little drawing-room, that Mr. Francis Breton was being entertained at tea by her sister and mother.

It was a quarter to seven now, so perhaps he had gone, but at any rate there would be a great deal that her mother and sister would wish to tell her about him. A week ago Mr. Francis Breton had come to live on the second floor in 24 Saxton Square, had put there his own furniture, had brought with him his own man-servant (a most sinister-looking man). These matters might have remained (although, of course, Miss Lizzie Rand's connection with the

Beaminster family made his arrival of the most dramatic interest) had not Miss Daisy Rand (Miss Lizzie Rand's prettier and younger sister) happened, one evening, to run into Mr. Breton in the dark hall; she screamed aloud because she thought him a burglar, became very shaky about the knees, and needed Mr. Breton's assistance as far as the Rand drawing-room. Here, of course, there followed conversation; finally Mr. Breton was asked to tea and accepted the invitation.

On this very afternoon must this tea-party have taken place. Lizzie Rand knew her mother and sister very well, and she had, long ago, learnt that their motto was, "Let everything go for the sake of adventure." That was well enough, but when your income was very small indeed, and you wished to do no work at all and yet to have your home pleasant and your life adventurous, certainly someone must suffer. Everything had always fallen upon Lizzie.

Mrs. Rand's husband had been a colonel and they had lived at Eastbourne; on his death it was discovered that he had debts and obligations to a lady in the chorus of a light opera then popular in London. The debts and the lady Mrs. Rand had covered with romance, because she considered that they were due to the Colonel's insatiable appetite for Adventure—but, romance or no, there was now very little to live upon.

They moved to London. Daisy was obviously so pretty that it would be absurd to expect her to work, and "she would be married in a minute," so Lizzie had, during the last five years, kept the family. It would be impossible to give any clear idea of the effect on Mrs. Rand that Lizzie's connection with the Beaminster family had. Mrs. Rand loved anything that was great and solemn and ceremonious; she loved Royalties, bands and soldiers gave her a choke in her throat, the "Society News" in the Daily Mail was like a fine picture or a splendid play. She was no snob; it was simply that she saw life as a background to slow stately figures gorgeously attired.

In all England there was no one like the Duchess of Wrexe; in all England there was no family like the Beaminster family.

Even Royalty had not quite their glow and glitter; Royalty you might see any day, driving, bowing, smiling. The Queen had a smile for everyone and was at home in the merest cottage; but the Duchess, the Duchess—no one, not even Lizzie, on whose shoulders the whole fortunes of the Beaministers rested, ever saw.

There was nothing about the Beaminsters that Mrs. Rand did not know, and so of course she knew all about the unhappy past history of Francis Breton. That any Beaminster should have behaved rather as her own dead colonel had once behaved gave one a link at once.

Mrs. Rand's mind was, at the best of times, a confused one, and, in the dead of night, she could imagine a scene in which the wonderful Duchess would send for her, give her tea, press her hands and say, "Ah! Dear Mrs. Rand, our men-folk—your husband and my grandson—what trouble they give us, but we love them nevertheless."

So romantic was Mrs. Rand's mind that she saw nothing extraordinary in the coincidence of Mr. Breton's arrival at their very doors. Of course he would arrive there! Where else could he arrive? And of course he would fall in love with Daisy, would reform for her sake; there would be a splendid marriage; the Duchess would thank Mrs. Rand for having saved her grandson.

Yes, Mrs. Rand had an incurably romantic mind.

Lizzie knew all about her mother's mind, and Daisy's mind. She dealt with them very much as she dealt with Lady Adela's mind or Lord John's mind. They were all muddled people together, and the clear-headed people had the advantage over them.

So with regard to her mother and sister Lizzie had developed a protective feeling; she wished to save them from the inroads of the clear-headed people who might so rob and devour them.

She saw also that her connection with the Beaminster family was a very bad thing for her mother and sister because it encouraged them to be romantic and muddled and idle. But, at present, at any rate, there was nothing to be done.

As she turned into the grey silence of little Saxton Square she did hope that her mother and sister would not behave too outrageously about Mr. Breton. She was interested, she would like to see him; his whole possible relation to the Duchess, to Lady Adela, to Miss Beaminster set her own imagination working. She did hope that her mother and sister would not behave so disgracefully that they would frighten Mr. Breton away so that he would never come near them again.

And then, as she reached the door of No. 24, she thought for a moment of Rachel Beaminster.

"I like her," she thought, "I'd like to know her. She's never spoken to me like that before."

III

No. 24 had three floors: the ground floor was occupied by the Rands, the first floor by Breton and the second floor by an old decrepit invalid called Cæsar and his son, who was a bank clerk.

Down in the basement lived Mr. and Mrs. Tweed, owners of the whole house; he had been a butler and she a housekeeper, and exceedingly respectable they were. Every floor had its own kitchen and every lodger found his own servants, but the hall was common for all the three floors, and if young Mr. Cæsar came in at two in the morning and banged the front door everybody knew about it.

It must have been a fine old house in its day, No. 24, and there were still fine carvings, good fireplaces and ceilings, high broad windows and thick solid walls. Mrs. Rand liked to think that her drawing-room had once seen fine eighteenth-century ladies reflected in its mirrors, heard the tapping of high-heeled shoes on its polished floors. The thought of those glorious days gave her own rather faded furniture a colour and a touch of poetry. Sometimes, Lizzie thought with a sigh, if her mother had inhabited a plain nineteenth-century house living within a small income would have been easier for her.

Lizzie, entering the drawing-room, knew at once that Mr. Breton was still there. She saw that he was tall and spare, that he had no left arm, that he had a rather small pointed brown beard and eyes that struck her as fierce and protesting. She did not know whether it were the beard or the eyes or the absence of the arm, but at her first vision of him she said to herself: "He's too dramatic; it's not quite real," and her second thought was: "He's just what mother will like him to be!"

He was standing against the window, and he wore a black suit, a little faded. The blinds had not been drawn, and the square beyond the window was elephant grey, with the lamps at each corner a dim yellow; there was a thin rather ragged garden in the middle of the square, and in the garden was a statue of a nymph, old and deserted, and some trees now faintly green. Over it all was a sky so pale that it was more nearly white than blue.

Although the curtains had not been drawn a lamp in the middle of the room was lit and the fire burnt merrily. The furniture had once been good and was now respectable. There were several photographs, a copy of "The Fighting

43

Téméraire," and a water-colour sketch of "Lodore Falls." There was a book-case with the works of Tennyson, Longfellow, and Miss Braddon, and on one of the tables two French novels, one by Gyp and one by Zola.

Mrs. Rand would have been handsome had her grey hair been less untidy and her clothes more uniform in design and colour. Her blouse was cut too low and she wore too many rings; her eyes always wore a lying-in-wait expression, as though she might be called on to be excited at any moment and didn't wish to miss the opportunity.

Daisy Rand was pretty and pink with light fluffy hair. All her clothes looked as though their chief purpose were to reveal other clothes. The impression that she left on a casual observer was that she must be cold in such thin things.

Lizzie, looking at Frank Breton, could not tell what impression her sister and mother had made upon him. "At any rate," she thought, "he's stayed a long time. That looks as though he had been entertained." She was introduced to him and liked the cool, firm grasp of his hand. She saw that her mother and Daisy were quiet and subdued—that was a good thing. She caught, before she sat down, his instinctive look of surprise. She knew that he had not expected her to be like that.

"We've been telling Mr. Breton, Lizzie," said Mrs. Rand, "all about the theatres. He's been away so long that he's quite out of touch with things."

Lizzie always knew when her mother was finding conversation difficult by the amount of enthusiasm and surprise that she put into her sentences.

"So terrible it must be to have missed so many splendid things."

"I assure you, Mrs. Rand," said Breton, "that I've been seeing other splendid things in other countries. Now I'm ready for this one again."

Mrs. Rand was silent and at a loss. Lizzie knew the explanation of this. Her mother had been trying to venture on to the subject of Breton's family and had found unexpected difficulty. Perhaps there had been something in Breton's attitude that had warned her.

They talked for a little while, but disjointedly. Then suddenly there was a knock at the door, and young Mr. Cæsar, a bony youth with a high collar and an unsuccessful moustache, came in. He had not very much to say, but

44

the result of his coming was that Lizzie found herself standing at the
window with Breton; they looked at the square now sinking into dusk.

He spoke; his voice was lowered: "I understand that you are secretary to my
aunt, Miss Rand?"

"Yes," she said.

"They haven't heard of my return with any great delight, I'm afraid?"

She noticed that he was trying to steady his voice, but that it shook a little in
spite of his efforts.

"I don't know," she said, looking up and smiling. "I'm far too busy to think of
things that are not my concern."

"They are giving a ball to-morrow night for my cousin?"

"Yes."

"Do you see much of her?"

"No—nothing at all. She's been abroad, you know."

"Yes, so I heard. But I saw her driving yesterday. She looks different from
the rest of them."

All this time, as he spoke to her, she was conscious of his eyes; if only she
could have been sure that the protest in them was genuine she would have
been moved by them.

She did not help him in any way, and perhaps her silence made him feel that
he had done wrong to speak to her about his affairs. They looked at the
square for a little time in silence. At last, speaking without any implied
fierceness, he said:

"You know, Miss Rand, I'm a wanderer by nature, and sometimes I find
cities very hard to bear. Do you know what I do?"

"No," she said.

"Turn them into other things. Now here in London, do you never think of
streets as waterways? Portland Place, for instance, is like ever so many rivers

I've seen, broad and shining. And some of those high thin streets beside it are like canals; Oxford Circus is a whirlpool, and so on— —"

He laughed. "I get no end of relief from thinking of things like that."

"You hate cities?" she asked him.

"No—not really. But it depends how they receive you. If they're hostile— —" He shrugged his shoulders.

"And this square?" she said. "What's this square?"

"A pool. All the houses hang over it as though they were hiding it. It's restful like a pool. There's no noise— —"

The statue of the nymph had disappeared. The trees were a black splash against the lamp-lit walls. Lights were in the windows.

He seemed suddenly conscious that it was late. When he had gone Lizzie stood, for some time, looking into the square and thinking how right he had been.

All that evening Daisy was out of temper.

CHAPTER V
SHE COMES OUT
I

Downstairs the dinner-party was at its height. Mrs. Newton, the housekeeper, went softly down the passages to give one last glimpse at the ballroom. There it lay, like a great golden shell, empty, expectant. The walls were white, the ceilings gold; on the white walls hung the Lelys, the Van Dycks, and at the farther end of the room Sargent's portrait of Her Grace, brought up, for this especial occasion, from the Long Drawing-room. There was the gleaming, shining floor, there the golden chairs with their backs against the wall, and there before each picture a little globe of golden flame ministering to its beauties, throwing the proud pale faces of the old Beaminsters into scornful relief, and none of them so scornful as that Duchess in the far distance, frowning from her golden frame.

Mrs. Newton was plump and important. She worshipped the Beaminster family, and it yielded her now intense satisfaction to see these rooms, that were used so seldom, given to their proper glory and ceremony. For a moment as she stood there and felt the fine reflection of all that light upon the shining floor, absorbed the silence and the space and the colour, she was uplifted with pride, and thanked her God that she was not as other women were, but had been permitted by Him to assist in no small measure in the glories and splendours of this great family.

Then, with a little sigh of satisfied approval, she softly walked away again.

II

Two hours later Rachel Beaminster, standing a little behind her aunt, saw the people pressing up the stairs. To those who watched her, she seemed perfectly composed, her flushed cheeks, her white dress, her dark hair and eyes gave her distinction against the colour and movement of the room.

Her eyes were a little stern, and her body was held proudly, but her hands moved with sharp spasmodic movements against her dress.

As she stood there men were brought up to her in constant succession and introduced. They wrote their names on her programme, bowed and went away. She smiled at each one of them. Before dinner she had been introduced to the Prince—German, fat and cheerful—and the second dance of the evening was to be with him. Some of the men who had been dining in the house she already knew—Lord Crewner, Roddy Seddon, Lord Massiter, and others—and once or twice now the faces that were led up to her were familiar to her.

The great ballroom seemed to be already filled with people, and still they came pressing up the stairs.

Rachel was miserably unhappy. For one moment before she had left her room, where her maid had stood admiringly beside her, when she herself had seen the reflection of the white dress and the dark hair and the flushed cheeks in the long mirror, for one great moment she had been filled with exaltation. This ball, this agitation, this excitement was all for her. The world was at her feet. The locked doors were at last rolling open before her and all life was to be revealed.

Pearls that Uncle John had given her were her only ornament. They laughed at her from the mirror, laughed and promised her success, conquest, glory. Life at that instant was very precious.

But, alas! the dinner had been a terrible failure. She had sat between Lord Crewner and Lord Massiter, and had no word to say to either of them. Lord Massiter was middle-aged and hearty and kind, and he had done his best for her, but she had been paralysed. They had talked to her about the opera, the theatres, hunting, books, Munich; she had had a great deal to say about all these things, and she had said nothing. Always within her there seemed to be rivalry between the Beaminster way of saying things and the other way. When Lord Crewner said to her, "What I like in music is a real cheerful little piece that one can go to after dinner, you know," there were a whole number of Beaminster observations to make. But as soon as they rose to her mouth something within her whispered, "You know that you don't mean that. That's at second hand. Give him your opinion." And then that seemed presumption, so she said nothing.

It was all wretched and quite endless. Uncle John sent her encouraging smiles every now and again, but she felt that he must be disappointed at her failure. The food choked her. The tears filled her eyes and it was her pride only that saved her. Through it all she felt that her grandmother upstairs in her bedroom was planning this.

Afterwards the Princess, seeing perhaps that she was unhappy, was kind and motherly to her, and told her funny stories about her childhood in Berlin. But all the time Rachel was saying to herself, "You're a fool. You're a fool. You've got no self-control at all."

She had been dreading the introductions to so many young men, but she found that that was easy enough. They were not young men; they were simply numbers on her programme and they vanished as soon as they came.

Then the band in the distance began to play an extra, whilst the young men wandered about and discovered their friends, and the sound of the music cheered her. It amused her now to watch the people as they mounted the stairs. She noticed that all the faces were grave and preoccupied until a moment before the arrival at Aunt Adela, and then a smile was tightly fastened on, held for a moment, and then dropped to give way to the preoccupation again.

The room was so full now that it seemed that it would be quite impossible for any dancing to take place. Uncle John was working very hard at introducing people to one another, and as she saw his good-natured face and his white hair her heart went out to him. If everyone were as kind as Uncle John how nice the world would be! Meanwhile her eyes anxiously watched the stairs, and as every woman turned the corner at the bottom the question was—"Was this May Eversley?"

There had been a battle about May. Aunt Adela did not like her, disapproved of her, would not hear of inviting her. Very well, then, Rachel would not come to the ball at all. They could give the ball for somebody else. If May were not asked Rachel would not come.

So Lady Eversley and May had both been asked, and of course they had accepted.

Rachel waited and gazed and was continually disappointed. The extra was over and soon the first dance would begin; with the second dance would arrive the Prince and Rachel would have no talk with May at all. It was too bad of May to be late. She had promised so faithfully—Ah! there she was with her air of one confidently conducting a most difficult campaign. She mounted the stairs like a general, gave Lady Adela the tiniest of smiles, and was at Rachel's side.

That clasp of May's hand filled Rachel's body with confident happiness. May's hardy self-control, her discipline derived from some stern old Puritans, dim centuries away, was all waiting there at Rachel's service.

"How late you are!"

"Mother was such a time. And then we couldn't get a cab. How are you, Rachel?"

"Dinner was terrible—all wrong. I hadn't a word to say to anyone. I'm better now that you've come."

"Is the Prince here?"

"Yes. I'm dancing the next dance with him. The Princess was very kind after dinner. Oh! May, dinner was a disaster, an absolute disaster!"

"Not nearly so bad as you thought, you may be sure. Things always seem so much worse."

And now May had been discovered. Gentlemen young and old dangled their programmes in front of her, were received, were dismissed. May had the air of a general, sitting fiercely in his tent and receiving reports from his officers as to the progress in the field. Confident young men were instantly timid before her.

The first dance was over. Against the white splendour vivid colours were flung and withdrawn. Threads and patterns crossed and recrossed, and then presently the glittering floor was waste and deserted; on its surface was reflected dark gold from the shining walls.

The second dance came, and with it the Prince. Rachel had now lost all sense of the ball having been given in any way for herself. The dancing, it comforted her to see, was not of the very best, and at once she found that she had herself nothing to fear. The Prince danced well, and soon she was lost to all sense of everything save the immediate joy of rhythm and balance, and the perfect spontaneity of the music and her body's acknowledgment of it.

When it came to an end, and they were sitting in a corner, somewhere, he was a fat middle-aged man again, and she Rachel Beaminster, but she knew now for what life was intended.

After that, for a long period, her dancers did not concern her. They were there simply to supply her with that ecstasy of rhythm and movement. Sometimes they could not supply her because they were bad dancers, and one of her partners was indeed so bad that she ruthlessly suggested, after one turn round the room, that they should sit out. Then she sat in a room near at hand, irritated by the sound of that glorious music, and paying very scant attention to the young man's stammered apologies, his information about his experiences of Paris and the way that he shot birds in Scotland.

She was to go down to supper with Roddy Seddon, and she was waiting that experience with some curiosity. If her grandmother were so fond of him, then he must be a disagreeable young man, and yet his appearance was not disagreeable.

He looked as though, like Uncle John and Dr. Chris, he were one of the comfortable people. Dr. Chris, by the way, had not arrived. He had told her that he might not be able to escape until late hours.

And so, as the evening advanced, her happiness grew; impossible now to understand that speechlessness at dinner, impossible to find reasons for that earlier misery. She danced now both with Lord Massiter and with Lord Crewner, and said exactly what she thought to both of them; impossible now to imagine anything but that the world was an enchanting, thrilling place especially invented for the happiness of Miss Rachel Beaminster.

III

Uncle John had been promised a dance; his moment arrived. He had watched her during the early part of the evening, and had been afraid that she was not at all happy.

She was so unlike other girls, and that first miserable hour seemed to him the most tragic omen of her future career.

"How is she ever to get on if she takes things as badly as this? I wish I could help her. I know so exactly how she must be feeling."

But imagine him now confronted with a figure that shone with happiness, with success, with splendour!

She caught his arm—"Come, Uncle John, we won't dance. We'll talk. Up here—There's no one in this room."

She ran ahead of him, found a corner for them both, and then, pushing him on to a sofa, twisted round in front of him, turning on her toes, flashing laughter at him, sitting down at last beside him, and then kissing him.

"Oh, my dear! I'm so glad," he said. "I thought you were miserable."

"So I was—at first—perfectly wretched. Now it's all splendid—glorious!"

This was to him an entirely new Rachel. In her movement, her excitement, her immediate glad acceptance of the life that an hour ago she had feared with such alarm, he perceived an element that was indeed foreign to all things Beaminster. And this new attitude reminded him with renewed sharpness that he could not now hope to hold the old Rachel with the intimate affection that had been his before. She was slipping from him—slipping ... even as he watched her, she was going.

She laid her hand upon his arm: "Uncle John, I'm a success! I am really. I can dance, dance beautifully! I can put these young men in their places. They're frightened!... really frightened."

"Of course—you're lovely—the biggest success there's ever been. But what was the matter with you at dinner?"

"Yes. Wasn't that dreadful? Everything went wrong, and the only thing I could think of was how glad grandmamma would be. I had a kind of paralysis."

Uncle John nodded his head. "I know exactly what it's like."

"Well, I shall never let myself be so stupid again—never! I swear it!" They sat in silence for some time, she, restless, straining towards the music, he a little overcome by her happiness.

There was a pause between the dances and then the band began once more.

"Have you danced with Roddy Seddon yet?"

"No. What's he like?"

"Oh! he's nice—you'll like him."

"I don't expect to. He's a friend of grandmamma's. Hark! There's the band again!... Come along, back we go!"

Smiling, radiant, she hung upon his arm. Afterwards, standing in a doorway, he watched her.

He sighed. "What a selfish old pig I am!... But she'll never be mine again."

IV

Uncle John held only for a moment Rachel's attention. No single person now, but rather a gorgeous pattern that the whole evening was weaving about her. She saw the lights, she heard the music, she felt the movement of her body, she gathered through a haze of happiness the faces of her uncles and Aunt Adela and others whom she knew, but now for the first time in her life she knew what happiness, happiness without thought, or doubt, or foreboding could be.

Thus it was that she came to Roddy Seddon, who was certainly enjoying himself: this, however, was not the first ball of his life nor even, if all the truth were known, his best. He had expected it to be solemn and sedate — you could not hope to find here the jolly kind of dance that they had had at the Menets', for instance, last week; that would not be possible in a Beaminster household.

It was all, to be honest, a little old-fashioned. Things were moving a bit faster nowadays. Waltzes and Lancers were all very well, but one might have had a cotillon, something unexpected! However, May Eversley and one or two other girls had had the right kind of go about them. He smiled a little and tugged at his short bristling yellow moustache, and then discovered that it was time to take Rachel Beaminster down to supper.

This event was of more than ordinary interest to him. He was perfectly aware that most of his friends and relatives thought that it would be a very good thing for him to marry Rachel Beaminster. He was, himself, not scornful of this idea.

He was thirty-two, and it was time that Seddon Court in Sussex had a mistress; his life had been varied and exciting and it was right now that he should make some ties. There were a number of other reasons in favour of his marrying.

As to Rachel Beaminster, she was not pretty, but she was interesting. She was unusual; moreover she was a Beaminster, and an alliance with that ancient family would be, past dispute, a magnificent alliance. But the element in it all that intrigued him most was the fact that nobody could tell him anything about Rachel, even May Eversley who knew her so well was not sure about her. "You'll go on being surprised," she had said.

Surprise, indeed, was waiting for him this evening. On the few occasions that he had seen Rachel he had seen her grave, shy, a little awkward, most reserved. Now she met him as though she had known him for years, glowing, almost pretty, so burning were her eyes. At supper she laughed, called across the room to May, agreed with everything that everybody said, and with it all was younger than any girl that he had ever known. The girls who were Roddy's friends talked about life at times more boldly than he would have talked with his men friends, and were, at all events, for ever hinting at the things that they knew.

Rachel hinted at nothing; she kept nothing back, she allowed him no disguises.

"Oh! don't I wish," she cried, "that this night could go on for ever just like this"—and he, taking the compliment to himself, agreed with her. He had expected to find someone haughty and cold, a young Aunt Adela with a dash of foreign temper.

He found someone entirely delightful. Afterwards, when they sat out on a balcony overlooking Portland Place, he was encouraged to talk about himself.

"I like all this, you know," he said, waving his hand at the grey mysterious street that the pale lamps so mournfully guarded. "I like this air comin' along from the park. I'm all for the open, Miss Beaminster—horses and dogs and rushin' along with the wind at your back. It's a rippin' little place I've got down in Sussex. I hope you'll see it one day—old as anything, with jolly Roman roads and such hangin' around, and the most spiffin' lot of gees. Look, the sun will be gettin' above the houses soon. I've seen some sunrises in my day. You ought to be on the Downs at night, Miss Beaminster."

Roddy was surprised at himself at the way that he was talking, but she really looked quite beautiful there in the window with her dark hair and her eyes and white dress.

"I can't tell you," she said, when it was time for them to part, "how much all you say interests me. I love horses too, and I adore dogs — —"

"I've got a dog I'd like you to have," he began. "It's a — —"

"Oh no," she answered. "Aunt Adela would never let me keep one here. Thank you all the same. But you'll let me come down to Seddon Court one day, won't you?"

"Let you!" Roddy could find no words.

She flung one glance at the square, where the dawn was beginning, and then was back in the ballroom again, dancing, dancing, dancing....

The sky was all pink above the roofs, and the birds were making a whirl of chattering, when her bedroom received her again.

Her maid was sleepy but proud.

"They all say it's been a great success, Miss Rachel."

"Success!" She stood for a moment in the middle of the room with her arms extended. "Oh! It's been glorious, glorious. I've never——"

She paused. Her arms fell to her sides—"Oh! Dr. Chris! Dr. Chris! He never came—he said that he mightn't be able. It was the only thing that was wrong"—Then more slowly, as she moved to her dressing-table—"And all the last part I never missed him."

"Well, I dare say," said Lucy, standing behind Rachel's chair and staring at the white face in the mirror, "that with his patients and the rest he couldn't get away——"

"Oh! But I ought to have missed him," said Rachel, and afterwards, lying in bed, sleepless with excitement, it was Dr. Christopher's face that she saw.

CHAPTER VI
FANS

"Il est doux de sommeiller a l'ombre chaude, sur le tiède oreiller d'un mal épicurisme et d'une intelligence ironique, très simple, assez curieuse, et prodigieusement indifferente, au fond."

Romain Rolland.

I

On the afternoon that followed the ball Lady Adela took Rachel to tea with Lord Richard.

It was a superb May afternoon; white clouds, bolster-shaped, were piled in the heavens and made, so rounded were they, the blue sky seem an infinite distance away. It was a day of sparkling dazzling gaiety—the air seemed electric with the happiness of the world, and, as they drove down to Grosvenor Street, Rachel felt that the little breeze that just touched the hats and coats of the people on the omnibuses was created simply by the joy of the beautiful weather.

As they moved slowly down Bond Street Rachel looked at the world and thought of last night. She looked at the men with their shining hats and shining boots; at the messenger boys and the young women with parcels and the young women without; at the old men who thought themselves young and the young men who thought themselves old; at the fish shops and the picture galleries, at the jewellers' and the book shops, at the place where they taught you Swedish exercises and the place where there was a palmist with a Japanese name, and it was all splendid and magnificent and simply carried on the glories of the night before. Before the turning into Grosvenor Street there was a great crush of carriages and a long pause. In the carriage next to Rachel there was a very stout, very richly coloured lady with a strong scent and a pug dog. A little farther away there were two young gentlemen in a smart little carriage, and their hats were so large and their expression so haughty and the top of their canes so golden that it seemed absurd that they should have to wait for anybody, and near them was a small boy on a little butcher's cart and near him an omnibus with a red-faced driver and any number of interested ladies, and all these incongruities seemed only to add to the haphazard happiness of this shining afternoon.

Rachel had many things to consider as she sat there. Aunt Adela did not interfere with her thoughts, because she never talked when she was in a carriage, but always sat up and looked wearily at the people about her. She had never very much to say, but the open air made her feel stupid.

Rachel was aware that last night had altered her point of view for all time. She was aware, as she sat there in sunshine, of a new world. By one glance at Aunt Adela was this new world made apparent. Aunt Adela had hitherto been important—Aunt Adela was now unimportant.

Had this afternoon been wet and gloomy, then Rachel might have doubted that passionate discovery of the world that she now felt was hers, but here with this blazing sun and sky the note was sustained. Surely never again would Rachel be afraid of her grandmother, surely never again would she be afraid of anyone. Holding herself very proudly in a dress that was a soft primrose colour and in a hat that was dark and shady, Rachel looked round about her on the world.

"There's Lady Massiter!" Lady Adela smiled lightly and bowed a very little—"Monty Carfax is with her."

Rachel thought of Lord Massiter, and wondered again at last night's dinner—"How could I have been like that? How could I?"

There passed them a very handsome carriage with a little dark handsome lady who looked happily round about her, all alone in her magnificence. Rachel did not know whether her aunt had seen or no: here was the Beaminster arch-enemy, Mrs. Bronson, a young American widow, incredibly rich, incredibly fascinating, incredibly bold. Mrs. Bronson had been in London only a year, had snapped her jewelled fingers at the Beaminsters and everything that they stood for, had laughed at snubs and threats, was intending, so it was said, to have London at her feet in a season or two.

Rachel considered her. She was like some jewelled bird of paradise. She was—one must admit it—better suited to this glorious day than was Aunt Adela.

Why need Aunt Adela refuse to be glad because the sun was shining? Why could not Aunt Adela have said something pleasant about last night's dance? Why must this absurd outward dignity be so carefully maintained? Why when one was looking attractive in a primrose dress could one's aunt not say so?

That reminded her of Roddy Seddon.

She liked him. He might be a real friend like Dr. Christopher. The thought of him made her, as she sat there in the sun, feel doubly certain that the world was a comfortable, reassuring place and that that vision of cold spaces and dark forests that had been so often with her was now to be banished like an evil dream never to return.

At the end of Grosvenor Street the trees were so green that they might have been painted, and here they were at Uncle Richard's house.

II

But, with the closing of Uncle Richard's doors the sun was taken from the world. Uncle Richard's house was always soft and dim, like one of those little jewel cases, all wadding and dark wood. Uncle Richard's carpets were so thick and soft that everyone seemed to walk on tip-toe, and the wonderful old prints in the hall and the beautiful dark carving on the staircase and the sudden swiftness of the doors as they closed behind you only helped to increase the impression that everything here, yourself included, was in for a beautiful exhibition, and that light might hurt the exhibits.

Uncle Richard's study, where they always had tea, was lined from roof to ceiling with book-cases, and behind the shining glass there gleamed the backs of the haughtiest and proudest books in the world. For, were they old and dingy, then they were first editions of transcendent value, and were they new and shining, then were they "Editions de luxe," or some of Uncle Richard's favourites bound in the most intricate and precious of bindings.

Some china on the mantelpiece was so valuable that housemaids must surely have a sleepless time because of it, and all the furniture was so conscious of its rich and ancient glories that to sit down on the chairs or to lean on the tables was to offer them terrible insults.

Two Conders and a Corot shone from the grey walls.

In the midst of this was Uncle Richard, elaborately, ironically indifferent to all emotions. "I have governed the country, yes—but really, my friends, scarcely a job for a fine spirit nowadays. I have collected these few things — yes, but after all what does it come to? Don't many pawn-brokers do the same?"

Rachel, as she stood in the room, felt that her newly found independence was slipping away from her. With the departure of the sun had fled also that consciousness of last night's splendours. About her again was creeping that atmosphere that was always with her in this room, something that made her feel that she was a wretched, ignorant Beaminster, and that even if she did learn the value of all these precious things, why then that knowledge was of little enough use to her.

Uncle Richard with his high white forehead, his long dark trousers, his grey spats and his great collar that bent back, in humble deference, before the nobility of his neck and chin, Uncle Richard required a great deal of courage.

"Well, dear, I hope you enjoyed your dance."

"Yes, Uncle Richard, thank you."

"I left early, but everything seemed to be going very well."

"Yes, I think it was all right."

How different this from the fashion in which she had intended to fling her enthusiasm upon him. What, she wondered, would have been the effect had she done so? How would he have taken it? Could she have pierced that melancholy ironical armour that always kept the real man from her?

Meanwhile she was now back again in the old, old world; tea was brought, the footman and butler moved softly about the room. Aunt Adela said a little, Uncle Richard said a little ... the lid was down upon the world.

Meanwhile, impossible to imagine that only a quarter of an hour ago there had been that gay confusion in Bond Street, impossible to believe Mrs. Bronson in her carriage anything but common and vulgar, impossible to prefer that dazzling sun to this cloistered quiet.

A wonderful lacquered clock ticked the minutes away. "I'm in a cage—I'm in a cage—and I want to get out," someone in Rachel Beaminster was crying, and someone else replied, "Thank God that you are allowed to be in such a cage at all. There's no other cage so splendid."

Her primrose gown was forgotten; when Uncle Richard asked her questions she answered "Yes," or "No." Her old terrors had returned.

Upon the three of them, sitting thus, Roddy Seddon was announced. Roddy had assaulted and conquered Lord Richard in as masterly a fashion as he had subdued the Duchess and Lady Adela. He had done it simply by presenting so boisterous and honest an allegiance to the Beaminster standard. Lord Richard's irony had been useless against Roddy's ingenuous appeal. Moreover, there was the Duchess's advocacy—young Seddon was the hope of the party.

Roddy brought to view no evidence of last night's energies; he was as fresh, as highly coloured, as browned and bronzed and clear as any pastoral shepherd, his skin was so finely coloured that clothes always seemed, with him, a pity. Lord Richard's melancholy cynicism had poor chance against such vigour.

His eyes, as they fastened upon Rachel, brightened. She gave that dim room such fresh pleasure, sitting there in her primrose frock with her serious eyes and long hands. No, she was not beautiful; he knew that his last night's impression had been the true one; but she was unusual, she would make, he was sure, a most unusual companion. "You wouldn't think it," May Eversley had said, "but there's any amount of fun in Rachel—you'll find it when you know her."

He was not sure but that he saw it now, lurking in her eyes, her mouth, as she sat there, so gravely, opposite to her uncle and aunt.

"How d'ye do, Lady Adela? How d'ye do, Miss Beaminster? How are you, sir? Thanks—I will have some tea. Pretty gorgeous day, ain't it? Rippin' dance of yours last night, Lady Adela."

Meanwhile, Rachel knew that she had nothing to say to him. Out there in the sunlight she might, perhaps, have maintained that relationship that had been begun between them the night before, but in here, with Aunt Adela and Uncle Richard so consciously an audience, with the air so dim and the walls so grey, Roddy Seddon seemed the most strident of strangers.

She sat, silently, whilst he talked to Aunt Adela. "I've never had so toppin' a dance as last night—'pon my soul, no. Young Milhaven, whom I tumbled on at Brook's at luncheon, said the same. Band first-rate, and floor spiffin'."

"I'm glad you liked it, Roddy," said Lady Adela, with a dry little smile. "I must confess to being glad that it's over."

Roddy glanced a little shyly at Rachel. "I suppose you're goin' hard at it now, Miss Beaminster?"

She looked across the tea-table at him. "There's Lady Grode's and Lady Massiter's, and Lady Carloes is giving one for her niece——"

"The Massiter thing ought to be a good one. Always do it well," said Roddy. "'Pon my word, on a day like this makes one hot to think of dancing."

He was perplexed. He had instantly perceived that he had here a Rachel Beaminster very different from last night's heroine. She was now beyond all contemplated intimacy. He had heard others speak of that aloofness that came like a cloud about her. He now saw it for himself.

After a time he came across to her whilst Lady Adela and her brother talked as though the world consisted of one Beaminster railed round by high palings over which a host of foolish people were trying to climb.

He stood beside her smiling in that slightly embarrassed manner of his, a manner that caused those who did not know him to say that they liked Roddy Seddon because he was so modest.

"Such a day it seems a shame to be in town."

"Yes—isn't it lovely?"

"The opera's pretty hot in the evenin' just now. Have you been yet?"

"I've been in Munich often. I've never been here."

"My word! Haven't you really? Wish I could say the same. I'm always bein' dragged——"

"Why do you go if you don't care about it?"

"Can't think—always askin' myself. Why do half the Johnnies go? And yet in a way I like some sorts o' music."

"What kind of music?"

"Sittin' in the dark, in a room, with someone just strokin' the piano up and down—just strokin' it—not hammerin' it. I don't care what the old tune is——"

Rachel laughed a little, but said nothing. Of course, she thought him the most thundering kind of fool, and this made him eager to display to her his wisdom and common sense.

61

But he could say nothing. There followed the most awkward silence. She did not try to help him, but sat there quietly looking in front of her.

Suddenly she said: "Uncle Richard, I want to see your fans again. I haven't seen them for a long time. I know you've added some lately. Sir Roderick, have you ever seen my uncle's fans?"

"No," he said. "I'd be delighted ― ―"

Lord Richard's eyes lifted. The lines of his mouth grew softer.

Rachel watched him. "Now he'll pretend," she said, "that he doesn't care. He'll pretend that they're nothing to him at all."

He went, in his solemn guarded manner, to a place in the room where a large cabinet was let into the wall. He drew this cabinet forward, and then, out of it, moving his hands almost pontifically, he pulled trays, and on these trays lay the fans.

The others had gathered around him. There were nearly five hundred fans ― fans Dutch and Italian and French and Chinese and Japanese; fans of the sixteenth and seventeenth centuries, of the eighteenth and of the Empire ― modern Japanese heavy with iron spokes, others light as gossamer, with spokes of ivory or tortoise shell. There were French fans, painted only on one side, with pictures of fantastic shepherds and shepherdesses; there were Chinese fans with bridges and mandarins and towers; Empire fans perforated with tinsel and such lovely shades of colour that they seemed to change as one gazed.

There they all lay in that rich solemn room, quietly, proudly conscious of their beauty, needing no word of praise, catching all the colour and the daintiness and fragrance that had ever been in the world.

Rachel drank in their splendour and then looked about her.

Uncle Richard's eyes were flaming and his hands trembling against the case.

Then she looked at Roddy Seddon. His head was flung back; with eyes and mouth, with every vein, and fibre of his body he was drinking in their glory.

His eyes were suddenly caught away. He was staring at her before she looked away ― Her eyes said to him, "Why! Do you care like that? Do those things mean that to you?"

She smiled across at him. They were in communion again as they had been last night.

He was surprised that he should be so glad.

CHAPTER VII
IN THE HEART OF THE HOUSE

"Our interest's on the dangerous edge of things
The honest thief, the tender murderer,
The superstitious atheist, demirep,
That loves and saves her soul in new French books —
We watch while these in equilibrium keep
The giddy line midway: one step aside,
They're classed and done with. I, then, keep the line —"
Bishop Blougram's Apology.

I

The Duchess could but dimly guess at the splendour of that fine May afternoon.

It had been her complaint lately that she was always cold and now the blinds and curtains were closely drawn and a huge fire was blazing. Her chair was close to the flame: she sat there looking, in the fierce light, small and shrivelled; she was reading intently and made no movement except now and again when she turned a page. Dorchester was the only other person there and she sat a little in the shadow, busily sewing.

From where she sat she could see her mistress's face, and behind her carved chair there were the blue china dragons and the deep heavy red curtains and a black oak table covered with little golden trays and glass jars and silver boxes.

Neither heat nor cold nor youth nor age had any effect upon Dorchester. No one knew how old she was, nor how long she had been with her mistress, nor her opinions or sentiments concerning anything in the world.

She was tall and gaunt and snapped her words as she might snap a piece of thread.

From Mrs. Newton and Norris downwards the servants were afraid of her. She made a confidant of no one, was supposed to have no emotions of any kind, absurd and fantastic stories were told of her; she was certainly not popular in the servants' hall and yet at a word from her anything that she requested was done.

With Miss Rand only was it understood that she had a certain friendly relationship; it was said that she liked Miss Rand.

Dorchester had witnessed the whole of the Duchess's career.

As she sat now in the shadow every now and again she looked up and glanced at that sharp white face and those thin hands. What a little body it was to have done so much, to have battled its way through such a career, to have fought and to have won so many conflicts! It seemed to Dorchester only yesterday that splendid time, when the Duchess had been queen of London. Dorchester also had been young then and had had an energy as enduring, a will as finely tempered as had her mistress.

What a character it had been then with its furies and its disciplines, its indulgences and its amazing restrictions, its sympathies and cold clodded cruelties, its tremendous sense of the dramatic moment so that again and again a position that had been nearly surrendered was held and saved. She had never been beautiful, always little and sharp and sometimes even wizened. But she gained her effects one way or another and beat beautiful and wise and wonderful women off the field.

And then sweeping down upon her had come disease. At first it had been fought and magnificently fought. But it was the horror of its unexpected ravages that had been so difficult to combat. She had never known when the pain would be upon her—it might seize her at any public moment and her retreat be compelled before the whole world. There had been doctors and doctors and doctors, and then operation after operation, but no one had done any good until Dr. Christopher had come to her, and now, for years, he had been keeping her alive.

Out of that very necessity of disease, however, had she dragged her drama. She had retired from the world, not as an old woman beaten by pain, but as a priestess might withdraw within her sanctuary or some great queen demand her privacy.

And it had its effect. Very, very carefully were chosen to see her only those who might convey to the world the right impression. The world was given to understand that the Duchess was now more wonderful than she had ever been, and it was so long since the world at large had seen her that every sort of story was abroad.

Certain old ladies like Lady Carloes who played bridge with her gained most of their public importance from their intimacy with her. It was rumoured that at any moment she might return and take her place again in the world, old though she was.

All this was known to Dorchester and she smiled grimly as she thought of it. The real Duchess! Perhaps she and Dr. Christopher alone in all the world knew the intricacies, the inconsistencies of that amazing figure. From the moment that illness had come every peculiarity had grown. Her self-indulgences, her temper, her pride, her egotism—now knew, in private, no restraint. And yet when her friends were there or anyone at all from the outside world she displayed the old dignity, the old grand air, the old imperious quiet that belonged to no one else alive.

But what, during these last years, Lady Adela had suffered! Dorchester herself had had many moments when it had seemed that she had more to control than her strength could maintain, but long custom, an entire absence of the nervous system, and a comforting sense that she was, after all, paid well for her trouble, sustained her endurance.

But Lady Adela had nothing.

The Duchess had always hated her children, but had used them, magnificently, for her purposes. They had all been fools, but they were just the kind of fools that the Beaminster tradition demanded.

Lady Adela had from the first been more of a fool than the others. She had never had the gift of words and before her mother was, as a rule, speechless, and it had been only by her changing colour that an onlooker could have told that her mother's furies moved her.

Often Dorchester had attempted interference, but had found at last that it was better to allow the fury to spend its force. Then also Dorchester had noticed a curious thing. The Duke, Lord Richard, Lord John, Lady Adela were proud of these prides and tempers. They were proud of everything that their mother did; they might suffer, their backs might wince under the blows, but it was part of the tradition that their mother should thus behave.

Dorchester fancied that sometimes there was flashed upon them a sudden suspicion that their mother was in these days only an old, ailing, broken woman—no great figure now, no magnificent tyrant, no mysterious queen of society. And then Dorchester fancied that she had noticed that when such a suspicion had come upon them they had put it hastily aside and locked it up and abused themselves for such baseness.

Curious people, these Beaminsters!

Well, it was no business of hers. And, perhaps, after all she had herself some touch of that feeling, some fierce impatient pride in those very tempests and rebellion. After all, was there anyone in the world like this mistress of hers? Was there another woman who would bear so bravely the pain that she bore? And was not that fierce clutch on life, that energy with which she tried still to play her part in the great game, grand in its own fashion?

Would not Dorchester also fight when her time came?

She looked across the firelight at her mistress. When would arrive the inevitable moment of surrender? How imminent that moment when in the eyes of all those about her the old woman would see that all that was now hers was a quiet abandonment to death!

Well, there would be some fine, savage struggling when that crisis struck into their midst. Dorchester smiled grimly, and then, in spite of herself, sighed a little.

They were all growing old together.

II

At five o'clock came Dr. Christopher, and Dorchester moved into the other room and left the two together. With his large limbs and cheerful smile he made the Duchess seem slighter and more fragile than ever, and she herself felt always with his coming some addition of warmth and strength; each visit, so she might have expressed it, gave her life for at least another tiny span.

That he, knowing so much of the follies and catastrophes of life, should yet be an optimist, would have proved him in her opinion a fool had she not known, by constant proof, that he was anything but that. "Well, one day he will discover his mistake," she would say, and yet, perversely, would cling to him for the sake of this very illusion. He helped her courage, he helped her battle with her pain, he gave her, sometimes, some shadowy sense of shame for her passions and rebellions, but, more than all this, he yielded her a reassurance that life, precious, adorable, wonderful life, was yet for a little time to be hers.

He knew well enough the influence that he possessed, and when, as on this afternoon, he felt it his duty to avail himself of it, he could not pretend that he faced his task with any exultation.

The Duchess of Wrexe

That he should rouse her fury, as he had one or twice already roused it, meant humiliation for him as well as for herself, and afterwards embarrassment for them both as they saw those scenes in retrospect.

She glanced up at him carefully as he came in and knew him well enough to realize that there was something that he must say to her. There had been other such occasions, she remembered them all. Sometimes she herself had been the subject of them, something that was injuring her health, some indulgence that he could not allow her. Sometimes the battle had been about others; she had fought him and on occasions it had seemed that their relationship was broken once and for all, that nothing could cover the words that had been spoken—but always through everything she had admired his courage.

The way had always been to stand up to her.

For a little time they talked about her health, and then there fell a pause. She, leaning back in her chair with her thin, sharp hands on her lap, watched him grimly as he sat on the other side of the fireplace, leaning forward a little, looking into the fire.

"Well," she said at last. "What is it?" Her voice was deep, but every word was clear-cut, resonant.

"There is something—two things," he answered her slowly. "You can dismiss me for an interfering old fool, you know. You often have been tempted to do it before, I dare say."

"I have," she said. "Go on."

But as she spoke she drew her hands a little more closely together. She was not quite so ready for these battles as she had once been. She was afraid a little now. A new sensation for her; she hated that restricting awkwardness that would remain between them for days afterwards.

She looked at his red, cheerful face and wondered impatiently why he must always be meddling in other people's affairs. She hated Quixotes.

"Your Grace," he began again, "has only got to stop me and I'll say no more."

"Oh yes, you will," she said impatiently. "I know you. Say what you please."

"I want to speak about Francis Breton——" He paused, but she said nothing, only for an instant her whole face flashed into stone. The firelight seemed for an instant to hold it there, then, as the flame fell, she was once again indifferent.

Christopher had grasped his courage now. He went on gravely:

"I must speak about him. I know how unpleasant the whole subject is to you. We've had our discussions before and I've fought his battles with all the world more times than I can count. You must remember that I've known Frank all his life—I knew his unhappy father. I've known them both long enough to realize that the boy's been heavily handicapped from the beginning——"

"Must you," she said, looking him now full in the face, "must it be this? Have we not thrashed it out thoroughly enough already? I don't change, you know."

He understood that she was appealing to his regard for their own especial relationship. But there was a note of control in her voice; he knew that now she would listen:

"I've cared for Frank during a number of years. I know he's weak, impulsive, incredibly foolish. He's always been his own worst enemy. I know that the other day he wrote a most foolish letter——"

"It was a letter beyond forgiveness," she said, her voice trembling.

"Yes, I would give anything to have prevented it. I know that when he was in England before I pleaded for him, as I am doing now, and that by a thousand foolhardy actions he negatived anything that I could say for him.

"I'm urging no defence for the things that he did, the shady, disreputable things. But he has come back now, I do verily believe, ready, even eager, to turn over a new leaf. I——"

She interrupted him, smiling.

"Yes. That letter——"

"Oh, I know. But isn't it a very proof of what I say—would anyone but a foolhardy boy have done such a thing? Sheer bravado, hoping behind it all to be taken back to the fold—eager, at any rate, not to show a poor spirit, cowardice."

"Over thirty now—old for a boy——"

"In years, yes. But younger, oh! ages younger than that in spirit, in knowledge of the world, in everything that matters—I know," he went on more slowly, smiling a little, "that you've called me sentimentalist times without number—but really here I'm not urging you to anything from sentimental reasons. I'm not asking you to take him back and kill the fatted calf for him.

"I'm asking nothing absurd—only that you, his relations, all that he has of kith and kin, should not be his enemies, should not drive him to desperation—and worse."

"If you imagine," she said steadily, "that his fate is of the smallest concern to me you know me very little. I care nothing of what becomes of him. He and I have been enemies for many years now and a few words from you cannot change that."

"I'm only asking you," he replied, "to give him a chance. See what you can make of him, instead of sending him into the other camp—use him even if you cannot care for him. There's fine stuff there in spite of his follies. The day might come, even now, when you will own yourself proud of him——"

But she had caught him up, leaning forward a little, her voice now of a sharper turn. "The other camp? What other camp?"

He caught the note of danger. "I only mean," he said, choosing now his words with the greatest care, "that if you turn Frank definitely, once and for all, from your doors, there may be others ready to receive him——"

"His men and his women," she broke in scornfully; "don't I know them? I've not lived these years without knowing the raffish tenth-rate lot that failures like Frank Breton affect——"

"No—there are others," Christopher said firmly, "Mrs. Bronson, for instance——"

At that name she broke in.

"Yes—exactly. Mrs. Bronson. Oh! I know the kind of crowd that Mrs. Bronson and her like can gather. They are welcome to Francis and he to them."—She paused. He saw that she was controlling herself with a great effort. For a little while there was silence and then she went on, more quietly:

"There, now you have it. That is why there can never be any truce between Francis and myself. It is more than Francis—it is all the things that he stands for, all the things that will soon make England a rubbish heap for every dirty foreigner to dump his filth on to. Hate him? Why, I'll fight him and all that he stands for so long as there's breath in my body——"

"But Frank is with you," Christopher urged eagerly, "if you'll let him be. He's only in need of your hand and back he'll come. He's waiting there now—longing, in spite of his defiance, for a word. Give him it and in the end I know as surely as I sit here that he'll be worth your while——"

"What can he do for me?"

"Ah! He'll show you. After all, he is one of the family; he's miserable there in his exile. He's got your own spirit—he'd die rather than own to defeat—but he'll repay you if you have him."

He saw then, as she turned towards him, that he had done no good.

"Listen," she said, "I've heard you fairly. Let us leave this now, once and for all. I tell you finally no word that God Almighty could speak on this business could change me one atom. Francis Breton and I are foes for all time. I hate not only himself and the miserable mess that he's made of his life, I hate all this new generation that he stands for.

"I hate these new opinions, I hate this indulgence now towards everything that any fool in the country may choose to think or say. In my day we knew how to use the fools. Took advantage of their muddle, ran the world on it. I loathe this tendency to make everyone as intelligent as they can be! Why! in God's name! Give me two intelligent men and a dozen fools and you'll get something done. Take a wastrel like Frank and turn him out. Take muddlers like my family and keep 'em muddled. Richard ran the country well enough for a time or two, and he's been a muddler from his childhood.

"All this cry to educate the people, to be kind to thieves and murderers! to help the fools—my God! If I still had my say—Whilst there's breath in me I'll fight the lot of them."

71

She leant back in her chair, waited for breath, and then went on more mildly:

"You may like all this noise and clamour, Doctor. You may like your Mrs. Bronson and the rest—common, vulgar, brainless—ruling the world. Every decent law that held society together is being broken and nobody cares.

"Frank Breton may find his place in this new world. He has no place in mine."

Then she added: "So much for that—what's the other thing?"

But he hesitated. Her voice was tired, even tremulous, and he was aware as he looked across at her that her emotions now treated her more severely than they had once done. At the same time he was aware that giving free play to her temper always did her good.

"Well—perhaps—another day——"

"No—now. I may as well take my scoldings together—it saves time!"

He stood up and, leaning on the mantelpiece with one arm, looked down upon her.

"Here," he said, "I'm afraid I may seem doubly impertinent, but it's a matter that is closer to me than anything in the world. You know that I'm a lonely old bachelor and that all those sentiments that you accuse me of must find some vent somewhere. I'm fonder of Rachel, I think, than I am of anyone in the world, and it's only that affection and the feeling that, in some ways, I know her better than any of you do that give me courage to speak."

He could see that now she was reaching the limits of her patience.

"Well—what of Rachel?"

"I understand—I know—that you—that all of you intend that she shall marry young Seddon——"

"Well?"

"I know that it is impertinent of me, but, as I have said, I think I know Rachel differently from anyone else in the world. She is strange—curiously ignorant of life in many ways, curiously wise in others. Her simplicity—the things

72

that she takes on trust—there is no end to it. The things, too, that she cannot forgive—she doesn't know how often, later on, she will have to forgive them—

"But the first man who breaks her trust——"

"Thank you for this interesting light on Rachel's character. What does it mean?"

"It means," he said abruptly, "that she mustn't be hurt. Your Grace may turn me out of the house here and now if you will, but Seddon is the wrong man for her to marry——"

"What are his crimes?" Her voice was rising, and her hand tapped impatiently on her dress.

"I know him only slightly, but common repute—anyone who is in the London world at all will tell you—his reputation is bad. I've nothing against him myself, but his affairs with women have been many. He is no worse, I dare say, than a thousand others. At least he's young—and I myself, God knows, am no moralist. But to marry him to Rachel will be a crime."

He knew as he heard his own voice drop that the scene that he dreaded was upon him. The air was charged with it. In the strangest way everything in the room seemed to be changed because of it. The furniture, the dragons, the tables, the very trifles of gold and silver, seemed to withdraw, leaving the air weighted with passion.

She was trembling from head to foot. Her voice was very low.

"You've gone too far. What business is this of yours? How dare you come to me with these tales? How dare you? You've taken too much on your shoulders. See to your own house, Doctor——"

He stepped back from the fireplace.

"Please—to-morrow——"

"No. Here and now." Her words flashed at him. "You've begun to think yourself indispensable. Because I've shown you that I rely upon you— Because, at times, I've seemed to need your aid—therefore you've interfered in matters that are no concern of yours."

"They are concerns of mine," he answered firmly, "in so far as this affair is connected with my friend."

"Your friend and my granddaughter," she retorted. "But it is not only that. I will return you your own words. You say that your friend is in danger — what of mine? You have dared to attack someone who is more to me than you and all the rest of the world put together. Someone whom I care for as I have never cared for my own sons. It was bold of you, Dr. Christopher, and I shall not forget it."

He took it without flinching. "Very well," he said. "But my word to the end is the same. If you marry Seddon to your granddaughter you do your own sense of justice wrong."

At that the last vestige of restraint left her. Leaning forward in her chair she poured her words upon him in a torrent of anger. Her voice was not raised, but her words cut the air, and now and again she raised her hands in a movement of furious protest.

She spared him nothing, dragged forward old incidents, old passages between them that he had thought long ago forgotten, reminded him of occasions when he had been mistaken or over-certain, accused him of crimes that would have caused him to leave the country had there been a vestige of truth in her words; at last, beaten for breath, gasped out: "Sir Roderick Seddon shall know of what you accuse him. He shall deal with you — —"

"I have nothing," Christopher answered gravely, "against Seddon — nothing except that he should not marry Rachel!"

"You have attacked him!" she gasped out. "He — shall — answer."

But her rage had exhausted her. She lay back against her chair, heaving, clutching at the arms for support.

He summoned Dorchester, but when he approached the Duchess feebly motioned him away.

"I've — done — with you — never again," she murmured.

She seemed then most desperately old. Her dress was in disorder, her face wizened with deep lines beneath her eyes and hollows in her cheeks.

Christopher waited while Dorchester helped her mistress into the farther room. For some time there was silence. The room was stifling, and, impatiently, he pulled back the heavy red curtains.

He sat, waiting, eyeing the stupid dragons, every now and again glancing at his watch.

Even now the room seemed to vibrate with her voice, and he could imagine that the French novel, fallen from her lap on to the carpet, winked at him as much as to say:

"Oh, we're up to her tempers, aren't we? We know what they're worth. We don't care!"

At last Dorchester appeared.

"Her Grace is in bed and will see you, sir," she said.

Her face was grave and without expression.

After another glance at his watch he passed into the bedroom.

CHAPTER VIII
THE TIGER
"For every Manne there lurketh
hys Wilde Beast."
Sardus Aquinas (1512).

I

Brun, meeting Christopher one day, had asked him to tea in his flat, and then, remembering his interest in the Beaminster history, invited him to bring Breton with him.

"I haven't seen him for years. I'd like to see him again."

Christopher had accepted this invitation, and now on a sultry afternoon in June found himself sitting in Brun's rooms. Brun's sitting-room had a glazed and mathematical appearance as though, from cushions to ceiling, it had been purchased at a handsome price from a handsome warehouse. It was not comfortable, it was very hot.... The narrow street squeezed between Portland Square and Great Portland Street lay on its back, the little windows of its mean houses gasping like mouths for air, the hard sun pouring pitilessly down.

No weather nor atmosphere ever affected Brun. His clothes as well as his body had that definite appearance of something outside change or disorder. He might have been, one would allow, something else at earlier stages before this final result had been achieved (as a painting is presented to the observer before its completion), but surely now nothing would ever be done to him again. Surveying him, he appeared less a man with a history, origins, destinies about him than an opinion or a criticism. He was designed exactly by Nature for cynical observation, and was intended to play no other part in life.

"Well, Christopher?" said Brun. "Hot, isn't it?"

"My word—yes. Breton's coming along presently."

"Good. I've asked Arkwright the explorer. Nice fellow." They sat in silence for a little. Then Brun said:

"Interested in writers, Christopher?"

"Not very much. Why?"

"Just been lunching with a young novelist, Westcott. What he said interested me. Of course, he's very young, got no humour, takes himself dreadfully seriously, but he asked my advice—and it is as a sign of the times over here that I mention it."

"Go ahead."

"He tells me that a number of young novelists are going to band themselves into a kind of Artists' Young Liberty movement—artists, poets, novelists, some thirty altogether—going to have a magazine, do all kinds of things. Some of the older men will scoff. At the same time——"

"Well?" said Christopher.

"They'd asked him to join. He wanted my opinion."

"What did you say?"

"He interested me—he was a kind of test case. It would mean that, commercially, from the popular point of view, it would put him back for years. Those young men will all be put down as conceited cranks. They will tilt at the successful popular men like Lawson and the others, will worship at the feet of the unsuccessful 'Great' men like Lester and Cotton. The papers will hate 'em, the public will be indifferent. The result will be that, in the end, they may do a big thing—at any rate they'll have done a fine thing, but they'll all die on the way, I expect."

Brun spoke with enthusiasm unusual for him.

"How was this a test of Westcott?" asked Christopher.

"Well—would he go or no? He's at the kind of parting of the ways. I believe success is coming to him, if he wants it; but he'll have to build another wall in front of his Tiger either before the success or after. If he joins this crowd of men, there'll be no walls for him ever again."

Christopher knew that when Brun had some idea that he was pleasantly pursuing and had secured an audience nothing would stay or hinder him.

He pushed a chair towards him.

"What do you mean by your Tiger?" he asked.

"My Tiger is what every man has within him—I don't mean, you know, a nasty habit or a degrading passion or anything of necessity vicious—only my theory is that every man is given at the outset of life a Beast in the finest, noblest sense with whom through life he has got to settle. It may be an Ambition, or a Passion, or a Temptation, or a Virtue, what you will, but with that Beast he's got to live. Now it's according to his dealings with the Beast that the man's great or no. If he faces the Beast—and the Beast is generally something that a man knows about himself that nobody else knows—the Beast can be used, magnificently used. If he's afraid, pretends the Tiger isn't there, builds up walls, hides in cities, does what you will, then he must be prepared for a life of incessant alarm, and he may be sure that at some moment or another the Tiger will make his spring—then there'll be a crisis!

"Over here in England you're hiding your Tigers all the time. That's why you're muddled—about Art, Literature, Government, everything that matters—and an old woman like the Duchess of Wrexe—sharp enough herself, mind you—uses all of you.

"No Beaminster has ever faced his or her Tiger yet, and they're down, like knives, on everyone who does and everything that shows the Tiger's bright eyes——

"But I see—oh, Lord! I see—a time coming, yes, here in England, when the Individual, the great man, is coming through, when the Duchess will be dead and the Beaminster driven from power and every man with his Tiger there in front of him, faced and trained, will have his chance—

"More brain, more courage, no muddle—God help the day!"

"You see things moving—everywhere?"

"Everywhere. These fellows, Randall and the rest, are bringing their Tigers with 'em. They're going to put them there for all the world to see. It's only another party out against the Duchess, she wants all the Tigers hidden—only herself to know about them—then she can do her work. She'll hate these fellows until they've made their stand and then she'll try to adopt them in order to muzzle them the better in the end.

"If Westcott hides his Tiger, forgets he's there, his way's plain enough. He'll make money, the Duchess will ask him to tea. Let him join these fellows and his Tiger may tear all his present self to pieces."

"What about yourself, Brun?"

"Oh, I'm nothing! I'm the one great exception. No Tiger thinks me worth while. I merely observe, I don't feel—and you have to feel to keep your Tiger alive."

Brun's little lecture was over. He suddenly drew his body together, clapped his mental hands to dismiss the whole thing and was drawing Westcott to the door.

"But I talk—how I talk! You bear with me, Christopher, because I must go on, you know. It means nothing—absolutely nothing. But they will have arrived now, so down we go. I go on in my sleep, exactly the same. And now tea—and I will talk less because Breton talks a great deal and so does Arkwright, and so do you...."

II

Arkwright came, and after a little, Breton. But the meeting was not a success. Arkwright had heard a good deal about Breton's reputation, and although, on the whole, he was tolerant of any backsliding in women, he made what he called his liking for "clean men" an excuse for much narrow-mindedness.

It is quite a mistake to suppose that living in solitude and danger makes a human being tolerant. It has the precisely opposite effect. Arkwright was more frightened of a man who was not "quite right with society" than of any number of enraged natives. With natives one knew where one was. Whereas with a man like this ...

Breton, anxious to please, made the mistake of showing his anxiety. Seeing an enemy round every corner he was a little theatrical, too demonstrative, too foreign. Arkwright disliked his beard and the movement of his hands. "He wouldn't have come, had he known...."

Breton had, of course, at once perceived this man's hostility. Returning to England had involved, as he had known that it must, a life of battles, skirmishes, retreats, wounds, and every kind of hostility. People did not forget and even had they desired to do so, his relationship family history prevented Breton's oblivion.

He was ready for discourtesy, however eager he may have been for friendship. But what the Devil, he thought, is this fellow doing here at all? If Brun brought him in he must have told him just whom he was to meet, and if he came with that knowledge about him, why then should he not behave like a gentleman? Breton's half timid advance towards friendliness now yielded to curt hostility.

Brun maintained his silence and only watched the two men with an amusement just concealed. Conversation at last ceased and the heat beat, in waves, through the open windows and the air seemed now to be stiffened into bronze. Beyond the room all the city lay waiting for the cool of the evening.

Christopher liked Arkwright and Arkwright liked Christopher.

Christopher had read one of Arkwright's books and spoke of it with praise and also intelligence, and nothing goes to an author's heart like intelligent appreciation from an unbiassed critic. But Breton was not to be won over. He sat deep in his chair and replied in sulky monosyllables whenever he was addressed.

Christopher soon gave him up and the three men talked amongst themselves.

The heat of the afternoon passed and a little breeze danced into the room, and the hard brightness of the sky changed to a pale primrose that had still some echo of the blue in its faint colour.

The city had uttered no sound through the heat of the day, but now voices came up to the windows: the distant crying of papers, the call of some man with flowers, then the bells of the Round Church began to ring for evensong.

Breton sat there, wrapped in sulky discontent. In his heart he was wretched. Christopher had deserted him; these men would have nothing to do with him. As was his nature everything about him was exaggerated. He had come to Brun's rooms that afternoon, feeling that men had taken him back to their citizenship again. Now he was more urgently assured of his ostracism than before. Who were these men to give themselves these airs? Because he had made one slip were they to constitute themselves his judges? These Beaminster virtues again—the trail of his family at every step, that same damnable hypocrisy, that same priggish assumption of the right to judge. Better to die in the society of those friends of his who had suffered as he had done, from the judgment of the world—no scorn of sinners there, no failure in all sense of true proportion.

Christopher got up to go. He gave Arkwright his card. "Come in and dine one night and tell me all you're doing——"

"Of course I'll come," Arkwright said. "Only you're much too busy ——"

"Indeed no," said Christopher. "One day next week you'll hear from me ——"

Breton got up. "I'll come with you," he said to Christopher.

The two men went away together.

When they were gone Arkwright said to Brun, "Now that's the kind of man I like ——"

"Yes," said Brun, laughing. "Better than the other fellow, eh?"

Arkwright smiled. "More my sort, I must confess."

III

Christopher and Breton did not speak until they reached Oxford Circus. Here everything, flower-women, omnibuses, grey buildings, grimy men and women—was drowned in purple shadow. It might be only a moment's beauty, but now beneath the evening star, frosted silver and alone in a blue heaven, sound advanced and receded with the quiet rhythm of water over sand. For an instant a black figure of an omnibus stood against the blue and held all the swell, the glow, the stir at a fixed point—then life was once more distributed.

Here, as they turned down Oxford Street Christopher broke silence. He put his arm through Breton's:

"Well, Frank? Sulks not over yet?"

Breton broke away. "It's all very well, but I suppose I'm to pretend that I like being insulted by any kind of fool who happens to turn up. Good God, Chris, you'd think I was a child by the way you talk to me."

"And so you are a child," said Christopher impatiently, "and a thankless child too. Sometimes I wonder why I keep on bothering with you."

Christopher was, like other Scotchmen, a curious mixture of amiability and irascibility; his temper came from his pride and Breton had learnt, many years ago, to fear it. In fact, of all the things in life that he disliked doing, quarrelling with Christopher was the most agreeable. Then there were stubbornness and tenacity that were hard indeed to deal with. But to-day he was reckless; the heat of the afternoon and now the beauty of the evening had both, in their different ways, contributed to his ill-temper. He knew, even now, that afterwards he would regret every word that he uttered, but he let his temper go.

"I wonder that you do bother," he said. "Let me alone and let me find my own way."

"Don't be a fool," Christopher answered. "There's nothing in the world for us to quarrel about, only I can't bear to see you giving such a wrong impression of yourself to strangers—sulking there as though you were five years old——"

"All very well," retorted Breton; "you didn't hear the way that fellow insulted me. I'll wring his neck if I meet him again. I'll——"

"Now, enough of that!" Christopher's voice was stern. "You know quite well, Frank, that you're hardly in a position to wring anyone's neck. You remember the account I gave you of my little dispute with your grandmother——"

"Thank you," said Breton fiercely. "You remind me rather frequently of the kind things you do for me."

And all the time something in him was whispering to him, "What a fool you are to talk like this!"

Christopher's voice now was cold: "That's hardly fair of you. I'm turning up here——" They paused. Breton looked away from him up into the quiet blue recesses of the side street. Christopher went on: "I only mean that if I were you I should drop hanging on to the skirts of a family who don't want you. I should set about and get some work to do, cut all those rotten people you go about with, and behave decently to strangers when you meet them. That's all. Good night."

And Christopher was gone.

Breton stood there, for a moment, with the tide of his misery full upon him. Then he turned down Oxford Street and drove his way through the crowds of people who were coming up towards the Circus. He was alone, utterly alone in all the world. Everyone else had a home to go to, he alone had nowhere.

Only a few weeks ago he had come back to England, with money enough to keep him alive and a fine burning passion of revenge. That family of his should lament the day of his birth, that old woman should be down on her knees, begging his mercy. Now how cold and wasted was that revenge! What a fool was he wincing at the ill-manners of a stranger, quarrelling with the best friend man ever had.

How evilly could Life desert a man and kill him with loneliness.

And then his mood changed; if Christopher and the rest intended to cast him off, let them. There were his old friends—men and women who had been ostracized by the world as he had been—they would know how to treat him.

He turned into the silence and peace of Saxton Square and there met Miss Rand, who was also walking home. The statue was wrapped in blue mist, the trees were fading into grey and the evening star seemed to have taken Saxton Square under its special protection.

"Good evening, Miss Rand."

"Good evening, Mr. Breton."

"Isn't it a lovely evening?"

"Yes. But hasn't it been hot?"

Miss Rand did not look as though she could ever, under any possible circumstances, be hot, so neat and cool was she, but she said yes it had been.

"Isn't it odd the way that as soon as it's fine people begin to complain just as they do when it's wet?"

"It gives them something to talk about—just as it's giving us something now," said Miss Rand, laughing.

Breton looked at her and liked her. She seemed so strong and wise and safe. She would surely always give one the kind of sensible encouragement that one needed. She would be a good person in whom to confide.

They were on the top doorstep now.

"No. I've got a key." He let her pass him.

They stood for a moment in the hall together.

He spoke, as he always did, on the instant's inspiration:

"Miss Rand?"

"Yes."

"I'm alone such a lot—in my evenings I mean. I wonder—might I come down sometimes and just talk a little? You don't know how bad thinking too much is for me, and if I might— —"

"Why, of course, Mr. Breton—whenever you like."

Seeing her now, he thought, just now, with her sudden colour she looked quite pretty.

"I expect you could advise me—help me in lots of ways— —"

"If there's anything mother or I can do, Mr. Breton, you've only got to ask— Good night— —"

The door closed behind her.

He went up to his room, a less miserable man.

CHAPTER IX
THE GOLDEN CAGE

"She gives away because she overflows. She has her own feelings, her own standards; she doesn't keep remembering that she must be proud." — The Lesson of the Master.

I

Those weeks were, to Rachel, a golden time. She did not pretend to deny or examine their golden quality — they were far, far better than she had imagined anything could ever be, and that was enough. She had never, very definitely, imagined to herself this "coming out," but it had been, at any rate, behind its possible glories, a period of terror. "All those people" was the way that, with frightened eyes, she had contemplated it.

And now the kindness that there had been! All the London world had surely nothing to do but to pay her compliments, to surround her with courtesies, to flatter her every wish. Even Aunt Adela had under the general enthusiasm, blossomed a little into good-will, even Uncle Richard had remembered to wish her well, even the Duke had cracked applause, and as for Uncle John! ... he was like an amiable conjurer whose best (and also most difficult) trick had achieved an absolute triumph.

And behind all this there was more. May, June and the early part of July showered such weather upon London as had surely never been showered before, and these brilliant days dressed, for Rachel, her brilliant success in cloth of gold and emblazoned robes. She felt the presence of London for the first time, as the hot weather came beating up the streets and the brilliant whites and blues and greens and reds flung back to the burning blue their contrast and splendour.

She felt, for the first time, her own especial London, and now the grey cool cluster of buildings at one end of blazing Portland Place and the dark green of the hovering park at the other end had a new meaning for her, as though she had only just come to live here and was seeing it all for the first time. In the streets that hung about Portland Place she noticed little shops — little bakers and little shoemakers and little tailors and little sweetshops — and they were all furtive and dark and shabby.

And these little shops led to the growth in her mind of an especial picture of her square of London life, Portland Place white and shining in the middle, with the Circus like a fair at one end of it, the park like a mystery at the other end of it, and, on either side, little secret shops and little dim squares hanging about it, and Harley Street sinister and ominous by its side.

Every element of Life and Death was there, the whole History of Man's Journey Through This World to the Next.

Behind all the joy and overflowing happiness of these weeks this sudden setting of London about her was consciously present.

II

Since that meeting with Miss Rand on the day before the ball Rachel had often spoken to her. They met at first by accident and then Rachel had gone to Lizzie's neat little sitting-room to ask for something and, after that, had looked in for five minutes or so, and they had talked very pleasantly about the hot weather and the theatres and the ways of the world.

Behind all the splendour there was, for Rachel, the dark shadow of suspense. Was it going to last? What was to follow it? When would those awkward uncertainties that had once kept her company return to her? Now whatever else might be doubtful about Miss Rand, one thing was certain, that she would last, would remain to the end the same clean, reliable, honest person that she was now.

Imagine Lizzie Rand unreliable and she vanishes altogether! Rachel welcomed this and she also admired the wonderful manner in which Miss Rand accomplished her gigantic task. To run a house like this one and at the end of it all to remain as composed and safe as though nothing had been done!

Rachel herself might carry off a difficult situation by riding desperately at it, stringing her resources to their highest pitch, but afterwards reaction would claim its penalty.

The penalties were never claimed from Miss Rand.

So, gradually, without any definite words or events, almost without active consciousness, they became friends.

Rachel, suddenly, on one afternoon early in July, determined to go and pay Lizzie Rand a visit in her house.

That house in Saxton Square had acquired a new romantic interest since Rachel had learnt that the abandoned, abominable cousin, who defied Grandmamma and whose name one was never to mention, lived there. Rachel had considered this cousin more than once during these last months.

She had resented, from the first, the fact that he was to be given, by the family, no chance of redemption. However bad he had been (and he had apparently been very bad indeed) his opportunity should have been offered to him. His life, she knew, had been hard, he was, like herself, an orphan, and he hated, as she did, her grandmother. Of course, then, he interested her.

She did not now say to herself that if this romantic cousin had not been staying in that house she would not have contemplated a visit to Lizzie. The Beaminster in her had just now the upper hand, and the Beaminster simply said that Saxton Square would be a nice place in which Uncle John, who was, this afternoon, taking her out for a drive, might leave her whilst he went to the club; later he could pick her up and take her home.

The Beaminster part of her did not acknowledge the cousin.

Quite casually she said to Uncle John, "I want you to leave me at Miss Rand's for half an hour this afternoon—she is helping me about some clothes."

Now Uncle John had during these last weeks continually congratulated himself on the disappearance of Rachel's irritable, unsettled self. Always lately one had been presented with her delightful young eager self and always she had been anxious to agree with Uncle John's proposals. The world had been going smoothly for him in other ways of late, and no one had been disagreeable. How pleasant to keep the world in this amiable condition and how dangerous to risk anyone's displeasure!

He had moreover almost (not quite) forgotten that his rascal of a nephew was living in the same house as Miss Rand, and, even if he did remember it, well, it was quite another part of the house, and in all probability Miss Rand had never spoken to Frank Breton, nor so much as said good day to him.

Finally it was so sumptuous a day, and Rachel was clothed in so radiant a happiness and so fluttering and billowing and chuckling a dress of white and blue, and he himself was looking so handsome in the most shining of top-hats, the broadest of black bow ties, the most elegant of pepper-and-salt trousers and the whitest of white spats, that complaining or arguing or disputing was utterly out of the question.

"Miss Rand's, my dear? What's the address?... Right you are—" so off they went.

She arrived to find Miss Rand, a round chubby lady in bright pink, and a stranger having tea together. The chubby lady was Mrs. Rand and the stranger was Francis Breton. She had not expected that her arrival would cause such a disturbance, nor that she herself would discover the right and easy words so difficult to say. The little room seemed to be crowded with furniture and tea-things, and she, quite deliberately, put off any consideration of her cousin until the atmosphere had been allowed, a little, to settle around them.

Miss Rand looked at her almost sternly and was, plainly, at a loss. Mrs. Rand was excited, and so nervous that her tea-cup rattled in her saucer and she stayed for quite a long time with her finger in the tea under the delusion that she was using a teaspoon.

Mrs. Rand's absence of mind was generally due to the fact that she read one novel a day all the year round and that her thoughts, her hopes, her despairs were always centred in the book of the day, although when to-morrow came she could not tell you the author nor the title nor any of the incidents. Had she been to a play, then, for twenty-four hours following, it was the drama that held the field.

She spent her life in an amiable desire to remember, for the sake of her friends, the plays and books of the past. But she was never successful. As she said, "The attempt to keep up with the literature and drama of the day, although praise-worthy, demands all one's time and energy."

The Beaminster family alone of all other interests in the wide world might be calculated to draw her out of the realms of the imagination, and Rachel's entrance scattered all plots to the four winds.

Rachel sat down and, for a little while, Mrs. Rand held the field. She told them all that this visit of Miss Beaminster was the most wonderful and unexpected thing, that it was like a novel, and that she would never forget it. "But I always do say, Miss Beaminster, that it's the unexpected that happens. Life's stranger than fiction is my opinion, and I don't care who contradicts me I shall still hold it."

At length Rachel had leisure to consider her cousin and then was, instantly, convinced that she had met him before. She also knew that she could not have met him before.

In the strangest way he was connected with those early dream years which, now, she struggled so sternly to forget. The snow, the bleak sky, the silence, the sleigh-bells, some strange voice speaking high in air as though from a distant summit, and all this coming to her with a poignancy that, even now, brought the tears to her heart and filled it to overflowing.

As she saw his thin body, his eyes, his head and the attitude of the boy in all his movements and gestures she knew that, for her, he belonged to that earlier world. She knew it so certainly that, although he had not yet spoken, she could be sure of the exact quality that his voice would have.

And confused with this recognition of him was the alarm that she always felt when her early life returned to her.

Also she was young enough to be pleased at the agitation into which her coming had thrown him. It meant, plainly, so much to him; although he was silent he leant forward in his chair, with his eyes fixed upon her, waiting for his opportunity.

Miss Rand, watching him, saw how tremendously this meeting with one of the family excited him, and, seeing him, her heart filled with pity. "He's so young. It is hard. He does want someone to look after him."

Rachel's happiness had, now, returned to her. She liked them all so much, it was all so cosy, it was so good of them to wish to see her. She talked with Mrs. Rand about the theatre and the opera.

"We're going to the opera to-night—the Meistersinger. I've heard it in Munich twice, but never with Van Rooy, who's singing to-night. I believe that's an experience one never forgets——"

Mrs. Rand did not really care about opera; everything in opera happened so slowly, except in Carmen, and even that was better simply as a play. She liked musical comedy because there you could laugh, or plays like The Mikado, for instance.

She was vague as to the Meistersinger and she had never heard of Van Rooy, but she said, "I agree with you, Miss Beaminster. There's nobody like him."

At that Breton struck in with something about music that he had heard in strange places abroad, and then Rachel, looking in his face for the first time, asked him about his travels.

As their eyes and voices met she was again overwhelmed with the vivid consciousness of their earlier meeting. She thought, "If I were to ask him whether he remembered that same snow and silence he would say yes — I know he would say yes."

Miss Rand, with eyes that were kind but very, very sharp, watched them. She noticed the eagerness of Breton and wished that he did not seem quite so anxious to please. "But that's because he's young," she thought again.

And, now that he had begun, the words poured from him. With gesticulation that was faintly foreign, ever so little dramatic, he unpacked his adventures. He spoke as though this were, beyond all time, the moment when he must make his effect.

He did it well, a born teller of tales. And yet Miss Rand wished that he had not had to do it at all, that there had been more reserve, less drama, less volubility.

Mrs. Rand, an older Desdemona, listened spellbound. This was as good as getting a circulating library without paying a subscription. As she said to her daughter afterwards: "He really was as good as those novels by what's his name — you know who I mean — those delightful stories about those foreign places — and the sea."

He spoke of the first time that he had actually been conscious of the jungle. "Of course I'd been into it dozens of times — often and often. But there was a day — I remember as though it were yesterday — when we went up in a boat — some river or another — That river was the most secret and sleepy green, and the place all closed about it as though we'd gone into a box, and they'd closed the lid. Nothing but the green river and all the forest getting closer and closer and darker and darker, all blacker than you can imagine, and worse still when it was lighter — a kind of twilight — and you could see enough to make you shiver — no sound but the animals, and the branches and the great plants and brilliant flowers all creeping and crawling — Suddenly — all in a flash — I wanted a lamp-post and a public house, a wet night shining on streets, the rattle of a hansom — I was suddenly ghastly frightened, and we got deeper and deeper into it, and human beings further and further behind, and only the beastly monkeys and the alligators and the hideous flowers. I can feel it still — —"

Rachel was enthralled. He called up, on every side about her, that stern life of hers. He knew and she knew — they alone out of all the world. All her gaiety, her happiness, her interest of the last weeks went now for nothing beside this experience. He was not now related to the Beaminsters — to Grandmother, to Aunt Adela, to Uncle John — but to her and to that part of her that had nothing to do with the Beaminsters at all. The room, the commonplace furniture, the pictures of "Lodore Falls" and "The Fighting Téméraire," the little glimpses of the square beyond the window, these things shared in the mystery.

Miss Rand had seen her caught and held. "She's very young too," she said to herself a little grimly and a little tenderly also—"All too sensational to be true," she thought. "There's a little bit of unreality in him all the way through."

Mrs. Rand said: "What do you think of alligators, Miss Beaminster? Don't you agree with me that they must be most unpleasant to meet? I always dislike their sluggish ways when I see them in the Zoological Gardens."

Then upon them all broke the little maid with a husky "Miss Beaminster's carriage, please, mem."

Rachel, as she said good-bye, was aware of him again as "her scandalous cousin." He too was now awkward and embarrassed. They said good-bye hurriedly and there was between them both a consciousness that no word of the family or their relationship had been mentioned.

"Well," said Mrs. Rand, when the door was closed, "no one in the world could have been pleasanter...."

III

They did not arrive at the opera that night until the beginning of the second act. It was Lady Carloes' box and she and Uncle John and Roddy Seddon were Rachel's companions.

All the way home in the carriage Rachel had been silent and Lord John, perceiving uneasily that some of the old Rachel was back again, had said very little.

Her mind was confused. At one moment she felt that she did not want to see him again, that he disturbed her peace and worried her with memories that were better forgotten. At another moment she could have returned, then and there, to ask him questions, to know whether he felt this or that: had he ever pictured such a place? Had he...?

And then sharply she dismissed such thoughts. She would think of him no more—and yet he did not look a villain. How delightful to persuade the family to take him back. Why should she not help towards a reconciliation?

91

She was herself so happy now that she could not bear that anyone should feel outcast or lonely—they were all very hard upon him.

It was not until she heard the voices of the apprentices that thought of her cousin left her. As she groped her way in the dark box and heard Lady Carloes' stuffy whisper (she had the voice of a cracknel biscuit), "You sit there, my dear—Lord John here. That's right—I knew you'd be late because ..." she was gloriously aware that quite close to her the music that she loved best in all the world was transforming existence. She touched Roddy's hand and then surrendered herself.

She had been to Covent Garden now on four or five occasions and from the first the shabby building with its old red and gold, its air of belonging to any period earlier than the one it was just then amusing, its attitude, above all, of indifference to its aspect—all this had attracted her and won her affection. London, she discovered, was always best when it was shabbiest and one could not praise it more highly than by declaring, with perfect truth, that it was the shabbiest city in the world. Now, feeling instinctively that English apprentices (she had had already some taste of the Covent Garden chorus) would act too much or too little, she closed her eyes.

Now, as the music reached her, the old red and gold seemed a cage, swinging, swinging higher and ever higher with old Lady Carloes and Roddy Seddon and all the brilliant people in the stalls, and all the enthusiastic people in the gallery, swinging, swinging inside it. She could feel the lift of it, the rise and fall, and almost the clearer air about her as it rose into the stars.

Then there came to her the voice for which she had surely all her days been waiting. It enwrapped her round and comforted her, consoled her for all her sorrows, reassured her for all her fears. It filled the cage and the air beyond the cage, it was of earth and of heaven, and of all things good and beautiful in this world and the next.

For the second time to-day her early years came back to her; the voice had in it all those hours when someone's tenderness had made Life worth living. "Life is immortal," it cried. "And I am immortal, for I am Love and Charity, and, whatever the wise ones may tell you, I cannot die." She felt again the space and the silence and the snow, but now with no alarm, only utter reassurance. And the cage swung up and up and there were now only the stars and the wind around and about them.

Then, in an instant of time, the cage, with a crash, was upon the ground. Across her world had cut Lady Carloes' voice—"Oh yes, and there's Lord Crewner—no, not in that row—the one behind—next that woman with the silver thing in her hair—four from the end——"

And Roddy Seddon's voice—"Yes, I see him. Who's he got with him?"

Lady Carloes again: "I can't quite see—Miss Mendle as likely as not.... You know, old Aggie Mendle's daughter...."

Rachel felt in that moment that murder was assuredly no crime. Her hands shook on her lap and one of those passions, that she had not known for many months, caught her so that she could have torn Lardy Carloes' hair from her head had the chairs been happily arranged.

Fortunately the interruption had been accompanied by Beckmesser's entrance: that other voice was, for the moment, still. Then, as Sachs caught up Beckmesser's serenade, there came again:

"Well, of course if you can't go that week-end I dare say she'll give you another. Only I know she's settling her dates now."

"Yes, but it's a bore havin' to fix up such a long way ahead and you don't know what old stumers you mayn't be boxed up with——"

Oh! It was abominable! She had been seeing a great deal of Roddy during these last weeks, and ever since that visit to Uncle Richard she had been conscious of an intimacy that she had certainly not resented.

But any favour that he may have had with her was certainly now forfeited. His voice was again superior to Beckmesser:

"And so of course I said that if they would go to such shockin' rot I wasn't goin' to waste my evenin's——"

She pushed her chair back against his knees: "Beg pardon, Miss Beaminster, afraid I jolted you——"

"Oh! Keep quiet! Keep quiet!"

Her whisper was so urgent, so packed with irritation that instantly there was, in the box, the deepest of silences.

She sat forward again, anger choking her: she could not recover any illusion. She hated him, hated him! The crowd came on with a whirl. Then there was that last moment when the old watchman cries to the genial moon and the silvered roofs.

Then the curtain fell.

Without a word, her face white, her hands still trembling, she rose to leave the box. She passed out into the passage and found that Roddy was by her side.

"I say, Miss Beaminster, I am most awfully sorry, most awfully. I hadn't any idea, really, that I was kickin' up that row. I could have hit myself."

She walked down the passage and he followed her. She was superb, she was indeed, with her head up, that neck, those hands, those flashing eyes. He had never seen anyone so fine. She ought always to be enraged. That instant decided him. She was the woman for a man to have for his own, someone who could look like someone at the head of your table, someone with the right blood in her veins, someone....

"I could beat myself," he said again.

"How dared you — —" she broke out at last. They were, by good luck, alone in the passage. "How could you? What do you come for if you care nothing for music at all? If you can hear a voice like that and then talk about your own silly little affairs.... And the selfishness of it! Of course you think of nobody but yourself!"

"Upon my word, Miss Beaminster!"

"No, I've no patience with you. Go to your musical comedy if you like, but leave music like this for people who can appreciate it!"

Oh! she was superb! Entirely superb! She ought to be like this every day of her life! To think that he should have the chance of winning such a prize!

Nevertheless she would not speak to him again and they went back to the box. She would not speak to Lady Carloes nor to her uncle.

Then as the loveliest music in all opera flooded the building her anger began to melt.

He had looked so charmingly repentant and, after all, the Meistersinger was long for anyone who did not really care for music—and then they all did talk. It was only in the gallery that one found the proper reverence.

Her anger cooled and then descended upon her the quintet, and she was once again swept, in her cage, to the stars.

Now she and all live things seemed to be opening their hearts together to God—no shame now to speak of one's deepest and most sacred thoughts. No fear now of God nor the Archangels nor all the long spaces of Immortality. The cage had ascended to the highest of all the Heavens, and there, for a moment, one might stand, worshipping, with bowed head.

The quintet ceased and Rachel felt that she could never be angry with anyone again. She wished to tell him so.

At last, the revels were over, the "Prieslied" had won its praises, Sachs had been acclaimed by his world, and they were all in the lobby, waiting for carriages, talking, laughing, hurrying to the restaurants.

Her face was lighted now with happiness. She touched his arm.

"I didn't mean to be angry—like that. It was silly and rude of me. Forgive me, please——"

He turned, stuttering. "Forgive you!" He took her hand—"I ought to have been shot—Yes, I'll never forgive myself. You—you——" And then he could say no more, but suddenly, raising his hat, bolted away.

As the door swung behind him Lady Carloes turned a perplexed face—

"Why! he said good night! And now I shall never find——"

But Lord John appeared just then and all was well.

Going back, in the dark brougham, Rachel put her head on her uncle's shoulder and, exhausted with excitement and happiness and something more than either of them, cried her eyes away.

CHAPTER X
LIZZIE AND BRETON

"What of Adam cast out of Eden?
(And O the Bower and the hour!)
Lo! with care like a shadow shaken
He kills the hard earth whence he was taken."
Dante Gabriel Rossetti.

I

To the ordinary observer Lizzie Rand was, during that hot July, as she had ever been.

The servants in 104 Portland Place could detect no change, but then they did not search for one, having long regarded Miss Rand as a piece of machinery, symbolized by that broad shining belt of hers, happily calculated to fit, precisely, the duties for which it was required.

But Miss Rand herself knew that there was a sharp, accurate, shrewd piece of machinery named Miss Rand, and a breathing, emotional, uncertain human being called Lizzie. There had always been those two, but since the inadequacy of her mother and sister had been confronted with the stern necessity of making two ends meet, Miss Rand had been in constant demand and Lizzie had only, by her occasional obtrusion, made life complicated and disturbing.

Miss Rand had told herself that Lizzie was now almost an anachronism, that the emotions in life that aroused her were bad cheap emotions, and that this was an age that demanded increasingly of women a hard practical efficiency without sentiments or enthusiasms.

These forcible arguments had for a time kept Lizzie in a darkened background; it was some years since Miss Rand had been disturbed. But now in the warm weather of 1898 Lizzie had not only reappeared, but had leapt, an insistent, shining presence, into urgent life. Miss Rand faced her—what had created her? A little, the weather, the beauty of those brazen days—A little, Rachel's coming out into the world, an adventure that had stirred the whole house into a new and sympathetic excitement—a little, these things. But chiefly, and no pretence nor shame could conceal the fact, did this new Lizzie owe her creation to the appearance of Francis Breton.

Lizzie Rand had had, from her birth, a romantic heart; she had had also a prosaic practical exterior, and a mind as hard and clear, if necessary, as her own most lucent typewriter.

The romantic heart had, throughout these years, been there, and now this romantic, scandalous, youthful, engaging unfortunate had called it out.

She was never so warmly attracted as by someone lacking, most obviously, in those qualities with which she herself abounded. That people should be foolish, impetuous, careless, haphazard commended them straight to her keeping. "Poor dears" had their instant claim upon her. Her mother and sister were "poor dears" and she had suffered from them now during many years. Francis Breton was most assuredly a "poor dear!"

Here the Duchess a little flung her shadow and confused the mind. Although Lizzie had never seen that splendid figure she was, nevertheless, acutely conscious of her. She was conscious of her through her own imagination, through her mother, finally through Lady Adela.

Her imagination painted the old lady, the room, the furniture fantastic, strangely coloured, always with dramatic effect. Her picture was never precisely defined, but in its very vagueness lay its terrors and its omens.

Miss Rand, the most practical and collected of young women, could never pass the Duchess's door without a "creep."

Through her mother the Duchess came to her as the head of society. Society had never troubled Lizzie's visions of Life. She had, in her years with the Beaminsters, seen it pass before her with all its comedy and pathos, and the figures that had been concerned in that procession had seemed to her exactly like the figures in any other procession except that they were dressed for their especial "subject." But oddly enough when, through her own observation, this life, seen accurately at first hand, amounted only to any other life, seen through the eyes of her mother, it achieved another size.

She knew that her mother was a foolish woman, that her mother's opinions on life were absurd and untrue, and yet that dim, great figure that the Duchess assumed in her mother's eyes, in some odd way impressed her.

Lastly, and most strikingly of all, came Lady Adela's conception to her. Lady Adela was in terror of her mother; everyone knew it, friends, relations, servants. Lizzie herself saw it in a thousand different ways—saw it when Lady Adela spoke of her, saw it in the way that Lady Adela addressed Dorchester when that grim woman was interviewed by her, saw it when Lady Adela was suddenly summoned to that room upstairs.

Lizzie, during the hours when she was writing from Lady Adela's dictation or working with her, found her dry, stupid, sometimes kind, never emotional. It was to her, therefore, the most convincing proof of the Duchess's power, this emotion, this alarm drawn from so dry a heart.

Now the influence that the Duchess had upon Lizzie was always a confused one. Persuasion from this source followed lines of reasoning that were false and led to some conclusions that were muddled and untrue.

Through such minds as her mother's and Lady Adela's no clear truth could come, and yet it was through such minds as these that the Duchess's influence descended upon Lizzie.

It descended now with regard to Francis Breton. It told Lizzie that Breton had been proved by society to be a scoundrel, that he should be no worthy man's friend, that he belonged to that world, the world of shadows and past misadventures, that no proper soul might, with honesty, investigate.

This was what the Duchess told to Lizzie and perhaps by so doing increased her sympathy with the sinner.

II

It must not be supposed that Mrs. Rand had not, at first, been unsettled by scruples.

The fact that Breton was, in the eyes of the Beaminster family, a ne'er-do-well who had brought disgrace upon the family name had, for a time, distressed her, but the romantic hope of being herself the agent of his restoration to his grandmother, and the delightful manners of the scoundrel when he appeared, killed her alarm. Mrs. Rand's mind was a dark misty place except when the candles of romance were lit; when they flamed, blown by the wind though they might be, there was, around the candlesticks at any rate, a real and even splendid blaze.

One afternoon, towards the end of July, Mrs. Rand meeting Breton on their doorstep was moved to ask him whether he would come in and spend the evening with them, if he had nothing better to do. They had only a simple little meal, and would he please not bother to dress? Breton said that he would be delighted.

Mrs. Rand had been, that afternoon, to a romantic comedy in which ladies and gentlemen with French accents had made love and escaped together and been caught together and been married together. Mrs. Rand had gone quite alone into the pit and had returned with tears in her eyes and affection for all the world.

So she had asked Mr. Breton to dinner.

After a while, however, she was a little uncertain. Daisy was away in the country with friends. How would Lizzie then like this unexpected visitor? Mrs. Rand was, quite frankly, frightened of Lizzie and complained of her a good many times a week to Daisy. Lizzie was for ever interfering with innocent pleasures; Lizzie was mean and unromantic and unimaginative; Lizzie was thoroughly tiresome.

The fact that Lizzie worked incessantly for her mother and her sister never occurred to Mrs. Rand at all.

Lizzie objected to all innocent amusement and she would, in all likelihood, object now.

However, when Mrs. Rand with a fearful mind said, "Oh, Lizzie dear, I've had such a delightful afternoon. I went to Love and the King and it was too charming—you ought to go, really—and Mr. Breton's coming to dinner to-night," Lizzie only smiled a little and asked whether there was food enough. Lizzie was so strange....

Alone in her bedroom Lizzie wondered at her excitement. She looked at her trim, neat figure in the glass, with the hair so gravely brushed, with her collar and her cuffs, with her compact businesslike air: what had she to do with excitement because a young man was coming to dinner? "It must be because I'm tired—this heat," she said to the mirror. And the mirror replied, "You know that you are glad because your sister Daisy is away."

And to that she had no answer.

When he arrived he was grave and seemed sad and tired, she thought. Dinner was a serious affair and Mrs. Rand, who disliked people when they refused to respond to her moods, wished, at first, that she had not asked him, and felt sure that there was much truth in what people said about his wickedness.

Then, when dinner was nearly over, he brightened up and told stories and was entertaining. Mrs. Rand noticed that he drank much claret, but this was, after all, a compliment to her housekeeping. By the end of dinner Mrs. Rand almost loved him and wished that Daisy had been here to entertain him.

Of course it must be dull for a man with only a plain cut-and-dried girl like Lizzie for company.

Lizzie, meanwhile, knew that he was waiting for an opportunity of speech. She had read an appeal in his eyes when he had first entered the room, and now she sat there, curiously, ironically amused at her own agitation. "Lizzie Rand," she said to herself, "you're only, after all, the kind of fool that you despise other people for being. What are you after in this galère?"

Nevertheless even now, in retrospect, how arid and sterile seemed all those other active useful days. One moment's little grain of sentiment and a life's hard work goes for nothing in comparison.

After dinner, when the lamp burnt brightly and the furniture seemed to be less anxious to fill every possible space and the windows were opened into the square with its stars and grey shadows, the room seemed, of a sudden, comfortable, and Mrs. Rand, sitting in an arm-chair, with a novel on her lap and spectacles on her nose, was almost cosy. She had left, before going to her matinee, Just a Heroine at one of its most thrilling crises, and Lizzie knew that the talk with Breton depended for its very existence on the relative strength of the play and the novel. If Love and the King were the more powerful, then would Mrs. Rand make a discursive third. But no, for a moment there was a pause, then, indecisively, Mrs. Rand took up her book. For a while she talked to Breton over its pages, then the light of excitement stole into her eyes, her soul was netted by the snarer, Breton was forgotten as though he had never been.

Their chairs were by the open window and a very little breeze came and played around them. In the square there was that sense of some imminent occurrence, a breathless suggestion of suspense, that a hot evening sometimes carries with it. The stars blazed in a purple sky and a moon was full rounded, a plate of gold; beneath such splendour the square was cool and dim.

"You mustn't think mother rude," Lizzie said with a little smile. "If she once gets deep into a book nothing can tear her from it."

He said something, but she could see that he was not thinking of Mrs. Rand. It was always in the evening, she thought, when uncertain colours and shadows filled the air, that he looked his best. He touched, now, as he had touched on that day of their first meeting, a note of something fine and strange—someone, very young and perhaps very foolish and impetuous, but someone armoured in courage and set apart for some great purpose.

He sat back in his chair, flinging, every now and again, little restless glances beyond the window, pulling sometimes at his beard, answering her absent-mindedly. Then suddenly he began, fiercely, looking away from her—

"Miss Rand, I've got an apology to make to you— —"

His voice was so low that she could only catch the words by leaning forward—"To me?"

"Yes—I've been wanting to speak all these weeks. It seemed right enough before, but since I've known you I've felt ashamed of it—as though I'd done something wrong."

"What is it, Mr. Breton?" Her clear grave eyes encouraged him.

"Why—I came to this house, took my rooms, simply because I knew that you were here— —"

"That I was here?"

"Yes. I was looking about in this part of the world for rooms. I wanted to be—near Portland Place, you know. I came here and old Mrs. Tweed talked a lot and then, after a time, I said something—about my grandmother. And then she told me that someone who lived here did secretarial work for my aunt— —"

He stopped abruptly.

"Well?" said Lizzie, laughing. "All this is not very terrible."

"Then, you see, I determined to stay. I was full of absurd ideas just at the time, thought that I was going to take some great revenge—I was quite melodramatic. And so I thought that I'd use you, get to know you and then, through you—do something or another."

Lizzie eyed him with merriment. "Upon my word, what were you going to make me do? Carry bombs into your aunt's bedroom or set fire to the Portland Place house? Tell me, I should like to know— —"

"Ah," he said, "it's all very well for you to laugh. It's very kind of you to take it that way, but lots of women wouldn't have liked it. They'd have thought it another of the things I'm always accused of doing, I suppose."

"No," said Lizzie gravely, "it was all perfectly natural. I understand. I should have done just the same kind of thing, I expect, if I'd been in your place."

The fierceness of his voice showed her that he had been brooding for weeks, and that life was, just now, harder than he could endure.

"You can trust me a great deal farther than that, Mr. Breton," she said.

"The other night," he began, "you said that I might talk to you. I've been pretty lonely lately—and it would help me if——"

"Anything you like," she assured him.

"Besides, there's more than that," he went on. "You've heard—of course you must have heard all kinds of things against me. You're in the enemy's camp and I don't suppose they measure their words. I don't know why you've been so decent to me as you have after what you must have heard——"

"Don't worry your head about that," she said. "We all have our enemies."

"No, but now that we're friends I'd like you to know my side of it all. I don't want to make myself out a hero or blacken all the other people, but there is something to be said for me—there is—there is——"

He muttered these last words with the deepest intensity. He seemed to fling them through the window into the square, as though he were standing out there, on his defence, before all those listening lighted windows.

"I've been a fool—a thousand times. I've done silly things often and once or twice bad, rotten things, but all these others—these virtuous people who are so ready to judge me, have they been any better?"

"My father was a scoundrel, although I loved him and would love him now if he came back—but he was just as bad as they make 'em and there's no use in denying it. He'd tell you so himself if he were here. He broke my poor mother's heart and killed her. I don't remember her—I was no age at all when she died—but I've got an old picture of her, kept it always with me; she must have been rather like my cousin Rachel, who was here the other day——"

102

Lizzie watched his face. There had left him now all that hint of insincerity, of exaggeration that she had noticed when he had talked before. She knew that he was telling her now absolutely the truth as he saw it.

"She died and after that I was taken about Europe with my father. We lived in almost every capital in Europe—Berlin, Paris, Rome, Vienna, everywhere. Sometimes we were rich, sometimes poor. Sometimes we knew the very best people, sometimes the very worst. Sometimes I'd go to school for a little, then I'd suddenly be taken away. My father was splendid to me then; the best-looking man you ever saw, tall, broad, carried himself magnificently— the finest man in Europe. I only knew, bit by bit, the things that he used to do. It was cards most of the time, and he taught me to play, of course, as he taught me to do everything else.

"When I was eighteen my eyes were opened—I tried to leave him—But I loved him and I verily believe that I was the only human being in the world that he cared for. Anyway, he died of fever and general dissipation when I had just come of age, and I came home to England with a little money and great hopes of putting myself right with the world."

As he had talked to her he had gathered confidence; her silence was, in some way to him, reassuring and comforting. Some people have the gift of listening without words so warmly, with such eloquence that they reassure and console as no speech could ever do. This was Lizzie's gift, and Breton, depending, more than most human beings, upon the protection of his fellows, gathered courage.

"My father had always taught me to hate my grandmother. He painted her to me as I have since found her—remorseless, eaten up with pride, cruel. I came home to England, meaning to lead a new life, to be decent—as I'd always wanted to be.

"Well, they wouldn't have me, not one of them. They pretended to at first; and my Uncle John at least was sincere, I think, and was kind for a time, but was afraid of my grandmother as they all were. Christopher—you know him of course—was a real friend to me. He'd stood up for my father before and he stood up for me now. But what was the use? I was wild when I saw that my grandmother was against me and was going to do her best to ruin me. I just didn't care then—what was the good of it all? Other people encouraged me. The set in London that hated my people would have done something with me, but I wouldn't be held by anyone.

"I'm not excusing myself," he said quietly, looking away from the window and suddenly taking his judgment from her eyes.

"I know you're not," she said, smiling back to him.

"Cards finished me. I'd always loved gambling—I love it still—my father had given me a good education in it. There were plenty of fellows in town to take one on and—Oh! it's all such an old story now, not worth digging up. But there was a house and a table and a young fool who lost all he possessed and—well, did for himself. It had all been square as far as I was concerned, but somebody had to be a scapegoat and two or three of us were named. It was hushed up for the sake of the young fellow's people, but everyone knew. Of course they all said, as far as I was concerned, 'Like father like son,' and I think I minded that more than anything——"

"Oh! I'm sorry, I'm sorry," Lizzie said.

"I give you my word of honour that it had all been straight as far as I was concerned—gambling just as anyone might. That's what made me so mad, to think of the rest of them—all so virtuous and good—and then going off to Monte Carlo and losing or winning their little bit—just as I'd done.

"I tried to brazen it out for a bit, but it was no good. Christopher still stuck by me—otherwise it was—well, the Under Ten, you know——"

"The Under Ten?"

"Yes—all the men and women who've done something—once—done one of the things that you mustn't do. It mayn't have been very bad, not half so bad as the things—the cruel, mean things—that most people do every day of their lives, but, once it's there, you're down, you're under. There's a regular colony of them here in London; their life's amusing. There they are, hanging on here, keeping up some pretence of gaiety, some kind of decency, waiting, hoping that the day will come when they'll be taken back again, when everything will be forgotten. They pretend, bravely enough, not to mind their snubs, not to notice the kind people, once their friends, who cut them now. Every now and again they make a spring like fish to the top of the water, see the sun, hope that the light and air are to be theirs again, after all—and then back they are pushed, down into the dark, their element now, they are told. Oh! there's comedy there, Miss Rand, if you care to look for it."

She said nothing; the fierce bitterness in his voice had made him seem older suddenly, as though, in this portion of his journey, be had spent many, many years.

"I must cut it short—you'll have had enough of this. I couldn't stand it. I left London and went abroad. After that, what didn't I do? I was everywhere, I did everything. Sometimes I was straight, sometimes I wasn't. I was always bitter, wild with fury when I thought of that old woman—of her complacency, sitting there and striking down all the poor devils that had been less fortunate than she. All those years abroad I nourished that anger and, at last, when I thought that I'd been abroad long enough, that people would have forgotten, perhaps, and forgiven, I came back. I came back to be revenged on my grandmother and to re-establish myself. I'd got some money, enough for a little annuity, and I was careful now—I wasn't going to make any mistakes this time." He laughed bitterly. "One doesn't learn much with age. What a fool I was! I've got the reputation I had before, whether I'm good or bad. It would all be hopeless—utterly hopeless—if it weren't for one thing——"

She looked up, and as she glanced at him, could feel the furious beating of her heart.

"I'd go back at once—I've almost gone back already—not abroad, that never again for long—but back to my friends, the unfortunates—" He laughed. "They're anxious to have me. They'll welcome me. I can have my cards and the rest then, with no one to object or to lecture—and I'll be done for quite nicely, completely done for."

Then he pulled himself together, squared his shoulders. "But one thing keeps me," he said. "Something's happened in the last few weeks—I've met somebody——"

"Yes," she said almost in a whisper.

"Somebody who's made it worth while for me to fight on a bit." She could feel his agitation: his voice, although he tried very hard to control it, was shaking. Then he laughed, raised his voice and caught and held her eyes with his.

"But there, Miss Rand. I've talked a fearful lot, only I wanted to tell you—I had to tell you. And now—if you feel—that you'd rather not know me, you've only got to say so."

105

She laughed a little unsteadily.

"Thank you for taking me into your confidence. You shall never regret it. I'm glad you're going to hold on, and, after all, we're all doing that more or less."

"It's done me a world of good talking like this. It's what I've been wanting for months."

She quieted her emotion. Looking out into the stars she knew that she believed every word that he had said. She thought that she valued Truth above every other quality; the directness that there was in Truth; its honesty and clarity. He might not always be honest with her, but she would never forget that he had, on this night, at least, spoken no falsehood.

Life—her work, her surroundings, Portland Place, her home—this was full of falsehood and deceit and muddle.

Here, this evening, at last, was honesty.

They said no more, but sat there silently and listened to the echo of dance music from some house.

Mrs. Rand, whom their conversation had lured into oblivion of them, was roused now by their silence.

She looked up. "It's quite splendid," she said, "you must read it, Lizzie. The part about the Riviera is lovely." Then, slowly remembering, "Really, Mr. Breton, I'm afraid you must consider me very rude."

He came towards her, assuring her that his evening had been delightful.

Lizzie was happy, happier than she could ever remember to have been before. She felt her cheeks burn. She leant out of the window to cool them. She flung back, over her shoulder:

"By the way, Mr. Breton—a piece of gossip. Your cousin is to marry Sir Roderick Seddon!"

She could not see him. He said nothing. Mrs. Rand said:

"Really, Lizzie! How interesting! How long's that been announced?"

"Oh! it isn't announced. I don't believe that he's even asked her, but all the house knows it. It's settled. I believe she likes him immensely and, of course, the Duchess is devoted to him."

Anything would do to talk about. What did it matter? Only that she should keep on talking so that they should not see how happy she was—how happy!

He said good night, rather sharply; his voice was constrained as though he too were keeping in his emotion.

After he had gone Mrs. Rand said, "I don't like him, my dear. I can't help it— you may laugh at me—but my impressions are always right. He hardly spoke to me all the evening."

"Why, mother, you were reading. How could he?"

"That's all very well, but I don't like him. And I believe he's in love with his cousin. He went quite white when you spoke about the engagement."

"Mother—how absurd you are. He's only seen her once——"

"Well, my dear, that's a book you ought to read; really, I haven't enjoyed anything so much for weeks. I simply——"

Up in her bedroom Lizzie flung wide her window and laughed at the golden moon. Then she lay, for hours, staring at the pale light that it flung upon her ceiling.

Oh! what a fool she was! But she was happy, happy, happy. And he needed someone to look after him—he did, indeed!

CHAPTER XI
HER GRACE'S DAY
I

The Duchess had suffered, during the last five or six years, from sleeplessness, and throughout these hot days and nights of June and July sleep almost deserted her. Grimly she gave it no quarter, allowing to no one that she was sleeping badly, pretending even to Christopher that all was well.

Nevertheless those long dark hours began to tell upon her. She had known many nights sleepless through pain, certain nights sleepless through anxiety, but they, terrible though they had been, had not worn so stern a look as these long black spaces of time when all rest and comfort seemed to be drawn from her by some mysterious hand.

To herself now she admitted that she dreaded that moment when Dorchester left her; she began to do what she had never in her life done before, to fall asleep during the daytime. Small mercy to anyone who might attract any attention to those little naps.

She fell asleep often towards six or seven and, therefore, without any comment, Dorchester, seeing her fatigue, left her to sleep until late in the morning. She had not for many years left her room before midday, but she had been awake with her correspondence and the papers by half-past seven at the latest. Now it was often eleven before she awoke.

She found that she did not awake with the energy and freshness that she had always known before. About her there always hovered a great cloud of fatigue—something not quite present, but threatening at any moment to descend.

On a certain morning late in July she awoke after two or three hours' restless sleep. As she woke she was conscious that those hours had not removed from her that threatening cloud: she heard a clock strike eleven. Dorchester was drawing back the curtains and from behind the blinds there leapt upon her a blazing, torrid day.

Her bedroom carried on the touch of fantasy that her other room had shown; she was lying in a red lacquer Japanese bed that mounted up behind her like a throne. Her wall-paper was an embossed dull gold and the chairs were carved Indian, of black ebony.

Lying in bed she appeared very old and ugly; the sharp nose was exceedingly prominent and her white hair scattered about the pillow gave her face the colour of dried parchment.

Dorchester brought her her chocolate and her letters and The Times and the Morning Post.

"Another terribly hot day, your Grace."

"Yes—I suppose so." As she took her letters she felt, for the first time in her life, that it would perhaps be better to lie in bed for the rest of her life and conduct the world from there.

She put the letters down and stared at the day—

"Draw the curtains again, Dorchester, and kindly ask Lady Adela if she will be so good as to come and see me in a quarter of an hour's time."

When Dorchester had gone she lay back and closed her eyes and dozed again, whilst the chocolate grew cold and the births and deaths and marriages grew aged and stale. She did not care, she did not want to see her daughter ... she did not want to see anyone, nor was there anything now in the world worth her energy or trouble. Her body, being now at ease, was called back to days, brighter days, days filled with thrilling events and thrilling people, days when the world was a world and not a dried-up cinder. Those were men ... those were women ... and then, suddenly, she was conscious first that her daughter was speaking and then that her daughter was a tiresome fool.

She sat up a little and her nightdress fell back showing a neck bony, crinkled and yellow.

"I said a quarter of an hour," she snapped.

"It is a quarter of an hour, mother," said Lady Adela.

Lady Adela hated and dreaded these morning interviews. In the first place she disliked the decorations of her mother's bedroom, thought them almost indecent, and could never be comfortable in such surroundings. She was also aware, by long experience, that her mother was always at her worst at this hour in the morning and many were the storms of temper that that absurd bed and those unpleasant black chairs had witnessed. Thirdly she knew that she herself looked her worst and was her weakest amongst these eccentricities and shadowed by this dim light.

She waited now whilst her mother fumbled her letters.

"There's your chocolate, mother," she said at last. "It'll be cold."

The Duchess was looking at her letters, but was absorbing only a little of their contents. She was summoning all her will to her aid; she wanted to order the blind to be pulled down, to command her daughter to avoid her presence for at least a week, to scatter her correspondence to the four corners of the earth, and to see none of it again; at the same time she was driving into her brain the fact that before Adela, of all people in the world, she must be alert and wise and wonderful; Adela, the ugliest and most foolish of living women, must see no weakness.

"Shall I read your letters to you, mother?"

She did not answer; slowly, steadily at last, her will was flooding her brain. She could feel the warmth and the colour and the strength of it pervading again her body. The day did not now appear of so appalling a heat and the weight of the things to be done was less heavy upon her.

Lady Adela, meanwhile, watching her mother was struck once again by that chill dismay that had alarmed her first on that May evening, after the visit to the picture gallery. In that half-light her mother did seem very, very old and very, very feeble. Lady Adela had a dreadful temptation to say in a brusque sharp voice, "What do you let your chocolate get cold like that for? Why don't you get someone to read your letters sensibly to you instead of groping through them like that?" and at the mere horror of such a thought a shudder shook her and her heart began wildly to beat. Let once such words as those cross her lips and an edifice, a wonderful, towering temple raised by submissions and subduals and self-denials, would tumble to the ground.

For some moments the struggle in Lady Adela's breast was sharp, then by a tense dominion of her will she produced once again for herself the Ceremonial, the Terror, the agitated, humble Submission.

"Julia Massiter," the Duchess said, "has asked Rachel for the last week-end in July—She'll go of course——"

"Yes," said Lady Adela.

"Roddy Seddon is going — —"

"Yes."

"Roddy is going to marry Rachel. He's coming to see me this afternoon."

Lady Adela was silent.

"A very suitable business. I'd intended it for a long time." Then, after a pause —

"You may tell Dorchester I will dress now."

Lady Adela, conscious, as she left the room, of the relief of her dismissal, joyfully yielded that relief as witness —

The Terror was still there, and she was glad.

II

Very different, however, at three in the afternoon. Now she sat in her high black chair waiting for Roddy Seddon. Very difficult now to imagine that early discourage of the morning. Magnificent now with her black dress and flashing eyes and white hair, waiting for Roddy Seddon.

This that she had long planned was at length to come to pass. Roddy Seddon was to be united to the Beaminster family, never again to be separated from it.

Of Rachel she thought not at all. She had never liked Rachel; indeed it was a more positive feeling than that. Alone of all the family was Rachel still in rebellion; even the Duke, although he was so often abroad or in the country (he hated London), was submissive enough when he was with them. But Rachel the old woman knew that she had not touched.

Frightened — yes. The girl hated that evening half-hour and would give a great deal to avoid it, but the terror that she showed did not bring her any closer to her grandmother's power; she stood outside and away.

The Duchess had attempted to influence the girl's brain, to catch some trait, some preference, some dislike, that she could hold and use.

Still Rachel's soul was beyond her grasp, beyond even her guessing at. But she knew Roddy Seddon—she knew Roddy Seddon as no one knew him. And Roddy Seddon knew her.

Even when he was a boy he had known her as no one else knew her. He had seen through all her embroideries and disguises, had known where she was theatrical and why she was so, had discovered her plots and prides, her defeats and victories—and together they two, Pagan to the very bone of them, had laughed at a credulous, superstitious world.

The London that knew Roddy Seddon thought him a country bumpkin with dissipated tastes and an amiable heart. But she knew him better than that. He was not clever—no. He was amazingly innocent of books, he had no intellectual attainments whatever—yet had he received any kind of education, she knew that he might have had one of the finest brains in the country.

He had preferred dogs and horses and the simple enjoyments of his sensations.

Bowing to the outward rules and laws of the modern world he was less modern than anyone she had ever known.

Pagan—root and branch Pagan. In his simplicities, in his complexities, in his moralities and immoralities, in his kindnesses and cruelties—Pagan.

When they were together it was astonishing the number of trappings that they were able to discard. They were Pagan together.

But Rachel? Rachel?

Well, Rachel did not matter. It would be a rather good sight to see Rachel suffer, to watch her proud spirit up against something that she could not understand.

And meanwhile the Beaminster family was strengthened by a great addition and the campaign against this new generation, that refused to be led, that wished to lead, that thought itself so very, very brilliant, should go victoriously forward....

"Sir Roderick Seddon, your Grace."

As she looked at the healthy and red-faced Roddy sitting opposite to her, for an instant, some sharp warning, some foreordained consciousness of trouble to come, bade her pause. She knew that a word from her, now, would be enough to prevent the match. He would not prosecute it were she against it. After all, ought Roddy to marry anybody? Could a girl, as ignorant of the world as Rachel, put up any fight against Roddy's simple complexities?

What, after all, did Roddy think of the girl? Did he imagine that he was in love with her? Did he know her, understand her?

Then, looking at him, the affection that she had for him—the only affection that she had for anyone in the world—swept over her. This marriage would bind him to her, would give her another ally before the world—yes, it should go on.

She smiled at him.

"Well, Roddy, have you no news for me, now?"

He had been silent, gazing before him, his brows puckered.

Now he smiled back at her.

"Well, there's been the usual doin's the last week or two. I've been dancin' every night till I'm tired. 'Bout time for the country agen——"

"Have you been down to Seddon at all?"

"Yes. Two nights last week—all dried up—Place wants me a bit oftener down there——"

"What's this I hear about young Olive Ormond marrying Besset Crewe's daughter?"

"So they say—can't imagine it myself. The girl's about eighty-four and a half and he's the most awful kid. Saw them at the opera the other night——"

"What about Scotland this summer, Roddy? Are you going?"

"Don't think so. Depends——"

Then there was silence. The little conversation had been as stiff as it was possible a conversation could be. The China dragons must have wondered — never before so constrained a dialogue between these two!

Now another pause, then suddenly Roddy, his hands clutching one another, his face redder than ever —

"I want — I wonder — dash it — have I your leave to ask your granddaughter to marry me?"

She laughed.

"Really, my dear Roddy, you've been very long about it — coming out with it, I mean. Didn't you know and didn't I know that that's what you came for to-day?"

"Well then, may I?"

She paused and watched his anxiety. Between both of them there hung, now, the recollection of so many things — conversations and deeds and thoughts known to both of them, so many, many things that no others in all the world could know. She waited for his eyes, caught them and held them.

"Are you in love with her?"

"Yes — that is — she's splendid — —"

"You haven't known her very long and you're a little impulsive, ain't you, Roddy, about these things?"

"No — I don't know her now. But we've seen a lot of one another these last months — a fearful lot. She's — oh! hang it! I never can say things — but she's a brick."

"Do you think she'll accept you?"

"How can any feller tell? I think she likes me — she's odd — —"

"Yes — she is — very. She's a mixture — she's very young — and she won't understand you."

His eyes were suddenly troubled and, as she saw that trouble, she was alarmed. He really did care....

"Yes, I know—I don't understand myself. I'm wild sometimes—I wish I weren't——"

"Marriage is going to make you a model character, Roddy. Of course I'm glad—but it won't be easy, you know. And she won't be easy."

"I want her though. I've never thought of marriage before. I do want her."

"My dear Roddy, you speak as though she were a sheep or a dog. It's only her first season. Don't you think you'd better wait a little?"

"No. I want her now."

"Well, you're definite enough—" She paused and then, in a voice that had, in spite of her, real emotion, "You have my consent. You've got my blessing."

He rose and came clumsily towards her.

"You don't know—I'm no use at words, but I'm dam' grateful—Rippin' of you!"

For a second he touched her dried, withered hand—how cold it was! and in this hot weather, too.

"You'll ask her at Julia Massiter's next week?"

"Expect so—I say you are——"

Then he sat down again. The room was relieved of an immense burden; once more they were at ease together.

"The other night—" he said, bending forward and chuckling ever so little.

III

Lady Carloes, Agnes Lady Farnet, and old Mrs. Brunning were coming to play bridge with her. The ceremonial was ever the same! They arrived at half-past nine and at half-past eleven supper for four was served in the Duchess's little green room, behind her bedroom (a little room like a box with a green wall-paper, a card-table and silver candlesticks). They played, sometimes, until three or four o'clock in the morning; the Duchess played an exceedingly good game and Mrs. Brunning (a bony little woman like a plucked chicken) was the best bridge player in London. The other two were moderate, but made mistakes which allowed the Duchess the free use of her most caustic wit and satire.

Lord John came just before dinner as he always did for a few minutes every evening. He stood there, fat and smiling and amiable and, as always, a little nervous.

"Well, John?"

She liked John the best of her children, although he was, of course, the most fearful fool, but she liked his big broad face and he was always clean and healthy; moreover, she could use him more easily than any of them.

"Bridge to-night, mother, isn't it?"

"Yes. Not so hot this evening. Just give me that book. Turn the lamp up a little—no—not that one. The de Goncourt book. Yes. Thank you."

"Anything I can get for you, mother? Anyone I can send to you?"

He was thinking, as he smiled down at her, "She's old to-night—old and tired. This hot weather...."

She looked up at him before she settled herself—

"Roddy Seddon came this afternoon ——"

"Yes. I know."

Suddenly his heart began to beat. He had known, during all these last weeks, of what the common talk had been. He knew, too, what his conscience had told him, and he knew, too, how perpetually he had silenced that same conscience.

"He asked me whether he had my permission to propose to Rachel ——"

"Yes."

"Of course I gave it him. I thought it most suitable in every way."

Now was Lord John's moment. He knew, even as it descended upon him, what was the right to do. He must protest—Roddy Seddon was not the right man to marry Rachel, Rachel who was to him more than anyone in the world—

He must protest—

And then with that impulse went the old warning that because his mother seemed to him older and feebler to-night than he had ever known her, therefore if he spoke now, it would involve far more than the immediate dispute. There was a sudden impulse in him to risk discomfort, to risk a scene, to break, perhaps, in the new assertion of his authority, all the old domination, to smash a tradition to pieces.

He glanced at his mother. She met his eyes. He knew that she was daring him to speak. After all to-morrow would be a better time—she was tired now—he would speak then. His eyes fell, and after a pause and a word about some indifferent matter, he said good night and went.

IV

Once, in some early hour of the morning when the candles were burning low, the thought of Rachel came to her.

Even as she noticed that her hand shone magnificently with hearts she was conscious that the girl stood opposite to her, there against the green wall, straight and fierce, all black and white, looking at her.

Christopher? John?...

For a second her brain was clouded. Might she not have attempted some relationship with the girl? Given her some counsel and a little kindness? She must have been lonely there in that great house without a friend. She was going now into a very perilous business.

She pushed the weakness from her. Her eyes were again upon the cards.

"Hearts," she said. The odd trick this game and it was her rubber. The dying flame rose in the silver sconces and the four old heads bobbed, wildly, fantastically, upon the wall.

CHAPTER XII
DEFIANCE OF THE TIGER—I
I

Rachel sat in the train with Aunt Adela and Uncle John: they were on their way to Trunton St. Perth, Lord Massiter's country house. It was a July day softened with cool airs and watered colours; trees and fields were mingled with sky and cloud; through the counties there was the echo of running streams, only against an earth fading into sky and a sky bending and embracing earth, sharp, with hard edges, the walls and towers that man had piled together showed their outlines cut as with a sword.

Over all the country in the pale blue of the afternoon sky a great moon was burning and the corn ran in fine abundance to the summit of the hills.

Rachel, as the train plunged with her into the heart of Sussex, was gazing happily through the window, dreaming, almost dozing, feeling in every part of her a warm and grateful content. Opposite to her Aunt Adela, gaunt and with the expression that she always wore in trains as of one whose person and property were in danger, at any instant, of total destruction, read a life of a recently deceased general whose widow she knew. Uncle John, with three illustrated papers, was interested in photographs of people with one leg in the air and their mouths wide open; every now and again he would say (to nobody in particular), "There's old Reggie Cutler with that foreign woman—you know"—or "Fancy Shorty Monmouth being at Cowes after all this year—you know we heard——"

Rachel had been having a wonderful time—that was the great fact that ran, up and down, through her dozing thoughts. Yes, a wonderful time. It was surely, now, a century ago, that strange period when she had dreaded, so terribly, her plunge.

That day, after her visit to the Bond Street gallery, when it had all seemed simply more than she could possibly encounter, those talks with May Eversley (who, by the way, had just announced herself as engaged to a middle-aged baronet) when the world had frowned down from a vast, incredible height upon a miserably terrified midget. Why! the absurdity of it! It had all been as easy, simply as easy as though she had been plunged in the very heart of it all her life.

Followed there swiftly upon that the knowledge that Roddy Seddon was to be, for this same week-end, at Lady Massiter's. Rachel did not pretend that, ever since that Meistersinger night at the opera she had not known of his attentions to her—impossible to avoid them had she wished, impossible to pretend ignorance of the meaning that his inarticulate sentences had, of late, conveyed, impossible to mistake the laughing hints and suggestions of May and the others.

She did not know what answer she would give did he ask her to marry him. At that concrete suggestion her doze left her and, sitting up, staring out at the wonderful day into whose heart muffled lights were now creeping, she asked herself what, indeed, was her real thought of him.

He was to her as were Uncle John and Dr. Christopher—safe, kind, simple. He appealed to everything in her that longed for life to be clear, comfortable, without danger. She loved his happiness in all out-of-door things—horses and dogs and fields and his little place in Sussex. Ever since that visit to Uncle Richard's fans she had suspected him of other appreciations and enthusiasms, perhaps she might in time encourage those hidden things in him.

Above all did she find him true, straight, honest. Lies, little mannerisms, disguises, these were not in him, he was as clear to her as a mirror, she would trust him beyond anyone she knew.

He did not touch in any part of him that other secret, wild, unreal life of hers, and indeed that was, in him, the most reassuring thing of all.

The Rachel who was in rebellion, to whom everything of her London life, everything Beaminster, was hateful, whose sudden memories and instincts, whose swift alarms and fore-warnings were so shattering to every clinging security that life might offer—this Rachel knew nothing of Roddy Seddon.

He was there to take her away from that, to drive it all into darkness, to reassure her against its return, and marriage with him would mean release, security, best of all freedom from her grandmother who knew, so well, that life in her and loved to play with that knowledge. Her colour rose and her eyes shone as she thought of what this so early escape from the Portland Place house would mean to her. Already, in her first season, to be free of it all—to be free of humbug and deception—Oh! for that would she not surrender everything in the world?

Roddy, as she pictured him, with his clean life, his love of nature, his kindliness, seemed, just then, the safest refuge that would ever be offered to her.

And at that, without reason, she saw before her her cousin Francis Breton. Several times she had met him since that first occasion at Lizzie Rand's. Once again at Lizzie's and twice in Regent's Park when she had been walking with May.

Yes—that was all. Thinking of it now the meetings appeared to her almost infinite. Between each actual encounter intimacy seemed to leap in its progress, and although, on at least two of them, he had only walked with her for the shortest period, yet, always with them, she was conscious of the number of things that, between them, did not need to be said—knowledge that they shared.

In all this there was, with her, a confusion of motives and sensations that, at present, refused to be disentangled. For one thing there was, in all of this, a furtiveness, a secrecy, that she loathed. Against that was the persuasion that it would be the finest thing in the world for her to bring him back into the Beaminster fold, not, of course, that he should remain there (he was far too strong and adventurous for that), but that, accepted there, he could use it as a springing-off board for success and fortune. Let her once, as the situation now was, say a word to Uncle John or the others, and that of course was the end....

She knew, quite definitely, that now she wished that she had never met him.

He had been, during these weeks, the only influence that had drawn that other Rachel to the light. It was always that other Rachel that met him — someone alarming, rebellious, conscious of unhappiness, and apprehensive, above everything, that in some hidden manner she was being untrue to her real self.

At such moments it was as though she had blinded some force within her, muffled it, stifled it, because her way through the world was easier with it so muffled, so stifled.

At some future time, what if there should leap out upon her that muffled figure, bursting its bonds, refusing any longer to be silenced, proclaiming the world no easy, comfortable place, but a battle, a fierce, unresting war?

When she thought of Breton it was as though she knew herself for a coward, as though he had threatened to expose her for one, and as though (and this was the worst of all) something in her was eager that he should—

Against this there was the peace, the security that Roddy could offer her....

Beaminster security, perhaps—nevertheless....

They were at Trunton St. Perth. The little station glittered in the evening air.
It was all suddenly thrilling. Who would be there? What might not happen
before Monday?

II

In the high beautiful hall where they all stood about and had tea she could
see who they were. There was a girl whom she had met on several occasions
this season, Nita Raseley, there was a large florid cheerful person who was,
she discovered, Maurice Garden, the well-known and popular novelist,
there was his wife, there was a thin intellectual cousin of Lady Massiter's,
Miss Rawson, old and plain enough for her cleverness to have turned to
acidity, Roddy Seddon and, of course, Lord and Lady Massiter.

Lord Massiter was large and florid like the novelist, and when they stood
together by the fireplace foreign customs and languages were suddenly
absurd, so English was the atmosphere. Lady Massiter was also large, but
she had the kind and warm placidity that makes some women the type of all
maternity. She would be, Rachel felt, a sure resource in all time of trouble
and she would also be entirely unsatisfactory as an intimate personal friend.
She would, like philanthropists and clergymen, love people by the mass,
never by the individual.

Nita Raseley was pink and white, with large blue eyes that confided in
everyone they looked at. Her laugh was a little shrill, her clothes very
beautiful, and men liked her.

So there they all were.

She had said good day to Roddy and then had moved away from him,
governed by some self-consciousness and the conviction that Nita Raseley's
blue eyes were upon her.

It was all very cheerful and very English as they stood talking there, and the
doors beyond the hall showed through their dark frames green lawns and
terraces soaked in evening light. It was all very, very comfortable.

As she dressed for dinner Rachel had her windows open, so hot was the
night, and she could watch the evening star that shone with a wonderful
brilliance above a dark little wood that crowned a rise beyond the gardens.
She had a maid who was very young indeed; this was her first place, but she

had, during the three months, learnt with great quickness and had attached herself to her mistress with the most burning devotion. She was a silent, unusual girl and kept herself apart from the rest of the servants.

Rachel as she sat before her dressing-table could see in that mirror the dark reflection of the twilit garden.

"It's a lovely place, Lucy——"

"Yes, Miss Rachel."

"Are you glad to get away from London?"

"It has been hot there these last weeks."

Rachel met in the glass the girl's black eyes. They were searching Rachel's face.

"Lucy, would you rather live in London or in the country?"

"I don't mind, Miss Rachel." Then after a little pause: "I hope I've give satisfaction these last weeks?"

"Why, yes, of course."

"Then I hope, miss, that you'll allow me to stay with you whether—in London or the country."

The colour mounted to Rachel's cheeks.

"I hope there'll be no need for any change," she said.

She found when she came down to the drawing-room that Monty Carfax had arrived. Monty Carfax was the chief of the young men who were, just at that time, entertaining London dinner-tables. About half a dozen of God's creatures, under thirty and perfectly dressed, with faces like tombstones and the laugh of the peacock, went from house to house in London and mocked at the world.

They belonged, as the mediæval jesters belonged, each to his own court, and Monty Carfax, certainly the cleverest of them, was attached to the Beaminster Court and served the Duchess by faith, if not by sight.

Rachel hated him and always, when she found herself next to him, wrapped herself in her old farouche manner and behaved like an awkward schoolgirl.

She was terribly disappointed at discovering that he was going to take her into dinner to-night; he knew that she disliked him and felt it a compliment that a raw creature fresh from the schoolroom should fail to appreciate him; on this occasion he devoted himself to the elderly Massiter cousin on his other side—throughout dinner they happily undressed the world and found it sawdust.

Rachel meanwhile found Maurice Garden her other companion. He genially enjoyed his dinner and talked in a loud voice and prepared the answers that he always gave to ladies who asked him when he wrote, whether he thought of his plots or his characters first, and "she did hope he wouldn't mind her saying that of all his books the one——"

He frankly liked these questions and was taken by surprise when Rachel said:

"I've never read any of your novels, Mr. Garden, so I won't pretend——"

He asked her what she did read.

"Have you ever read anything by an author called Peter Westcott?"

"Westcott? Westcott?... Let me see ... Westcott?... Well now—One of the young men, isn't he?"

"Yes. He wrote a book called Reuben Hallard."

"Ah yes. I remember about Reuben Hallard—had quite a little success as a first book. He's one of your high-brow young men, all for Art and the rest of it. We all begin like that, Miss Beaminster. I was like that myself once——"

She looked at him coolly.

"Why did you give it up?"

"Simply didn't pay, you know—not a penny in it. And why should there be? People don't want to know what a young ass thinks about life if he can't tell a story. All young men think the same—green leaves, moons and stars and lots of symbols, you know—all good enough if they don't expect people to pay for it."

"I think Reuben Hallard's a fine book," she said, "and so are some of the others. After all, everyone doesn't want only a plot in a book."

He looked at her with patronizing kindness. "Well, you see if your Mr. Westcott doesn't change. Every writer wants an audience whatever he may pretend, and the best way to get a audience is to give the audience what it wants. It needs unusual courage to sit on a packing-case year after year and shave in a broken looking-glass——"

She looked round the table. Everyone was happy. The butler was fat and had the face of a Roman emperor, the food was very, very good, Nita Raseley and Roddy laughed and laughed and laughed—

Suddenly Rachel's heart jumped in her body. Oh! she was glad; glad that Roddy cared for her and would look after her, because otherwise she didn't know what violence she might suddenly commit, what desperations she might not engage upon, what rebels and outlaws she would not support—

What Outlaws! And then, looking beyond the thickly curtained windows, she could fancy that she could see one gravely standing out there on the lawn, standing with his one arm and his pointed beard and his eyes appealing to be let in.

Then there was an ice that was so good that Peter Westcott and Francis Breton seemed more outcast than ever.

III

After dinner, when the men had come into the drawing-room, they all went out into the gardens. It was such a night of stars as Rachel had never seen, so dense an army that all earth was conscious of them; the sky was sheeted silver, here fading into their clouded tracery, there, at fairy points drawing the dark woods and fields up to its splendour with lines of fire. The world throbbed with stars, was restless under the glory of them—God walked in all gardens that night.

At first Nita Raseley, Monty Carfax, Rachel and Roddy went together, then, turning up a little path into the little wood that rose above the garden, Rachel and Roddy were alone.

They found the trunk of a tree and sat down—Behind them the trees were thin enough to show the stars, below them in a dusk lit by that glimmering lustre that starlight flings—a glow that would be flame were it not dimmed by distance immeasurable—they could see the lawns and hedges of the garden and across the dark now and again some white figure showed for an instant and was gone. The house behind the shadows rose sharp and black.

Roddy looked big and solid sitting there. Rachel sat, even now uncertain that she did not see Francis Breton in front of her, looking down, as she did, into the shadowy garden.

"I hope," she said abruptly, "that you don't like Monty Carfax."

"I've never thought about him," he said. "He's certainly no pal of mine—why?"

"Because I hate him," she said fiercely. "What right has he got to exist on a night like this?"

"He's always supposed to be a very clever feller," Roddy said slowly. "But I think him a silly sort of ass—knows nothin' about dogs or horses, can't play any game, only talks clever to women——"

"I can't bear that sort of man and I don't like Mr. Garden either. He's so fat and he loves his food."

"So do I," said Roddy quite simply. "I love it too. It was a jolly good dinner to-night."

She said nothing and then, when he had waited a little, he said anxiously:

"I say, Miss Beaminster, we've been such jolly good friends—all these weeks. And yet—sometimes—I'm afraid you think me the most awful fool——"

She laughed. "I think you are about some things, but then—so am I about a good many things—most of your things——"

"Look here, Miss Beaminster—I wish you'd help me about things I'm an ass in. You can, you know—I'd be most awfully glad."

"What," she said, turning round and facing him, "are the things you really care about?"

"The things? ... care about?"

"Yes—really——"

"Well! Oh! animals and bein' out in the open and shootin' and ridin' and fishin'—any old exercise—and comin' up to town for a buck every now and again, and then goin' back and seein' no one, and my old place and—oh! I don't know," he ended.

"You wouldn't tell anyone a lie, would you, about things you liked and didn't like?"

"It wouldn't be much use if I did," he said, laughing. "They'd find me out in a minute——"

"No, but would you? If you were with a number of people who thought art the thing to care about and knew nothing about dogs and horses, would you say you cared about art more than anything?"

"No," he said slowly. "No—but sometimes, you see, pictures and music and such do please me—like anything—I can't put into words, but I might suddenly be in any old mood—for pictures, or your uncle's fans, or dogs or the Empire or these jolly old stars—Why, there, you see I just let it go on—the mood, I mean, till it's over——" Then he added with a great sigh, "But I am a dash fool at explainin'——"

"But I know you wouldn't be like Mr. Garden or Mr. Carfax—just pretending not to like the thing because it's the thing not to. Or like Aunt Adela, who picks up a phrase about a book or picture from some clever man and then uses it everywhere."

"I should never remember it—a phrase or anythin'—I never can remember what a feller says——"

"Oh! I know you'd always be honest about these things. I feel you would—about everything. It's all these lies that are so impossible: I think I've come to feel now after this first season that the only thing that matters is being straight. It is the only thing—if a person just gives you what they've got—what they've got, not what someone else is supposed to have. May Eversley used to say that people's minds are like soup—thick or clear—but they're only thick because they let them get thick with other people's opinions—you don't mind all this?" she said, suddenly pausing, afraid lest he should be bored.

"It's most awfully interestin'," he said from the bottom of his heart.

"There are some men and women—I've met one or two—who're just made up of Truth. You know it the minute you're with them. And they'll have pluck too, of course—Courage goes with it. Our family," she ended, "are of course the most terrible liars that have ever been—ever— —"

"Oh! I say— —" he began, protesting.

"Oh! but yes—they run everything on it. My uncle Richard ran through Parliament beautifully because he never said what he meant. And Aunt Adela—and Uncle John, although he's a dear. But then my grandmother brought them up to it. My grandmother would have about three clever people and then muddle all the rest so that the three clever ones can have everything in their hands— —"

"Look here," he broke in, "I'm most awfully fond of your grandmother— we're tremendous pals— —"

"You may be—I hate her. Oh! I don't hate her with melodrama, I don't want to strangle her or beat her face or burn her, but I'm frightened of her and she's always making me do things I'm ashamed of. That's the best reason for hating anyone there is."

"But she's such a sportsman. One of the old kind. One— —."

"Oh! I know all that you can say. I've heard it so many times. But she's all wrong. There isn't any good in her. She's just remorseless and selfish and stubborn. She thinks she ran the world once and she wants to do it still."

"That's all rather fine, I think," said Roddy. "I agree with her a bit. I think most people have got to be run—they just can't run themselves, so you have to put things into them."

"Well, that's just where we differ," she said sharply. "It isn't so. That's where all the muddle comes in. If everyone were just himself without anything borrowed—Oh! the brave world it'd be— —"

Then she laughed. "But I'm all wrong myself, you know. I'm as muddled as anyone. I've got all the true, real me there, but all the Beaminster part has slurred it over. But I've got a horrid fear that Truth gets tired of waiting too long. One day, when you're not expecting it, it comes up and says—'Now you choose—your only chance. Are you going to use me or not? If not, I'm going'—How awful if one didn't realize the moment was there, and missed it."

127

She was laughing, but in her heart that other woman in her was stirring. For a startled, trembling second the wood seemed to flame, the gardens to blaze with the challenge:

"Are you, for the sake of the comfort and safety of life, playing false? Which way are you going?"

She burst into laughter, she caught Roddy by the arm. "Oh! I've talked such nonsense—It's getting cold—we've got to go in. Don't think I talk like that generally, Sir Roderick, because I don't—I——"

She was nervous, frightened. The stars were so many and it was so dark and Roddy no longer seemed a protection.

"I know it's late—Look here, I'm going to run—Race me——"

She tore for her very life out of the little wood, felt him pounding behind her, seized, with a gasp of relief, the lights and the voices—

She knew, with joy, that Roddy was closing the door behind her and that the garden and the stars and the wood were shut into silence.

For a little while, in the drawing-room, she talked excitedly, laughed a great deal, even at Monty Carfax's jokes.

She knew that they were all thinking that she was pleased because she had been with Roddy. She did not care what their thoughts were.

At last in her room she cried to Lucy—"Pull the curtains tight—Tighter—Tighter—Those stars—they'll get through anything."

When at last Lucy was gone she lit her candle and lay there, hearing the clocks strike the hours, wondering when the day would come.

CHAPTER XIII
DEFIANCE OF THE TIGER—II
I

Roddy, dozing after a night of glorious sleep, lay on his back and swung happily to and fro.

The footman who was valeting him had pulled up the blind and drawn aside the curtains, and the garden came to him, not as on last evening, weighed with its canopy of stars, but now asserting its own happiness and colour and freshness.

The man said: "The bathroom is the last door down the passage on your right, sir. Breakfast is at half-past nine. It has just gone eight. What clothes, sir?"

Roddy stared at him and smiled. After a little time, the man enquired again: "Which suit will you wear this morning, sir?"

"Dark blue." Roddy, still happily floating somewhere near the ceiling—floating with delicious lightness—"Dark blue—Dark blue—Dark blue——"

For a little while the man, a strange vague shape, pulled out drawers and closed them and walked about the floor, like Agag, delicately. Roddy, from the ceiling watched him and resented the fact that every sharp click of a drawer pulled him nearer to the carpet.

The man's final shutting of the bedroom door plumped Roddy into his bed, wide awake.

"Damn him! What a wonderful day!"

He lay back and watched how waves of light danced on the walls. A fountain splashed in the gardens and the long mirror on the right of the bed had in it the corner of the green lawn and the cool grey stones of an old wall.

Roddy lay on his back and allowed his sensations to run up and down his body. It was for moments such as this that his life was intended. He lived, deliberately and without any selfishness in the matter, for the emotions that the good old god Pan might choose to provide for him.

He did not know Pan by name except as a silly fancy dress that Monty Carfax had once worn at a fancy-dress dance and as Someone alluded to

129

every now and again, vaguely, in the papers, but even though he did not call him by name he, nevertheless, paid, without question, his daily homage.

When, as on this beautiful morning, one had only to lie down and be instantly conscious of a thousand things—sheep moving slowly across hills, cattle browing in deep pools, those Downs that he loved rising, slowly, like aged men, to greet a new day—then one questioned nothing, one argued nothing, one needed no words, one was happy from the crown of one's head to the toes of one's feet.

On this especial morning these delights were connected with the fact that, during the day, he intended to propose marriage to Rachel Beaminster. He thought of her, now, as she had looked last night, sitting in that wood, in a pale blue dress, with the stars behind her, staring, so seriously, down into the garden. She had been very beautiful last night, and it had been a splendid moment—not more splendid than other moments that he had had, but splendid enough to remember.

He was always prepared for the necessity of the short duration of his sensations. He had discovered, when he was very young, that nothing lasted and that the things that lasted the shortest time were generally the best things, and therefore he had, quite unconsciously, trained himself to store his memory with splendid moments; now, although he had no memory at all for any sort of facts or books or histories, he could recall precisely, in all their forms and colours, scenes, persons, adventures that had, at any time, thrilled him.

He could remember days; once when, as a little boy, he had been overtaken by night on the Downs and had sheltered in a deserted house, black and evil, that had, he afterwards discovered, been, in the eighteenth century, a private mad-house; once when the sea had been green and purple, the sky black, and he had discovered a star-fish for the first time (very young on that occasion); once when his horse had run away with him and the danger had been exceeded by the glorious speed through the air ... many, many others, all to be counted by him to their very least detail, and now, of some of them, Rachel Beaminster was the central figure.

He had had relations of many kinds with many different women and never until now had he supposed, for an instant, that these relations would be permanent. Even now, although he was intending to marry Rachel Beaminster, he was not so foolish as to imagine that the freshness and novelty of the feeling that he now had for her would last more than a very short time.

130

Quite deliberately he treasured up in his mind a thousand pictures of her, as he had seen her during the last two months, so that when the time came for seeing her no longer in that way, he would have his memories: there was the time of her first ball, all excitement and happiness, the day at her uncle's when she had looked at him over the top of the fans, the night at the opera when she had been so angry with him, last night —

She had, through all this time, remained elusive. He did not know her, could not reconcile one inconsistency with another — but he thought that she cared about him and would marry him.

He had always known that he must one day marry. That necessity was, in no way, connected with the emotional side of him, it rather had its relationship with the common sense of him, the part that believed in the Beaminsters and all their glory.

He must marry because Seddon Court must have a mistress, because he himself must have children, because he would like to have someone there to be kind to. That need in him for bestowing kindness upon someone was always most urgent, and all sorts of animals and all sorts of persons had shared it — now one person would have it all. He could not bear to hurt anyone or anything, and the crises of his life were provided by those occasions when, in the delight of one of his emotional moments, hurting somebody was involved — there was always then a conflict.

He knew that it was just here that the Duchess failed to understand him. She liked hurting people and expected him to be amused when she told him little stories about her having done so. He had now a kind of dim feeling that it was because the Duchess hoped that he was going to hurt Rachel that she had prosecuted so strenuously his marriage.

He trusted with all his heart that he would never hurt Rachel, he intended always to be very, very kind to her; it was indeed a thousand pities that the present quality of his attitude to her must, like all attitudes, eventually change.

But he was always — he was sure of this — going to be good to her and give her everything that the mistress of Seddon Court should have.

At the same time, vaguely, he wished that the old Duchess had had nothing to do with this; sometimes he wondered whether the side in him that found pleasure in her was really natural to him.

131

Whenever he thought of her, she, in some way, confused his judgment and made life difficult.

She was doing that now....

II

When he came down to breakfast he found that he was the last. He sat next to Nita Raseley and was conscious, after a little time, that she was behaving with a certain reserve. He had known her in the kind of way that he knew many people in his own set in London, pleasantly, indifferently, without curiosity. She had, however, attracted him sometimes by the impression that she gave him that she was too young to know many men, but, however long she lived, would never find anyone as splendid as he: she had certainly never been reserved before. Finally he realized that she expected to hear of his engagement to Rachel Beaminster at any moment. "Well, so she will," he thought, smiling to himself. Meanwhile he avoided Rachel quite deliberately.

He was now self-conscious about her and did not wish to be with her until he could ask her to marry him. No more uncertainty was possible. He felt, not frightened, but excited, just as he would feel were he about to ride a dangerous horse for the first time.

He seized, with relief, upon the proposal of church; he wanted the morning to pass; his prayer was that she would not walk to church with him, because he had now nothing to say to her except the one thing. When he heard that she was staying behind and walking with Nita Raseley he was surprised at his own sense of release.

Lady Adela was kind to him this morning in a sort of motherly way and apparently seized on his going to church as an omen of his future married happiness.

"They're all waiting to hear," he said to himself.

They were to walk across the park to the little village church, and when they set out he was conscious that Lord John, like a large and amiable bird, was hovering about him: finally, Lord John, nervous apparently, most certainly embarrassed, settled upon him.

"Going to church, aren't you, Roddy?"

"Yes, Beaminster."

"Well, let's strike off together, shall we?"

Roddy liked Lord John best of the Beaminster brothers; the Duke he could not endure and Lord Richard was so superior, but Johnny Beaminster was as amiable as an Easter egg and fond of race meetings and pretty women, and not too dam' clever—in fact, really, not clever at all.

But Johnny Beaminster embarrassed was another matter and Roddy found soon that this embarrassment led to his own confusion.

Lord John flung out little remarks and little whistles because of the heat and little comments upon the crops. He obviously had something that he very much wanted to say—"Of course," thought Roddy, "this is something to do with Rachel—he's very fond of Rachel."

Although Johnny Beaminster had not, in strict accuracy, himself the reputation of the whitest of Puritans, yet Roddy wondered whether perhaps he were not now worrying over some of Roddy's past history, as rumoured in London society.

"Doesn't want his girl to be handed over to a reg'lar Black Sheep, shouldn't wonder," thought Roddy, and this led him to rather indignant consideration of the confusion of the Beaminster mind and its muddled moralities.

The walk to the church was not very long, but it became, towards the close of it, quite awful in its agitation.

"Dam' hot," said Lord John.

"Very," said Roddy.

"Wouldn't wonder if this weather broke soon——"

"Quite likely."

"Makes you hot walking to church this hour of the morning."

"Yes—don't it? Farmers will be wantin' rain pretty badly. Down at my little place they tell me it's dried up like anythin'——"

"Reg'lar Turkish bath——"

133

"Well, the church ought to be cool— —"

"You never know with these churches— —"

Roddy thought "He's afraid of his old mother. Doesn't want me to marry Rachel, but he's afraid of his old mother."

"Massiter's getting fat— —" This was Lord John's contribution.

"Yes—so's that novelist feller— —"

"Oh! Garden! Yes—ever read anything of his?"

"Never a line. Never read novels."

"Not bad—good tales, you know."

"He's probably," Roddy thought, "had a row with the old lady about me— —
"

Then, strangely enough, the notion hit him—"Wish it was he wanted me to marry Rachel and the Duchess didn't—Wish she didn't, by Gad."

As they entered the church Roddy might have seen, had he been gifted in psychology, that there was in Lord John's face the look of a man who had fought a battle with his dark angel and been, alas, defeated.

III

After luncheon Roddy said:

"Miss Beaminster, come for a walk?"

"A little way," she said, looking at him with her eyes in that straight direct way that she had.

"She must know," said Roddy to himself, "that I'm going to do it now. They all know. It's awful!"

Some of the others had gathered together under a great oak that shaded the central lawn, and now as he climbed the hill with his capture he felt that from beneath that tree many eyes watched them.

They did not go very far. At the top of the hill, above the little wood and the gardens and the house, there was a grassy hollow, and under this grassy hollow a great field of wheat, a sheet of red-gold with sudden waves and ripples in it as though some hand were shaking it, ran down to the valley.

"Let's stop here," Rachel said. "I was out all this morning with Nita Raseley and it's too hot for any exertion whatever."

A tree shaded them and they sat down and watched corn.

"What sort of a girl do you think she is—Nita Raseley, I mean?" asked Rachel.

"Oh! I don't know—the ordinary kind of girl—why?"

"She seems to want to know me. Says that she hasn't many friends. Is that true? I thought she had heaps——"

"You never can tell with girls. You're all so uncertain about one another—devoted one moment and enemies the next."

"Are we?" said Rachel slowly. "I don't think I'm like that—Oh! how hot it is!" She lay back against the grass with her arms behind her head.

"Do you like me?" Roddy said suddenly.

"I?... You!"

She slowly sat up and he saw at once that she knew now what he was going to say. At that moment, sitting there, staring at him, with her breasts moving a little beneath her white dress and her hands pressing flatly against the grass, in her agitation and the look in her eyes of some suddenly evoked personality that he did not know at all she was more elusive to him than she had ever been—

She was frightened—and also glad—but the change in her from the girl he had known all the summer was so startling that he felt that he was about to propose to someone he had never seen before.

"Do I like you?" she repeated slowly, and her lips parted in a smile.

"Yes," he said, looking at her hands that seemed to belong to the earth into which they were pressing—"Because I want you to marry me——"

The moment of her surprise had come before—now she only said very quietly—

"Why—what do you know about me?"

"I know—enough—to ask you," he said, stumbling over his words. He was now afraid that, after all, she intended to refuse him, and the terror of this made his heart stop. No words would come. He stared at her with all the fright in his eyes.

"Roddy" (she had never called him that before), "do you care——"

Then she stopped.

She began again. "I don't want to talk nonsense. I want to say exactly what I feel. I suppose most girls would want to be free a little longer, would want to have a good time another two or three seasons—but I don't—I hate being free—I want somebody to keep me, to prevent my doing silly things, to look after me ... and ... I'd rather you did it—than anybody else...." Then she went on quickly—"But it is more than that. I do like you most awfully, only I suppose I'm not the kind of girl to be frantically excited, to be wild about it all. I'm not that. I do like you—better than any other man I know—Is that enough?"

"I think—we can be most awfully good pals—always," he said.

"Oh!" she cried suddenly, putting her hand on his and looking straight into his face. "That's what I want—that, that—If that's it, and you think we can, why then, I'd rather marry you, Roddy dear, than anyone in the world."

"Then it's settled," he said. But he did not take her hand or touch her. They sat for quite a long time, looking at the rippling corn and the house, that was like a white boat sailing on the green far below them.

They said no word.

Then, without speaking, they got up from the grass and walked down the path to the little wood. But when they came to the place where they had been the night before he caught her to him so furiously that his own body was bent back, and he kissed her again and again and again.

BOOK II
RACHEL

CHAPTER I
THE POOL AND THE SNOW
"For now doors open, and war is waged with the snow.
And trains of sombre men, past tale of number,
Tread long brown paths, as toward their toil they go:
But even for them awhile no cares encumber
Their minds diverted; the daily word is unspoken,
The daily thoughts of labour and sorrow slumber
At the sight of the beauty that greets them, for the charm they have broken."
Robert Bridges.
I
In the early days of the December of that year, 1898, the first snow fell.

Francis Breton, standing at his window high up in the Saxton Square house, watched the first flakes, as they came, lingering, from the heavy brooding sky; as he watched a great tide of unhappiness and restlessness and discontent swept over him. His was a temperament that could be raised to heaven and dashed to hell in a second of time; life never showed him its true colours and his sensitive suspicion to the signs and omens of the gods gave him radiant confidence and utter despair when only a patient quiescence had been intended. During the last three months he had risen and fallen and risen again, as the impulse to do something magnificent somewhere interchanged with the impulse to do something desperate — meanwhile nothing was done and, standing now staring at the snow, he realized it.

He had never, in all his days, known how to moderate. If he might not be the hero of society then must he be the famous outcast, in one fashion or another London must ring with his name.

And yet now here had he been in London since the end of April and nothing had occurred, no steps, beyond that first letter to his grandmother, had he taken. He had not even responded to the advances made to him by his old associates, he had seen no one save Christopher, Brun once or twice, the Rands and his cousin Rachel.

Throughout this time he had done what he had never done before, he had waited. For what?

A little perhaps he had expected that the family would take some step. Looking back now he knew that the shadow of his grandmother had been over it all. He had always seen her when he had contemplated any action, seen her, and, deny it as he might, feared her. She confused his mind; he had never been very readily clear as to reasons and instincts—he had never paused for a period long enough to allow clear thinking, but now, through all these weeks, he had been conscious that that same clear thinking would have come to him had not his grandmother clouded his mind. He felt her as one feels, in a dream, some power that prevents our movement, holds us fascinated—so now he was held.

The other great force persuading him to inaction was Rachel Beaminster, now Rachel Seddon.

Long before his return to England the thought of this cousin of his had often come to him. He would speculate about her. She, like himself, was by birth half a rebel, she must be—She must be. He had sometimes thought that he would write to her, and then he had felt that that would not be fair. Behind all his dreams and romances he always saw some destiny whose colours were woven simply for him, Francis Breton, and this confidence in an especial personally constructed God had been responsible for his wildest and most foolish mistakes.

Often had he seen this especial God bringing his cousin and himself together. Always he had known that, in some way, they two were to be chosen to work out, together, vengeance and destruction against all the Beaminsters. When, therefore, that meeting in the Rands' drawing-room had taken place he had accepted it all. She was even more wonderful than he had expected, but he had known, instantly, that she was his companion, his chosen, his fellow-traveller; between them he had realized a claim, implied on some common knowledge or experience, at the first moment of their meeting.

From the age of ten, when he had been petted by one of his father's mistresses, his life had been entangled with women; some he had loved, others he had been in love with, others again had loved him.

He did not know now whether he were in love with Rachel or no—he only knew that the whole current of his life was changed from the moment that he met her and that, until the end of it, she now would be intermingled with all his history.

At first so sure had he been of the workings of fate in this matter that he had been content (for the first time in all his days) to wait with his hands folded. During this period all thought of action against the Beaminsters on the one hand or a relapse into the company of the friends of his earlier London days on the other, had been out of the question. This certainty of Rachel's future alliance with himself had made such things impossibly absurd.

Then had come the announcement of her engagement to Seddon. For a moment the shock had been terrific. He had suddenly seen the face of his especial God and it was blind and stupid and dead....

Then swiftly upon that had come thought of his grandmother. This was, of course, her doing—Rachel was too young to know—She would discover her mistake: the engagement would be broken off.

During this time he had met Rachel on several occasions, and although the meetings had been very brief, yet always he had felt that same unacknowledged, secret intimacy. After every meeting his confidence had risen, once again, to the skies.

Then had come the news of her marriage.

From that moment he had known no peace. At first he had wildly fancied that this had happened because he had not come to her and more plainly declared himself; his picture of her idea of him was confused with all the dramatic untruth of his idea of her; then, interchanging with that, had come moods when he had seen things more plainly as they were and had told himself that all relations between herself and him had been invented by himself, that any kindness that she had shown him had been kindness sprung from pity.

During the early months of the autumn Rachel and her husband were abroad, and during this time, Breton told himself that he was waiting for her return before taking any action. Then a certain Mrs. Pont, a lady whose beauty had been increased but her reputation lessened by several scandals and a tiresomely querulous Mr. Pont, had suggested to Francis Breton a continuation of certain earlier relationships.

He knew himself well enough to be sure that one evening in Mrs. Pont's company would put an end to his struggles, so weak was he in his own knowledge that the only possible evading of a conflict was by the denial of the enemy's very existence.

He denied Mrs. Pont and, throughout those dark gloomy autumn weeks, clinging to Christopher and Lizzie Rand, waited to hear of Rachel's return.

Although he would confess it to no man alive, he longed now, with an aching heart, for some sort of reconciliation with the family. He would have astonished them with his humility had they given him any sign or signal. He fancied that Lord John or even the Duke might come.... Once admitted to his proper rank again and what a citizen he would be! Vanish for ever Mrs. Pont and her tribe and all that dark underworld that waited, like some sluggish but confident monster, for his inevitable descent. Wild phantasmic plans crossed his brain every hour of every day—nothing came of it all; only when at last it was announced that Sir Roderick and Lady Seddon had returned to England he discovered that he had nothing to do, nothing to say, no step to take.

That return had been at the end of October; from then until the end of November he waited, expecting that she would write to him; still, by this anticipation, were Mrs. Pont and Mrs. Pont's world kept at bay.

No word came. Driven now to take some step that would shatter this silence, he wrote to her a long letter about nothing very much, only something that would bring him a line from her.

For ten days now he had waited and there had come no word. As these first flakes of snow softly, relentlessly, fell past his window the nebulous cloud of all the uncertainties, disappointments, rebellions, of this pointless wasted thing that men called Life crystallized into form—"I'm no good—Life, like this, it's impossible—I'm no good against it—I'd better climb down...."

And here the irony of it was that he'd never climbed up.

The awful moments in Life are those that threaten us by their suspension of all action. "Just feel what's piling up for you out of all this silence," they seem to say. Breton's trouble now was that he did not know in what direction to move. His relation to Rachel was so nebulous that it could scarcely be called a relation at all.

He only knew that she alone was the person for whom now life was worth combating. He had told her in his letter that she could help him, and the absence of an answer spoke now, in this threatening silence, with mighty reverberating voice. "She doesn't care."

Well then, who else is there? Almost he could have fancied that his grandmother, there in the Portland Place house, was withdrawing from him all the supports in which he trusted.

Now the snow, falling ever more swiftly, ever more stealthily, seemed to be with him in the room, stifling, choking, blinding.

He felt that if he could not find company of some kind he would go mad, and so, leaving the storm and the silence behind him in his room, he went to find Lizzie Rand.

II

Lizzie Rand did not conceal from herself now that she loved him. So long had her emotional life been waiting there, undesired, that now it could be kept by her utterly apart from her daily habit, but it became a flame, a fire, that lighted with its splendid warmth and colour the whole of her accustomed world. She indulged it now without restraint, through the long dark autumn she had it treasured there; she did not, as things then were, ask for more than this splendid knowledge that there was now someone upon whom she loved to spend her care. She had not loved to spend it upon her mother and sister, but that had been a duty defined and necessary. Now everything that she could do for Breton was more fuel to fling to her flame. That further question as to whether he might care for her she kept just in sight, but nevertheless not definite enough to risk the absolute challenge.

At least, now, as the weeks passed, he sought her company more and more. She helped him, she cheered and comforted him, enough for her present need.

Even, beyond it all, could she survey herself humorously. This the first love affair of her life made her smile at her capture and defeat.

"Well, I'm just like the rest—And oh! I'm glad, I'm glad that I am."

Finally she knew that there was still a step that might be taken, between them, at any moment. He had, she knew, something to tell her. Again and again lately he had been about to speak and then had caught the impulse back.

This too she would not examine too closely, but from the moment that he should demand from her definite concrete assistance, from that moment she would be to him what she knew no one now living could claim to be.

Breton was glad when the little maid told him that Mrs. Rand was out, but that Miss Lizzie was at home. He saw her in the warm cosy room, sitting before the fire with her toes on the fender and her skirts pulled up, drying her shoes.

141

She looked up and smiled at him and told him to sit down, but did not move from her position.

"Mother's out at a matinee with Daisy. I got away early this afternoon. Do you hate snow, Mr. Breton?"

"I hate it to-day. I've got the dumps. I had to find someone to talk to or I'd have gone screaming into the street — —"

"Couldn't find anyone better, so took me — thank you for the compliment. But I like the snow. Your pool's more like a pool now than ever, Mr. Breton."

He went across to the window and stood there looking at the little square now white with the gaunt trees rising black from the heart of it and the grey houses that hemmed it in. Over it the snow, yellow and grey and then delicately white, swirled and tossed.

He came back and sat down beside her and wondered at her neat comfort and air of calm control of all her emotions and desires.

She, looking at him, saw that he was ill. Dark lines beneath his eyes, his cheeks pale and an air of picturesque melancholy that made her want first to laugh at him and then mother him.

"I know what's the matter with you," she said, nodding her head.

"What?"

"Something to do. That's what you want." She turned towards him, looking at him with a little smile and yet with grave seriousness in her eyes. "Oh! Mr. Breton, why don't you? What is the use of sitting here month after month, doing nothing, just waiting for something to happen — something that can't happen unless you make it? Things don't fall into people's mouths just because they sit with them open."

He coloured. "Everybody's always scolding me," he said. "Christopher — you — everybody. Nobody understands — how difficult...."

He broke off. So intangible were his difficulties that no words would define them, and yet, God knew, they were real enough.

"I know—" she said, nodding her head. "It's the thought of them all at Portland Place that's holding you back. You began by fancying that you wanted to cut their throats, and you still wouldn't mind slaughtering them if only they in their turn would do something definite. It's their doing nothing that just holds you up. But really as long as your grandmother's alive I'm afraid that it's no good thinking of them. When she's dead—and she can't live for ever—anything may happen. Meanwhile why not show them what you can do?"

"But what can I do?" he answered her fiercely. "I've never been brought up to do anything—except what I oughtn't—There's my arm and one thing and another—Besides, there's more than that in it, Miss Rand. It's the fact that— well, that there's nobody that cares that's—so freezing. If only somebody minded——"

As he spoke Rachel rose, beautifully, wonderfully, before him. There, as she had been on that first day when she had had tea there, bending forward, listening, her dark wondering eyes on his face.

Lizzie at the sound of the appeal in his voice had felt her heart expand, beat, so that her body seemed to hold, suddenly, some great possession that hurt her by its force and urgency.

But she answered almost sharply:

"Nonsense, Mr. Breton. Excuse me, but I've no patience with that kind of thing. People are meant to stand alone, not to go leaning about for other people's support. You're cursed with too much imagination, Mr. Breton, and you remember too clearly everything that's happened before. Begin now, as though you were born yesterday, and startle the family by your energy——"

"Now you're laughing at me," he said hotly. "I dare say I deserve it, but I don't feel as though I could stand—very much of it from anyone to-day——"

Then he was astonished by the sudden softness of her voice. "No, no, please," she said; "I understand so well. But indeed you have got friends who believe in you. Dr. Christopher, myself, if you'll count me, and lots more. You'll win everyone in time if you're not impatient and don't despair. Don't think of your grandmother too much. The mere fact of your not seeing her makes you imagine her as something portentous and dreadful, and she weighs you down, but she isn't really anything at all. She can't stop one's energies if one's determined to let them go. Please, please don't think I'm laughing. I only want to help——"

"I know you do," he answered warmly, "I owe you more than I can say. All these last weeks you and Christopher have been the two people who've held the world together for me. But there's more than you know, Miss Rand. There's— —"

He bent towards her. She knew that the confidence was at last to be hers. It needed her strongest control to prevent the trembling of her hands. His eyes were alight, his whole body eloquent. At the thought of what he might be about to tell her the room turned before her.

Voices in the little hall. Then the door opened and in came Mrs. Rand and Daisy. They had been to the play—Such nonsense. One of these new, serious plays with long, long conversations—Mrs. Rand wanted tea. Daisy wanted admiration.

Between Lizzie and Breton the precious cup had fallen, smashed to the tiniest atoms.

Meanwhile aimless conversation was more than he, in his present mood, could endure.

He made some excuse and, scarcely knowing what he did, found his hat and coat and went out into the square.

III

There had come to him one of those agonies of loneliness that no argument, no reasoning can destroy.

The absence of any letter from Rachel seemed to show that she had abandoned him. In all this vast thickly peopled world there was now no one to whom his presence or absence, his fortunes or disasters mattered. The snowstorm gathered him into its folds; the snow fell against his mouth, his eyes, and before him, behind him, around him there was a world deserted of man, houses blind and without life.

The snow might fall now to the end of time. It would creep up and up, falling from the heavens, rising from the earth, swallowing all creation—the end of the world.

He pressed into the park and there under the trees stretching like gallows against the throttling sky temptation to give it all up, to go under and have done with it all, leapt, hot and fierce, upon him. Mrs. Pont and the others

were waiting for him. They would be good to him. The Upper World would
not hear nor see nor think of his disasters, and slowly, with the others, life
would recede, he would crumble and decay and cease to care, and death
would come soon enough.

Then the wind smote his face and tore at his coat: the snow died away,
beyond the black bare trees a very faint yellow bar threaded the thick grey —
promise that the storm was at an end.

Suddenly with the cessation of the storm the long field of white seemed
good and restful, and beyond the park the houses showed light in their
windows.

The yellow spread through the sky, and stars, very slowly, came and the
wind died away.

Courage filled him. Rachel might never come or write or care, but he would
make the thought of her the one true thing in his heart, and with that he
would do battle so long as he could.

Christopher and Miss Rand ... he thought of them as he trudged his way
home—and when he saw the white silence of Saxton Square and the golden
sky breaking above its peace and quiet he thought that, for a time longer, he
would keep his place and hold his own.

CHAPTER II
A LITTLE HOUSE

"Each in the crypt would cry,
'But one freezes here! and why?
'When a heart, as chill,
'At my own would thrill
Back to life, and its fires out-fly?
'Heart, shall we live or die?
The rest ... settle by-and-by!'"
Robert Browning.

I

Rachel at Seddon Court watched, from her window, that first fallen snow.

Seddon Court is about three miles from the town of Lewes and lies, tucked and cornered, under the very brow of the Downs. It is a grey little house, old and stalwart, with a courtyard and two towers. The towers are Norman; the rest of the house is Tudor.

Beyond the actual building there are gardens that run to the very foot of the Downs, with only a patch and an old stone wall intervening. Above the house, day and night, year after year, the Downs are bending; everything, beneath their steady solemn gaze, is small and restless; as the colours are flung by the sun across their green sprawling limbs the house, at their feet, catches their reflected smile and, when the sun is gone and the winds blow, cowers beneath their frown; everything in that house is conscious of their presence.

Rachel had been at Seddon Court for a month and now, at the window of her writing-room, looking across the garden, up into their dark shadows, she wondered at their indifference and monotony. Anyone who had known her before her marriage would be struck instantly, on seeing her now, by a change in her.

Her whole attitude to the world, during her first season in London, had been an attitude of wonder, of expectation, of the uncertainty that comes from expectation.

With that expectation were also alarm, distrust, and it was only when some sudden incident or person called happiness into her face that that distrust vanished.

Now she was older, that hesitation and awkwardness were gone, but with their departure had vanished, too, much of her honesty. Her dark eyes were as sincere as they had ever been, but to anyone who had known her before her attitude now was assumed. Nothing might catch her unprepared, but what experiences were they that had taught her the need for armour?

Sitting in her room looking on to a lawn that would soon be white and to Downs obscured already by the thick tumbling snow, she knew that she was unhappy, disappointed, even alarmed. Suddenly to-day the uneasiness that had been gathering before her throughout the last weeks assumed, on this afternoon, the definite tangibility of a challenge.

"What's the matter—with me, with everything?... What's happened?"

Her room, dark green and white, had no pictures, but a long low book-case with grave handsome books, an edition of someone in red with white paper labels and another edition of someone else in dark blue and another in gold and brown, an old French gilt mirror, square, with a reflection of the garden and the foot of the Downs in it, an old Queen Anne rosewood writing-table, some Queen Anne chairs, a gate-legged table—a very cool, quiet room.

At her feet with his head resting on her shoe there lay a dog. This dog about a fortnight ago she had found in a field near the house with a kettle tied on to his tail, and his body a confused catastrophe of mud and blood.

She had carried him home; it had needed some courage to introduce him into the household, for Roddy possessed many dogs all of the finest breeds, and this was a mongrel who defied description. He was very short and shaggy and stumpy. He was much too large for a Yorkshire terrier and yet that was undoubtedly his derivation. There was something of a sheep-dog in him and something of a Skye; his hair fell all over his face and, when you could see them, his eyes were brown. His nose was like a wet blackberry and his ears were long and full of emotion; when he ran his short tail, on which the hairs were arranged like branches on a Christmas tree, stuck up into the air and he resembled a rabbit.

In the confusion of the moment Rachel had called him Jacob, because she thought that Jacob was, in the Bible, the "hairy one".... After all, you could not call a dog Esau.

Yes, to retain him had needed courage. Thinking of Roddy's attitude to the dog brought so many other attendant thoughts in its train. Roddy in his devotion to animals (and oh! he was devoted), had no room for those that were not of the aristocracy.

Concerning dogs who were mongrels he was kind but thought them much better dead. Unkind he would never be, but the way in which he ignored Jacob was worse than any unkindness.

Jacob, sensitive perhaps from early suffering, knew this and avoided Roddy, ran out of the room when he came into it, showed in every way that he must not expect to rank with the other dogs.

Very characteristic this attitude of Roddy, but very characteristic, too, the affection that Jacob was now receiving from his mistress. There was something that Jacob drew from Rachel that none of the fine, noble dogs of the house was able to secure.... Why?... What, again, was the matter? Why was Rachel unhappy?

Rachel was unhappy, and the answer came quite clearly to her as the room was darkened by the great storm of snow now falling over the Downs and the garden, because marriage with Roddy had not lessened in any way that uneasy disquiet that had stirred, without pause, beneath her life before her marriage; that uneasiness had, indeed, during the last three months, increased....

Was this her fault or Roddy's?

Attacked now by a scrutiny that refused dismissal she delivered herself up to the investigation of these months of her married life.

She knew that she had only once been happy since her marriage—that was on the first evening, when, the noise and clamour of the London wedding having died away, she had walked with Roddy in the peace of the Massiter garden (Lady Massiter had lent her house for the first weeks of the honeymoon), had felt his arm about her, had believed that there had really come to her that comfort and safety for which she longed.

After that there had followed a fortnight of great unreality—the strangest excitement, the most adventurous wonders, but a wonder and excitement that were from herself, the real Rachel Beaminster, most absolutely removed. It was as though she had watched closely but detached the experiences of some other girl. Roddy had, during those times, been a most ardent and passionate lover; she had tried to respond and had hidden, as best she could, her failure.

Then, suddenly, with the time of their going abroad, passion had left him; it had left him as swiftly as the passing of wind over a hill. It was there—it was gone.

But he remained the perfect husband. His kindness, his charm, his simplicity, his affection for her—an affection that could never for an instant be doubted—these things had delighted her. He was now the friend, the strong reliant companion that she had wanted him to be. During those first weeks in Italy and Greece happiness might have come to her had she not been stirred by her remembrance of the earlier weeks. The passion that had been in him, although it had not touched her, now in retrospect lit fires for her imagination. Instantly back to her had come the whole disquiet and unrest. The things that Roddy called from her now, she suddenly discovered with a great shrinking alarm, were all the Beaminster things. All the true emotions, qualities, traditions that made up her secret life were roused in her by their own inherent vitality, never by his evocation of them. He was Beaminster—Roddy was Beaminster. With his kindness and courtesy his eyes saw the world with the eyes of his ancestors, his tongue spoke the language that had in it no sincerity, his heart wished for all the ceremonies and lies that the Beaminster had believed in since the beginning of time.

But her discovery did not lead her much further. She had, in her heart of hearts, always known that Roddy was a Beaminster. Why then had she married him? She had married him because she had been untrue to herself, because she had herself encouraged the Beaminster blood in her to blind her eyes, because she had desired deceit rather than truth, because she had wanted the comfort that the man could give her rather than the man himself, because she had muffled and stifled and silenced that Power in her—the Power that made her restless and unquiet; the Power that was as hostile to the Beaminster faith as heaven is to hell—

And yet this vehemence of explanation did not altogether explain Roddy. Roddy was not simply a Beaminster like Uncle John or Uncle Richard or Aunt Adela. There was an elemental direct emotion in Roddy that was exactly opposed to Beaminster conventionality.

These two elements in him puzzled and even frightened her. His attitude during that first fortnight of their marriage she saw, again and again, in lesser degrees during their time abroad. She had seen him so primitive in his joy and excitement over places and people and moments—colour, food, storms, towns, passers-by, anything—that she had been astounded by the force of it. Emotions swept over him and were gone, but, whilst they were there, she knew that she counted to him for nothing. Strangest of ironies that when he was least a Beaminster, then was she farthest from him — strangest of ironies that her link with him should be the Beaminster in him.

She was frightened of his primitive passions. She had in her the instinct that one day they would touch his relationship to her and that that contact would rouse in her the full tide of the unhappiness of which she was now so conscious, and that then ... what might not happen?...

And yet behind it all she felt a strange, almost pathetic satisfaction because he, after all, had in him, just as she had, his two natures at war. There at least they found some common link; her eagerness to find some link was evidence enough of the affection she had for him.

After their return to England the wilder nature in him had extended and broadened. Everything to do with Seddon Court drew it out of him; his passion for the place was wonderful to witness. Every stone of the little grey building was a jewel in his eyes; the servants, the cattle, the horses, the dogs, the flowers, the villagers, even the townspeople of Lewes drew sentiment from him.

"My old place," he would say, cuddling it to himself; he was never "sloppy" about it, but direct and simple and straightforward. It was obviously the great emotion above all other emotions.

He was most anxious that Rachel should share this with him, and during her first weeks there she thought that she would do so. Then the disquiet in her spread to the place. The house spread itself out before her now as the lure that had from the beginning tempted her.

"It was for this place and quiet that you were false to yourself — —"

Roddy felt that she did not share his enthusiasm, and their difficulty over this was exactly their difficulty over everything else; simply that Roddy was the least eloquent person in the world. He could explain nothing whatever of the vague unhappiness or dissatisfaction at his heart. Rachel could have explained a great many things, but Roddy, she felt, would only look at her in his kind puzzled way and wonder why she couldn't take things as they were.

Perhaps during these last weeks he had himself felt that all was not well. Rachel thought that sometimes now through, all his kindness she detected a floating, wistful speculation on his part as to whether she were happy.

He wanted her to be happy—most tremendously he wanted it—and did she explain to him that she was not happy because she was, now, for ever attended by a sense of her own disloyalty to all that was best in her, he would have suggested a doctor or have made her a present.

Had she been some stranger and had the case been presented to him he would have probably dismissed it by saying that "having made her bed she must lie on it." "After all, she married the feller—Well then, that's her look-out."

So, perhaps, if this had been simply her trouble she would have done her bravest best to endeavour.

But there was more behind it all—far, far more.

She saw her marriage to Roddy, her struggling for self-respect, her present morbid introspection as a stage in what was now developing into a duel between herself and her grandmother.

Her grandmother had planned this marriage. Her grandmother was determined to destroy the honesty and truth in her and had chosen a Beaminster for her agent and now waited happy for the death of Rachel's soul.

But Rachel's soul should not so readily die! During all these weeks the thought of her grandmother had been continually with her. How she hated her, and with what fervour did Rachel return that hatred!

There was no melodrama in this hatred. When she had been a very little girl Rachel had somehow believed that her grandmother had been very cruel to her mother and father—She had hated her for that. Then she had seen that her grandmother disliked her and wished to tease her—so she had hated her for that also.

Her older amplification of this into principles and instincts had not altered the original vehemence of the passion, it had only given it grown-up reasons for its existence.

And so, thinking of her grandmother, she thought also of Francis Breton.

Some weeks ago she had received a letter from him and that letter was now lying in the desk of her writing-table.

She had thought that her marriage would have snapped her interest in her cousin because it would have broken that hostility with her grandmother upon which her relationship with her cousin so largely depended. But now when she saw that marriage had only intensified her hostility to the Duchess, so therefore it had intensified her perception of Breton. His letter had aroused in her, just as contact with him aroused in her, everything in her that now, for her own peace of mind, she should keep at bay. His letter had amounted to this:

"You are a rebel as I am a rebel. We have said very little, but you have recognized in me the things that I have recognized in you. You have escaped through marriage, but for me there is no escape, and if you would, for the sake of those things that we have in common, keep me from going utterly under, then you must help me—as only you can."

He did not say this nor anything at all like this. He only, very quietly, congratulated her on her marriage, hoped that she would be very happy, said that London was a little desolate and difficult, hoped that she would not think more harshly of him than she could help, and, at the very end, told her that meeting her made him feel that he was not entirely abandoned by everybody.

It was the letter of a weak man and she knew it, but it was the letter of a man who was weak exactly in the places where she also failed. And this, more than anything else, moved her.

They two alone, it seemed, were struggling to keep their feet in a world that did not need them. It had been, through these months, Rachel's sharpest unhappiness, the consciousness that Roddy and indeed everything at Seddon Court could get on so very well without her.

Nobody in London needed her—nobody here needed her. If you accepted the Beaminster doctrine, then no wife would demand more from a husband than Roddy gave Rachel—but was this not simply another proof that Rachel had made a Beaminster marriage?

Rachel had been flung straight from the schoolroom into marriage and the sensitive agonizing cry of a child to be loved by somebody—the cry that had always been so urgent in her—was urgent still.

It was exactly this comfortable sense of being a help that Roddy had not given her. Now this letter gave it to her.

But if this letter was an appeal, just as the mongrel Jacob, now at her feet, was an appeal, on the part of someone wounded and outcast, to her pity, so also was it an invitation to rebellion.

It was also a temptation to deceit and, did she answer the letter, she encouraged Breton to write again; she opened up not only a new relationship to him, but also a new relationship to all the forces that were most hostile to Roddy and her married happiness. May Eversley had once said to her: "Sit down and see, without any exaggeration or false colouring, what you've got. Take away, ruthlessly, anything that you imagine that you've got but haven't. Take away ruthlessly everything that you imagine that you would like to have but are not confident of securing—See what's happened to you in the past—Take away ruthlessly any sentimental repentances or sloppy regrets, but learn quite resolutely from your ugly mistakes."

Long ago she had written this down—now was the first necessity for applying it.

The doctrine of Truth—Truth to Oneself, the one thing that mattered. She knew that the pursuit of Truth was to her, and to every rebel against the Beaminsters, the restive Tiger. In marrying Roddy she had been untrue to herself. In writing to Breton she would be true to herself but untrue to Roddy. She was fond of Roddy although she did not love him, nor did he, really, love her. The anxiety on both their parts to avoid hurting one another was proof enough of that, she thought.

There then was the whole situation. As she felt Jacob's warm head against her foot a great agitation of loneliness and dismay and helplessness swept over her.

Tears were in her throat and eyes—Then with a strong disdain she pushed it all from her. She was growing morbid, losing her sense of humour and proportion. Here in the house there was Nita Raseley staying; in the country there were people to be called upon, to be invited, to be interested in, there was Roddy, a perfect husband.

She strangled that other Rachel, there in her room. "Now you're dead," she felt, and seemed to fling a lifeless, crumpled figure out into the snow —

She looked at herself in the glass.

"You're not Rachel Beaminster now—you're Rachel Seddon. Act accordingly and don't whine—" She washed her face and brushed her hair, and combed Jacob's hair out of his eyes, and then, determined to be sensible and cheerful and civilized, went down to tea.

II

The room called the Library was the pleasantest room in the house; an old, long, low-ceilinged room with windows that stretched from floor to ceiling, with a large stone open fireplace and book-cases running from end to end and old sporting prints above them.

Before the great fireplace the tea was waiting and there also was Nita Raseley, very charming and fresh and pink in the face and golden in the hair. It was strange that Nita Raseley should have been their first guest since their marriage, because Rachel, most certainly, did not like her; but, after that meeting at the Massiters' the girl had flung a passionate and incoherent correspondence upon Rachel and had ended by practically inviting herself.

Roddy liked her; Rachel knew that—so perhaps after all it had been a good thing to have her there. Rachel's dislike of her was founded on a complete distrust. "She's all wrong and insincere and beastly. I'll never have her here again...." And yet, really, Miss Raseley had behaved herself, had been most quiet and decorous and most affectionate.

The electric light was delicately shaded, the curtains were drawn, outside was the storm, here cosiness and shining comfort.

"Oh! darling Rachel—I am so glad you've come—I do so want tea——"

"Where's Roddy?"

"Just come in—He'll be here in a minute——"

Rachel came over to the fire and was busy over the tea-table.

"Well, Nita, what have you been at all the afternoon?"

"Oh! that silly old book. Rachel, how could you tell me——"

"What book?"

"Oh! you know—you lent it me. Something like drinking—you know. By that man Westcott—such a silly name."

"The Vines!—Didn't you like it?"

"Like it! My dear Rachel, why, they go on for pages about each other's feelings and nothing happens and I'm sure it's most unwholesome. They're all so unhappy and always hating one another. I like books to be cheerful and about people one knows—don't you?"

"Well, Nita dear, it's a good thing we don't all like the same things, isn't it? Sugar?"

"Yes, dear, you know—lots—Darling, have you got a headache? You do look rotten—you do really."

Rachel knew that she must keep an especial guard to-day: she was irritable, out of sorts. She would have liked immensely to send Nita to have her tea in the nursery, were there one.

"No, I'm all right. But I wanted to get out and this storm stopped me."

"You do look dicky! Oh! what do you think! Roddy's taking us over to Hawes to-morrow to lunch if the weather's anything like decent. He's just fixed it up—sent a wire——"

"To-morrow? But I can't.... He knows. I've got Miss Crale coming here——"

"Only old Miss Crale? Put her off——"

"I can't possibly—I've put her off once before. She wants to talk about her Soldiers' Institute place—" Then Rachel added more slowly, "But Roddy knew——"

"Oh! he said you'd got some silly old engagement, but he knew you'd put it off!"

"He knows I can't. He was talking about it this morning. He knew how——" Then she stopped. She was not going to show Nita Raseley that she minded anything.

But Roddy had always said that they would go over together to Hawes— one of the loveliest old places in the world—He had always promised....

She knew perfectly well what had occurred. Nita had caught Roddy and clung on to him and persuaded him—Roddy was such a boy—But she was hurt and she despised herself for it.

"Oh," she said, laughing. "That's all right. You two must just go over together—that's all! I'll go another time——"

"Well, you see, Roddy did send a wire and the Rockingtons would hate being put off at the last moment.... Oh! You beastly dog! He's been licking my shoe, Rachel. Really he oughtn't to, ought he? So funny of you, Rachel, when he's such a mongrel and Roddy's got such lovely darlings—Of course Jacob's a dear, but he is rather absurd to look at——"

Jacob glanced at her, shook his ears and then, hearing a step that he knew, retired, instantly, under a sofa in a far corner of the room.

Roddy came in and stood for a moment laughing across at them. He was in an old tweed suit with a soft collar and his face was brick-red; looking at him as he stood there, the absolute type of health and strength and cleanly vigour, Rachel wondered why she felt irritable. She certainly was out of sorts.

"Hullo, you two," Roddy said, "you do look cosy! Talkin' secrets, or will you put up with a man?"

"Oh! Roddy," said Nita Raseley, "why, of course. Rachel's only just come down, hasn't been any time for secrets. Come and get warm."

Room was made for him. Rachel smiled at him as she gave him his tea. "Well, Roddy, what have you been doing? I've been trying to write letters and Nita's been abusing a novel I lent her. I hope you've been better employed——"

"I've been botherin' around with Nugent over those two horses he bought last week. And—oh! I say, Rachel, you'll come over to Hawes to-morrow, won't you?"

"You know I can't. I've got Miss Crale coming to luncheon——"

"Oh, I say! Put her off——"

"Can't—I've put her off before and she doesn't deserve to be badly treated——"

"Oh! dash it! But I've gone and wired. The Rockingtons won't like my changin'——"

"Well, don't change—you and Nita go over——"

"No, but you know we'd always arranged to go over together. You see, I felt sure you'd put old Miss Crale on to another day. She won't mind——"

"No, Roddy, thank you. That's not fair on her. It can't be helped. You go over with Nita."

Then there occurred between them one of those little situations that were now so frequent. Rachel was hurt, but was determined to show nothing; Roddy knew that she was hurt, but was quite unable to improve relations, partly because he had no words, partly because "a feller looks such a fool tryin' to explain," partly because there was in him a quality of sullen obstinacy that was mingled, most strangely, with his kindness and sentiment.

He was absolutely ready to fling Nita and the Rockingtons into limbo, but he was quite unable to set about such a business.

Moreover now there was Nita Raseley—It was at this moment that Jacob, having fought in the dark recesses of the sofa between his dislike of Roddy and his love of tea, declared for his stomach and walked slowly, and with the dignity required by the presence of an enemy, across the room.

"Hullo! there's the mongrel—" Roddy endeavoured to cover earlier awkwardness by easy laughter, but the laughter was not easy and his attempt to pat Jacob was frustrated by a sidling movement on the dog's part.

Then Nita Raseley laughed.

Roddy now thought that women were damnable, that his wife had no right to drag a mongrel like that about with her, that he'd show them if they laughed at him, and that if Rachel couldn't come to-morrow, why then, she must just lump it—The last thought of all was that Rachel was always finding a grievance in something.

He waited a little while, talked in a stiff and unnatural fashion and then went.

"This weather is very trying, dear, isn't it?" said Nita. "If I were you I really would go and lie down. You do look so seedy!"

"I think I will," said Rachel.

As she went slowly upstairs to her room she knew that she would answer Francis Breton's letter.

CHAPTER III
FIRST SEQUEL TO DEFIANCE
"He began to love her so soon, as he perceived that she was passing out of
his control."

Jane Austen.

I

Next morning Rachel wrote the following letter to Francis Breton:

"Dear Mr. Breton,

It was good of you to write to me and I must apologize for allowing your
letter to remain so long unanswered, but, on my return from abroad, there
were naturally a great many things to do and a great many people to see.

My husband and I enjoyed our time abroad immensely: it was my first visit
to Greece and Italy and I loved every bit of it—Athens is to me more
wonderful than now, here so snugly in England, seems possible; Florence
and Rome very beautiful of course but spoilt, don't you think, by tourists
and the modern Italian who has learnt American habits—

How is London? I've not yet had a good look at it since I came back, but we
shall be coming up soon, I expect, and have taken a flat in Elliston Square,
between Portland Place and Byranston Square.

Your letter sounds a little dismal; it is kind of you to say that I can help you,
but, indeed, if writing to me helps do so. It is only fair to say that at present
my husband shares the family point of view and, so long as that is so, I
cannot ask you to come and see me, but I hope that soon he will see the
whole affair more sensibly.

Yours very sincerely,

Rachel Seddon."

She was not proud of this letter when she read it. She whose impulse was for
truth seemed to be flung, at every turn, into direct dishonesty. No, she
would not seize on the excuse of some vague tyrannical fate.

She was herself her own agent in this affair and she bitterly, from her heart,
condemned herself ... and yet, strangely, this letter to Breton seemed, in

159

obedience to some inward impulse, her most honest action since her marriage.

Yet why did she not go to Roddy now and say to him that she had written to Breton and was determined to act as his friend?

Roddy would forbid any further relationship; she knew that. And then?...

No, she could not see beyond—

She banished the letter from her mind, saw the two of them off to Hawes, and entertained Miss Crale to luncheon. Miss Crale was a broad and shapeless old maid with huge boots, a bass voice and a moustache. She was behind most of the charitable affairs in the county, was popular everywhere, and the most energetic character Rachel had ever met—

Rachel liked her and she liked Rachel, and after she had departed, breathless and red-faced, on some further visit concerned with some further charity, Rachel felt braced and invigorated and happier than she had been for many weeks.

It was a day of frosted blue and the sun flashed fire on to the great field of snow that stretched from sky to sky. The Downs lay humped against the blue and the whole world was frozen into silence.

The only sounds were the soft stir the snow, falling from branches or walls, made and the sharp cries of some children playing in a field near at hand.

When Miss Crale had gone Rachel went off for a walk. Jacob was with her. She struck up the winding path on to the Downs. The snow was hard and yielded a pleasant friendly crunch beneath her feet. Shadows that were dark and yet were filled with colour lay across the snow; beneath her a white valley against which trees and buildings seemed little wooden toys and, in the far distance, hills rising, cut, with their iridescent glow, the blue sky.

No clouds; no movement; no sound: and soon the sun would be golden and then hard and red, and then across all the snow pink shadows would creep and the evening stars would burn—

In the heart of the snow, a valley between the shoulders of the Downs, a black clump of trees clustered; she could see, now, Seddon Court like a grey box at her feet, very tiny and breathing rest and peace.

The Duchess of Wrexe

Some of her trouble slipped from her under this clear sky and in this sharp air; from these quiet hills she saw all her introspection as an evil thing, morbid, cowardly; from here it seemed to her that her trouble with Roddy had been because he did not know what introspection meant and could not understand the appeals that she made to him.

But was it not unfair that men should have so many things that could take the place of love? For Roddy there were a thousand emotions to give meaning to life: for Rachel all experience seemed to come to her only through people and her relations with people.

Soon the valley and the little toy houses were behind her and she had only the white rise and fall of the hill on every side. Dropped into a hollow was a little dark deserted house with bare trees about it; otherwise there was no dwelling-place to be seen.

This absence of human life suddenly drew up before her, as sharply and with as living an actuality as though some mirage had cast it there— London—

Three months in the country had flung the London that she knew into a vivid perspective that was quite novel to her. By the London that she knew she did not mean the London of parties and theatre, the London of Nita and her kind, but rather the actual London of the streets and squares and fountain and parks and dusty plane trees and tinkling organ-grinders.

She felt now quite a thrill of excitement to think that, in another week or two, she would be back in it all and would see all the lamps coming out and the jingling cabs and the heavy lumbering omnibuses, and that she would hear again the sharp crying of the newspaper boys and the ringing of church bells and the thud of the horses down the Row and the hum of voices above the orchestra during the intervals of some play.

She thought of Portland Place and the park and the Round Church and the little shops and Oxford Circus and the buses tumbling down Regent Street into Piccadilly and then tumbling down again into Pall Mall. From Portland Place she seemed to look down over the whole of London and to see it like a jewel, with its glow dazzling the night sky—

She knew now that although she hated her grandmother she did not hate the Portland Place house and she was glad that Roddy had taken a flat near there. No other part of London would ever be quite the same to her as that

161

was: it would always be home to her more than any other place in the world, with its space and air and sense of life crowding around it.

And, as she walked, she was fired with the desire to have some real active share in the London life; not in the sham life of pleasure and entertainment, but to be working, as all kinds of men must be working, with London behind them, influencing them, sometimes depressing them, sometimes exalting them, always moving within them.

That was a fine ambition to work towards a greater London, a greater, finer, truer world, and whether you were politician or artist or journalist or merchant or novelist or clerk or philanthropist, still by your working honestly you would deserve your place in that company.

If she could have some share in such things, then her miserable doubts and forebodings would vanish in a vision too bright and glorious to contain them—

As she walked her face glowed and her body moved as though it could continue thus, swinging through the clear air, for all time.

She determined that on this very evening she would tell Roddy about Breton. Whatever might be the result life in the future should be clear of Beaminster confusions. She would even ask Roddy to help her about Breton, to influence, perhaps, her grandmother with regard to him—

Then, in a few days, Nita Raseley would be gone, and, afterwards, she would discipline all her wit and energy towards establishing a fine relationship with Roddy.

Something had, throughout all these months, been wrong; she would discover where that wrong lay—She would curb her own impatience, would fling herself into his interests, would learn the things that Roddy wanted from her and give them to him—

Then, as the sun sank lower and the yellow shadows crept up the sky, she felt desolate and lonely. Vigour left her—She had descended now into the valley and had come to the deserted house with the stark frowning trees. This place, she had heard, had in the eighteenth century been a private mad-house, and now behind its darkened windows she could have fancied shapes and down the wind the echo of voices.

She fought with all her might against a great tide of loneliness that was now sweeping up about her. There had always been so many people around her and yet she had always been lonely. Even May and Dr. Christopher had not helped her there. She had a sense now of all the people in all the world who were waiting for the other people who could understand them; they were always missing one another, so near sometimes, sometimes touching, and then, after all, going through life alone.

Those were the people with feelings and emotions—and as for the people without them, of what use was life to them?

Either way, except for the fortunate way, Life was a futile business.

Then, climbing up from that sinister little valley and seeing that the sky had turned to violet and that the evening star was there burning as she had known that it would, she laughed at her morbidity.

She shook herself free from it, thought once more of the things that she would do with Roddy, thought of London and the fun that she would have there, thought of Christopher and Uncle John and even Aunt Adela; then, as she turned down the little crooked path towards the house, she thought again of her cousin; she would work without ceasing to bring him back into the family.

That, at any rate, was work upon which she might commence on her return to London, and as she clicked the little wicket-gate, a side-entrance to the garden, behind her, she was almost happy again.

The dusk was deepening into darkness, the moon had not yet risen above the hill. She had entered the garden on the further side of the house and passed through a long laurel path, her feet silenced by the snow.

Jacob had stayed, some way behind. She could see the white lawn and beyond it the lighted house; she was about to step out of the dark shadow of the laurels when she found, just in front of her, almost touching her, hidden by the black depth of the trees, two figures.

She was upon them with a startled cry. A man had his arms about a woman; bending back a little he had pulled her forward against him and was kissing her so fiercely that her hands were buried deep in his coat to steady herself.

Rachel knew them instantly; they were her husband and Nita Raseley—

The Duchess of Wrexe

She stepped past them on to the lawn and at that instant they were conscious of her—

Then she walked swiftly into the house.

II

She went up to her bedroom. No thought came to her, her mind was blank, but she noticed little things, put some of the silver things on her dressing-table in order, pulled her blind a little lower, moved to the fire and pushed the logs into a blaze. She sat there for a long, long time.

When the dressing-bell echoed through the rooms she was still sitting there, thinking nothing—

Her maid came to her; she told her the dress that she would wear and after a while sat staring into her mirror whilst her hair was brushed.

Lucy said, "The snow's begun again, my lady. Coming down fast——"

Then some absence of light in her mistress's eyes frightened her and she said no more.

Someone knocked on the door: a note for her ladyship. Rachel read it:

"It was all a horrible, horrible mistake. Darling Rachel, you know it was only fun—just nothing at all. Shall I come and explain? If you'd rather not see me just now say so and I shall quite understand. I've been so upset that I think I won't come down to dinner, if it isn't too much bother having just a little sent up to me. It was all such a silly mistake, as you'll see when we've explained.

Your loving

Nita."

When she came to "we" Rachel coloured a little. Then she said, "Lucy, bring me the local railway-guide. In my writing-room."

Lucy brought it to her. Then she wrote:

"Dear Nita,

164

No explanations necessary. There is a good train up to town from Hawes at 9.30 to-morrow morning.

Yours,

Rachel Seddon."

"I want this taken to Miss Raseley, Lucy—now. She's not very well, so ask Haddon to see that dinner is sent up to her room, please."

Then she finished dressing and went down to Roddy.

III

He had perhaps expected that she would not come down, but there was no opportunity given them for speech because the butler announcing dinner followed her into the library. They went in.

He sat opposite her, looking ashamed, with his eyes lowered, and the red coming and going in his sunburned cheeks.

They talked for the sake of the servants, and she asked him whether Hawes had been as lovely as ever and whether Lady Rockington's nerves were better, and how their youngest boy (delicate from his birth) was now.

Whilst she spoke her brain was turning, turning like a wheel; could she only, for five minutes, think clearly, then might much after disaster be avoided. She knew that in the conversation that was to come Roddy would follow her lead and that it would be she who would be responsible for all consequences.

She knew that and yet she could not force her brain to be clear nor foresee what the end of it all was to be.

The dessert and the wine came at last and she went—

"I'll be in the library, Roddy," she said.

He gave her a quarter of an hour, and in that pause, with the house quite silent all about her and the fire crackling and the lights softly shining, she strove to discipline her mind.

She had known as soon as she had seen them there that the most awful element in it was that this had in no way altered the earlier case—it merely precipitated a crisis and demanded a definition. Nothing could have proved to her that she had never loved Roddy so much as her own feeling at this crisis towards him. Therein lay her own sin.

It was simply now of the future that she must think. The awful chasm that might divide them after this night, were not their words most carefully ordered, shook her with fear; peril to herself, for she could stand aside and see herself quite clearly: and she knew that if to-night she and he were to say things that they could neither of them afterwards forget, then, for herself, and from her deep need of love and affection, there was temptation awaiting her that no disguise could cover.

Then, as more clearly she figured the scene in the garden, patience seemed difficult to command.

She hated Nita Raseley—that was no matter—but she despised Roddy, and were he once to-night to see that contempt she knew that his after remembrance of it would divide them more completely than anything else could do.

When he came in she had still no clearer idea of what she intended to say, or how she wished things to go. She was sitting in an arm-chair by the fire with her hands shielding her face, and he sat down opposite her and stared at her and cleared his throat and wished that she would take her hands down and then finally plunged:

"Rachel—I don't know—I can't—hang it all, what can I say? I've been a beastly cad and I'd cut my right hand off to have prevented it happening——"

She took her hand down and turned towards him—

"Let's cut all the recrimination part, Roddy," she said. "It was very unfortunate—that was all. It was rather beastly of you, and as for Nita——"

Here he broke in—"No, I say, you mustn't say anythin' about her. She wasn't a little bit to blame—It just——"

"Well, we'll leave Nita. She isn't of any importance, anyway. The point is that things have been wrong for months between us, and as we haven't been married very long that's a pity. This has just brought things to a head, that's all——"

"No," said Roddy firmly. "No, Rachel, that ain't fair to Nita. I know it isn't nice, but I must put that out fair and square—fair and square to Nita.

"We'd had a jolly old drive to Hawes—rippin' day, cold as anythin', with the horse just spankin' along, and then the Rockingtons were jolly and the lunch was jolly and back we came. We looked about the house for you and heard you were still out walkin', so we just strolled about the garden a bit and then—Well, anyway, Nita simply had nothin' to do with it. It was so rippin' and jolly after the drive and all, that I just kissed her. All in a second I just felt I had to ... beastly weak of me," he finally added in a contemplative tone.

"Well, that disposes of Nita," said Rachel. "Don't let's mention her again. Meanwhile what sort of life am I going to have if 'things' are going to sweep over you like this continually? Besides, it's rather early days, isn't it? We haven't been married half a year yet."

"No," said Roddy slowly, "no, we haven't and it's simply beastly. I'm a perfect swine. When I married you the one thing I meant to do was to be just as kind to you as I jolly well could be, and give you a perfectly rippin' time, and here I am hurtin' you like anything——"

She moved impatiently. "Never mind that, Roddy. You have been very kind and I'm sure you'd have given anything for me not to have come into the garden just when I did, so as to have avoided hurting me. But what I do know is that you're not straight with me. You know I told you before we were married that the one thing that mattered was Truth—truth to oneself and truth to everyone else—Well, we haven't been straight with one another for a single instant. You've done any number of things that would be wrong to you if I knew about them, but wouldn't be in the least wrong if I didn't."

"Of course," said Roddy, "no feller tells his wife everything—that would be absurd. I think things are worse if people know about 'em whom it hurts to know—much worse."

She was suddenly confronted now with a Roddy whose assurance and confidence in his own personality startled her. Because he had never been gifted with words and liked to be in the company of dogs and horses she had fancied that he had no ideas about anything.

Rachel was a great deal younger than she knew and a great deal more contemptuous of the other half world than her experience of it justified. Strangely enough this confidence on Roddy's part angered her more than anything else could have done.

"The fact is that since our marriage we've never got to know each other in the least. We talk and go to places together and you give me things and I give you things—and that's all. I don't know you and now, after to-day, I can't trust you——"

He coloured a little at that, but said nothing.

She went on, rather fast and her breath coming between her words: "But I'm not going to be so silly as to make a scene because I saw you kissing Nita Raseley. She's simply not worth thinking about,—but you ought to be straighter to me all the way round. If you've wanted to be kind to me as you say, then you might have taken me more into your life——"

"Well," said Roddy slowly, "if you'd managed to love me a bit, Rachel, things might be different."

This answer was so utterly unexpected that it took her like a blow. That Roddy should attack her when he had, only a few hours before, been discovered so abominably!

"What do you mean, Roddy?" she stammered angrily. "Love you? But——"

"Yes," he persisted doggedly, "I know when you accepted me you said you didn't and I know that I hadn't any right to expect it, but I believe if you hadn't thought me such a silly ass and hadn't looked all the time as though you were just indulgin' my silly fancies until somethin' more sensible had come along, things might have been different. I'm the sort of feller," Roddy said, choosing his words carefully, "that you could have made anythin' out of, Rachel. I'm weak in some ways—most men are—and when a thing comes dancin' along lookin' ever so temptin', why, then I generally have to go after it. But you could have kept me, Rachel, more than anyone I've ever known——"

She was not touched nor moved, only angered that he, so obviously in the wrong, should attempt justification.

"Yes," she said hotly. "And I suppose in another moment you'll be telling me that it's silly of me to be angry at what I saw this afternoon?"

He thought it out a moment, then answered: "No, it was perfectly natural of course—only I don't think you ought to mind much. If you really cared, you wouldn't. It don't matter really so much what I do if I still like you best.

Moments don't count—it's what goes on all the time that matters. Why, I might kiss a hundred women and still you'd be the only woman who mattered to me. I've never cared for one so long before," he added simply.

Then as she said nothing he went on: "I've never been sort of educated— never cared enough for anyone to give things up. I would have given things up for you if you'd wanted me to, but you didn't really——"

"Aren't we a little off the point, Roddy?" she flung back. "The point is how are we going to get along all the years and years we've got in front of us? What are we going to do?"

"Everybody's just the same," said Roddy quietly. "It takes a lot of years before married people settle down. We can't expect to be any different——"

But although he spoke so quietly he watched her, hoping for some yielding on her part; in an instant, had she come to him, she would have seen a Roddy whom she had never seen before and from that moment onwards would have had a power over him that nothing could have shaken.

So delicately hung the balance between them. But she was filled with a sense of her own wrongs, her loneliness, the injustice of it all. At that moment all affection for Roddy had left her, she would only have been glad if she had known that she was never to see him again. His slow voice, his way of thinking out his sentences, his thick clumsy hands and his red face, everything came to her now as a continuation of the chains that she had worn all her days.

She got up and confronted him—

"Yes," she said fiercely, "that's exactly it. Life is to be like everyone else. We're to say the things, do the things that our neighbours say and do. Because your friends at Brooks's kiss their wives' friends, therefore you are to do so. Because the men you know never say what they mean and lie about everything they do, therefore you do the same. Oh! I know! Haven't I heard it all my life? Haven't my precious family lived on lies? You've caught it all from my delightful grandmother! I congratulate you!"

"What if I have?" he said. "She's a friend of mine, Rachel. She's been dashed good to me—You're not to say a word against her."

"I hate her," Rachel cried passionately. "All my life she's been over me—for years she's been my enemy. If she stands for everything that you believe, then it isn't any wonder that we have nothing in common, that you should be proud of this afternoon, that—that——"

She was biting her lips to keep back the tears. Over his face had crept a sulky obstinate look that might have told her, had she seen it, that she was driving him very far.

"She's fine," he said. "She's made England what it is. You're all for ideas, Rachel, and for Truth and lots of things, but you're difficult to live with."

"Very well, Roddy. Thank you. Now we know how we stand. I at least owe Nita a debt for having cleared up the situation. If you find it difficult with me I can at least return the compliment—and I have at any rate this added advantage, that I speak the truth."

As he looked at her across the room he saw in her that same figure that he'd seen once just before proposing to her—someone foreign, unknown—He felt as though he were quarrelling with a stranger....

She turned and went.

For a long while he stood gazing into the fire, his hands in his pockets. How had it all happened? Why had they let it come to that kind of quarrel when they might so easily have prevented it?

And she, crying bitterly in her room, asked herself the same question.

CHAPTER IV
RACHEL—AND CHRISTOPHER AND RODDY
I

Christopher had snatched his first holiday for two years and was abroad during the January of 1899 when the Seddons were in town.

February, March and April they spent at Seddon Court, and it was not therefore until early in May that Christopher saw Rachel.

She had dreaded with an almost fantastic alarm this meeting. No other human being knew her so honestly and accurately as did Christopher, and the change in her that he would at once discern would, when she caught the reflection of it in his eyes, mark definitely the sinister country into which these last months had carried her.

It had seemed as though some malign spirit had been determined to make the most of that quarrel that Nita Raseley had provoked.

Both Roddy and Rachel hated scenes—upon that, at least, they were agreed—and from their determination never to have another arose a deliberate avoidance of any plain speaking. Rachel, longing for honesty, found herself caught in a thousand deceits—Roddy, avoiding any kind of analysis, found that everything that he provided in conversation seemed to lead to danger.

He was now always ill at ease in Rachel's company; he had stood on that fatal evening, more strongly for the Beaminster interest than he had intended, but from his very determination to maintain his new independence, he produced the Duchess for Rachel's benefit at every turn of the road.

Roddy knew that the Duchess feared that Rachel would lead him from her side and that she received with rejoicing every sign on his part of irritation against Rachel. She had wanted him to marry her granddaughter because that bound him more closely to her, but she had not, perhaps, been prepared for the probable effect of Rachel's character upon him.

The Duchess therefore made, throughout these months, a third member of their company. Roddy, finding Rachel's society a growing embarrassment, spent more and more of his time with his animals and his tenants and labourers. But all this time he was conscious, in a dumb way, of unhappiness and a puzzled dismay, so that his very affection for Rachel produced in him a growing irritation that it should be so needlessly thwarted. Things were all wrong and his resentment of his own failure to right them reacted, without his will, upon the very person whom he wished to propitiate.

For Rachel these months were baffling in their hideous discomfort. Her affection for Roddy was there, but it was swallowed by her desperate efforts to analyse a situation that was, in definite outline, no situation at all.

As Roddy withdrew, her loneliness wrapped her round, and in every day that added to her distance from Roddy she saw the active and malignant agency of her grandmother. She was intelligent enough to be aware that in this constant vision of the Duchess she was outstepping the probabilities; but her early years and the precipitation with which she had been shot out of them into an atmosphere that unexpectedly resembled their own earlier surroundings seemed to point to some diabolical agency.

"Oh! when I get free of this," had been her earlier cry, and now the foreboding that she was never to be free of it until she died terrified her with its possibility. Imagine her brought up in a stuffy house with windows tightly closed, in full vision of a high road, imagine her promised the freedom of the road at a future time; imagine her liberated, at last, rushing into the new life and finding that, after all, the walls of the house were still about her, and about her now for ever.

Her one reserve during the early months of the year at Seddon had been her letters to Francis Breton. His letters to her had been a series of self-revelation; he had restrained himself in so far as appealing to her simply on the score of their relationship and his enmity to the head of the house. She had replied revealing her sympathy, hinting at rebellion on her own side and feeling, after the writing of every letter, a hatred of her own deceit, a curiously heightened sense of affection for Roddy, above all a conviction that impulses were, of their own agency, working to some climax that she could not, or would not, control.

The foreign blood in her, the English blood in him, baffled their advances toward one another. Everything that Rachel did now seemed to Roddy so close to melodrama that it was best to use silence for his weapon. All Roddy's actions were to Rachel further illustrations of Beaminster muddle and second-rate personality.

Had Roddy called out of Rachel the great depth of passion and reality that she inherited from her mother her own love of him would have solved everything but that he could not call from her, nor ever would.

For Rachel, she saw in him now a possibility of perpetual infidelity, and at every suspicion of it her disgust both at herself and him grew because that possibility did not move her more.

They came up to London at the beginning of May and hid, very successfully from the world, the widening breach.

To Rachel, it was sheer terror to discover the thrill that the adjacence of Elliston Square to Saxton Square gave her. In this one self-revelation there was enough to present her with night after night of sleepless misery. She visited the Duchess and found that her presence was continually demanded. Every visit was a battle.

"Show me how you are treating him, whether he cares for you. Have you found him out? Tell me everything — —"

"I will tell you nothing. I will come here day after day and you shall gather nothing from me. I have escaped you."

"Indeed you have not escaped me. My power over you is only now beginning — —"

No word between them but the most civil. There was no trace in the old woman now of her earlier irony — no sign in Rachel of irritation or rebellion.

But the girl knew that war was declared, that her only ally was one in whose alliance lay, for her, the very heart of danger.

All these things she might hide from the world — from Christopher she knew that she could hide nothing.

II

It was on an early afternoon in May that Christopher had tea with Rachel. He had waited for his visit with very real anxiety; the letters that he had had from her had been unsatisfactory, not because they were actively expressive of unhappiness, but because there was an effort in every word of them — Rachel had never found it difficult to write to him before.

He was also uneasy because he had been against this marriage from the beginning. He did, as he said to the Duchess, know Rachel better than anyone else knew her; he knew her from his love for her, and also from that scientific study that he applied in his profession. And he had found, too, in her, as he had found in Breton, some strain of fierce helplessness, as of an animal caught in a trap, that especially moved his interest and affection —

Was Rachel's marriage a disaster? If so she had certainly managed to conceal it, for even the Duchess did not know — of that he was sure.

If Rachel were indeed unhappy would she come to him as she used to come to him?

What change had marriage wrought in her?

It was one of those May days when the weather is hot before London is ready. It was a day of tension; buildings, streets quivered beneath a sun in whose gaze there was no kindliness nor comfort. Christopher drove from Eaton Square, where, for some hours he had been engaged in preventing an old man from dying, when both the old man himself and all his friends and relations were convinced that death was the best thing for him —

Sloane Street ran like white steel before his eyes, not dimly veiled as he had so often seen it; Park Lane offered houses that stared with haughty faces upon a world that would, they knew, do anything for money —

Elliston Square itself was white and sterile; the town was, on this afternoon, irritated, sinister ... feet ached upon its pavements and hearts were suddenly clutched with foreboding.

As he ascended in the lift to her flat he knew that, did he find that this marriage was, truly, a misadventure for Rachel, then, until his death, he would reproach himself for some weak inaction, some hesitation when first he had heard that it was to be.

He had protested, but now he felt that he should have done more.

Soon he had his answer to all his questions.

He saw at once that Rachel was no longer the impulsive, nervous girl whom he had always known. She was a girl no longer.

Her eyes greeted him now steadily, she seemed taller and her body was in perfect control — very tall and slim and dark, her cheeks pale but shadowed a little with the shadow deepening beneath her eyes. Her mouth, that had always been too large, had had before a delightful quality of uncertainty, so that smiles and frowns and alarms, distress and happiness all hovered near. It was now grave and composed.

Her limbs had always moved unsteadily and with the awkward lack of control of a child, now there was no kind of impulse, every movement was considered, and that was the first thing that Christopher saw, that nothing that Rachel now did or said was spontaneous.

There was less in her now to remind him of her foreign blood.

The flat was comfortable, but more commonplace than it would have been had it been Rachel's only.

He kissed her, as he had always done, and he fancied that she clung for a moment to him, as her hands went up to his coat.

He settled his big loose body and looked across at her.

Christopher was no subtle analyser of other people's emotions. His own feelings were never complicated and he expected life to run on plain and simple lines of likes and dislikes, sorrow, anger, love and hatred. If someone of whom he was fond made a direct appeal to him his simple remedies were often wonderfully useful—he was no fool and he had been brought, during a great number of years, into the most direct relations with men and women, but, if that direct appeal was not made, then he was frightened and baffled.

He was frightened of Rachel now; he knew instantly that instead of appealing she would defend herself from him.... Some mysterious conviction seemed to forebode that he would not be able to help her. He was, essentially, of those who, believing in goodness and virtue and the glorious Millennium, are contented, quite simply, with that belief and might, if they stated those simplicities, irritate the scoffers. But he was saved because he made statements on the rarest occasions and lived his life instead.

Here, however, was a crisis in his relations with Rachel that no platitudes could satisfy. Did he not touch her now he might never touch her again.

In a situation that was beyond him he was always hopelessly self-conscious. His love for Rachel was so tremendous a thing in him that a statement of it should surely have been the simplest thing in the world. But he saw in her eyes that to challenge her with—"My dear, you know how I love you. Tell me what's the matter," would frighten her to absolute silence. "I'm going to tell you nothing," she seemed to say to him, "unless you move me in spite of myself. But, if I don't tell you now I shall never tell you."

"Well, my dear," he said, smiling at her, "how are you after all this time?"

"I'm all right," she answered, smiling back at him. "It is good to see you again. Tell me all about your holiday."

"Tell me about yours first."

"Oh! There isn't very much to tell. I enjoyed it all enormously, of course."

"What did you enjoy most?"

"Oh! some of the smaller towns—Rapallo, for instance.—Oh! yes, and Bologna was fascinating."

"Not Rome and Florence?"

"In a way. But there were too many tourists. Rome one's got to stay in, I'm sure. That first view was disappointing."

"And how did Roddy—if I may call him Roddy—enjoy it?"

"Immensely, I think. He liked the country better than the towns though."

"You saw lots of pictures?"

"Heaps. Roddy enjoyed them enormously. I'd no idea he knew so much about them. Oh! it was all lovely, and such colours, such light—London seems like a cellar, even in June."

There followed then a pause that swelled and swelled between them until it resembled some dreadful monster, horribly stationed there to separate them.

Christopher looked at Rachel, but she refused to meet his eyes.

"I've lost her. I shall never see her again!" he thought with despair. Two years ago he would have gone to her, put his arms around her, kissed her and drawn from her at once her trouble.

He could not do that now.

"Your turn, Dr. Chris dear. Tell me about your holidays."

"Oh, mine don't count. I went to Brittany first, then up to St. Andrews with another man to play golf."

"You're looking splendidly well and you're thinner. What was Brittany like?"

"Delightful. Have you ever been there?"

"Never. I must get Roddy to take me. Just suit him, I should think."

To Christopher's intense relief tea was brought. He came to the table and then, for an instant, he did catch her eyes, saw tears in them, and behind the tears some appeal to him to help her. Her hand was shaking.

"How silly of me to spill your tea. I'm so sorry. Let me pour it back...."

"Rachel——" he began, but a servant entered with something and he waited. When they were alone again, standing over her as though he were afraid that she would escape him, he plunged.

"Rachel dear. We're talking as though we'd never met before. You've never been shy with me like this. If marriage is going to make a stranger of you, I shall break young Seddon's neck——"

"No," she said in a voice that was between laughter and tears. "Of course, Dr. Chris. Things are just the same between us, only, only—well, I'm married and—one thing and another, you know."

He caught both her hands.

"You're perfectly happy?"

She met his eyes.

"Perfectly."

"Happier than you've ever been in your life?"

She dropped her eyes.

"Happier than I've ever been in my life."

"And you'll come to me just the same if there's any kind of trouble?"

"Of course."

"You promise?"

"I promise."

They talked then, for a little time, of other things. But he was not satisfied. Rachel's soul, caught away in alarm, was still beyond his grasp.

At last, feeling that the moments were precious and that Roddy might at any instant appear, he sat down on the sofa beside her.

"Rachel dear. Something's worrying you. You won't tell me?"

"Nothing's worrying — —"

"Ah, but I know — well, if you won't you won't — but if you knew how much I loved you you'd feel that you were cruel not to let me help you."

"Dear Dr. Chris — but there is nothing."

But her eyes were full of tears.

"Look here," he said. "Perhaps you'll feel later on you can talk to me. Just come straight away if you do feel that."

He went on. "Don't be frightened, my dear, if there are a whole heap of new emotions, new instincts, stirred in you by marriage. Just take them all as they come. It's all progress, you know. Don't be frightened of anything. Just take the animal by the head and look at it."

That led him to speak about Brun's Tiger. He explained it — the force in people, the way they either grappled with the creature, and at last trained it to help them with their work in the world, or ignored it, silenced it, allowed it at last to die, and so, cosy and lazily comfortable, passed to their day's end, but had, nevertheless, missed the whole purpose of life.

He enlarged on that and showed the connection of the individual Tiger with the welfare of the world, so that everyone who denied his Tiger added to his world's muddle and confusion, and at last there would come an inevitable crisis when war would spring up between those who had grappled with their Tiger and those who had not.

"One knows one's own Tiger—absolutely of oneself one knows it and has, of oneself, the choice whether to grapple or not—at least that's what I gathered he meant—I know it struck me at the time."

"Oh," she said, with a sigh that quivered through her whole body. "It's so easy to talk.... But it's true what he says. I know it."

At last Christopher got up to go. He did not know whether he had done any good; he felt that he was a miserable failure, and he had a foreboding that one day he would be ashamed indeed that he had not helped her.

"Do something," a voice seemed to tell him. "You'll regret ... all your life you'll regret."

He turned and held again her hands in his.... "Rachel—dear—tell me——"

Her hands were chill and lifeless. Her voice caught. "Oh! Dr. Chris!..." Then she suddenly stepped back from him—

"It's all right.... I'm all right. Come again soon, Dr. Chris dear—come soon."

He left her and found his way into the hot, breathless street.

After he had gone Rachel sat, staring beyond the room out on to the white walls of the houses and the green branches of the trees in the square.

Roddy came in.

All the afternoon he had been thinking about her; at one moment he was furious with the discomfort that life was now becoming to him, at another moment he was imagining little plans that would sweep all the discomfort away.

All this spring they had been miserable together. Now was beginning a time that was always jolly in London and yet he could not enjoy a moment of it. Did she dislike him instead of liking him, or did he like her instead of loving her, it would all be so easy—just the same as any other couple.

Ever since that silly Nita incident there had been this restraint, and yet how could that be the cause?

Rachel had made nothing of it; it was because it had meant so little to her that he had chafed so at the remembrance of it.

She was fond of him—he knew that—she was miserably unhappy.

He loved her—and he was miserably unhappy.

Damn this weather.

He looked at her, wondered what would happen did he cross over and suddenly kiss her, knew that he would see her struggle to be kind, to give him what he wanted, knew that that would hurt most damnably, and that he would be in a bad temper for the rest of the evening and would wonder why—

So, with a muttered word he went out and up to his dressing-room, had a bath, and then lay reading with serious brows The Winning Post until his man told him that it was time to dress.

Slowly and with the absorbed care that he always gave to these preparations he made himself ready for the Beaminster dinner.

CHAPTER V
LIZZIE'S JOURNEY—I

"So thy great gift, upon misprision growing,
Comes home again, on better judgment making;
Thus have I had thee, as a dream doth flatter
In sleep a king; but waking no such matter."
William Shakespeare.

I

During this year Lizzie Rand was glad that she had so much to do. As she had never until now given the romance in her an opportunity for freedom, so had she never before realized the amazing invasion upon life that that same romance might threaten.

Indeed by the early summer months of 1899 "threaten" was no longer an honest definition, for, now this same Romance had invaded, had conquered, had confronted the very citadels of Lizzie's heart, citadels never surveyed nor challenged at any time before.

Nevertheless, even now, Portland Place noticed no change in Miss Rand. Norris, Mrs. Newton, Dorchester would still, had they been challenged, have protested that Miss Rand had no conception of the softer, more sentimental side of life; she was there for discipline and order—Norris had been known to be led a fearful dance by young women "time and again"—Mrs. Newton had passionately adored the late Mr. Newton until a sudden chill had carried him to St. Agnes, Bare Street Cemetery, whither Mrs. Newton, every Sunday, did still make her stately pilgrimage—even Dorchester had once, it was said, paid grim attentions to a soldier who had, unhappily, found in some fluffy young woman a more hopeful comfort.

Here, above and below stairs, passion had marked its victims ... Miss Rand only could have felt no touch of it.

She sometimes wondered at herself that she could so calmly and dispassionately separate the one life from the other. Never, within that neat stern room at Portland Place, was there a shudder or sudden invading thrill at some flashing recollection or imagination. To her work every nerve, every energy was given. Now, indeed, more than ever before in her experience of it did 104 Portland Place demand her presence. Increasingly throughout these months of 1899 was the solemn heavy air unsettled.

Lizzie, to whom all impression came with sharpening acuteness, had seen in the appearance, success and marriage of Rachel Beaminster the disturbing

181

elements at work—"Things will never be the same here again"—she had said to herself.

It was, of course, through Lady Adela that Lizzie studied the house. The Duchess she never saw, but it was Lady Adela's attitude, before and after those interviews with her mother, that told their story. Lady Adela had never until now appeared an interesting figure to Lizzie, but now forth, from the dry sterile husk of her, a life, pathetic, struggling against heritages of dumb years, tried to come.

Lady Adela was unhappy; the very foundations of her existence threatened to dismay her, at any moment, by their insecurity. Within her the Beaminster tradition urged, before Lizzie Rand at any rate, the maintenance of dignity and indifference, but the novelty to her of all this disturbance brought with it a hapless inability to deal with it, and again and again little exclamations, little surprised wonders at what the world could be coming to, little confused clutchings at anything that offered stability, showed Lizzie that trouble was on every side of her. Then through the house rumour began to twist its way—Her Grace was not so well—"The Old Lady was breaking up" (this, in the close security of shuttered rooms below stairs).

No one could say whence these whispers gathered. Dorchester would admit nothing. Her own position in the servants' hall was that of a lofty uncompromising female Jove, and she knew well enough that her supremacy over Norris and Mrs. Newton depended on her mistress's supremacy over the world in general. Not for her then to admit ill health.

"Indeed no—Her Grace has been better of late than for years past."

But Norris and Mrs. Newton were not to be taken in. They were truly proud now of their alliance with the Beaminster family royal, but, supposing Her Grace were to leave this world to rule in a better one ("Here to-day, gone to-morrow 'igh or low," as Norris remarked), why, then "Le Roi est mort—Vive le Roi," and the Crown might, in the meanwhile, have passed elsewhere.

"You mark my words," Mrs. Newton said to Norris, "'er Grace will go, old Victorier will go, and where'll the Beaminster crowd be then, I ask you? Times are movin' too quick. I wouldn't give a toss for your Birth and Debrett and all in another twenty years."

To Lizzie also there came other signs of the times. She noticed that now the relations and friends of the family gathered more frequently together than ever before within her memory. The Duke, Lord Richard were continually in the house, and the adherents, Lady Carloes, Lord Crewner, the Massiters and all the others, called, dined, came to tea.

Throughout it all there was no expression of any change in the family policy. To Lizzie Lady Adela admitted nothing, only there were occasions when, almost against her will, she asked for advice, was uncertain a little, vague a little, even appealing a little.

Here Lizzie was exactly right, assisted and yet admitted no need for assistance. Her tact was perfect.

Lizzie had also Lady Seddon to besiege her attention.

To her considerable surprise Rachel had written to her three times during this year. On each occasion there had been some definite reason for writing, but behind the reason there had been some implied friendliness and Lizzie had, in her turn, sent answers that were more than businesslike replies.

Lizzie had seen Rachel several times in January and at each meeting her impression of Rachel's unhappiness had grown.

"There've been three of you," Lizzie said to herself. "There was the girl in the schoolroom, and a fierce awkward difficult creature she was. There was the girl in her first season, and a delightful, joyful, radiant creature she was. And now—well, there's a girl married, fierce again, suffering again—above all, afraid of herself."

In May Rachel asked Lizzie to go and see her, and Lizzie went. That meeting was in no way personal: Rachel seemed less friendly than she had been on that day, a year ago, when she had been to Lizzie's, but behind all that outward stiffness the appeal was there.

"She wants me to help her," thought Lizzie. "She's too proud now to ask me: the time will come though."

All this was connected, she knew, with the fortunes of the house. Through Lord John, Lord Richard, the Duke, Lady Adela, Dorchester, Norris, Mrs. Newton the spirit of uneasiness was abroad.

The Duchess, during these months, more than ever before, was present in every room and passage of the house—

The shadow of some coming event hovered.

II

Over Lizzie's other life, also, the Duchess hovered. Were any disaster to snatch Her Grace from the domination of this world into a comparatively humble position in the next, Lizzie did not doubt that the Beaminsters would once more take Francis Breton into their ranks. It was the Duchess who held the gate against him.

The romantic side of her did not hold complete dominion. She knew that were Francis Breton once more accepted by the family, his distance from her would be greatly increased. Were he, on the other hand, to marry her whilst he was yet an exile, then had she no fear of after consequences. She could hold her own with anyone.

She had now very little doubt that he loved her. She had seen, during the last year, the flame of some passion burning in his eyes, increasingly he depended upon her and found opportunities for being with her. There was no other woman whom he saw, of that she was convinced.

Often he had been about to tell her some secret and then had refrained; she thought that he was waiting until he could be quite assured that she loved him, and she had fancied that since that day in last December when the first snow had fallen and they had had that little talk together he had been much happier, as though he were now convinced of her love for him.

The spring passed and still his confession did not come. With the early summer he seemed to be once more unhappy and unsettled, and throughout May she scarcely saw him.

Then in July he asked her whether she would dine with him and go to the theatre. He had two dress circle tickets for Mrs. Lemiter's Decision.

Something told her that on this evening he would speak to her.

As she dressed her fingers trembled so that buttons and hooks and laces were of terrible difficulty. In the glass she saw her cheeks flaming; she wished she were taller, not so sturdy. The lines of her face, she thought, were all so set as though they knew well for what purpose they were there. "Business we're here for ..." they seemed to say.

For once she envied her sister's fair rounded fluffiness. Her black evening dress was fashionable, almost smart, but just a little stern: she fastened some dark red carnations into her waist and hung around her throat a chain of tiny pearls, her only piece of jewellery. Her hair was restrained and disciplined—she could not extract from it any waves or soft indulgencies.

At the end, staring at her reflection, she let herself go.

"He's seen me all this time as I am. How silly to try to alter things!" Her face glowed, the pearls and carnations seemed to smile encouragement to her.

What possibilities had this new, this wonderful Lizzie Rand! What a life might be hers! What a happy, fortunate woman she was!

God, how grateful she was!

Mrs. Rand saw them off in a four-wheeler with an air of reluctance. It always hurt her that anyone should go to the theatre without her.

Of course Lizzie was old enough by now to look after herself, but at the same time this Mr. Breton was no safe character and it would have been altogether "nicer" if Lizzie had suggested her company—

Lizzie had not suggested it; with a shiver Mrs. Rand resigned herself to an evening made hideous by a vision of a world crowded with theatres through whose portals gay audiences were pouring—

"Of course it's selfish of her," she said again and again to Daisy—"Selfish is the only word."

Meanwhile the cab was, for Lizzie, a chariot of happiness. He looked splendid to-night, more romantic than he had ever been, with his pointed beard, his armless sleeve buttoned across on to his coat, his top-hat shining, his clothes fitting so perfectly. Poor though he was, he always stood up as smart as anyone, the Duke or Lord John were no smarter.

Did he realize, she wondered, that the edge of his hand touched the silk of her dress? Did he notice the absurd way that the pearls jumped up and down on her throat? Did he feel the little shiver of happiness that ran through her body and out at her toes and fingers?

The chariot was dark, but beyond it there were piled lighted buildings; before these ran streets that flung dark figures, here one by one, now in throngs, against the glittering colour.

She could not believe that anyone there by the lumbering cab could show happiness that could equal hers.

Had she been coldly surveying, from the careful distance of an outside observer, these emotions in some other woman she would have demanded her reasons for such expectation of happiness, but it was her very inexperience of any other such affair in her life that allowed her now to rest assured. As he touched her hand to help her into the restaurant she was sure, by the beating of her heart, that she could not be deceived.

The restaurant was in Pall Mall, and as she went in she noticed the string of faithful people waiting round the corner of Her Majesty's Theatre; she was glad that there were so many others enjoying themselves to-night.

They sat at a little round table on a balcony and below them other happy people were laughing and talking—Flowers, lights, women not so beautiful that they disheartened one, and, from the open windows, a whir, a rattle, a shout, a cry, a bell, a hurdy-gurdy, a laugh—Oh! the world was turning to-night!

There was a beautiful dinner, but she was far too happy to eat much. He seemed to understand. They both talked a little, but it was, it appeared, implied between them that their real conversation should be postponed.

She was, to herself, an utterly new Lizzie Rand to-night, inarticulate, uncertain, confused.

"What's this the papers say about South Africa?"

"Yes, it looks as though there were going to be trouble there. But you can trust Milner—a strong man——"

"Yes, I suppose so—but it seems a pity that this Conference that they hoped so much from has all fallen through, doesn't it? They do seem obstinate people."

"Well, they are. I was out in Pretoria in '95—obstinate as mules. But there won't be much trouble—a troop or two of our fellows have only got to show their faces——"

"Yes, of course. Isn't that a pretty woman down there? There to the right—with the black hair and the diamonds—tall—"

186

But tall women with black hair and Boers in South Africa were merely points to catch hold, and, for an instant, the thrill of the contact and the anticipation and the glorious vision of the wonderful future.

Him all this time she closely observed. He was not entirely at his ease, when she had been in public with him before she had noticed it, his glance at every new-comer, his conscious summoning of control lest it should be someone whom he had once known, someone who might now, perhaps, not know him.

It made him in her eyes all the younger, all the more happily demanding her protection; how terribly she loved him she had never, she thought, realized until this moment.

The Haymarket Theatre, where Mrs. Lemiter's Decision had been given to a grateful world for nearly two hundred nights, was next door.

In a moment they were there and the band was playing and the lights were up, and then the band was not playing and the lights were down, and she was instantly conscious of the places where his body touched hers and of his hand lying white upon his knee.

She, Lizzie Rand, most perfect of private secretaries, most sedate and composed of women, found it all that her self-control could secure that she should not then and there have touched that hand with her own.

It was not really a good play. There was a lady, Mrs. Lemiter, who had once done what she should not have done. There were a number of ladies and gentlemen, placed round her by the author, in order that she should, for the benefit of as many audiences as possible, confess what she had done.

During the first and second acts Mrs. Lemiter made little dashes towards escape and the author (naturally omniscient) always placed someone in front of her just in time and there were cries of "Not this way, my good woman." At the end of the third act, Mrs. Lemiter, thoroughly bored and exasperated, turned on them all and, for a good twenty minutes, told them what she thought of them.

During the fourth act they all assured her that they liked her very much and that, as it was now eleven o'clock and she'd lost her temper so successfully that the house would certainly be filled for many months to come, they'd all better have tea or dinner, whilst a young couple, who had throughout the play loved one another and quarrelled, made it up again.

When the play was at an end Lizzie did not know what it had been about. She took his hand and when he was about to hail a cab stopped him.

"Let's walk," she said, "it's such a lovely night."

He eagerly agreed and they started.

III

She knew that her moment had come; he knew too—she could tell that because all the way up the Haymarket he said nothing.

Piccadilly Circus was a screaming confusion. A music-hall invited you to come and hear "Harry and Clare, drawing-room entertainers." Lights—red and green and gold—flashed and advised drinks and hair-oil and tobacco. Ladies, highly coloured and a little dishevelled; stared haughtily but inquisitively about them, boys shouted newspapers and dived under horses and appeared, miraculously delivered from the wheels of omnibuses.

It was a rushing, whirling confusion and through it his arm led her, happier in his secure guard than in anything else under heaven.

Regent Street was quiet and softly coloured above the maelstrom into which it flowed. He suddenly began:

"I've got something I want to tell you—something I've wanted to tell you for a long time. You must have seen — —"

Her voice coming to her as though it were a stranger's, said, "Yes." At the same time, looking about her, almost unconsciously, she registered her memory of the place and the hour—the shelving street, rising with its lamps reflected, before them, a bank of dark cloud that had suddenly appeared and hung, sinister against the night sky, behind the white houses, a slip of a silver moon surveying this same cloud with anxiety because it knew that soon its darkness would engulf it.

"I've wanted to tell you," he began again, "this long time. It's needed courage, and things during this last year have rather taken my courage away from me."

"You needn't be afraid," she said with a little laugh. "You ought to know by this time that you can tell me anything, Mr. Breton."

"Yes, I do know," he said earnestly. "Of course I know. What you've been to me all this last year—I simply can't think how I'd have kept up if it hadn't been for you."

"Oh, please," she said.

"No, but it's true. Even with you it's been a bit of a fight."

He paused. She saw that the black cloud had already swallowed up the moon and that a few raindrops were beginning to fall.

He went on: "You must have seen that all this time something's been helping me. I've never spoken to you, but you've known— —"

The moment had come. Her heart had surely stopped its beat and she was glad, in her happiness, of the rain that was now falling more swiftly.

"I don't know—" he stammered a little. "It's so difficult. It's come to this, that I must speak to somebody and you're the only person, the only person. But even with one's best friends—one knows them so slightly—after all, perhaps, you'll think it very wrong— —"

At that word it was as though a great hammer had, of a sudden, hit her heart and slain it. The street, shining with the rain, rose ever so little and bent towards her.

"Wrong?" she said, looking up at him.

"Yes. I don't know about your standards—you've been always so kind to me and put up with my faults and so I've been encouraged— —"

Her relief should have awaked the gods of Olympus with its triumph.

"I've meant everything I've ever said— —"

"Yes, I'm sure you have and that's why I think you'll understand. As I say, I've got to tell someone or I'll burst. It's just this—it's my cousin Rachel— Lady Seddon. Ever since we first met in your room she's been my whole world. Nothing else has mattered. It's she that's kept me all these months from going under. She's my life, my whole existence now and in the world to come, if there is one. Oh! Thank God!" he cried. "I've told someone at last. If you don't approve I can't help it. I know you'll keep my secret and, after all, it's nothing very terrible. I'm content to go on like this, just seeing her sometimes, writing to her sometimes. Now you know, Miss Rand, what's been my secret all this time. I've felt it's been between us and that's why I had to tell you. We'll be twice the friends that we were now that I've told you. And I must, I must have someone to talk to about her sometimes. It's been killing me, getting along without it."

Now that he had begun words poured from him. He did not know that it was raining; he saw only Rachel with her white face and dark hair.

Lizzie pulled her wrap about her; she was very cold and the rain was coming fast.

He was suddenly conscious of this.

"I say, what a brute I am! It's pouring!" He called a passing hansom and they climbed into it.

He was aware that she had said nothing.

"There!" he said, "you wish I hadn't told you. I know you do. You're shocked."

"No," she said, struggling to prevent her teeth from chattering.

He felt her shiver. "Why! you're shaking with cold! We oughtn't to have walked, but I did so want to speak to you about this. We must talk about it another time. But, I say, you aren't really horrified about it, are you?"

"No," she said again. "Another time though—There must be thunder. This storm makes my head ache."

She could say no more. The rest of the drive was in silence. In the hall she thanked him for her delightful evening.

She looked through the drawing-room door and wished her mother and sister good night, but did not stay to discuss incidents.

"Well," said Mrs. Rand, who had a fine list of questions ready about the play—"There's selfishness!"

Lizzie locked her door, undressed and lay down.

Like a sword jagging through and through her brain and piercing from there down to her heart stabbed the refrain:

"Oh! I hate her! I hate her! I hate her!"

So, wide-eyed, she lay throughout the night.

CHAPTER VI
ALL THE BEAMINSTERS

"We must expect change," returned Mrs. Chick.

"Of weather?" asked Miss Tox in her simplicity.

"Of everything," returned Mrs. Chick. "Of course we must. It's a world of change. Anyone would surprise me very much, Lucretia, and would greatly alter my opinion of their understanding, if they attempted to contradict or evade what is so perfectly evident. Change!" exclaimed Mrs. Chick, with severe philosophy — "Why, my gracious me, what is there that does not change! Even the silkworm, who I am sure might be supposed not to trouble itself about such subjects, changes into all sorts of unexpected things continually."

Dombey and Son.

I

At four o'clock on the afternoon of Wednesday, October 11th, in this year 1899 war between England and South Africa was declared.

At that same hour on that same afternoon an afternoon party was given by Lady Adela Beaminster at 104 Portland Place, and all the more important believers in the Beaminster religion were present.

The Long Drawing-room had the happy property of extending to accommodate its company and now, shadowy as its corners always were, it yielded the impression still of size and space, its mirrors reflecting its dark green walls that receded from the figures that thronged it.

The Duchess (now Ross's portrait of her) hung above the Adams fireplace and a little globe of light shone, on this dark October day, up into that sharp and wizened face and lit those bending fingers and flung forward the dull green jade and the dark black dress.

Many people were present. The Duke, Lord John, Lord Richard of course — also, of course, Lady Carloes, the Massiters, Lord Crewner, Monty Carfax, Brun, Maurice Garden the novelist, and his wife — also a fine collection of ladies and gentlemen, important in politics, in the graver camps of society — also a certain number who belonged by party to those whom Brun had once called the Aristocrats, the Chichesters, the Medleys, the Darrants. Old Lady Darrant was there looking like a cook, and Fred Chichester and his kind and

freckled features, and Mrs. Medley who had married Judge Medley's only
son.

Of the Democrats—of the Ruddards, the Denisons, the Oaks, not one to be
seen.

The men and women who stood about in the room seemed strangely, oddly,
of one family. No human being present was without his or her self-
consciousness, but it was a self-consciousness that had about it nothing
vulgar or strident. No voice in that room was raised, the very laughter
implied, "Here we are, in the very Court of our Temple; we may then relax a
little. For a time, at any rate, we know who we all are."

This security was implied on every hand. It was: "Young Rorke's going
out—he's the son of Alice Branches—he married old Truddits' daughter,"
or—

"No, I don't know him personally, but Dick Barnett has seen him once or
twice and says he's a very decent feller," or—

"Well, I should go carefully, if I were you. Neither the Massiters nor the
Crawfords know her and, in fact, I can't find anyone who does."

Had a stranger penetrated into the fastnesses of the Chichesters or the
Medleys he would have been overwhelmed with courtesy and politeness
and, unless he had full credentials, would have been utterly excluded at the
end of it. Had he boldly invaded the Denisons he would, unless he could
prove his contribution to the entertainment of the day, have been told
frankly that he was not wanted.

Had he passed the doors of No. 104 and had no proof of his Beaminster faith
upon him, Norris would have exchanged with him a quiet word or two and
he would have found himself in the bright spaces of Portland Place.

Rachel and Roddy had come to the party. Rachel sat on a high chair and
looked stiff and pale; Lady Darrant, bunched up in an arm-chair, was beside
her. Lady Darrant's emotions were divided between the welfare of the
church in her parish in Wiltshire and the welfare of her only son, a boy aged
twenty who, supposed to be studying for the Diplomatic Service, was really
interested in race meetings and polo. Lady Darrant had, like most of the
Aristocrats, a tranquil mind. Sorrow, tragedies, perplexities might come and
go, the plain surface stability was in no way disturbed. She would have liked
to possess more money that she might bestow it upon the church, and she

193

would have preferred that her son should place foreign languages above horses, but, since these things were not so, God knew best and the world might have been much worse: none of her friends were ever agitated, outwardly at any rate. Life was calm, sure, proceeding from a definite commencement to a definite conclusion and—God knew best. Rumours came to her of atheists and chorus girls and American millionaires, but she was neither alarmed nor dismayed.

At a Beaminster entertainment she felt that she was among strangers. Her account of such an affair given afterwards to friends implied that this world into which she had glanced was not her world. Lady Adela frightened her and the mere suggestion of the Duchess, whom she had never seen, threatened more fiercely her tranquillity than any other event or person.

Now, every minute or so, she flung little agitated glances at the portrait. At the back of her mind, this afternoon, was the reflection that there was going to be a war and that quite certainly her boy, Tony, would insist on helping his country.

She was proud that he should insist, but, had she not been quite so confident of God's care for her, would have been very near to most real agitation.

She looked at Rachel timidly and wondered whether that strange, fierce, pale girl would be sympathetic. She had heard of Rachel and her marriage, and she knew that that rather stout healthy-looking young man standing and talking to Lord John Beaminster was the husband.

He looked kinder than she did, Lady Darrant thought.

"It's terrible about this horrid war, isn't it?" she said at last.

Rachel, watching the room, was absorbed by her own thoughts; she scarcely noticed the little woman beside her.

She saw Uncle John, his white hair and happy smile and large rather shapeless body, his way of laughing with his head flung back, the look of him when he was thinking, his face precisely that of a puzzled pig—simply to see him there across the room brought back to her a flood of memories.

She knew that she had avoided him lately and she knew, too, that he was unhappy about her. He was unhappy, poor Uncle John, about a number of things—always behind his laughter and cheerful greetings there was the little restless distress as though Life were offering him, just now, more than he could control.

Rachel looked and then turned her eyes away.

"Yes," she said to Lady Darrant, "I hope it won't be very much. They say that a week or two will see the end of it."

Truly, for herself, this afternoon was almost too difficult for her. She had received, that morning, a letter from Francis Breton asking her to go to tea with him in his rooms, one day within the following week.

She had never been to his room; she had not met him once during the whole year.

She had known, during all these last twelve months, that meeting him had nothing at all to do with the especial claim that they had upon one another. That claim had existed since that day of their first coming face to face and nothing now could ever alter it.

But the next time that they met must be, for both of them, a definite landmark. She might either decide, now, once and for all, never to see him again, or grasp, quite definitely, the possible result of her going to him.

The writing of this letter brought, at last, upon her the climax that she had been avoiding during the last year.

Sitting there in the Beaminster camp it was difficult to act without prejudice. With the exception of Uncle John and Roddy she hated them all.

After all if she were to refuse to see Francis Breton did it solve the question? Did it help her—and that was the great need of her present life—to love Roddy any better?

And if she went to his rooms and saw him, would not the truth emerge from that meeting and the miserable doubts and temptations that had shadowed her since her marriage be cleared away for ever?

She liked Roddy and did not love him—nothing could alter that.

Breton and she belonged to a world that was hostile to this world that she was now in—nothing could alter that.

Yes, she would go and see Breton. She got up, smiled at Lady Darrant and went across the room to talk to Uncle John.

On this afternoon she had a great overpowering longing for someone to love her, to care for her, to pity her, to take her into their arms and whisper comfort to her. It was so long—oh! so long, since Dr. Chris and Uncle John had done that.

And yet—the irony of it—there was Roddy eager to do it all: and from him, the fates had decreed that it should mean nothing to her.

"Why can't he touch me? Why can't he give me what I want? Is it my fault? Whose fault is it?"

And when she came to Uncle John she was almost afraid to look at him lest he should see the unhappiness in her eyes.

But, in spite of her unhappiness, she could be satirically observant. Her grandmother, up there on the wall, controlled, like the moon, this tide of human beings. They flowed forward, they retreated. About them, around them, behind and in front of them hovered this War....

Rachel knew that it was the Beaminster doctrine that anything that occurred to the nation was to be attributed, in the main, to Beaminster principles. She could tell at once that they had seized upon this war as an example of Beaminster government. Had diplomacy prevented it, behold the triumph of Beaminster diplomacy; now, as it had not been prevented, a swift and total triumph would assert the genius of Beaminster militancy.

"A week out there ought to be enough.... It's tiresome, of course, but they'll soon have had enough of it...."

Even Rachel, looking up at the portrait, might, not too fantastically, imagine that this war presented the last great manifestation of power on the part of that old woman.

Everyone in the room, perhaps, felt the same.

II

Many eyes were upon her as she moved across to Lord John. This girl, with the foreign colour and bearing, having, apparently, so little of the Beaminster about her and making so quickly so conventional a marriage

("One hadn't expected her to care about a man like Seddon"), stirred their curiosity.

Monty Carfax, licensed transmitter of public opinion, reported her unpopular. "Met her one week-end at the Massiters'—that very time when Seddon proposed. Didn't like her and, really, can't find anyone who does. Conceited, farouche. It's my opinion Roddy Seddon finds her difficult." "Yes, but she's interesting," someone would reply, "unusual. Dissatisfied-looking—not at all happy, I should say."

Lady Adela, stiff, awkward but important, in an ugly grey dress found Lord Crewner the only helpful person in the room. He seemed to understand the way that worries accumulated about one and yet refused to be defined.... He stayed near her throughout the afternoon. She saw Rachel moving across to her brother and the sight of her stirred all her discomfort.

"Why need she look as though she hated everyone?" she thought.

Rachel came at length to Uncle John and found him talking to Maurice Garden. That large and prosperous gentleman hastily proclaimed his delight in meeting Rachel again, but she had very little to say to him.

He left them, secretly determined that he would never speak to the girl again if he could help it.

Uncle John regarded her with an air of supplicating nervousness.

"Come along, my dear," he said. "We haven't had a talk for weeks. Let's find a corner somewhere— —"

They found a corner and then were both of them uncomfortable. The girl whom Uncle John had known and loved had had her tempers and intolerances, but she had also had her wonderful spontaneous affections and tendernesses.

Now she sat there looking straight before her and replying only in monosyllables to his questions.

She was saying to herself: "Shall I go? Shall I go?"

At last he said timidly:

"You'll see mother before you leave?"

"Yes," Rachel said.

"I'm afraid she's not very well."

"Not very well?" Rachel looked up at him sharply, Lord John stared away from her. No one had ever said that publicly before, Lord John himself wondered at his words when he had spoken them.

"Of course she doesn't admit it," he said hurriedly. "No one says anything about it—even Christopher. I oughtn't perhaps to have said anything myself—but I thought— —" He broke off. Rachel knew that he meant that she should be kind and considerate on this visit.

Before she could say anything the Duke came up and joined them.

It always amused Rachel to see her two uncles together. The Duke was a little dried-up wasp of a man, absolutely selfish, with a satirical tongue and a self-conceit that nothing could pierce. He wore high white collars, over which his brown sharp face searched for compliments. He walked on his toes, his hands were most wonderfully manicured and his trousers were so stiff and rigid over his thin little legs that they looked like iron. The one soft spot in him was a strangely tender affection for his sister Adela which was in no way returned; for her, and for her alone, he would forget his selfishness. Richard and John he despised.

"Well, John," he said. "Well, Rachel?"

"Well, Uncle Vincent," she said. The Duke was afraid of Rachel because her tongue was as sharp as his, but he respected her for that.

"Going up to see mother?"

"Yes," said Rachel. Should she go? Should she go?

Suddenly, arising, as it seemed, out of that crowd of moving figures and coming and standing there in front of her, was her answer.

Yes, she would go. All these months of indetermination should be ended. She should know, once and for all, what this Francis Breton meant to her, what that other life of hers meant to her, and so, in opposition, what Roddy meant to her. She would, as Christopher would have put it, grapple with her Tiger....

198

Instantly, the relief, the glad, happy relief showed her how wretched life had been.

"What about this war, Uncle Vincent?" she said.

"Well—hem—well—no need to worry—I assure you—no need to worry!"

"It seems a pity," said Lord John, still looking furtively at Rachel and wishing that he could carry her off into some other corner and just ask her whether she were really happy or no.

"Why, John," said the Duke, cackling. "You'll have to go out, 'pon my word, you will—fight 'em, by Jove—Ha! ha! You'd make a fine soldier, old boy."

Rachel got up, hating Uncle Vincent very much. She put her hand on Uncle John's fat arm.

"You may go, Uncle Vincent," she said. "We all give you leave—Uncle John we love too much: if it's a question of bravery he'd be quite certainly the first of this family." She gave his arm a squeeze.

Uncle Vincent looked at her, smiling—

"Well," he said. "None of us would dream of going ... we're all much too comfortable."

"I'll see you before I go, uncle dear," she whispered to Lord John. Then she moved away.

Slowly making her path through the room she left it and climbed the great stone staircase.

III

Outside her grandmother's door she paused; so she had always paused, and now, as she waited there, all the procession of other days when she had stood there came before her. Conditions might be changed, but her agitation was the same. Never until she died would she open that door without wondering, in spite of common sense, whether she might not be caught by some disaster before she closed it again.

She went in and found her grandmother sitting back in her stiff chair and looking at some patterns of bright silks that lay on a little table beside her.

A great fire was burning and the room seemed to Rachel intolerably hot; she noticed at once that what Uncle John had said was true. Before she had heard Rachel's entrance the Duchess looked an old, tired woman. Her head was drooping a little over the blue and purple silks; she seemed half asleep.

But at the sound of the door she was alert; when she saw that it was her granddaughter who stood there, tall and stately, her large black hat shadowing her face, she seemed in a moment to be transformed with energy and life—her head went up, her eyes flashed, her hands stiffened on her lap.

"May I come in for a moment, grandmother?" Rachel said.

By the door she had wondered—how could she be afraid of this old sick woman? Now as she crossed over to the fire her sternest self-command was summoned to control her alarm. She was frightened by nothing but this—here it was indeed as though there were some spell that seized her.

"Certainly, my dear—come in." The Duchess gave a last look at the silks and then turned to her granddaughter. "I'm afraid you'll find it very hot—I must have a fire, you know."

She had a trick of drawing in her lower lip as she spoke, so that her words hissed a little over her teeth. She did not do this with everybody and Rachel believed that it was only because she had noticed that Rachel as a little girl had been frightened of it that she did it now.

Rachel sat down opposite her and the heat of the fire and a scent of something that had violets and mignonette in it—a scent that was always in the room—stifled her so that her head began to swim and the rings on the Duchess's hand to hypnotize her.

"There's a great party going on downstairs," she said.

"Yes. I know. John came up for a moment and told me about it—and how are you?"

"Very well, thank you, grandmamma. Roddy and I have been ever so sociable lately, given several dinner-parties and one musical thing."

"You're not looking very well. Roddy here?"

"Yes."

"Hope he'll come and see me before he goes. Hasn't been to see me much lately."

Their eyes met. Rachel held her ground and then, beaten as though by a physical blow, lowered her gaze.

"Oh! hasn't he? He's been here a lot, I thought. He's been very busy over some horses that he's had to go up and down to Seddon about."

"H'm. Well—I dare say he'll remember me again one day—so we're in for a war?"

"Yes. They don't seem to think it very serious though—Uncle Richard says—
—"

"Your Uncle Richard knows nothing about it—nothing. However, I don't think anyone need be alarmed."

There was in this last sentence a ring in the Duchess's voice that flung her words out for the nation to grasp at. "No need, my good people, for you to worry—I have this in hand."

"Well, I'm very glad," said Rachel. "It's such a long while since anything has happened that it seems quite odd for everyone to have something to talk about except dinner-parties and scandal——"

The old woman looked across at her and then very slowly a smile rose, stiffened between her old dried lips and stayed there—

"What would you say, my dear, if Roddy thought it his duty to go and defend his country?"

There was, suddenly, the sharp ring in her voice that Rachel knew so well.

"I know," Rachel said quietly, "that Roddy would do his duty, and of course I would want him to do that."

The Duchess, with her eyes still upon her granddaughter's face, said—"I've heard a good deal about a young friend of yours lately."

"Who is that, grandmamma?" Rachel said, and, in spite of herself her hand trembled a little against her dress.

"Nita Raseley."

Rachel caught her breath.

"I gather that you and she haven't seen so much of one another lately."

"Oh! I think we have. We never were great friends, you know."

"Did she enjoy her time at Seddon? A clever little thing. I shouldn't drop her, Rachel, if I were you."

"She seemed to enjoy Seddon, grandmamma. I must be going, I'm afraid, with the patient Roddy waiting for me. Shall I tell him to come up?"

The old hand struck the arm of the chair and the rings flashed.

"No, thank you, my dear. If he can't come of his own accord, I'd prefer that he had no prompting. There was a time when it was otherwise."

Rachel got up. Their eyes met again, and their hatred for one another was so settled, so historic, so traditional an affair, that their glance now was almost friendly.

Then Rachel bent down very slowly and kissed her grandmother's cheek. How much, she wondered, did she know of the Nita affair? Nita's spite would, assuredly, have found a happy ground in which to plant its seed. Oh! how she loathed this thick clouded atmosphere, this deceit, this deceit! It seemed that, at every turn since her marriage, she had been dragged into an atmosphere of disguise and subterfuge and double-dealing.

Well, she was soon to be done with it. At the thought of what her grandmother would say did she know of her friendship with Breton her heart beat triumphantly. There at any rate was a weapon!

"Well, good-bye, my dear. Come and see me again soon."

"Yes, grandmamma—good-bye."

IV

In the carriage with Roddy she suddenly laughed.

All those people, moving so solemnly with such self-importance about that room. The Duke, Lord Richard, Aunt Adela ... Norris, the footman....

Over them all that fierce commanding portrait. And upstairs that old, sick woman....

And beyond, away from that house, a war that that old woman and those self-important people saw only as a means of increasing their own self-importance.

It was all as a box of tin soldiers and a parcel of stiff china-faced dolls—

What were they all about? What did they think they were all doing? What, after all, was she, Rachel? Had they no conception of the sawdust that they all were beside this real, swiftly moving, death-dealing War that was suddenly amongst them?

"What is it?" said Roddy.

"Grandmother—grandmother—my dear, delightful, wonderful grandmother. To think of her sitting all alone up there in her bedroom and all those people moving about downstairs—all so conscious of her. And yet she does nothing—nothing." Rachel, in her excitement, struck her knee with her hand. "She isn't even clever, really—She's never in all her life been known to say a witty thing—never. She doesn't really know much about politics.... She just sits there and acts—That's what it's always been, acting the whole time. If it's effective to be old and feeble she is old and feeble—if it's effective to be fantastic she is fantastic—She just sits still and takes people in. Why, if she'd wanted she could have been going out all these thirty years, I believe!"

"You're always unfair to her, Rachel," said Roddy. "You know she has ghastly pain often and often."

"Yes. I'll give her that," said Rachel. "She's brave—brave as anything. And after all," she added, "she couldn't affect me more if she were the wittiest woman in the world— —"

Roddy yawned—"Dam dull party," he said.

CHAPTER VII
RACHEL AND BRETON

"We are the Pilgrims, master; we shall go
Always a little farther: it may be
Beyond that last blue mountain barred with snow,
Across that angry or that glimmering sea.
... but surely we are brave
Who make the Golden Journey to Samarcand."
The Golden Journey to Samarcand.
James Alroy Flecker.

I

Rachel now awaited her meeting with Breton with restless impatience. It should afford her, beyond everything, a solution. She was young enough and inexperienced enough to make many demands upon life—that it should be romantic, that it should, in the issues that it presented, be honest and open and clear, that it should allow her to settle her own place in it without any hurt to anyone else, that it should, in fact, arrange any number of compromises to suit herself and that it should nevertheless be so honest that it would admit of no compromises at all.

She approached life with all the reckless boldness of one who has never come into direct contact with it. Neither her relations with her grandmother nor with Roddy had as yet taken from her any of her youngest nor simplest illusions. Were life drab and uninteresting, why, then one turned simply to the place where it promised colour and adventure.

She had not yet discovered that when we go deliberately to grasp at happiness we are eternally eluded.

But in spite of her desire for honesty she refused to face the actual meeting with Breton. She knew him so slightly as Francis Breton and so intimately as an idea. What she felt in her heart was, that her grandmother had hoped to catch her by marrying her to Roddy and that nothing could prove so eloquently that she had not been caught as her friendship with Breton.

"I will show her and I will show Roddy that I am my own mistress, free whatever they may say or do."

Breton—seen dimly as a rebel against a harsh dominating world—was the figure of all romance and freedom. "Roddy doesn't care what happens to me. He'll do anything grandmother tells him to...."

She was now out to attack the Beaminster fortress; she did not as yet know that half of her was urgent for its defence.

II

When the afternoon arrived she took a cab and was driven to Saxton Square. She mounted the stairs, knocked on the door and was admitted by his ugly man-servant.

"Is Mr. Breton at home?" she asked.

"Yes, my lady," he answered and smiled; she disliked his smile and before she passed into the room had a moment of wild unreasoning panic when she wished that she were not there, when Roddy's face came to her, kind and loving and homely.

She stepped forward into the room, heard the door close behind her and felt rather than saw him as he came forward to greet her.

Then she heard him say —

"Oh, I'm so glad you've come. I was so afraid lest something should stop you."

His windows, although only on the first floor, had a wide sweeping view; a world of chimneys and towers glittering now beneath the sinking sun.

His room was simple and had the effect of cleanly emptiness; a table arranged for tea, two rather faded arm-chairs, a dark green carpet, a book-case, two large framed photographs on the walls, one of some street in Bombay, the other of the Niagara Falls.

The sunshine lit the bare room and their faces and she was suddenly comfortable and at ease.

He drew one of the easy chairs forward to the window.

"Sit down in the sun; Marks will bring the tea in a moment."

She sat back in the chair and looked out on to the shining roofs and towers, not glancing towards him, but acutely aware of him, of all his movements. He sat down upon the broad window-seat near her and looked at her.

She knew that she had never been conscious, physically, of anyone before. Roddy's clumsy hands and rather awkward body had always simply belonged to Roddy and stayed at that; now she felt as if Francis Breton's hand, close, as she knew, to hers, was joined to her by a running current of attraction.

Although he was not touching her, it was as though she were chained to him. If he moved she felt that she must move with him and every motion that he made seemed to rouse some response in her.

She was aware, of course, as she was always aware with him, of the way that intimacy between them had moved since their last meeting. All her romantic evocation of life as she wanted it to be helped her to this. It was as though she said to herself, "Here at least is my true self free and dominant. I must make the most of it"—and yet, with that, something seemed to warn her that freedom too easily obtained carried at its heart disappointment. The ugly man-servant brought in tea and then disappeared. Breton moved about, waited upon her, then sat down closer to her, leaning forward and looking into her eyes.

It was part of his temperament that he should take her coming to him as an instant acknowledgment of the complete fulfilment of his wishes. He always saw life as the very rosiest of his dreams until it woke him to reality. He was ruled completely by the mood of the moment, and his one emotion now was that Rachel was divinely intended for him alone of all human beings—

But he could not wait.... He knew, by this time, that reflection was always a period of disappointment. He was unhappily made in that he yielded to his impulses of regret as eagerly as to his impulses of anticipation—One mood followed so swiftly upon another that collision might seem inevitable.

They were, both of them, young enough to see life as something that would inevitably, in a short time, condemn them both to years of sterile monotony. Rachel indeed felt that she was already caught....

They must, both of them, therefore, make the best of their time.

"I was so afraid," he repeated again, "lest something should have stopped you."

"I would have asked you to come to us, only I'm afraid that my husband still——"

"Oh! I quite understand."

"It's natural—Roddy's like that. If he wants to do a thing he doesn't care for anybody and just does it. But if nothing makes him especially want to do it, then he just takes other people's opinions. Now he might ask you suddenly to come and see us—simply because he took it into his head. Then nobody could stop him.... He's very obstinate."

She was rather surprised at herself for talking about Roddy. She had a curious feeling about him as though she were going on a journey and had just said good-bye to him and had a rather desolate choke in her throat because she wouldn't see him again for so long.

"Oh! but I'm glad you've come! If you knew the times and times when I've imagined this meeting—thought about it, pictured——"

She saw that his hand was trembling on the window-ledge—

"I oughtn't to have come, perhaps—But I don't know. I've felt so indignant at the way that grandmother is treating you. I wanted to show you that I was indignant...."

"You don't know," he said, "what a help you've been to me already—You showed me the very first time that we met that you did sympathize...."

His voice was tender, partly because her presence moved him so deeply and partly because the sympathy of anyone about his own affairs made him instantly full of sorrow for himself—When anyone said that they thought that he had been badly treated he always felt with an air of surprised discovery: "By Jove, I have been having a bad time!"

"Yes—Wasn't it strange, that first meeting in Miss Rand's room? We seem to have known one another all our lives."

She looked at him. "That you should hate grandmamma so," she said, "was a great thing to me. I'd been all alone—fighting her—for so long."

Rachel felt, in the glow of the occasion, that, all her days, there had been active constant war-to-the-knife in the Portland Place house.

"She's been the curse of my life," he said bitterly. "Always keeping me down, making me unable to do myself justice. Why should she hate me so?"

"She hates us," cried Rachel, "because we're both determined to be free. We wouldn't have our lives ruled for us. She wants everyone to be under her in everything."

They glowed together, very close to one another now, in a glorious assertion of rebellious independence. He put his hand upon the back of her chair—

"Now," he said, his voice trembling, "now that we've got to know one another, you won't go back on it, will you? If I couldn't feel that you were behind me, after being so encouraged, it would be terrible for me—worse than anything's ever been for me."

"You needn't be afraid," she said, not looking at him, but tremendously conscious of his hand that now touched her dress. Then there was a long and very difficult silence during which events seemed to move with terrific impetus.

She was overwhelmed by a multitude of emotions. She was past analysis of regret or anticipation. Somewhere, very far away, there was Roddy, and somewhere—also very far away—there was her grandmother, but, for herself, she could only feel that she was very lonely, that nobody cared about her except Breton and that nobody cared about him except herself— and that she wanted urgently to be comforted and that he himself needed comfort from her.

She knew that if she were not very strong-minded and resolute she would cry; she could feel the tears burning her eyes.

"Perhaps I oughtn't to have come—Oh! it's all so difficult—with grandmother—and everything—I thought I could—could manage things, but I can't—We oughtn't—I wanted to do what was best. I—I didn't know— You——"

Then the tears came—She tried desperately to stop them, then they came rushing; she buried her head in her hands and abandoned herself to weeping that was partly sorrow for herself and partly sorrow for Breton and partly, in the strangest way, sorrow for Roddy.

He was on his knees by her chair, had his arm about her, was crying:

"Oh! Rachel—Rachel—Rachel—I love you. I love you—Don't cry—Don't— Rachel——" He kissed her again and again and she clung to him like a frightened child.

III

After a time her crying ceased, she got up from the chair, moving gently out of his embrace, and then went to the looking-glass above the fireplace and stood there wiping her eyes.

Then, smiling, she looked back at him—He was standing in front of the window and behind him the reflection, from the departed sun, flooded the town with gold. He seemed a man transformed, gazing upon her with an ecstasy of triumph, exaltation, happiness.

"My dear—my dear—Oh! how glorious you are!"

But she did not move.

He stirred impatiently, and then, looking at her with adoring eyes, he whispered, "Oh! my dear! but I love you!"

"I must go," she said, her eyes, large and frightened, appealingly upon him—

He smiled at her, his eyes laughing.

"Yes, Francis—let me—let me. Now while I can still see what I ought to do."

"There's only one thing that you ought to do. You belong to me now." She plucked nervously with her hands one against the other.

"Francis, let me go—please—please——" He saw then that she was unhappy and the laughter died from his eyes. His voice, fallen from its happiness, was almost harsh, as he replied—

"You know we love one another, have loved one another ever since that day when we met in Miss Rand's rooms? You know it as well as I do. You knew it when you came to these rooms to-day."

"I oughtn't to have come." Her voice had gathered strength. "It's only because I realize now what you are to me that I want to go. I thought I was so strong, that I could be fair to Roddy and to you too ... I didn't know——"

"Then stay—stay—" he whispered urgently. "It's a thing that you've got to face anyhow—We can't stay apart, you and I, now. We can try, but you know—you know as well as I—that we can't do it."

"We must—That's what I meant before. That's why I must go now, because soon I shan't be strong enough. But we've got to part—we've got to."

"Oh, this is absurd," he cried. "We're human beings, not figures to hang a theory on—Now just as we realize what we are to one another——"

"Yes, because of that," she broke in swiftly, urgently. "You know that I love you—I know that you love me. We've got that knowledge that nothing can take away from us—and we've got the love—nothing can touch it. But my duty is with Roddy."

"You knew that," he said, "when you came here to-day."

Her face flamed—"That's not fair of you, Francis."

"No, I beg your pardon. It isn't——" He suddenly came to her, caught her and kissed her, holding her with his arm close to him, murmuring in her ear. At first she had struggled, then she lay absolutely still against him, making no response.

He felt her passive against his beating heart. He released her and watched her as she went across to the window and looked out into the darkening city.

"I don't care," he said roughly, "I love you. There's no talk about it or anything else. You belong to me."

"I belong to Roddy," she answered quietly. "It's all quite clear. My duty is to him until ... unless, life with him becomes impossible. I've got absolutely to do my best and while I'm doing that you've got to help me."

"What do you mean?" he said, his eyes upon her.

"Help me by our not meeting, by our not writing, by our doing nothing—nothing——"

"No—No," he answered her, his eyes set upon her.

"You don't get me any other way. Francis, don't you see that we're not the sort of people, either of us, to put up with the deceits, the trickeries, the lies that the other thing means? Some people might—lots of people do, I suppose—but we're not built that way. We're idealists—We aren't made to stand quietly and see all the quality of the thing vanish before our eyes—just to take the husk when we've known what the kernel was like.

"Besides, it isn't as though I hated Roddy. If I did I'd go off with you now, in a minute if you wanted me, although even then it would be a hopeless thing for us to do. But I'm very fond of Roddy. I'm not in love with him—I never have been—I told him from the first—But I'm going to do my best by him."

"Why did you come here?"

"I came here because I was driven towards you. I wanted to hear you say that you loved me—I wanted to tell you that I loved you. We've both of us said it. We know it now—and we've got to keep it, the most precious thing in the world."

"But we should soon hate one another if we destroyed one another's ideals. For many people it wouldn't matter—For us, weak as we are, it matters everything."

"All this talk," he said. "I'm a man. I'm here to love you, not to talk about it. I've got you and I'm going to keep you."

"You haven't got me," she cried. "You've got a bit of me. There'll be times when I'm away from you when I shall think that you've got all of me. But you haven't—no one's got all of me....

"And I haven't got you either—You think now for the moment that it is so—But I know what it would be if we were hiding about on the Continent or secretly meeting here in London—That's not for us, Francis."

"I've got you," he repeated. "I'm not going to wait any longer——"

"It's the only way you'll ever have me," she answered, "by letting me do my duty to Roddy—I promise you that. If ever life is impossible—if it's ever better for both of us that I should go, I'll come to you—But I shall tell him first."

"Tell him! But he won't let you go."

"He won't stop me—if it comes to that."

He pleaded with her then, telling her about his life, its loneliness, his unhappiness, how impossible it would be now without her.

But she shook her head.

"Don't you think," she cried, "that grandmother would be delighted if we went off? Both of us done for—you never able to return again ... Ah! no! For all of us, for every reason, it's not to be."

"I won't let you go—I've got you. I'll keep you."

"You can't, Francis——"

"I can and I will——"

Then looking up, catching a vision of her framed in the window with the lighted city behind her, he saw in her eyes how unattainable she might be....

He had, he had always had, his ideals. There was a long silence between them, then he bowed his head.

"You shall do as you will—anything with me that you will."

"Oh, my dear," she whispered, "I love you for that."

Then hurriedly, moving as though she feared her own weakness, she went to put on her wraps—He came to her.

"Let me write—let me."

"No—Better not."

"Just a line—Nothing that any ordinary person——"

"No, we mustn't, Francis."

He put her furs about her neck, then his hand rested on her shoulder. Her head fell back.

"Once more"—she said. He kissed her throat, then her eyes, then their lips met.

"Stay," he whispered, "stay"—Very slowly she drew away from him, smiled at him once, and was gone.

CHAPTER VIII
CHRISTOPHER'S DAY

"I judge more than I used to—but it seems to me that I have earned the right.
One can't judge till one is forty; before that we are too eager, too hard, too
cruel, and in addition too ignorant."

Henry James.

I

The War had the City in its grip. There was now, during these early weeks of
November, no other thought, no other anxiety, no other interest. The shock
of its reality came most severely upon those whose lives had been most
unreal. Here, in the midst of their dining and their dancing, was the sure fact
that many whom they knew and with whom they had been in the habit of
playing might now, at any moment, find death—

Here was a reality against which there was no argument, and against the
harshness of it music screamed and food was uninteresting.

During that first month of that war, so new a thing was the horrid grimness
of it, that hysteria was abroad, life was twopence coloured. For everyone
now it was the question—"What might they do?"

Something to help, something to ease that biting truth—"Your life has been
the most utterly useless business—no purpose, no strength, no unselfishness
from first to last—what now?"

Christopher's life had not been useless and he knew it. The reality of it had
never been in doubt and death—the haphazard surprise of it and the pathos
and melodrama and sometimes drab monotony of it—had been his
companion for many years.

Christopher, although he had been a hard worker from his childhood, had
always taken life lightly. He loved the gifts of this world—food and
amusement and exercise and pleasant company. He loved, also, certain
people whose lives were of immense concern to him. He also believed in a
quite traditional God about Whom he had never argued, but Whose definite
particular existence was as certain to him as his own.

He had faults that he tried to cure—his temper—his pleasure in food and
wine.

213

He had three great motives in his life—His love of God, his love of his friends and his love of his work. He hated hypocrites, mean persons, cruel persons, anyone who showed cowardice or deceit or arrogance. He was dogmatic and therefore disliked anyone else to be so. He was humble about his work, but not humble about his position in the world, which he thought, quite frankly, a very good one.

His interest in his especial friends was compounded of his love for them and also of his curiosity about them, and he always loved someone the more if he or she gave him the opportunity to practise his inquisitiveness upon them.

After Rachel Seddon he cared more, perhaps, for Francis Breton than anyone in the world. He had also of late been interested in Roddy, who was a far better fellow than he had expected.

One puzzle, meanwhile, obstinately and continually beset him. What had happened to Breton during this last year? Something, or in surer probability someone, had been behind him. Christopher might have flattered himself that he had been the influence, but he knew that, if that had been so, Breton's attitude to him would have implied it. Breton was fond of him, but did not owe that to him. Who then was it?

On one of these November days he invited a friend and Breton to luncheon together.

Christopher's geniality and the supreme importance of the war over everything else helped amiability. Christopher's little house in Harley Street showed, beyond its consulting-room, a cheerful Philistine appreciation of comfort and love. There was old silver, there were old prints, sofas, soft carpets, book-cases, whose glass coverings were more important than their contents. Also a luncheon that was the most artistic thing that the house contained, save only the wine.

At the side of the round gleaming table Christopher sat smiling, and soon Breton told the friend about India and the friend told Breton about Africa.

Meanwhile Christopher watched Breton. He knew Breton very well and, in the old days, he would have said that that nervous excitement that the man sometimes betrayed meant that he was on the edge of some most foolish action.

He knew that light in the eyes, that excited voice, that restlessness —these things had meant that Breton's self-control was about to break.

To-day there were all these signs, and Christopher knew that after luncheon Breton would escape him.

Breton did escape him, went off somewhere in a hurry; no, Christopher could not drive him —he was going in the opposite direction.

Whilst Christopher drove, first down to Eaton Square, then back to 104 Portland Place, he was wondering about Breton....

II

It seemed that, on this afternoon, he was unduly sensitive to impression. The house struck him with a chill, deserted air. There seemed to be no one about as Norris led him up to the Duchess's rooms, the old portraits grinned at him, as though they would have him to know that, very soon, the house would be once more in their possession and Beaminsters dead and gone be of more importance than Beaminsters alive.

At any rate it was a cold November day, and always now the streets seemed to echo with newsboys crying out editions.

Even through these stone walls, those cries could penetrate; he could hear one as he climbed the stairs.

The Duchess, looking peaked and shrivelled, received him with an eagerness that showed that she was longing for company. The room was close, but, in spite of that, now and again she shivered a little.

As he sat opposite her the glance that she flung him was almost pathetic — struggling to maintain her pride, but showing, too, that she might now, in his company, a little relax that great effort.

"I'm not so well," she said; "I've slept badly."

"I'm sorry for that," he said; "what's the trouble?"

"It's this war," she said, taking her eyes away from his face. "This war—I don't think I've ever felt anything before, but this—Oh! I'm old, old at last," she said almost savagely.

"Everybody's feeling it just now," Christopher answered her quietly. "I suppose I'm as level-headed as most people, but even I have been imagining things to-day — Nerves, simply nerves — — "

"Nonsense," she answered him — "Don't tell me, Christopher. What have I ever had to do with nerves?"

"Wait a little. All we want is to get used to War: it's a new experience for all of us — — "

She laughed sharply —

"It's ludicrous, but really you'd think if you studied my family that I was responsible for the whole thing. It's positively as though I'd made some huge blunder which they would do their best to excuse. Adela, John — I'm now to them an old sick woman who's got to be kept quiet and away from worry. They wouldn't have dared let me see that six months ago — "

Her voice was trembling.

She went on again, more quietly. "Every hour now one hears some horrible thing. This morning that young Dick Staveling dead, shot in some skirmish or another — Fine boy he was. They're all going out, one after the other — Not useless idiots who aren't wanted here like John or Vincent — but boys, boys like — like Roddy."

Again her voice trembled.

For the first time in his knowledge of her some pity for her stirred in him, for the first time in her knowledge of him she definitely looked to him with some appeal.

"Roddy came to see me yesterday," she said.

"Yes?" said Christopher.

"He had not been so often as he used — I told him so; he made some feeble apology, but I can see that he will not come again so often — — "

He would have interrupted her, but she went on — "He's not happy, but he loves her madly — madly. He did not tell me so, but I could see that. That was something I had never reckoned on."

"You prefer," Christopher said sharply, "to imagine that he is not happy. I know, unfortunately, what your feeling is about Rachel. Fond of him though you are you'd prefer that he was unhappy with her."

"I know that he is unhappy. He would not care for her so much if she returned it. I know Roddy. But she's clever enough — —" She broke off.

"If Roddy were to go out to South Africa," she said, "I think I would kill Rachel—then die happy — —"

"Forgive me," Christopher said, "but this is sheer melodrama. Rachel is devoted to Roddy and Roddy to Rachel. I've the best means for knowing — —"

Even as he spoke he saw her mouth curve with that smile that was always the wickedest thing about her. He had seen it on many occasions and it always meant that, then, in her heart there was something cruel or remorseless.

It gave her now an elfin look so that, amongst the absurd furniture of the room, she took her place as some old witch might take hers amongst the paraphernalia of her incantations—her cauldron, her bones, her noxious herbs.

"That shows, Christopher my friend, that you know very little. I've a piece of news that will surprise you."

He said nothing, but, in his heart, made ready for some blow.

"What would you say if our Rachel—your Rachel and my Rachel—had found a new friend in my worthy, most admirable nephew, Francis?"

"Rachel—Rachel and Breton?"

The Duchess watched him with amusement. "Exactly. I have the surest information — —"

"What does your—information—say?"

He hated her at that moment as he had never hated her before.

"It says—and I know that it is true—that for more than a year now they have been meeting and corresponding—The other day Rachel went to tea with him—alone. Was with him alone for some time—I'm sure that Roddy knows nothing of this——"

"It's impossible—impossible! Rachel is the soul of honour——"

"I know that you have always thought so. But what more likely? Their feeling about myself would, alone, be enough...."

But he would not let her see how hardly he was taking it. He deprived her of her triumph, did not even question her as to what she would do with it, turned the conversation into other channels, and left her at last—seeming there, amongst her candles, with her nose and thin hands, like some old bird of most evil omen.

III

But for him there was to be no more peace.

It was now about four o'clock and already the dusk was closing in about the town. He decided that he would go and see whether Rachel were in.

He was determined that he would ask Rachel nothing; if she wished to speak to him he would help her, but it must be of her own free will—that was the only way at present.

For how much was the Duchess's malignity responsible? What exactly did she know? What did she intend to do?

Oddly enough, for a long time past some subconscious part of him had linked Rachel and Breton together, perhaps because they were the two persons in all the world for whom he most cared, perhaps because he had always known in both of them that rebellious discontent so unlike that Beaminster acquiescence.

As he drove through the evening streets, he felt that never, until now, had he known how dearly he loved Rachel. In his mind there was no judgment of her, only a sense of her peril; if she would speak to him!...

When he asked at the door of the flat for Lady Seddon he was told that she was out.

"Sir Roderick is at home, sir." He would see Roddy.

Roddy was sitting in the little box-like room known as the smoking-room, poring over a war map. About the map little flags were dotted; he had two in his hand and, with one hand lifted, was hesitating as to their position.

"That was a damned bad mess——" Christopher heard him say as he came in.

At the sound of the door Roddy looked up, straightened himself, and then came forward.

"Hallo! Christopher," he said. "Delighted. Splendid! Rachel's out, but she said she'd be back to tea."

He was not looking well—fat, his cheeks pale and puffy, lines beneath his eyes.

"I'm jolly glad you've come," he said. He drew two arm-chairs to the fire and they sat down.

Roddy then talked a great deal. He was always a little nervous with Christopher because he was well aware that the doctor had disapproved of his marriage.

Christopher had lately shown him that he liked him, but still Roddy was not at his ease. He talked of the war, then of golf, then polo, then horses, Seddon Court—abruptly he stopped and sat there gazing moodily into the fire.

"You're not looking well, Seddon," Christopher said quietly.

"I'm not very—Nobody's at their liveliest just now with fellers one knows droppin' out any minute.... One feels a bit of a worm keepin' out of it all—skunkin' rather——"

Moodily he sat there, his head hanging, dejected as Christopher had never seen him before.

Suddenly he said—"That ain't quite the truth, Doctor. I am a bit worried——"

"My dear boy," Christopher said, putting his hand on the other's knee—"If there's anything in the world I can do for you, tell me."

"Thank you. You're a brick. I'm damned unhappy, Christopher, and that's the truth——"

"Rachel——" said Christopher.

"Yes—Rachel. I got to talk to somebody. I've been goin' along on my own now for months and I know you're fond of her——"

"I am," said Christopher, "more than of anyone in the world——"

"I know. That's how I can talk to you. I wouldn't have you think I'm complainin' of her. I'm gettin' nothin' but what I asked for, you know. But it's just this. When she took me she never said she loved me, in fact she said she didn't, but I thought that it wouldn't matter—all you wanted in marriage was just to be pals and show up about the town together and treat one another honourably. Well," said Roddy, taking now a melancholy interest in his discoveries concerning himself, "damn it all, if I haven't rotted the bargain by fallin' in love with her. Jove! Why, I hadn't a ghost's guess at what Love meant before Rachel came along. Of course it isn't her fault. You couldn't expect her to love an ordinary sort of chap like me, just like a million other fellers knockin' about—but she's so unusual there ain't another woman in the world so surprisin' as Rachel—

"She's fond of me," he went on, "I know that, but what I want she just can't give me and that's the long and short of it.

"Lately it's been terrible hard. She's not happy and that makes me wild, and every day that passes I seem to want her more. Nothin' else, no one else matters now. I've been playin' golf, ridin', sittin' down to this bridge they're all getting mad about, doin' every blessed thing—it isn't any use. Do you know, Christopher," he said slowly, "I'd give my soul to make her happy and I just can't——"

"I know——" said Christopher.

"But it's worse than that—" Roddy went on, taking up the poker and knocking on the fire—"Lately she's been having a room of her own. Started it a while ago as a temporary thing and now she sticks to it. Up here, in this damned town, we hardly see one another; always a crowd either here or outside. I know Rachel don't like it and I don't like it, but there it is—

"Next week we're going down to Seddon and things may get better there—But I can't stand it much more—not like this."

"Wait a bit. It'll come all right." Christopher spoke confidently. "I've know Rachel since she was a small child. She's half Russian, you know—you must always remember that—and Russian and Beaminster make a strange mixture—Wait——"

"That's so easy to say—" Roddy answered, shaking his head. "It's so easy to say, but I don't see just what's goin' to make things different from what they are——"

"No—one never sees," said Christopher. "And then Destiny comes along and does something that we call coincidence and just settles it all. Your trouble will be settled, Roddy, if you're patient——"

"Perhaps," Roddy said slowly, "you could see her a bit—find out——" he stopped.

"Anything in the world I can do I will. We'll find a way. Meanwhile, Seddon, there is a bit of advice I can give you——"

"What's that?" asked Roddy.

"Go and see the Duchess more than you've been doing. See her a lot—more than you did ever——"

"Oh! the Duchess!" Roddy sighed. "I don't know, but it all seems different with her now. I've changed, I suppose. All her ideas are old-fashioned and wrong; I used to think her rather splendid——"

"Yes—but she's ill and old, and you're the only person in the world she cares about."

"Yes, I'll go," said Roddy slowly. "I've known I ought to go."

Voices broke in upon them; the door opened and Rachel, followed by her friend May Cremlin, once May Eversley, came in—

"Oh! Dr. Chris! You dear!" she cried, and came forward and flung her arms about him and kissed him.

Her cheeks were flushed, from her black furs her eyes shone at him. Some thought caught him. He knew where he had seen that excited glitter already to-day—Breton at luncheon—

They all talked. Then Christopher said that he must go.

Rachel came with him to the door. In the hall she looked at him defiantly, that flash he knew so well.

"You never come now, Dr. Chris: you've given me up."

"I don't care for you in a crowd very much. There's always a crowd now — — "

"Ask me alone and I'll come," she said, but still her eyes were defiant.

"No," he said gravely. "I'll do no asking, Rachel. When you want me I'm there for you at any time — at any time — — "

For answer she flung her arms again about him and hugged him. Her heart was beating furiously. Then without another word she left him.

IV

He could not go back to Harley Street yet. The sense of apprehension that had been growing with him all day would give him a melancholy evening, were he to spend it alone. He thought of Brun. Someone had told him that the little man was in London.

He found him in his rooms, reading, with a cynical expression on his face, a French review.

"I came to see—" said Christopher, "whether you happened to be free to-night and would dine with me. I'm a pessimist for once this evening and it doesn't suit me!"

Brun was very, very sorry, but he was dining with a Russian princess; it was most tiresome that he should have to waste his time with a Russian princess when he'd come over to London on this occasion expressly to study the English people at this interesting crisis of their affairs, but there it was — he'd no idea how he'd let himself in for it, and how much rather would he spend the evening with his friend, Christopher.

Christopher said that he would smoke one cigarette and that then he must go.

"And so you feel pessimistic?" said Brun, looking at Christopher curiously—
"It's the war, Je crois bien—How alike you all are!"

"No," said Christopher, "I don't think the war's much to do with it. I dare say
the war's a very good thing for all of us."

"Didn't I tell you—?" said Brun, greatly excited—then pulled himself up—
"No, it wasn't you. It was Arkwright. More than a year ago we were in a
picture gallery looking at your Duchess's picture, and coming home we
talked. I said then that something would come, that something must come,
and that then everything, everything would crumple up. And behold!" cried
Brun, his eyes flashing—"See, it crumples!"

"That's a little previous of you," said Christopher. "Nothing crumpled yet.
We're disturbed of course——"

"It is most lucky," Brun said, "most lucky. Here we are, you and I, ordinary
people enough, with the end of a Period with its death and the way it takes
it, all for us to watch. Most lucky...."

"End of Victorian Age ... Voilà!" and with a little dramatic gesture he waved
his hand as though he were flinging the Age and its lumber away, out of the
window.

"You know, Christopher," he went on, "I've seen things coming over here for
so long. All you people, you couldn't have gone on very much longer so
remote from life. And now this—it will finish your Duchess, your
Beaminsters, your queen in her bonnet, your Sundays and your religion and
your Whigs and Tories, and all your hypocrisies—No names any more taken
just because they've always been taken, but new names made by men who're
doing things. Nothing taken for granted any more.

"Your Beaminsters will vanish, and then you'll have your Denisons and
Oaks and Ruddards on top. Then you'll see a time. You'll all be spinning like
a top, dancing, dancing like dervishes. Then while you're busy dancing up
the other people will quietly come—all the real people, the Individualists—
Women will have their justice—no man will skunk behind his garden hedge
because he doesn't want to be bothered. No more superstition, no more
inefficiency——"

"You're a wonderful fellow, Brun," said Christopher, getting up and flinging
away the end of his cigarette. "You've always got any amount to say—but do

you never think of people as people, not as theories or movements or developments— —"

"No, thank God, I don't. That's for the sentimentalists like you, Christopher. People are all the same, fools or knaves."

"Well, I'm glad I don't think so," said Christopher.

"Tell me," Brun put his little hand on the other's elbow, "your Beaminsters now, how are they?"

"They're all right."

"The Duchess? I hear she's not so well— —"

"Oh! nonsense—Well as she's been any time these last thirty years."

"Yes? So—I'm glad. But the other Beaminsters? Ah! I must go quickly and call—To see them burst asunder, that will be most amusing— —"

Christopher laughed. "You won't see the Duke or Richard Beaminster burst," he said—"They're like you—no personal feeling."

"And the girl?"

"Lady Seddon?"

"Yes. She'll stir things up. She's not a Beaminster, or only enough of one to make her hate the family. And she does hate them, hein?"

"Oh, my dear Brun, you've got an absurdly exaggerated view about everything. You'd twist the Beaminsters into anything to make them fit your theory."

"Oh, they'll fit it right enough. But I must be in at the death. We'll meet there together, Christopher. Things will occur before we're much older, my sentimentalist."

Christopher shook his head. "There's something sinister about your appearances in the City, Brun. 'Where the carcases are, there will....'"

Brun nodded. "It's true enough this time," he said.

CHAPTER IX
THE DARKEST HOUR
"So God help us! and God knows what disorders we may fall into.... Home
and to bed with a heavy heart."

Diary of Samuel Pepys.

I

During that terrible December week in 1899, England suffered more defeats
to her arms than during any other week of the century. Magersfontein,
Stormberg, Colenso, their names leapt one after another on to the screen.

London was dismayed; London was impatient. Easy enough to declare that
the most criminal blunders had been perpetrated, easy enough to explain
how one would oneself have conducted this or that, man[oe]uvred hither or
thither some pawn in the game.

Dismay remained—a wide active alarm at the things that Life, so suddenly
real and dominating and destructive, might in the future be preparing.

To Lord John this terrible week was simply the climax to a succession of
disturbing revelations of reality. All his days had he been denying Life,
wrapping it up in one covering after another, calling it finally a box of
chocolates or a racing card, a good cigar or a pretty woman, knowing, at his
heart, that somewhere in the dark forest the wild beast was waiting for him,
hoping that he might survive to the end without facing it.

Now it was before him and its glittering eyes were upon him.

He had gone on the Friday of this week, to pay a week-end visit at a country
house near Newmarket. Many jolly, happy week-ends he had spent at this
same house on other occasions, now, from first to last, it was nightmare.

On the Monday morning at breakfast a sudden conviction of the impossible
horror of this world struck at his heart. It came as a revelation, life was for
him never to be the same again. His hostess, a large-bosomed white-haired
lady, planted at the end of the table like an enormous artificial toy in the
middle of whose back some key must be turned if the affair is to amuse the
crowd, suddenly horrified him; the women of the party, their noses a little
blue, their cheeks a touch too white, their voices hard and sharp, the men,
red and brown, boisterously hearty about the animals they hoped to kill
before the day was done, the cold food in a glazed and greedy row, the hot
food—kidneys, fish, bacon, sausages, sizzling and scenting the air—: the

table itself with its racks of toast and marmalade and silver and fruit: the conversation that sounded as though the speakers were afraid that the food would all disappear were they spontaneous or natural—all these things suddenly appeared to Lord John in a very horrible light, so that, in an instant, racing and women and clothes and food were banished from a naked biting world in which he was a naked solitary figure.

He caught a train as one flies from some horrible plague: he arrived in London, breathless, confused, miserable, the foundations of Life broken from beneath him.

Here he found Lady Adela in a like condition.

He had never cared very greatly for his sister, he had not found her sympathetic or amusing, she had never appealed to him for assistance, nor challenged his violent opposition. He had never enquired very deeply into her interests; she had much correspondence and many acquaintances. She ran, he supposed, the house or, at least, directed Miss Rand to run it for her.

He thought her a rather stupid woman, but then all the Beaminsters thought one another stupid because they believed so intensely in the Duchess and she had always made a point of seeing that, individually, they despised one another, although collectively they faced the world.

Finally, Adela had always seemed to him unsympathetic towards Rachel and that he found it very hard to forgive—but then, he often reflected they were all, with the exception of himself, a most unsentimental family. He wondered sometimes why he was so different.

On the afternoon of his return from Newmarket, however, he began to wonder whether, after all, Adela had not more in common with him than he had ever expected. He had lunched at the club, had plunged down into the City to enquire about some investments, it had begun to rain, and he had returned with the weight of that gloomy day full heavily upon him.

He did not, as a rule, have tea, but to-day he needed company, and he found Adela in the little sitting-room next to the library, a little room with faded wall-paper, faded pictures (groups, some of them, of himself and Vincent and Richard at Eton and Oxford), faded arm-chairs and faded chintzes—a nice, cosy, friendly room, full of old associations and old hopes and despairs.

This room did not often see either Lady Adela or John, but to-day Norris, for reasons best known to himself, had put tea there and, to both of them, as they sat over the fire with the great house so still and quiet about them, the shabby intimacy of the little place was grateful.

John, disturbed, himself, out of his normal easy geniality, noticed that Adela also was disturbed.

That dry and rather gritty assurance that had all her life protected her from both the praise and abuse of her fellow-men and women was, to-day, absent. She seemed really grateful to John for coming to have tea with her to-day. He wondered whether she felt as he did that this war, with all its horrors, foreboded, in some manner, special disasters upon the Beaminster family, as though it were a portent, to be read of all men, of the destruction and ruin of that family.

"Poor Adela," he thought, "she's very plain. If she asks me to help her I will. She's got something on her mind."

"Rachel's here," Lady Adela said, looking at her brother nervously.

"Now?"

"Yes, she's with mother. She came to say good-bye to her. She and Roddy are going down to Seddon to-morrow."

"Yes, I know— —" said John.

"She's very queer—very odd. I don't pretend to understand her."

"We're all queer just now," said John. "Down at the club to-day it was too awful. No other subject—fellows killed, fellows going out to be killed. Blunder, blame, disgrace—all the time. But what's Rachel been doing odd?"

"You understand her better than I do," said his sister. "She always liked you better. I did my best with her, but she never cared about me. But now I understand her less than ever. She's so excited and hard and unnatural. Something's happened to her that we don't know about, I'm sure."

John said nothing. He was unhappy enough about Rachel, but he did not intend to talk to Adela about it. He would rather not talk to anyone about it because talking only brought it more actually in front of him. Besides, he did not know what to say. He knew that he had been cowardly about Rachel. He had tried to pretend to himself that she was happy when he had known that she was not and so, for the sake of his comfort, he had stifled the most genuine emotion in his life; that indeed was the Beaminster habit.

"She's not happy," continued Adela. "I'm sure I don't know why—Roddy's very good to her—very good. She's so queer. She wants to have Miss Rand down with her at Seddon for Christmas."

"Miss Rand?"

"Yes—she asked me whether I'd let her go. She's got to give a dance and a dinner-party or two and asked me whether she might have her help. Of course I said 'Yes.' Miss Rand hasn't been looking at all well for some time now. A change will do her good."

"What did Miss Rand say when you told her?"

"Oh, she was odd. She has been odd lately. At first she thought she wouldn't go. Then she said she would. I told her it would do her good."

"How's mother been the last two days?"

"Oh! the same. She won't say anything—she confides in nobody."

John looked at his sister and wondered why it was that he had never, during all these years, considered her as a personality or as anything actively happy or miserable. She had had, he suddenly supposed, a life of her own that was, in a way, as acute and sensitive as his and yet he had never realized this.

He had always taken his mother's word for it that Adela was a dried-up stick who resented interference; now he was sure that that judgment was short-sighted, and then, upon this, came criticism of his mother; therefore, to banish such disloyalty, he said hurriedly:

"I didn't enjoy the Massiters a bit—longed to get away—Sunday was miserable——"

Adela said—"I never could bear them—John——" she stopped.

"Yes," he said, looking across at her. His large good-tempered eyes met hers and then the colour mounted very slowly into her cheeks. He had never seen her agitated before—

"John—" she began again. "I must do something. I can't sit here—just quietly—going on as though nothing were happening. I know—all one's life one's stood aside rather, I've never wanted to interfere with anyone. But now, this war has made one feel differently, I think."

"Well?" said her brother.

"Well—an organization is being formed—women, you know—to help in some way. They're going to do everything, make clothes, have sales and concerts and get money together. It's to be a big thing—Nelly Ponsonby, Clara Raddleton, lots of others.... They've asked me to be on the committee——"

"Well?" said John, "why not?"

She looked at him appealingly. "Mrs. Bronson's on it too—one of the originators of it."

"Oh!" John was silent. Here was, indeed, a question. Mrs. Bronson, the Beaminster arch-enemy. Mrs. Bronson, who had snapped her bejewelled American fingers at the Duchess—Mrs. Bronson, who called the Beaminsters the most insulting names. Why, a fortnight ago any alliance with such a woman was unthinkable, incredible—

"I believe," went on Lady Adela, "that she herself proposed that I should be asked...."

A fortnight ago ... and now—

John knew that he was glad that Adela wished to join the committee, he knew that he was closer to Adela now than he had ever been at any moment during their lives together.

He looked across at her and their eyes met and in that glance exchanged between them barriers were broken down, curtains turned aside—they would never be strangers again.

"Mother isn't well." Adela said quite firmly. "Hasn't been well for a long time—we've all known it. She has felt this war and—and other things very much. She will feel my going on to the same committee as Mrs. Bronson— she will certainly feel it. But I think it's my duty to do so. After all, on an occasion like this family feeling must give way before national ones." Why did not the walls and foundations of No. 104 Portland Place rock and quiver before the horrid sacrilege of such words? John, himself, almost expected them to do so and yet he was of his sister's opinion.

"I think you are perfectly right, Adela," he said.

"Oh! I'm so glad that you do. I don't want to worry mother, just now. I'm frankly rather nervous about telling her—but it must be done."

"It's odd, Adela," said John, leaning back in his chair and crossing his fat legs. "But something real like this war, a ghastly day with boys shouting horrors at you followed by another ghastly day with more boys shouting more horrors, it does shake one's life up. I've been very cowardly, Adela, about a number of things. I see that now. I've never really wanted to see it before. It makes one uncomfortable."

"I don't think one ought to give way," said Adela with a slight return to her gritty manner, "to one's feelings too much. But certainly one is beginning to see things differently, which is a dangerous thing for people of our age, John."

"Yes," said John, "I suppose it is." He paused and then brought out—"There's Francis, Adela. We've all been very wrong about Francis. I've felt it for a long time, but hadn't the courage.... He's been behaving very well all this time— One oughtn't to hold aloof—altogether— —"

"Mother refuses to have his name mentioned— —"

"We must take into account," John said very slowly and now without meeting his sister's eye—"that mother is not so well—scarcely so sure in her judgment— —"

He broke off. There was a long pause and they looked away from one another, as though they had been guilty conspirators. Norris came in to take the tea away.

"Has Lady Seddon gone?"

"Yes, my lady. She was with Her Grace a very short time— —"

Adela turned impatiently to John. "So like Rachel. She might at least have come to say good-bye to us."

When Norris had gone John got up and walked a little about the room.

He stopped beside his sister and put his hand on her shoulder:

"If there's anything I can ever do to help you, Adela, tell me — —!" he said.

"Thank you, John," she answered.

II

Rachel had never understood why it was that she was driven so constantly into her grandmother's presence. The impulse that drove her had in it, perhaps, something of defiance and something of challenge as though she cried to some weakness in her that it should not master her and that she would just show it how little those visits mattered to her. It had all begun from some reason of that kind, and lately, when she grew older, she discovered that her grandmother was more terrible through imagination than she was through actual vision.

There was never absent from Rachel a lurking presentiment of what her grandmother might one day do, and she went to see her now to discover what she might be at, to prove to her that, whatever she be doing, Rachel was "up" to her.

On this particular occasion the visit was a very brief one, but there was one moment in it that after events always produced for Rachel as a most definite and (on the part of the Duchess) omniscient omen.

Rachel had said that she had come in only for a moment to say good-bye. She had talked a little and then, rising, stood by the fire.

As she stood there her grandmother suddenly looked at her — a glance that Rachel had not been intended to catch. There was there a malicious humour, a consciousness of some power, of some disaster that could be delivered, triumphantly, at an instant's notice.

Very swiftly Rachel gathered her control, but she had felt what that look conveyed.

"Francis ... she knows ... what is she going to do?"

She strung her slim, tall figure to its finest restraint and without a quiver in her voice (her heart was beating wildly), "Good-bye, grandmamma. I promised Roddy to be back."

231

But the old lady looked at her—

"How you do hate me, my dear," she said almost complacently.

Rachel compelled the other's eyes. "Would I come to see you so often if I did?" she said.

"Yes, my dear, you would. You've got a sense of humour hidden somewhere although, God knows, we've seen little enough of it lately. Oh! yes, you'd come all right—if it were only to see me growing older and older."

Rachel turned flaming. "There, at any rate, you're unjust. It's you that have always hated me from the beginning—since I was small. Hated me, been unjust to me——"

Her body trembled with agitation—she was not far from one of her old tempests of passion.

But the Duchess smiled. "You exaggerate, Rachel, your old fault. At any rate, I'll be gone soon, I suppose—it will seem trivial enough one day...." Then as Rachel, turning to the door, left her—"But hurt a hair of Roddy's head, my dear, and—well, you'll hate me more than ever——"

III

When Rachel had gone the Duchess felt very ill indeed. She had only to touch a bell and Dorchester would be with her, but she did not intend to summon Dorchester before she need.

She felt now, at this minute, that her spirit of resistance had almost snapped. Again and again, throughout the last months, the temptation to lie down and surrender had swept up, beaten about her walls and then sunk, defeated, back again.

But this last week of disaster had tried her severely. Her pride in life had been largely her pride in the arrangement of it and now all that arrangement was tumbling to pieces and she powerless to prevent it. For the first time in all her days she felt that she would like to have someone with her who would reassure her—someone less acid than Dorchester.

Why had she never had a companion—a woman like Miss Rand who would understand without being sentimental?

The Duchess of Wrexe

There was pain in every muscle and nerve of her body: it swept up and down her old limbs in hot waves.... She clutched the arms of her chair.

Even her brain, that had always been so sharp and clear, was now confused a little and passed strange unusual pictures before her eyes. That girl ... yes ... Dorchester had been very clever about that: Dorchester had been in communication with Breton's man-servant for a long time past. To go to tea there ... to be alone with him ... Roddy—

And at that dearly loved name all was sharp and accurate. Night and day she was terrified lest she should suddenly hear that he was off to South Africa. She believed that that would really kill her. Roddy—her Roddy—to go and make another of those ghastly tragedies with which the newspapers were now full. But let Rachel disdain him and he would go merely to show her how fine a fellow he was—what idiots men were!

Or let this other thing become a scandal, then surely he would go.

She shook there in her chair and then with her eyes fixed on the fire prayed to whatever gods or devils were hers that he might not go. Anything, anything so that he might not go. Break him up, hurt him—only, only he must not go.

She prayed, thrusting her whole soul and spirit into her urgency—

Then, even as she sat there, her darkest hour was suddenly upon her. It leapt upon her, as it were a beast out of some sudden darknesses—leapt upon her, seized her, tore her, crushed her little dried withered soul in its claws and tossed it to the fire.

She was held by the sudden absolute realization of Death. She had never seen it or known it before. Others had died and she had not cared; many were dying now and it did not concern her.

But this beast crouching in front of her, with its burning eyes on her face, said to her: "All your life I've been beside you, waiting for this moment. I knew that it would come. I have waited a long time—you have played and thought yourself important and have cared for meddling in the affairs of the world, but Reality has never touched you. You have gathered things about you to pretend that I was not there. You have mocked at others when they have seen me—you have enjoyed their terror—now your own terror has come."

233

Death.... She had never—until this instant—given it a thought. Everything was gone before its presence. In a week or two, a month or two, silence—

Rachel—she saw her standing there by the fire, full of life and energy, so young, so strong.

She, the Duchess of Wrexe, the great figure, courted by kings, princes, artists, all the men and women of her time, now must crumble into the veriest dust, be forgotten, be followed by others, banished by this new world.

She and her Times were slipping, slipping into disuse. Who cared now for those other glories? What minds now were fit to tackle those minds that she had known? What beauty now could stand beside that beauty that had shone when she was young?

The beast crouched nearer. The room darkened. She could feel the hot breath, could be dazed by the shining of those eyes. Behind her, around her, the trumpery toys that she had gathered faded.

Darkness rose; a great space and desolation was about her—She tried to summon all her energy.

She cried out and Dorchester, coming in, found that her mistress had, for the first time in her life, fainted, bending, an old, broken woman, forward in her chair.

CHAPTER X
LIZZIE'S JOURNEY—II
I

The world, during all these months, had seemed to Lizzie Rand a very silent place. Before that July night it had been loud with incident, coloured with possibilities, strange and varied and thrilling. Now she was only conscious of the duties that must be fulfilled between daybreak and darkness; she was unconscious of all life and movement, only she was aware of the demands on her deliberate activity—these demands she obeyed.

Slowly, as the dreary autumn dragged its days past her, she accustomed herself to forestall the horrid moments that would leap from some hidden darkness upon her. There was the moment when a something said: "Fancy caring for someone who had never asked nor shown any sign...." Another moment when something said: "Remember how here you stood, with your heart beating, waiting for him to come—There you caught some light in his eyes and fancied it a sign...."

Burning shame was in those moments did she indulge them—a realization, too, of the bare grey desolation of a world without movement or vision. She could not see the people about her, her mother, her sister, Lady Adela, Dr. Christopher (always kind to her), other friends—they were not there for her at all.

Only two things were there—that she must cling, at all possible costs, to her pride and that she hated Rachel. Her pride had been called to her defence before, but to hate anyone was new to her. She had never hated any human being and now the restlessness that this new emotion brought confused her.

Night after night stretched ironically before her, banishing sleep. All her life she had slept from the moment that her head was upon the pillow; now, at that instant, her brain sprang to fire, thought after thought, memory after memory, passed in dancing procession before her.

She saw him as little as possible, she supposed that in time she would not care, would be indifferent to him; she hoped so.

Meanwhile she went out when he came in; saw his kind distress because he thought that she was not well, and shuddered at it.

Then Lady Adela told her that Rachel had asked whether she were free for Christmas.

She received a letter:

"Dear Miss Rand,

I wonder whether by any chance you would care to come to us here for three weeks at Christmas time? I should be so grateful if you would come and help me a little with some tiresome social things here. May I add that I have for a long time wanted to know you better than the London rush ever gives time for? My aunt says that you have been overworking lately, she thinks. If you come here you shall have all the rest and quiet possible.

Yours sincerely,

Rachel Seddon."

A funny little letter—stiff and then suddenly impulsive and friendly.

Of course she would go—she had never doubted that. Here at last was some food for the burning restlessness that was always at her breast—Through these months she had longed for some step that would help to kill the pain.

Now she would watch Rachel and discover her heart and perhaps find from that discovery some way for her own release. For her shame, night and day, was that she still cared, cared, yes, as deeply as she had ever done—that caring must die.

Perhaps the sight and knowledge of this other woman would kill it.

At least here at last was action after the terrible silence and remoteness of those many months.

She would go to Seddon and she would not leave it without finding some way by which she might still make some use of life.

II

She had really stayed at very few houses before. The anticipation at any other time would have excited her, now nothing mattered except that she would meet Rachel.

Her mother and sister had watched her during these past months with a dismay stirred by the sudden absence of her genial friendliness.

They had taken so much of her kindliness for granted and now when she refused them the sympathy that they had always demanded for a thousand unimportant incidents they, clamorously, missed it.

At first it was easy to say that Lizzie was callous and selfish, afterwards that she was ill and overworked, finally they hailed with relief the promise of a three-weeks' holiday. "She'll come back," said Mrs. Rand, "as fresh as paint, and taken out of herself."

Meanwhile no solution of Lizzie's trouble occurred to them; that she should ever feel the tyranny of love, like more sentimental mortals, was, at this time of day, impossible. "We know Lizzie, thank you," said Mrs. Rand.

They watched her, on the afternoon of the 23rd of December, depart in a cab for Seddon Court. She was grave and pale and beautifully neat. "I do admire Lizzie, you know," said Daisy, returning with her mother into the house. "I can't get that kind of tidiness. Her things go on for years, looking as good as new."

"Men like a bit of disorder," said Mrs. Rand. "It seems more agitated. All the same I'd like to know what is worrying Lizzie."

It was a wet and gusty day and the wind blew the rain with hard impatient spurts against the windows of the cab. Few people were about: Hyde Park Corner was grey and deserted, umbrellas like black mushrooms started here and there from the shining ground.

Victoria Station also had, on this afternoon, nothing beautiful to offer. She found her way to her train, chose an empty carriage, sat in her corner with her hands upon her lap, waited for the train to move.

People, grey people with white faces, hurried past her carriage. She wondered whether they too had something in their hearts that made every thought, every movement a danger.

Because the train would not move and because for the first time in all these months she found herself without any occupation, she could not hold thought at bay. She resisted, she tried to sweep her brain empty, she surrendered. She, Lizzie Rand, always so fond of her self-discipline and restraint, found control now slipping from her. Before she had met Breton her duties, the skilful manipulation and arrangement of detail, her work and her place as a worker, these had supplied her needs. Now all those things were dust and ashes; high and lofty above them shone that bright fire whose warmth and colour she had, for an instant, felt and seen. What was life going to be, through all the years to come, if she were never to recapture her tranquillity?

The train moved off and she sat there, her eyes bright and shining, her little body stiff and resolute. Somewhere, a long way away, like a rounded coloured cloud, hovered emotion—emotion that would break her heart, would tear her to pieces and then perhaps build up for her a new life. But her eyes now were dry and her heart was cold.

The train went whir-whack—whack-whir and the telegraph wires flew up, hung, hesitated, were coming down, flew higher, then with a rush were buried below the window, and with the noise and movement there danced before her eyes the questions, "Does she love him?" "Does she love him? Has she told him that she loves him? What will her husband do? Does she love her husband?" And then, beyond that, "Why did she come and take from me all that I had, she who had already so much?"

And then, most bitter of all, "Ah, but you never had him. She took nothing from you. He never thought of you except as someone to whom he could talk——"

She had no doubt that these weeks were intended for a crisis. Something was going to happen at Seddon.... Something in which she was to have her share. She felt as though she had known that she would be sent to meet Rachel—It had to be....

Then her thoughts left, for a time, her own miserable little history. She wondered how Lady Adela would manage without her. Lady Adela had never been alone before and now that the Duchess had had, a fortnight ago, that fainting fit, they were all unsettled and alarmed. What would happen if the Duchess died? Then all the dignity and splendour of 104 Portland Place would pass away! other people might inhabit it, but the soul of that house would be dead.

Everything on every side of her seemed to be hastening to a climax and Lizzie could see that old woman fighting, behind her closed doors, for Life, beaten at last, dead, swept away, others laughing in her place—a new world to whom she was only a portrait cleverly painted by some young artist.

Yes, there were other histories developing now besides Lizzie's and she felt as though she had been whirled, during the last months, into a wild, tossing medley of contacts and revelations—all this after a life so grey and quiet and steadily busy.

As the train plunged into Sussex the rain stayed for a little and the shining earth steamed upwards to a grey sky broken here and there to saffron. Little towns quietly rested under the hills and many streams ran through the woods and the roads drove white like steel through the crust of the soil. White lights spread in the upper air and the heaving grey was pushed, as though by some hand, back into the distant horizon. For a moment it seemed that the sun was bursting through; trees were suddenly green where they had been black and fields red where they had been sombre dark—Light was on all the hills.

But the hand was stayed. Back the grey rolled again, heavily like chariots the clouds wheeled round and drove down upon the earth—The rain fell.

The carriage was very cold. Lizzie's hand and feet were so chill that they seemed not to belong to her at all. Pictures of houses at Brighton and the dining-car of some train and two public-houses at the bottom of a hill stared at her.

The sense of some coming disaster grew with her. It was as though someone were telling her that she must prepare to be very brave and controlled and wise because, very soon, all her restraint and wisdom would be needed. She summoned now, as she had learnt to do, a stern armoured resolution that sat always a little oddly upon her. Any observer who had seen her sitting there would have noticed the mild softness of her eyes, the tenderness of some curve at the corners of her mouth, and would have smiled at the lines of resolution as though he had known that the sternness was all assumed.

But she was saying that nothing should touch or move her down here at Seddon; her heart should be closed. She must grow into a woman who had no need of emotion—and even as she determined that some vision swept her by, revealing to her the happy dear uses that she could have made of love and sympathy had life been set that way for her. How she could have cared!... A dry little sob was at her throat and burning pain behind her tearless eyes. God, the things that other people had and did not value!

The train stopped at a wind-swept deserted station and a man and woman with a little child, the three of them tired, wet, bedraggled, entered the carriage.

The man was gaunt with a beard and large helpless eyes, the woman shapeless, loose-breasted, little eyes sunk in her cheeks, an old black straw hat tilted back on her head. These two did not glance at Lizzie, nor was there any curiosity of interest in their eyes, but the small child, yellow wisps of hair falling about her dirty face, detached herself from them, crept into the furthest corner of the carriage and from there stared at Lizzie.

The train droned on through a country now shrinking beneath a deluge of rain. The child moved a little, looked at the woman, looked again at Lizzie, crept to Lizzie's side of the carriage, at last, still without a word, came close and, finally, stole fingers towards Lizzie's dress.

Lizzie turned and smiled at the child, who stared back at her, now with wide terrified eyes. Lizzie looked away, out of the window, and after a long time, felt the grimy hand upon her knee.

Once the woman said, "Come away, Cissie. You're worrying the lady."

"No. Please," said Lizzie. She took the hand in her own and smiled again at the wide baby face. The child was very, very young and very, very dirty —

No child had ever come near her before. She wondered why it had come now.

III

At Lewes a carriage was waiting for her and, in a moment, it seemed that she was driving through a dark village street and in front of her, like a great wall topping the skies, the Downs rose.

When the carriage entered the courtyard and stopped before the broad stone door Lizzie was seized with terror. She wished, oh! she wished that she had not come. The sense of descending trouble was so strong with her that she felt for the first time in her life that she was going to prove unequal to her task.

Her life was over and done with! Why had she allowed herself to be pushed back again into all these affairs of other people?

She was ushered into a square lighted hall where they were all having tea round a wide open fireplace. She was conscious of Rachel rising, slim and tall, to greet her, of the square ruddy-faced country-looking man who gripped her hand, jolly hard, and was, of course, Sir Roderick; of a handsome, athletic-looking girl in a riding-habit, of a man or two and an elderly smartly dressed woman.

They were all immensely cheerful and friendly and to Lizzie, white and tired, noisy and horribly robust. She would have liked to have slipped up to her room and stayed there alone until dinner, but Rachel said:

"Oh! you must be perished after that wet journey. Tea's just at its hottest and its freshest. Quick, Roddy—the toast—Never mind the rest of us, Miss Rand—just drink that tea and get warm."

They allowed her to sink back into an easy chair somewhere in the shadow and the tea was very comforting and the stern hall with its crackling fire and its cosy solid shape most friendly. She listened to them all noisily discussing people and dances and horses and dinners. She watched Rachel Seddon, sitting a little gravely, straight in her chair, throwing in a word now and again.

This was the woman.... This was the woman....

She felt a warm tongue that licked her hand. She looked down and saw at her side the oddest dog, a dog like a mat, shapeless with two brown eyes behind its hair and a black wet nose.

There was something about the eyes and the way that the warm body was pressed against her dress that won her instant affection.

"What an adorable animal!" she said to Roddy, who was sitting next to her.

"Oh! Jacob!" he said, laughing. "He really oughtn't to be in here at all—servants' hall's his proper place—If you care for dogs, Miss Rand, I'll show you some——"

As he spoke she caught the dog's eyes and saw in the depths of them shame. He had been sitting, very square and upright, with his eyes gravely fixed, with great interest, upon the company. Then, at the sound of Roddy's voice his head had dropped, instantly he became furtive, his eyes searching for some place of escape.

Her hand caught his rough coat and she drew him to her side and stroked his ears.

"I think he's perfectly delightful," she said. "I'm afraid I prefer mongrels to better dogs."

"Do you really?" said Roddy, looking kindly at her. "'Pon my word, Miss Rand, I must show you my little lot. I don't think you'll have much use for that animal there afterwards."

At last the girl in the riding-habit and the other woman and the young man noisily departed.

Rachel took Lizzie upstairs. "Are you sure," she said, "you'd like to come down to dinner? Wouldn't you rather, to-night, go early to bed and have it there?"

"No, thank you, Lady Seddon." Lizzie looked about the room. "This is all splendid, thank you. I'm not a bit tired."

"I'm so glad you've come," said Rachel, searching for Lizzie's eyes. But Lizzie had turned away.

At last she was alone.

Her room was splendid—so wide, and high, and such a fire!

She flung up her window. There the Downs were, black, huge before her; the rain came down hissing from the sky and a smell of wet earth and grass stole up to her.

"That's the woman ..." she said again to herself—"What shall we say to one another?"

Then as she stared into the fire she thought, "She wants me to help her."

Afterwards she heard a scratching at the door. A maid had been sent to her, but she had dismissed her, saying that she would manage for herself.

She went to the door and found outside it the shaggy, square dog.

He walked into her room, sniffed for a time at the bed, pricked up his ears at the noise that the fire made, listened to the sound of the rain, at last sat down in a distant corner with one leg stretched at right angles to his body and watched her.

She was indignant with herself for the softness in her heart that his company brought to her.

CHAPTER XI
RODDY IS MASTER
"I and my mistress, side by side,
Shall be together, breathe and ride,
So, one day more am I deified,
Who knows but the world may end to-night?"
Robert Browning.

I

Introspection had been always to Roddy a thing unknown. He had never regarded himself as in any way different from the other men whom he met, and he would have been greatly distressed had he thought that he was different.—"What you writin' fellers," he had once said to Garden, "can find amusin' in inventin' people for I can't think; you've got to make 'em odd for people to be interested in 'em and then they aren't like anyone."

Now, however, for the first time in his life he would have been glad of help from someone who knew a little about the motive of human beings. He was worried, distressed, perplexed; slowly his temper was rising—a temper roused by his irritation at not being able to deal with the situation.

It was not his way to ask for help from anyone and he always had all the inarticulate self-confidence of the healthy Englishman, but now, as the days crept towards Christmas he was increasingly aware that something must soon happen to prevent his patience giving away.

He might as well not be married to Rachel at all—and that was an intolerable position for him as husband, as lover, as master of his house. Beyond doubt, he knew Rachel less now than he had known her when he married her. Her very kindness to him, her strange alternations of silence and affection perplexed him; for a long time he had told himself that he knew that she did not love him and that he must make companionship do, but ever since that quarrel about Nita Raseley the division between them had grown wider and wider.

Because he loved her he had been very patient with her—very patient for Roddy, who had always had what he wanted and shown temper if he were refused.

But Roddy's character was of a very real simplicity. The men and women and animals whom he had known had also been, for the most part, of a simple character and, in all his life, there had only been one horse and two women who had been too much for him, and even these, at the last, he had beaten by temper and dogged determination.

244

Rachel was utterly beyond him. The strange way that she had of suddenly becoming quite another woman baffled him; had he only not loved her he was sure that it would have been easier, much easier.

But now, as the days passed at Seddon, his irritation thrived. Women were all the same. They seemed obstinate enough, but there was nothing like brute force to bring them to heel. He was growing surly—cross with the servants and the animals. He didn't sleep. His discontent made him silent so that, when they were alone, instead of talking to her and interesting her and winning her, perhaps, in that way, he would sit and look at her and answer her in monosyllables, and, afterwards, would be furious with himself for behaving so absurdly.

This trouble sent him out of doors and away over the Downs on his horse. Fiercely he hurled himself into his fields and lanes and farms, getting up sometimes very early and riding out to some distant place, thinking always, as he rode, of Rachel and what he was to do.

His devotion for the country round Seddon, a devotion that had stirred his heart since his first conscious sight of the outside world, nobly now rewarded him. The land seemed to understand that he was suffering, and drew closer to him and watched him with gentle and loving eyes, and soothed his soul.

Before Christmas there came some sharp, frosty mornings; he would go out very early and would see, first, the garden, the lawn crisp and white, the grey jagged wall that divided his land from the sweeping Downs, the grey house behind him so square and solid and comfortable. At the end of the garden away from the road there was an old iron gate with stone pillars, and upon these pillars sat old stone gryphons. These gryphons had been there since long ago and he liked the friendliness of their faces, the strength of their crouching bodies and the way that they would look out so patiently, over a great expanse of fields and hedges, until their gaze rested on the white chalk hollows in the rising hills away behind Lewes.

Roddy, standing with the Downs so immediately behind him and this green spread of land in front of him, was always conscious of happiness. Here he was at home. He knew those fields, the streams that ran through them, the farmers, the labourers, the horses and dogs that lived upon them. No fear here that "one of those clever fellers" would wonder at his stupidity, no sudden "letting you down" or "showing you up." Behind him was his house, before him the land that he had always known; here he was safe.

He had, too, beyond this, some unformulated recognition of a service and a worship that here he was called on to pay. He had always declared that he could understand those Johnnies who worshipped the sun and the earth. "Damn it all—there's something to catch on to there."—He did not, in his heart, believe in all this civilization, this preserving of the sick and tending of the maimed and halt. "You've got to clear out if you're broken up" was his opinion. "If you can't do your bit, can't see or smell or anything, you're just in the way."—What he meant was that the halt and maimed were simply insults to the vigour and vitality of his fields and sky.

But indeed, what would he have done during these days had he not had his riding, farms to visit, shepherds and farmers for company? At first Rachel had ridden with him and they had been closer together during those rides than at any other time, but lately she had refused, on one excuse or another, to come with him.

He went a good deal now to other houses, but it was awkward because Rachel would not come with him. She asked people to Seddon and was charming when they came, but she would not often go out with him when the country people invited them.

Since the Nita Raseley episode he had thought that she might show jealousy did he ride and drive with some girl in the country. He hoped that she would be jealous, that would have filled him with tingling happiness—but no, she seemed to be glad that he should find someone who could take her place.

Over all these things he brooded and brooded. He would look at his old friendly gryphons and feel, in some dumb confused way, that they were being insulted.—"Poor old beggars—I bet she doesn't know they're there"— And through all of this, he loved her more and more, and was, daily, more wretched and unhappy.

II

The coming of Miss Rand puzzled him. He had, of course, known of her for a long time—"Adela Beaminster's secretary, most capable woman, simply runs the whole place."—As a human being she simply did not occur to him.

Now she seemed to be the one person whom Rachel wished to know. Another instance of Rachel's unexpectedness. When Lizzie came he was still more astonished. This tidy, trim little woman looked as though she ought always to have a typewriter by her side; her sharp eyes were always restlessly discovering things that were out of order. Roddy found himself fingering his tie and patting his hair when she was with him—not, he would have supposed, the sort of woman for whom Rachel would have cared.

Then after a while he discovered another astonishing thing. Miss Rand did not like his wife, did not like her at all. He watched and fancied that Rachel soon discovered this and was doing her utmost to force Miss Rand to like her.

Miss Rand was always pleasant and polite; she was an immense help about dinners and this dance that was to be given early in the New Year, but she yielded to none of Rachel's advances, was always reserved, unresponsive.

Roddy was afraid of her but believed in her. She liked animals and loved the house and the Downs and the country.—"She's all clean and bright and hard," he thought; "no emotion about her, no sentiment there. A man 'ud have a stiff time love-making with her."

But it gradually appeared that, whatever her feelings might be towards Rachel, she was ready to like Roddy. She walked with him, asked him sensible questions, listened attentively to his rather lumbering explanations. After a time, he almost forgot that she was a woman at all—"Damn sensible and yet she never makes you feel a fool."

He liked her very much, though she obviously preferred Jacob, the mongrel, to all other dogs in the place. He wondered as the days passed whether she might not help him with Rachel. He would not speak to anyone living about his own feelings for Rachel and his unhappiness, but he thought that, perhaps, in a roundabout way, he might obtain from Miss Rand some general wisdom that he could apply to his especial case.

The afternoon of Christmas Eve was cold and foggy and Roddy and Lizzie sat over the fire in the hall waiting for Rachel, who had gone out for a solitary walk. Roddy looking at his companion approved of the sharp delicate little face with the firelight touching it to colour and shadow; her dress was grey with a tiny brooch of old gold at her throat, and she wore one ring of small pearls; the look of her gave him pleasure.

"I wonder," Miss Rand said, "that you don't go where you'll get better hunting—you don't hunt round here at all, do you?"

"A bit"—Roddy looked gravely at the fire—"I go very little though. You see, Miss Rand, it's a case of bein' born down here and likin' the place, don't you know. Of course I'd love to have been born in a huntin' country, but bein' here I've got fond of it, you see, and wouldn't leave it for any huntin' anywhere."

She looked at him sharply: "You do love the place very much—I envy you that."

Even as she spoke her consciousness of "the place" faced her; she had always known that she was more acutely aware of the personality of her surroundings than were most of her friends, but her experience here was different from anything that she had ever known before.

She remembered that in the train she had been warned of some coming event and now, sitting opposite to Roddy beside the blazing fire, she was sharply and definitely frightened.

Rachel had already appealed to her; Roddy was appealing to her now, but stronger than either of these demands was some force in herself, warning her and raising in her the most conflicting, disturbing emotions.

The very silence of the house about them, the long green stretches of the level fields, came almost personally and presented themselves to her, and in her heart, growing with every moment of passing time, was her hatred of Rachel and, from that, tenderness for Roddy, who could thus be left, so pathetically unhappy, so eloquently without words that might express his unhappiness.

Something she knew was soon to occur that would involve all three of them in a common crisis.

It was almost as though she must leap to her feet and cry to the startled and innocent Roddy, "Look out!" her finger pointing at the closed door behind him.

Meanwhile Roddy had been considering her. She said that she envied him the place. That was pleasant of her, and he warmed to the urgency with which she had said it. If she felt in that way about such things, why then, all the more, he thought, he could speak to her about his trouble with Rachel. Perhaps, too, although this he would not admit to himself—his conviction that Lizzie disliked Rachel gave him more courage.

Everyone thought Rachel so wonderful—wonderful of course she was, but a complete sense of that wonder must blind the looker-on to Roddy's point of view.

"Places," he said moodily, "ain't everythin'—course I love this old bit o' ground, but when you love anything a lot you're disappointed because every feller don't see it exactly as you do."

Lizzie looked at him.

"I should have thought, though, Sir Roderick, that you were a very, very happy person."

Roddy considered, then slowly shook his head—"No, Miss Rand, not exactly—no, you know, I shouldn't say that exactly—but then, I suppose, no man on this earth is absolutely happy."

"Well," said Lizzie, "a great many people would envy you—your health, your home, your wife, you've got a good deal, Sir Roderick."

As she spoke her anxiety to help him seized and held her. He wanted advice so badly, advice that she could give him, and this English strain in him prevented him from speaking. Had she gone more deeply into her motives she would have known that her anger with Rachel, even more actively prompted, it seemed, by the stones and the fields and the hills around her, was urging her interference.

"People envy me," said Roddy, "but then, Miss Rand, people don't know. It's all my own fault, mind you, that I'm not perfectly happy. It's all because I'm such a fool, not able to see what people are gettin' at, always blunderin' in at the wrong moment and blunderin' out again when I ought to be stayin' in, and that sort o' thing. I used to think," he concluded, "that all the talk about people's feelin's, studying them and so on, was rot, but now I'm not so sure. I'd give anythin'—" he stopped abruptly.

"It is all rot," Lizzie said sharply—"I can only speak as a woman, of course, but I know that what every woman ever born into this world has wanted is just to be taken by someone stronger than herself and be beaten or kissed, loved or strangled as the case may be. Believe me, it is so."

Roddy looked at her, some new thought, perhaps a prologue to some new determination, shining from his eyes.

249

"By Jove!" he said. "I believe you're right, Miss Rand—I do indeed. Every woman, would you say?"

"Every woman," said Lizzie firmly.

Their eyes met. The sure steadiness of her gaze, the way that she sat there, her little body so sure and resolute, her very neat composure an argument against lightheaded reasoning, encouraged him beyond any help that he had yet found.

Their gaze seemed long and intimate; the colour rose and flushed his brown cheeks and into his eyes there crept that consciousness of a victory about to be won, although the odds were hard against him. The door opened behind him and he turned at the sound and saw that Rachel had come in.

Her entry gave him now, as it always did, a conviction that during her absence he hadn't had the least idea as to how splendid she really was. She brought into that little stone hall a wild colour, a strong, fine challenge to anything small, or shackled or conventional.

Her walk had given her cheeks a flame, the black furs round her throat, the black coat falling below her knees, a red feather in her round black fur cap, all these things set off and accentuated the brilliant fire and energy of her eyes.

As she came towards them then so splendid was she that Lizzie was herself for an instant lost in admiration—She lit the hall, she lit the house, she lit the country and the evening sky.

To Roddy, as he looked at her, there stole the spirit of some pagan ancestor telling him that here was his capture, that this fine creature was his to bind, to burden, to chastise, as his lordly pleasure might be.

Rachel, meanwhile, had come in from her walk, unappeased, unsated; the exertion had only succeeded in stirring in her a deeper, more urgent uneasiness. During these last weeks she had known no moment of peace. She had come down to Seddon determined to do her duty to Roddy; she had found that at every turn her duty to Roddy involved more than any determination could force her to give.

She had not known what that last interview with Breton would do to every situation that followed it. It seemed to her then that those last words with him would make her duty plain, they had only made her duty harder.

She could not now act, think, sleep, move but that last kiss, those last words of his, that last vision of him standing, struggling so finely for control—these things pursued her, caught her eyes and held them.

All her duty to Roddy could not hide from her now that she had, at one flaming instant, known what life at its most intense could be. She had felt the fire—how cold to her now these antechambers, these passages so chill, so far from that inner room. Lizzie had then occurred to her as the strongest person she knew. She sent for Lizzie, found instantly that Lizzie disliked her, suspected then that Lizzie knew about Breton.

She knew Lizzie for her enemy.... During the last week also she had detected a new attitude in Roddy; she had felt in him some active growing impatience that quite definitely threatened her safety. That wild lawlessness in Roddy that she had always known, that had produced the Nita episode and others, was now turning towards herself.

But most of all did she fear her thoughts of Breton. She drove him again and again and again from her mind, she called all her strength, mental, moral, and physical, to her aid—always, with a smile, with one glance from his eyes he defeated her.

Day and night he was with her, and yet at her heart she did not even now know whether it were Francis Breton whom she loved, or the life with Roddy, the whole Beaminster scheme of things that she hated. Every day it seemed to her that Lizzie was more watchful, Roddy more impatient, Breton more insistent—but afraid of them all as she was, fear of herself gave her the sharpest terror.

She rang for tea, reproached them because they had waited for her. Then they were—all three of them—silent.

One of the footmen brought in the five o'clock post with the tea and laid Rachel's letters on the table at her side.

Lizzie had leant across the table for something and saw, as though flashed to her by some special designing Providence, that the letter on the top of the pile was in Francis Breton's handwriting.

Rachel, busied with tea, had not looked down. Now she did so; the handwriting rose, as though she had at that instant heard his step beyond the room, and filled first her eyes, then her cheeks, then her heart.

Her eyes met Lizzie's and for the barest moment of time their challenges met. Rachel seemed to hesitate, then, gathering up her letters, looked round at Roddy and said, "I think I'll just go up and take my things off, this fire's hotter than I expected—I'll be back in a moment."

She walked slowly across the room and up the broad staircase.

III

She did not switch on the light. The evening dusk left the room cool and dim, but by the window, standing so that green shadows met the grey and through them both a pale light trembled before it vanished, she took the letter in her hand, allowing the others to drop and be scattered, white, on the floor at her feet.

She held the envelope; he had written and he had sworn to her that he would not do so—she should have been furious at his broken word, scornful of him for his weakness, indignant at his treating her so lightly.

But she could not think of that now, she could only think of the letter. The envelope was so precious to her that it seemed to return the caress that his fingers gave it and to have of itself some especial individuality. She traced his hand on the address, treasured every line and mark, and then at last tore it open. It was not a very long letter. He had written to her:

"You will despise me for breaking my word. Perhaps you won't read this— but I can't help it, I can't help it, and even if I could I don't think that I would. I know that my writing to you is just another of the rash, foolish, silly weak things that I've gone on doing all my life, but let it be so. I don't pretend to be fine or brave and I have tried all these weeks, tried harder than you can know. I've written to you every day letter after letter, and torn them up—torn them all up. I've fancied that perhaps you've forgotten by now and then I've known that you've not and then I've known that it were better if you did.

I love you so madly that—(here he had scratched some words out)—I must tell you that I love you so that you can hear me and not only my walls and furniture and my own self. I'm trying not to be selfish. I know that I'm doing something now that is hard on you, but my silence is eating me, thrusting, killing—I shall be better soon—I will be sensible—soon—I will be— —

But now, oh, my darling! for a moment at least I have caught you and held you throbbing against me, and put my hands in your hair and stroked your cheeks and kissed your eyes.

Don't write to me if you must not, don't be angry with me for this.

I will try not to break my word again."

As the letter ended so silence came back into the room that had been beating and throbbing with sound.

The pale light had gone, only the Downs were dim grey shapes against a darker sky—the ripple of some water slipping and falling came from the garden.

The letter fell from her hands and lay white with the others on the floor.

She tumbled on to her knees by the window and her heart was the strangest confusion of triumph and fear, exultation and shame.

For a little time she lay there and felt that she was in his arms and that his lips were on her mouth and that her hand pressed his cheek.

She got up, turned on the lights, took off her walking things, brushed her hair and washed her hands, picked up the other letters, but put his in the inside of her dress—then went down to the others.

IV

She found Lizzie sitting alone—"Where's Roddy?"

Lizzie looked up at her. "He had to go and see about a horse or something."

Rachel came down to the table and poured out some tea and then sat smiling at Lizzie; Lizzie smiled back.

"I hope you liked your walk."

"Yes, there's a storm coming up. You've no idea how deeply one gets to care for these Downs—their quiet and their size."

They were silent for a little and then Rachel said:

"Miss Rand—I do hope—that this really has been something of a holiday for you, being here, away from all your London work!"

Lizzie's eyes were sharp—"Yes—It's delightful for me. The first holiday I've had for years...."

"Don't think it impulsive of me—but I've asked you here hoping that we'd get to know one another better. I've wanted to know you, to have you for a friend—for a long time. I've always admired so immensely the way that you've helped Aunt Adela—done things that I could never possibly have done——"

She stopped, but Lizzie said nothing—Then she went on more uncertainly—

"You see, I hoped that perhaps you'd teach me a little order and method. I've married so young—I've hoped...." Then almost desperately—"But you know, Miss Rand, I don't feel as though your coming here has helped us to know one another any better."

The storm had come up and the sky beyond the house was black. Lizzie's face, lighted by the fire, was white, sharp and set—there was no kindness in her eyes.

"Perhaps, Lady Rachel," she said slowly, "I'm not a very emotional kind of woman. If one's worked, as I have, since one was small—had to earn one's living and fight for one's place—it makes one perhaps rather self-reliant and independent of other people—Our lives have been so different, I'm afraid," she added with a little laugh, "that I'm a dried-up, unsatisfactory kind of person—I know that my mother and sister have always found me so."

"Yes," Rachel said, "our lives have been different. Perhaps if mine had been a little more like yours—perhaps if I had had to work for my living—I...."

She broke off—a little catch was in her voice—she rose from her chair and went to the window and stood there, with her back to Lizzie, gazing into the darkening garden.

She knew that Lizzie had repulsed her; she was hardly aware why she had made her appeal, but she was now frightened of Lizzie and to her overstrung brain it seemed that she could now see Lizzie and Roddy in league against her.

She heard a step and turning round found Peters, the butler, large, square, of an immense impassivity.

"Please, my lady, might I speak to you a moment?"

She went out.

Lizzie, left in the darkening room, could think now only of the letter. The sight of that handwriting had stirred in her passions that she had never before imagined as hers—that first pathetic appeal of Roddy and then the sight of that letter!

Her brain, working feverishly, showed her the words that that letter would contain—the passion, the passion! There in the very face of her husband, Rachel was receiving letters from her lover, letters that she could not wait a moment to read, but must go instantly and open them.

This hour brought to a crisis Lizzie's agony. Had such a letter been written to her!

She tortured herself now with the picture of him as he sat there in his room in Saxton Square writing it! It appeared to her now as though they two— there in the very throne of their triumphant love—had plotted this insult, this snap of the fingers, to show her, Lizzie Rand, how desolate, how lonely, how neglected and unwanted she was!

That then, after this, Rachel should appeal to her for friendship! The cruel insult of it.

She felt as she heard the fast drops of rain lash the window-frames, that no revenge that she could secure would satisfy her thirst for it.

V

Roddy, meanwhile, had gone out to the stables. That little talk with Lizzie had determined a resolution that had been growing now within him for many weeks.

That little woman, with her assured air and neat little ways, knew what she was about—knew moreover what others were about. She had watched and had given him the tip—He would take it.

Roddy's mind was of far too simple an order to admit of more than one point of view at a time. He saw Rachel now as a dog or horse, of whom he

255

was very fond, who needed, nevertheless, stern discipline. He wondered now how it was that he had allowed himself for so long to remain indecisive.

"London muddles a feller," he concluded; "the country's the place for clear thinkin'."

He looked at his horses with great satisfaction, they were in splendid condition—he had never known them better. He also was in splendid condition—never been better.

As he walked away from the stables and turned towards the end of the garden bounded by the gryphons and the stone gate, he felt his body at its most supreme perfection. He thought, on that afternoon, that he was strong enough for anything, and perhaps never before in his life had he been so conscious of the glories of physical things; of all that it meant to have fine muscles and a strong heart and lungs of the best and thews and sinews as good as "any feller's."

"I'm strong enough for anythin'——" He turned back his arm and felt his muscle. He cocked his head with a little conceited gesture of satisfaction—"I was gettin' a bit fat in London—got rid of all that."

To walk, to ride, to fight, to swim, to eat and sleep, to love women and drink strong drink! God! what a world!

And then, beyond it all, Rachel, Rachel, Rachel! He had her now—she should be under his hand, she should be his as she had never been since the first week of their marriage.

"No more nonsense, by God!" he said triumphantly to himself—"no more nonsense."

He leaned on the stone gate and looked out over the fields—The gryphons regarded him benevolently.

He was conscious, as he stood there, of the Duchess—what was the old lady doing? He'd like to see her. He felt more in sympathy with her than he had been for a long time past. "She's right after all. You've got to stand up and run people. No use just lettin' them handle you."

There was a storm coming up. The white lights of the higher sky were being closed down by black blocks of cloud that spread, from one to another, merging far on the horizon above the hills into driving lines of rain. The white chalk hollows above Lewes stood out sharp and clear; the dark green of the fields was now a dull grey, the hedges were dark and a thin stream that cut the flat surface of the plain was black like ink.

Roddy welcomed the storm. Had he been superstitious the physical energy that now pervaded him might have frightened him. He felt as though with one raising of his arm he could hold up those black clouds and keep them off. The rain and the wind had not more force than he—

Life was a vast pæan of strength—"The weak must go"—He was, at this hour, Lord of Creation.

As he went back to the house the rain met him and whipped his cheek.

"By Gad, I'd like to find the old lady sittin' in the house, waitin' for a chat," he thought.

When he came down to dinner, he came as one who rules the world. That simple clear light was in his eyes that was always there when he had found the solution to something that perplexed him. His expression too was one that belonged to Rachel's earlier experience of him, one that she had not seen on his face for a long time past. His strong but rather stupid mouth had somewhere in its corners the suspicion of a smile. His chin stuck out rather obstinately—the light in the eyes, the smile, the set lips, these things revealed the old Roddy.

After dinner Lizzie went off to her room.

For a while Roddy and Rachel sat there—She read some book, her eyes often leaving the page and staring into the fire.

Then she got up and said good night. She came over and bent down and kissed him. He caught her arm and held her.

"I say, old girl, it's time we had the same room again—much more convenient." He heard her catch her breath and felt her tremble. She tried to draw her arm away, but he held her.

"Oh! but soon, Roddy—Yes—but not just now—I— —"

"Yes—now. I'll see about it to-morrow." She stepped back from him, dragging herself away, and then put her hand to her forehead with a desperate gesture.

"No, no—not——"

He got up and smiling, swaying a little, faced her—

"Yes—I've made up my mind—all this business has got to come to an end— Been goin' long enough."

"What business?"

"Seein' nothing of you—nothing from mornin' till night. You know, old girl, it isn't fair—if we didn't care about one another——"

"Yes, I know—but don't let's discuss it to-night. I'm tired, headachy—this storm——"

He said nothing—She looked at him and at the steady stare in his eyes and the smile at his mouth turned away.

She moved towards the door—He said nothing, but his eyes followed her.

"Good night," she said, turning round to him—but he still said nothing, only stood there very square and set.

For a long time he sat, looking into the fire—Then he went up to his room and very slowly undressed. Afterwards he came out, carefully closing the door behind him, then, in dressing-gown and pyjamas, went down the passage to Rachel's door.

The house was very still, but the storm was raging and the boughs of some tree hit, with fierce protesting taps, a window at the passage-end.

He knocked at her door, waited, then heard her ask who was there.

"It's I, Roddy," he said. There was a pause, then the door was opened. He came in and stood in the doorway. Rachel was sitting up in bed, her face very white, her eyes fixed on him.

"I'm sleepin' here to-night, Rachel," he said.

258

Her voice was a whisper—"No, Roddy—no—not—not——"

"Yes," he said firmly.

"No, not to-night."

"Yes—to-night—now."

He walked carefully across the room, took off his dressing-gown, and hung it over a chair. He looked about the room.

"Too much light"—he said and, going to the door, switched off all the lights save the one above the bed.

CHAPTER XII
LIZZIE'S JOURNEY—III

"Exile of immortality, strongly wise,
Strain through the dark with undesirous eyes,
To what may be beyond it. Sets your star,
O heart, for ever? Yet behind the night,
Waits for the great unborn, somewhere afar,
Some white tremendous daybreak."

Rupert Brooke.

I

That night Lizzie had a dream and, waking in the early hours of the grey dim morning, saw before her every detail of it. She had dreamt that she was lost in the house. No human being was there. Every room was closed and she knew that every room was empty.

It was full day, but only a dull yellow light lit the passages. —She could not find her way to the central staircase. A passage would be familiar to her and then suddenly would be dark and vague and menacing. She opened doors and found wide dusty empty rooms with windows thick in cobwebs and beyond them a garden green, tangled, deserted.

She knew that if she did not escape soon some disaster would overtake her, some disaster in which both Roddy and Rachel would be involved. She knew also that, in some way, Rachel's safety absolutely depended upon her—She felt, within herself, a struggle as to whether she should save Rachel. She did not wish to save Rachel.... But some impulse drove her....

She ran down the passage, stumbling in the strange indistinct yellow light— She knew that, could she only reach the garden, Rachel would be saved.

She reached a window, looked down, and saw below her, like a green pond, the lawn overgrown now with weeds and bristling with strange twisted plants.

She flung open the window and tried to jump, but a cold blast of some storm met her and drove her back. The storm screamed about her, the dust rose in the room, the plants in the garden waved their heads ... the wind rushed through the house and she heard doors banging and windows creaking.

She knew suddenly that she was too late—Rachel was dead.

She stood there thinking, "I thought that I hated her—I know now that I loved her all the time."

The storm died down—died away. A voice quite close to her said, "You made a mistake, Miss Rand. People have souls, you know—having a soul of your own is more important than criticizing other people's.... People have souls, you know."

She woke and heard a clock strike seven. As she lay there a sense of uneasiness was with her so strongly that she repeated to herself, half sleeping, half waking, "I wish to-day were over, quite over, quite over. I want to-day to be over."

She was completely wakened by a sound. She lay there for a little time wondering what it was. Then she realized that something was scratching on the door.

She got out of bed, opened the door and found the dog, Jacob, sitting in the long dark passage, looking through his tangled hair into space as though the very last thing that he had been doing had been trying to attract her attention. Jacob was nearer to a human being than any animal that she had ever known. He had attached himself to Miss Rand and she had decided, after watching him, that he knew more about the situation in the house than anyone else. To catch him, as he watched, with his grave brown eyes, Roddy or Rachel as they spoke or moved was to have no kind of doubt as to his wisdom, his deep philosophy, his penetration into motives.

He liked Miss Rand, but she knew well that his feeling for her had nothing of the passionate urgency with which he regarded Roddy or Rachel. All tragedy—the depths and the heights of it—she had seen in that dog's eyes, fixed with the deepest devotion upon Roddy.—"He knows," she had often thought during the last week, "exactly what's the matter with all of us."

He always slept, she knew, in a basket in Rachel's room, and she wondered why he had been ejected. He sat now in the middle of the floor and seemed deeply unhappy. He sat square with his legs spread out, his hair hanging in melancholy locks over his eyes, his small beard giving a last wistful touch to his expression. He did not look at Lizzie or show any interest in her, he only stared before him at the pattern on the wall.

Lizzie did not attempt to pat him—she went back to bed, and, lying there, saw the light gather about the room.

Once Jacob sighed. Otherwise he made no movement until the maid came in with Lizzie's tea—Then he crawled under the bed.

II

When she came down to breakfast she felt that she could not endure another day of this place. She wished now for no revenge upon Rachel, she had no longer any curiosity as to the particular feelings of any one of these people for any other ... she felt detached from them all, and utterly, absolutely weary.

She was weighed down with a sense of disaster and she felt that she must, instantly, escape from it all, fling herself again into her London work, deal with the tiresome commonplaces of her mother and sister—she must escape.

Roddy was sitting alone at breakfast and she saw at once that he was uneasy. He seemed to avoid her eyes and he coloured as she came towards him.

"Mornin', Miss Rand," he said, "Rachel's not comin' down. Bit of headache— rotten night."

"I didn't have a very good night either. That storm made me sleep badly."

"Yes, wasn't it a corker? It's all right to-day though."

She looked through the wide high windows and saw out over a country painted as in a delicate water-colour—The softest green and dark brown lay beneath a pale blue sky, very still, very gentle. Tiny white puffs of cloud were blown, like soap bubbles across the sun, so that bright gleams floated and passed and flashed again.

She drew a deep breath—"Nothing terrifying in such a day as this."

"Yes, it's beautiful—beautiful! I'm off for the day," Roddy said, "ridin'——"

She helped herself to some breakfast and sat down.

Roddy said, "Well, no one would ever believe you'd had a bad night, Miss Rand."—"You're fresh as a pin."

"Thank you," she said, laughing. "But, all the same, I did sleep badly."

"I'm not feeling princely myself," he confessed, "that's why I'm goin' off for a ride, nothin' like a ride to take you out of yourself. Don't you ever feel, Miss Rand, that you want to get right away from yourself and be someone else?"

She looked at him. Roddy was in real trouble. His very physical strength showed the more clearly that he was unhappy. His fingers moved restlessly, his eyes were never still. She looked at her letters. There was one from Lady Adela.

"Oh! I'm sorry—I'm afraid I shall have to go back almost immediately—The Duchess is much less well—They're worried about her."

"The Duchess!" Roddy started up and then sat down again. "I'm sorry—I was thinking about her only yesterday. What's the matter?"

"Lady Adela doesn't say, but she asks about you—the Duchess, I mean. Got it into her head, Lady Adela says, that you're not well or something."

"I'll write to her." Roddy spoke slowly as though to himself—"I've not treated her very well lately and she's always been such a brick to me." He left his breakfast, walked backwards and forwards once or twice—"Always been such a brick to me, the old lady has," he repeated.

Lady Adela really did want Lizzie to return. This horrid war was getting on her nerves, the house was all in disorder and nobody seemed either well or happy.

"Somebody really does want me," thought Lizzie with a certain grim satisfaction.

But she was terribly restless that morning. She could settle down to nothing and ended by walking up and down the garden paths, watching the pale winter light cross the Downs in sweeping shadow, seeing the bare branches, all black and sharp against the blue distance.

How she loved life and how, at every turn, life was thrust from her! For that other woman, there inside the house, two men were ready, eager to die—for herself, in all the world, no one cared.

There came up to her again, borne as it were on the sharp winter air, a determination to drive down Rachel's defences. The very sense that now, after Lady Adela's letter, she must shortly return to London, hardened her resolution.

Before breakfast she had felt that she did not care, now, quite suddenly she was determined that she would confront Rachel and drag the truth from her.

How much did Rachel care? Was Rachel already involved in a liaison with Breton?

And, at that thought, a pain so fierce clutched her heart that for a moment she could not see and the garden and the sky mingled like coloured smoke before her eyes.

Suddenly, coming to the end of the garden by the stone gate she saw that a strange thing had happened — one of the gryphons, perched there for many centuries, had tumbled to the ground and lay in the path, beyond the garden, broken into two pieces.

The storm of last night must have driven it down. But what had broken it?

She was sorry. She knew how deeply attached Roddy was to those gryphons; she remembered his pride when he had pointed them out to her.

The other gryphon looked very lonely.

"He will be distressed." The dead leaves on the path were trembling over the broken pieces of stone and whistling, in little excited groups, above it — "Just as though they are glad," she thought.

She and Rachel had a very amiable conversation at luncheon. Rachel confessed to a bad night.

Lizzie told her about Jacob.

"How tiresome of him to come and bother you — yes, I couldn't sleep and he was very restless too, so I put him into the passage. It was after six — I meant him to go down to the servants' hall. I'm so sorry, Miss Rand."

"Oh, he didn't worry me at all. I was awake." That appeal was in Rachel's eyes to-day more than ever. Lizzie saw it and steeled her heart. "I must know," she thought. "I must know."

"I'm afraid," she said, "that I'll have to go back to London to-morrow. I heard from Lady Adela this morning — The Duchess is not so well."

"Oh!" Rachel caught her breath — "oh, Miss Rand, no, no, oh! I hope not! You must stay! I— —!" her colour came and went. "There's the dance. I don't know what I shall do without you." And she went on more desperately, catching Lizzie's eyes and evading them. "We are just beginning to be so happy here. My husband likes you so much. I do hope — —"

She stopped and the colour left her again; her hands were trembling on the white tablecloth.

The strangest impulse flooded Lizzie's breast, an impulse to go to her and put her arms about her and kiss her and let her, there and then, unburden her heart —

Lizzie drove the impulse down, buried it. Her eyes were cold and her voice hard as she answered —

"I'm so sorry, but I think I must go. I can't leave Lady Adela if things are really difficult. I'll come this afternoon, shall I? and we might go over the dance — —"

Rachel had been thinking; she looked up sharply and stared at Lizzie, staring as though she had been some stranger whom she saw for the first time.

"Yes — Come to the Chinese room at four, will you? We'll have tea up there."

"Yes," said Lizzie, "at four."

They were both of them aware that something, now quite irrevocable, had been settled by these words.

There was a little old library up in one of the towers, and there Lizzie went. She had a desperate need of some place where, during the next hour, she might think and decide upon some plan. The room had little diamond-paned windows that looked down, on one side, over the courtyard, and on the other over the garden and the Downs. The shelves went from ceiling to floor and were filled with books that dimly shone with their old gold and were dusky in their rich, faded bindings.

It was very seldom that anyone came here; Lizzie was quite alone as, perched up in one of the deep-seated windows, she looked down at the garden, saw the stone gate with the solitary gryphon, watched the swiftly fading afternoon light fill the green lawn as a pot is filled with water.

Even now, early though it was, the little room was growing dark.

265

She strove now, resolutely, to discipline her mind. Although the very thought of Francis Breton now shamed her, it was for him that she must care. "Poor dear," he was even now, in her heart. "Foolish, indiscreet — must plunge from one mess into another, needs someone — Oh, so dreadfully — to help him out."

Her hostility to Rachel did not prevent her from feeling that here was someone very young, terribly inexperienced, most unhappily impulsive — the very last in the world to prevent Breton from having another catastrophe as bad as the early ones.

She must know absolutely what it was that he and Rachel were doing, and only Rachel could tell her that — And here her feeling about Rachel was compounded of the strangest mixture of anger and suspicion, of tenderness and compassion, of sympathy and hard callous indifference.

"Oh!" Lizzie thought, "why has all this come to me? Why wasn't I allowed just to go on with my life as it was — My life that was so safe and sure and dull?" —

She was conscious, as she sat there, that she was listening for something. She felt, in an odd way, that the day had been a direct continuance of the dream that she had had in the night; all the morning she had been aware that her ears, in spite of herself, had been waiting for some sound, a message, or an arrival.

She sat now in the swiftly darkening room, as though she had been told that someone was coming at such and such an hour and she had heard the clock strike and was listening for the grating of the wheels on the cobbles of the courtyard.

The calm winter's day passed now into a purple twilight — lights were coming in the windows —

She thought she heard a step in the passage and was startled as though someone had been suddenly, unexpectedly within the room.

She opened the window and listened — "Someone — several people — will come down that garden path in a minute — I know they will."

But the air was very cold and she closed the window; even as she did so a clock struck four.

266

She got up and went to Rachel.

III

The Chinese room was so called because its walls were covered with a stiff golden Chinese paper. It had wide windows looking on to the garden; Rachel used it a great deal.

Lizzie fixed upon her mind, very deliberately, all the details of her surroundings. Rachel was dressed in black with red round her throat and her waist, and this brilliant colour made her face seem white and there were deep, heavy black marks under her eyes.

She looked up when Lizzie came in, seemed, with a violent effort, to compel control.

They sat there for some time and discussed the dance; the dusk filled the room, then tea was brought. There was a light in their corner; slowly the rest of the room grew dark.

They finished tea, it was taken away, and Lizzie, sitting quite close to Rachel, on a little sofa that had a window just behind it, was aware that again, in spite of herself, her ears were straining for some sound. The house and all the world were profoundly still.

When the servant had at last left them alone, Rachel said — "Miss Rand, you mustn't go away to-morrow — Aunt Adela can manage for another week. After all, she did promise that you should stay for me over the ball."

"Why did you ask me here, Lady Rachel?" Lizzie said. Her speech was a direct challenge and, instantly, when she had spoken she knew that they had entered upon those personal relations that they had, during all these weeks, feared.

"I asked you because I wanted you for a friend — I've no friend — no woman friend — whom I can trust. I knew that I could trust you — I hoped that you could help me — —"

"I've been here for some time now and you have told me nothing."

"No — because you have held me off, have shown me so plainly that you disliked and distrusted me. You didn't always dislike me — what have I done?"

"That's only my way. As I told you this morning, Lady Seddon, I'm not an emotional person. But I feel more than I show. I would like to help you, if you will let me."

Rachel leaned forward and caught first Lizzie's arm, then her hand. Then she spoke, her voice quivering as though she were forcing upon herself the most intense control.

"Oh! you're so strange, so odd I don't know what you feel, whether you care, but these last months have been so hard for me that even though you hate me, despise me, it doesn't matter—nothing matters if only I can get away from myself, you're so different—so dry, so hard, but you are, you are!—just as hard——" she stopped—Lizzie drew her hand away.

"Please—don't tell me things if you feel about me like that. It hasn't been my fault, has it, that we don't get on? I didn't ask to come here, to know you—let me go—let me go back. Don't bother about me—leave me alone," she at last brought out.

But Rachel said more urgently—"No, don't go now. Even though you don't care, even though you hate me, help me. I've no one else. If only you knew the things I've suffered these past weeks, how I've hated myself for my indecision, for my weakness and shame. I don't know why I feel as though you were the only person to whom I could talk. I'm being driven, I suppose, by this long silence—and then you're so absolutely to be trusted—even though you dislike me—you're straight all through—I've always known that."

At Lizzie's heart again now that strange confusion of sensation, and with it a sure conviction that fate had this scene between them in hand, and that events now, whatever the hours might bring forth, were beyond her control.

"Yes, you may trust me," she said drily—"I'm useful, at any rate for that."

Lizzie watched her as, in the little pause that followed, Rachel struggled for concentration and for the point of view that would make the strongest appeal. That, Lizzie grimly knew, was the thing for which the girl was struggling and it yielded her the pleasanter irony because she was, herself, so surely aware of that one fact that all Rachel's confessions contained—

For herself she had only confidently to sit and wait.... Then Rachel plunged—

"I'm unhappy," she said, "in my married life, miserably unhappy, and entirely, utterly by my own fault. I've tried, or fancied that I've tried. I've done what I've thought was my best—Things have happened now, at last, that have made it impossible—I can't go on any longer."

She spoke as though she were, very urgently, endeavouring to deliver a fair honest statement. There was in her voice a note that showed that life had truly, of late, been very hard for her—

"I married, in the beginning, for a wrong reason. I knew then that I didn't love my husband. I married because I wanted to escape. I had always hated my grandmother and she had always hated me—you knew that, Miss Rand; everyone who had anything to do with us knew it. She had done more than hate me, she had made me frightened—frightened of life and people. Someone came along who was kind and easy and comfortable, and everyone said it would be a good thing, and so I, not because I loved him, but because I wanted to escape from my grandmother, married him. Because I had to silence everything that was honest in me I'm paying now."

"It was all quite natural," Lizzie said. "Most women would have done the same."

"It was horrible from the beginning; I found that I had not escaped from my grandmother at all. She had arranged the marriage and now was always, and in some curious way, influencing it.

"I soon saw what I had done—that I had been false to myself and therefore false to everything else. My husband was in love with me—He was very patient and good to me, but I found that everything that I did or thought or said in connection with my husband was false. What made it so hard was that I was, and I am, very fond of him. My training—the training of all our family had always been—to learn how to be sham, so that one's real self never appeared all one's life. It ought to have been easy enough—but I've never been like one of my family—I'd always been different.

"I had determined that this year I would do my duty to Roddy—But it's harder than any determination can govern. It's bad for Roddy, it's deadly for me ... at last things have happened that have made it impossible for me—I've made up my mind this morning. I must leave Roddy, let him divorce me, give him a better chance with someone else."

She spoke with the desperate immediate determination of youth, staring in front of her, her hands clenched. Like flame at Lizzie's heart leapt this knowledge.

"She and Breton are going — only you can stop them — she and Breton."

"Don't you think," said Lizzie, "a little of your husband?"

"I'm thinking of him all the time — It's for his sake — that he should have a better chance with someone who cared — —"

"No, that isn't true," said Lizzie — "It's because you love someone else — —"

Rachel, with her head down, whispered, "Yes — it's because ... someone else."

"Francis Breton."

"Yes, Francis Breton."

That whisper of his name had in it confidence, worship, defiance ... all these things were torture to Lizzie sitting there, very composed, very stern, very quiet. She should have been able to say that name with just that precious intimacy, and she saw, in Rachel's eyes, beyond her trouble the glad pride that the pronouncing of the name had given her.

"You know?" Rachel asked at length.

"Yes — —"

"You've known a long time."

"Yes — a long time."

"Oh! If you'd only spoken to me! — All this time I've been wanting you to — You must have known."

"Yes — I knew." Then Lizzie brought out slowly, letting her grave eyes wander over Rachel's face —

"You yourself insisted on telling me. You have brought it upon yourself if I say what I must...."

Rachel caught the hostility.

"Yes?" she said sharply.

"I'm older than you—older in every way. You know so little yet, the harm that you can do.... You must leave Francis Breton alone, Lady Seddon."

Rachel laughed—"Of course I knew that you—that it was the kind of way that you must look at it. But don't you see, we've got past all that first stage—It isn't, in the very least, any good looking at it from any general point of view. It's simply the individual happiness of the three of us, my husband, Francis Breton, myself—It's better for all of us that I should go."

"No ... not better for Francis Breton."

Rachel moved impatiently—"He—he and I—can judge that, Miss Rand——"

"No—You can't—you're too young. You don't know—I have a right to speak here, I know him—I have known him all this time——"

Lizzie broke off. Rachel, suddenly looking up, gazed at her—Lizzie, fiercely, also proudly as though she were guarding something very precious that they were trying to take from her, returned her gaze.

"All this time," Rachel said slowly. "You've known him—of course ... at Saxton Square...."

Then, as though the revelation had suddenly broken upon her, "Why you—you——!"

"Yes," said Lizzie, now fiercely indeed, hurling back at the girl the naïveté of her surprise. "Yes—it's odd, isn't it? I'm not the kind of woman, am I, ever to care for a man, or to have a man care for me?—To have any feeling or desire or affection. But it is not so strange as it may seem—I love him every bit as well as you do—I've cared more patiently perhaps, more unselfishly even. But there it is ... it gives me the right."

Nothing more surprising than that on this special circumstance Rachel had never reckoned. Feeling it now, blazing there before her, the way that she was to deal with it was beyond her experience. In an instant Lizzie Rand was, to her, a new creature. Always she had seen Lizzie patiently, with method, with discipline, putting things in order—that was her world and dominion. Lizzie had appeared, to Rachel, to stand for all the things that she herself was not. Rachel had often envied that absence of emotion, that security from impulse and passion, and it was upon that very security that Rachel had wished to depend. It was that that had driven her to seek Lizzie's friendship. She herself so unsure, so caught and destroyed by powers too potent for her resistance, had looked with wonder and desire upon Lizzie's safety—

Now Lizzie Rand was no longer Lizzie Rand. She was of Rachel's number, she might, as easily as Rachel, be swept, whirled away,—after death and destruction.

But there was more than that. There was the realization that Lizzie must hate her, that Lizzie was the last person in the world to whom she should have given her confidence, that Lizzie would fight now to the last breath in her body to keep Francis Breton from her.

During a long silence they sat facing one another—the little room was now nearly dark and it was only by the faint pale shadow from the sky beyond the window that they could catch, each from each, their consciousness of their new relationship.

It was during that silence that Lizzie was again aware that her ears were straining to catch some sound....

"I didn't know," Rachel said at last very softly; "it must seem brutal to you now that I should have told you all this. I wouldn't of course have spoken."

"Ah! you needn't mind," Lizzie said grimly. "He's never seen anything of it. You must never give him any reason to suspect—I trust you for that. No one in this world knows but you, and you should never have known if it had not been that I had to prove my right to interfere. Perhaps even now, you don't see that I have a right, but whether I have one or no, you've got to reckon with me now——"

"And you've got to reckon," Rachel answered, with some of Lizzie's own fierceness, "with a power that's beyond your power or mine or anyone's. Don't you imagine that we, all of us, haven't tried hard enough. Why! all these last two years we've done nothing but try. Now it's simply stronger than we are. If Roddy," she went on, speaking now more slowly, "hadn't forced it.... If he'd not been impatient—but now—after what's just happened, it's right—it isn't fair to him, to myself, to any of us, that things should go on as they are——"

"I'm thinking," Lizzie answered quietly, "simply of Francis Breton."

"Well! isn't it fairer too for him? He's been living, as we have, all this time, a life that's denying all his own real self. Anything's better than being false to that—life may be hard for us if we go away together, but at any rate it will be honest— —"

"Ah! that just shows how young you are! Don't I know that pursuit of truth and honesty as well as you? Don't I know that when life's beginning for us, the one thing that seems to matter is exposing ourselves, showing ourselves to the world just as we are! At first it seems such an easy thing—Just round that corner the moment's coming when the real person in us is going to stand up and proclaim itself just as it is, fine and splendid? but always something just comes in the way and stops it—the years go on and we're further off from truth than ever.

"You think that if you go off with Francis Breton now, you'll, both of you, be leading, suddenly, honest brave lives before the world. I tell you it isn't so. Things will be just as crooked, just as shadowed—issues just as confused—it will be worse than it was."

"But you don't know— —"

"I know Francis Breton. Don't you know too the kind of man that he is? Don't you know that he's as weak as a man can be, weaker than any woman ever could be? He's the kind of man who must have society to bolster him up. If the men of his world are supporting him then he's as good as gold, as fine as you like. Let them leave him and down he goes. All his life the world's been down on him and that's why he's been down. Lately he's been quiet—he's been winning his place back. Soon, if he's patient, they'll all come round him again. But let him go off with you and he's done, finished—absolutely, utterly. 'Ah!' everyone will say, 'that's what we expected. That's what we always knew would happen.' Don't you know what kind of effect that will have upon him? Don't you know?... Of course you do. It will break him up. His old life abroad, creeping from place to place, will begin again, only now he'll have the additional knowledge that he's done for you as well as for himself. It will be the end, utterly the end of him. And I, who love him, will not let it be."

Lizzie's speech had roused in Rachel one of those old storms of anger. She was exerting now her utmost self-control, but her heart seemed bound tight with some cord so slender that one movement, one impulse, would snap it—Then.... She saw in Lizzie now, only moved by a sense of jealous injury—

273

"She sits there, knowing that I've taken him from her. That's it.... That's what she's feeling—she's lost him. She can't forgive me for that."

But when she spoke her voice was quiet and controlled.

"That isn't so," Rachel said; "it won't, I think, be like that. There's so much more between us than you can understand. There's all our early life—not that we were together, but we seem to have it all in common, to have known it all together. We're unlike our family—all the Beaminsters—we're together in that—we are together in everything."

But Lizzie's voice went on, so coldly, with such assurance that, with every word, the flame of Rachel's anger climbed a little higher, grew stronger and steadier.

"There's another thing too. I watched you, more than you know. No, no man—no man in the world—will ever keep you altogether—there's something—I can't tell you what it is—there's something in you that demands more than just a personal relationship like that—Perhaps it's maternity—it is, with many women,—perhaps it's a great cause, a movement of a country—

"But I know, with certainty, that you will never love Breton as you should love a man. Realization will never be the thing to you that anticipation and retrospection are. I believe if you were to lose your husband now, you'd find that you loved him—All thoughts of Francis Breton, would go——"

At that, because at the very heart of her determination burnt the knowledge that Lizzie's words were true, Rachel's control was abandoned, her anger leapt: "You think you know—you think ... why ... why ... you don't know me at all!—you can't know me—we're strangers, Miss Rand—now—always....

"Nothing, nothing can ever make us friends again—I'll never forgive you for what you've said—the poor creature that you take me for—no doubt you'd have done better had the chance been yours, but you go too far——"

"That was unfair of you," Lizzie said very low—"You may say to me what you please—That's of no importance to anybody. But Francis Breton's happiness, his success, that is more to me than anything or anyone.—You shall not break his life into pieces for your own pleasure. There are more important things than your personal happiness, Lady Seddon——"

They were both standing, but they could not see one another, save, very
faintly, their hands and faces —

"It's too late, Miss Rand," Rachel laughed. "I shall write to him to-morrow. I
myself shall tell my husband — there is nothing that you can do — —"

They stood there, conscious that a word, a movement on either side might
produce an absurd, a tragic scene. Lizzie had never known such anger as the
passion that now held her. Rachel was taunting her with the thing that she
had missed; she stood there, before the world, as the woman for whom no
man cared — she stood there with the one human being who mattered to her
on the edge of complete disaster — nothing that she could do could prevent
it — and the woman at her side was the cause.

A sudden sweeping consciousness of the things that it would mean if Rachel
were dead flowed over her. Her heart stopped — that way — at least — Francis
Breton might be saved....

The room, dark as pitch before her, was filled now with a red glow — Her
hands, clenched, were ice in a world that was all of an overpowering heat.

Lizzie never afterwards could remember what then exactly happened.

She was worked to a pitch of anger, she was thinking to herself, "What
would be a way? ... anything to save him...."

"She shouldn't have taunted me with that" — when, suddenly, exactly as
though someone had taken her brain and emptied it, she had forgotten
Rachel, had forgotten her own personal injury, forgotten her anger, was only
aware that, with every nerve in her body on edge, she was waiting for some
sound —

Like an answer to an invocation, the sound, through the closed window,
came —

IV

She must have made some startled noise, because she heard Rachel say,
"What is it?"

She fled to the window and opened it. She could see nothing, but she could
hear, as she had known all day that she would hear, steps, stumbling, falling
heavily, upon the heavy gravel path.

She felt Rachel's hand upon her sleeve: "What is it?" Rachel said again—"Lizzie, what is it?"

Both women were seized and held by fear. Their feelings for one another were lost, sunk in the cold, shattering sense of disaster that had come, through the open window, into the room.

They could see lights now and figures—There were murmuring voices—

"Oh, Lizzie, what is it?" Rachel said for the third time, and then after a moment—"Roddy!"

Lizzie said—"Wait there. It may be nothing. I'll see—Don't you come for a moment."

She crossed the dark room, and opening the door saw Peters hurrying down the passage towards her. His face was in complete disorder—the face of someone who, throughout his life, has had only one kind of face that has served most admirably for every kind of occasion—suddenly a situation has arisen for which that face will not serve—

His body was shaking—

"Oh! Miss Rand, the master!"

Lizzie felt Rachel follow her, brush past both of them, down the passage and out of sight—

"An accident—flung from his horse and dragged along—been hours on the hill—a shepherd found him."

"Is he dead?"

"No, miss, not dead—not yet, thank God!"

"The doctor?"

"Dr. Crane from Lewes—we caught him, miss, most fortunately, on the way from another patient—he's downstairs now."

"Quick, Peters, things will be wanted."

Lizzie passed to the head of the stairs, Peters behind her said, "They've taken Sir Roderick into the green drawing-room, miss, so as not to have to go upstairs."

She came down the stairs and then stood, waiting in the hall. That was, for the moment, deserted, but the house wore an air of dismay, surprised alarm, so that every sound was of momentous import. Somewhere, a long way away, someone — perhaps a frightened kitchen-maid — was sobbing — the hall door was still open and little gusts of cold wind came in and stirred and rustled the pages of some illustrated papers on one of the tables.

Lizzie went to the door and closed it — what should she do? To go into the room and ask whether she could be of use? Her quarrel with Rachel had made any movement now on her part difficult — Rachel might resent her presence —

Someone came into the hall: she saw that it was the doctor. He stood, looking about him, as though he were searching for someone, and Lizzie went up to him —

"Doctor, please tell me — I'm staying in the house — is there anything — anything at all — that I can do?"

The doctor was tall, thin, black, like an elongated crow.

"Ah yes — no, I think there is nothing for the moment — there are two of us here — we instantly wired to London and the London men should be here if they catch the seven o'clock in an hour and a half. Lady Seddon is with her husband."

"There's hope?"

"Oh yes — I think Sir Roderick will live — It's the spine that's damaged."

He seemed to realize Miss Rand's efficiency. This was no ordinary country-house visitor. He went to the hall door and opened it. "I'm waiting for the things from Lewes. I just came on with what I'd got. Yes, the spine ... afraid will never be able to get about again — such a strong fellow too."

"There's nothing I can do?"

"Nothing anyone can do for the moment. Lady Seddon's taking it wonderfully, but she'll want you later. I advise you to get some quiet in the next hour—it's afterwards that they'll need your help——"

Lizzie went up to her room and lay down on her bed. She did not light the candles, but lay there in the darkness striving to compel some order out of the turmoil that rioted in her brain—her first thought was of Roddy. Roddy had always been to her the supreme type of animal spirits and vigour—that had been, above everything else, what he stood for. That he should have been struck down like this!

The cruelty, the irony of it! Much better that he should die than be compelled to lie on his back for the rest of his life—anything better for him than that—

If he died Rachel would be free. Lizzie faced that thought quite calmly! her quarrel with Rachel seemed to be now very, very long ago, something distant and remote, something whose very conditions had been torn asunder and flung aside—

As she lay there tenderness for Rachel came sweeping about her—"She must want someone now—she's so young and so ignorant—never had any crisis like this to deal with—hard for this to happen to him just after she'd thought those things ... that must be terrible for her.... Oh! she'll need someone now."

Something reminded Lizzie of other things, of Francis Breton, of Rachel's words, of Lizzie's anger, then—

"Ah, but that's all so long ago. It doesn't seem to count. There are things more important than all of that. What will she do now? Perhaps she still hates me—won't let me come near her—it's my own fault after all; I kept away for so long, wouldn't let her come near me. Oh! but she must have someone to help her!"

After a while Lizzie thought—"She won't be practical—she won't know the things that ought to be done—I'll wait a little and then I'll go."

Then she slept. She awoke with a clear active brain; she felt as though she could be awake now for weeks—a tremendous energy filled her....

She left her room and at the turn of the passage met a thick-set clean-shaven man whom she knew for Cramp—one of the most famous of the London doctors, a man whom she had sometimes seen with Christopher at the Portland Place house.

She stopped him—"I'm Miss Rand, Doctor—Lady Adela's secretary—we've met in London—I want you to tell me how I can help."

He shook hands with her, eyeing her with approval—

"Why, yes, of course—How do you do, Miss Rand? Yes, you're just the sort we want. For the moment Lady Seddon's my chief anxiety—she's borne up splendidly so far, but now I am a little afraid. I've got her to go and lie down—would you go to her, Miss Rand? Just be with her a little and let me know if anything happens——"

"Sir Roderick?"

"Pretty bad, I'm afraid—He'll live, I think—afraid will never run about, though, again."

Lizzie made her way to Rachel's bedroom. She paused outside the door. This was the very hardest thing that she had ever, in all her life, had to do. If Rachel were to repulse her now it would surely be the final absolute proof that she was of no use, no use to anyone in this whole wide world.

She knocked on the door and went in. "Who's that?"

"It's I—Lizzie."

The room was dark, but she saw that Rachel was lying on the bed—she went up to her—Rachel did not move.

"I came," Lizzie said, "to see whether I could help—if I could do anything——"

Rachel said nothing—

"If you'd rather—if you don't want to see me, of course just say...."

Rachel turned over and Lizzie heard her say—"I did it—I wanted him—it was my fault—it was my fault."

Lizzie knelt down beside the bed. "Rachel dear, you mustn't think that. It was nothing to do with anyone. But you can help him now, Rachel—He'll want you, he'll need you now as he's never wanted anyone."

Rachel gave a bitter cry—Her hand touched Lizzie's, then she flung up her arm, caught Lizzie's neck, drew her towards her, put both her arms around her and held her, held her as though she would never let her go.

BOOK III
RODDY

CHAPTER I
REGENT'S PARK—BRETON AND LIZZIE
"Yes," said Mrs. Bright, "he missed it all the time."

"Missed what?" asked Miss Rankin.

"'Is good luck," sighed Mrs. Bright.—Henry Galleon.

I

Francis Breton had known, during the weeks that preceded his letter to Rachel, torture that became to him at last so personal that he felt deliberate malignant agency behind its ingenious devices.

At first it had seemed that that wonderful hour with Rachel would satisfy his needs for a long time to come; he had only, when life was hard, dull, colourless, monotonous, to recall it—to see again her movements, to hear her voice, to remember to the last and tiniest detail the things that she had said, to feel that clutch of her hand upon his coat, and instantly he was inflamed, exultant.

So, for a time, it was. Into every moment of his daily life he worked this scene—Rachel was always with him, never, for a single instant, did he doubt that, in some fashion or another, she was coming to him. He had purchased an interest in some little business that had to do, for the most part, with candles, and down to the City now every morning he went. The candles prospered in a small but steady fashion and he found them of a more thrilling and romantic interest than he would once have believed possible. He had always known that he had a business head and now that his life was equable and regular he was astonished at the useful man that he was becoming.

He liked the men with whom he worked, he found that some of his friends of the old days sought him out ... he was assured that he had only to wait for the death of his grandmother for his restoration to the Beaminster bosom.

He was, during these first weeks, tranquil, almost happy, feeling that Mrs. Pont and the rest were, with every hour, passing more surely from his world, nourishing always, like hoarded treasure, his consciousness of Rachel....

Then a faint, a very faint restlessness crept upon him. The repetition of those precious moments was growing dry; from the very frequency of their recounting came impatience. His assurance that she would, ultimately, come to him grew chill.

He needed now something more tangible, and gradually there grew with him the conviction that she would write. She had said, very clearly and distinctly, that she would not—but, if she cared as he knew that she did, then this silence must be as impossible for her as for himself.

His state of mind now was that he expected a letter. When he came back from the City at half-past six or seven he expected to find lying there on the green tablecloth, the letter—In the morning his man appeared with a jug of hot water in one hand and the letters in the other—There, one of those tantalizing, mysterious envelopes, must be the letter.

At first disappointment was reassured with "Oh! it will be there to-morrow." But as the days passed and the silence grew the torture developed. Now after that first search in the morning, after that swift sharp glance to the green tablecloth came physical pain—sickened heavy drooping of the spirits when the world looked one vast deserted plain of monotonous dullness, when the hours and hours and days and days that yet remained to life seemed intolerable in their dreary multitude.

He would go to bed early in order that the morning letters might come the sooner; he fled home from the City, his heart beating like a drum, as he mounted his stairs.

Only one line, one line, would have been sufficient. It needed only the reassurance that she thought of him, that she still cared ... such a short letter would have given him all the comfort he needed.

The need for some sign came as much from his impatience with the whole situation as from his love for Rachel, but this, because he always saw himself as a fine coloured centre of some passionate crisis, he naturally did not perceive. His whole idea of Rachel was, as the days passed, increasingly a picture that was far enough from reality—On the one side Rachel—on the other side his restoration to his family ... now as he waited it seemed to him that he was in danger of losing both the one thing and the other.

There was nothing that so speedily drove Breton to frenzy as enforced inaction.

282

The Duchess of Wrexe

After all, they had been together so little —

Breton was cursed with his imagination. All his instability of character came from his imagination. He looked ahead and saw such wonderful events, he knew why people did this or that; he could see so clearly what would happen did he act in such and such a way.... He traced future action through many hazardous windings into a safe, fair Haven, and for the sake of the Haven embarked on the preliminary dangers — discovered, of course, too late, that the Haven was a dream. He saw Rachel now, sitting alone, thinking of him, loving him, forcing herself to be fair to her blockhead of a husband, feeling at last that she could endure it no longer, and so writing! or he saw her falling in love with that same blockhead, forgetting everyone and everything else.

In all of this his grandmother played her part. He was aware that behind all the attraction that he had had for Rachel was the consciousness that he was a rebel against the Duchess — they were rebels together — that, he knew, was the way that she thought of it.

He was aware, however, that he was a rebel only because he was forced to be one. Let his grandmother hold out her old arms to him and into them he would run! He would be restored to the family — horribly he wanted it! The spirit with which he had returned to England was one of hot vengeance that would, indeed, have suited the finest of Rachel's moods, but that spirit had, he knew, subtly changed — Here then, with regard to Rachel, he felt a traitor — Would she come to him, why then he would do anything for her even to pulling the Duchess's nose — but if she would not come to him, why then he would rather that the Beaminsters should take him to themselves and make him one of them.

But he felt — although he had no tangible arguments to support his feeling — that the old lady was "round the corner" — "she knows, you bet, all about things — what I'd give for just one talk with her.... I believe we'd be friends — —"

His weakness of character came, as he himself knew, from his inability to allow life to stay at a good safe dull level. "To-day's dull — Something must happen before evening; I must make it happen," and then he would go and do something foolish —

London excited him — the lighted shops, the smell of food and flowers and women and leather and tobacco, the sky — signs flashing from space to space, the carts and omnibuses, the shouts and cries and sudden silences, the confused life of the place so that you could never say, "This is London," but could only, in retrospect say, "Ah, that must have been London," and still know that you had failed to grasp its secret.

The dirt and shabbiness and lack of plan and good humour and crime and indecency and priggishness—its life!

Many things out of all this glory called him—racing, women, drink, the gutter one minute, the stars the next—from them all he held himself aloof because of Rachel ... and Rachel meanwhile perhaps did not care.

As Christmas approached he became utterly obsessed by this one thought— that he must have a letter. His obsession had been able, during these weeks, to clutch the tighter in that he had seen nothing of Lizzie Rand. Throughout the autumn he had encountered her very seldom—

Ever since that night in the summer when he had taken her to the theatre she had avoided him, and he decided that she had been shocked at his confession about Rachel—"You never know about women—I shouldn't have thought that would have shocked her—But there it is; you never can tell." Lizzie had been very good for him; he missed her now. He would tackle her, he said, one day.

Then not only with every day, but with every hour the torture grew. He avoided Christopher, because Christopher might see things. His work faded like mist from before him—He could not sleep, but lay on his back thinking of what she would say if she did write, whether she were thinking of him— how she found his own silence and what she felt about it.

Then he heard the astonishing news that Lizzie Rand had gone down to Seddon to stay.... At first he thought that he would write to her and beg her to find out for him all that she could as to Rachel's mind.

But Lizzie's avoidance of him checked him there—if she had been shocked at his just telling her, why then she would not be likely to help him now—No, that would not be fair to Rachel....

It occurred to him then that Rachel had asked Lizzie in order that she might speak of him, have with her someone who could tell her about his daily life, and so, without breaking her word, yet be in some kind of communication with him—

Soon this became with him a certainty. It assured him that her patience was exhausted and that she would forgive, and more than forgive, a letter from him.

He wrote—then in an agony would have snatched it back again, and yet was glad that the post had taken it from him. He had broken his word, and shown himself for the miserable poor creature that he was. She would never trust him again, but surely now she would write were it only to dismiss him for ever.

He waited and the agony once again grew phantasmal in its terrors; then swiftly came word first that Roddy Seddon had been flung from his horse and was hovering between life and death, then that he would not die, but— "Paralysis of the spine—always have to lie on his back, I'm afraid" (this from Christopher)—then, finally this note:

"Seddon Court,

Near Lewes,

Sussex.

Dear Mr. Breton,

I have to come up to London next Tuesday for the day—I shall return here that same evening. I have a message for you. Could we have tea together that afternoon—or what do you say to a walk in Regent's Park? Perhaps we could talk there more easily—I'll meet you at the entrance to the Botanical Gardens about 3.30 unless I hear from you.

Yours sincerely,

E. Rand."

II

The effect upon him of Roddy's accident was indescribable. He was sorry, terribly sorry—dreadful for a man whose whole interests are in physical things to be laid on his back, like this, for ever. Surely it would be better for him to die, and then, at that, sober thought would forsake him—He did not wish Seddon to die, but around the possibility of it, always turning, wheeling, his mind fluttered.

He did not know what Lizzie would have to say to him, but, at his heart, he expected triumph—with so little encouragement, he would wait so faithfully—

It was a cold windy afternoon of early spring and up to the gates of the Botanical Gardens little eddies came sweeping: twigs and dust and pieces of paper tossing, under a grey sky, beneath branches that creaked and strained; Breton stood there impatiently; he was ten minutes before his time; this biting windy world took from him his confidence ... a dirty little brown dog walked round and round, wagging, now and again, a pessimistic tail.

There at last she was, coming, as orderly and neat as ever, up the road; her grey dress, her little shining shoes, her hair that no breeze could disturb, her expression as though she were ready for anything and would be surprised at nothing—these all, to-day, irritated him. Good heavens! was she so surely tied to her typewriter that she could understand nothing of the emotions that an ordinary human being might be feeling? Had she no imagination? Because she had never herself known sentiment about anyone alive was it beyond her to consider what others might encounter?

Breton would have preferred any other ambassador in this affair than the neat, efficient Miss Rand, forgetting that there had been a time when he had chosen her as his one and only confidante.

"How do you do, Mr. Breton?" she said, giving him her little gloved hand.

"It's just struck—I was a little early," he answered, feeling confused and hating himself for his confusion—

"Let's go round to the left here and turn over the bridge and then out past the Zoo and back—That makes quite a good round."

"Yes"—he said.

"I chose the Park because I thought that we could talk better—We might have been interrupted at home."

He caught then a little tremor in her voice and was grateful for it. She did feel a little that this was important for him; she sympathized perhaps more than he should have expected.

"Let's come straight to the point, Miss Rand," he said, "you have a message for me."

She nodded, felt in the pocket of her dress and produced an envelope, which she gave him.

"She thought it better that I should give it you like this because then I could say something as well—something she had asked me to say——"

His hand trembled as he saw the writing on the envelope—"Francis Breton, Esq., 24 Saxton Square"—During what months and months he had longed for that handwriting and how often had he imagined that letter lying, just as it lay now, in his hand—

He read it, Lizzie walking gravely at his side—

"This letter is not easy to write and you must realize that and forgive me if I have not put things properly. These last weeks have all made such a demand on me that I'm tired out....

"I said once, Francis dear, that I would not write to you until I meant to come to you. Now I have broken my word—This is to tell you that everything, anything, that we have felt for one another must be ended, now and for ever.

"Don't think that I am angry with you for writing to me. Perhaps I should have been, but I understood—Only now all my life must be always, entirely, devoted to my husband. That is now all that I live for. I feel as though in some way I had been responsible for the disaster; at any rate his bravery and pluck are wonderful and it is a small thing that I can do to make his life as easy as I can, but it will take the whole of me.

"Perhaps after a time we shall meet—one day be friends—I can't look ahead or look back; I only know that I am now absolutely, entirely, my husband's—

"Don't hate me for this—it was taken out of our hands. I've asked Lizzie Rand to give you this. She knows everything and it would make me happy to think that you two had become great friends."

They had crossed the little bridge, left behind them the strange birds that chattered beneath it, and had passed into the wide green spaces, often given up to cricket or football, now empty of any human being—the Zoological Gardens, a deserted bandstand, a fringe of trees on which the first tiny leaves were showing; above them the grey sky had broken into blue and white, the cloud shaped with ribs and fleecy softness like a huge wing stretching above them from horizon to horizon.

Over the two of them, so tiny on that broad expanse, this wing brooded tenderly, gravely —

Breton had crushed the letter in his hand and stood looking in front of him, but seeing nothing. His one thought was that he had been brutally treated, — she had simply, without a thought, without a care, flung him aside.

He had, of course, known that this accident to her husband must, for a time, hold her, but now, in this fashion, she had passed on without hesitation — leaving him anywhere, anyhow; was it so long ago that she had said to him that, whether she came to him or no she would always love him? Had she already forgotten that kiss, that moment when she had clung to him, held to him?

He stood there, filled with self-pity. This restraint, this self-discipline all done for her and now all useless. It was not wanted; he was not wanted....

Had she only preserved some relationship, told him to wait, assured him that he meant something to her, anything but this —

But there was greater pain at Breton's heart than thought of Rachel brought him. To every man comes in due time the instant of revelation; it had flashed before Breton now.

He saw that his relationship with Rachel was at an end, utterly — However he might delude himself that, in his soul, he knew. There had been a moment when they had met and the moment had passed. But he saw more than this. He saw that he was a man to whom life had always been a succession of moments — moments flashing, stinging, flying, gone — he, always, helpless to grasp and hold.

Had he, on that day, been strong, held Rachel, conquered her, made her his.... He was weak through the fine things in him as surely as through the base — His ideals forced his purpose to tremble as often as his regrets....

Standing there, he faced himself and saw that, whether for good or evil, Life for him had always been evasive, fluid, a thing grasped at but never caught.

Rachel was not for such as he —

Lizzie had watched him and her face had grown very tender—"I know I'm a nuisance just now," she said—"it hasn't, naturally, been a very pleasant thing for me to have to do—but I thought that I could tell you a little about her—I've seen her through all of this."

He strode along fiercely, his eyes staring in front of him; he looked, she thought, like a boy who had been forbidden some longed-for pleasure; she found it difficult to keep pace with him.

"She's so very, very young," Lizzie went on, "I expect you forget that—she's filled, above everything else, with a determination to express her own individuality, a protest, you know, against its having been squashed by her family.

"Anything that helps her to express it she seizes on. You helped her—she seized on you. Now all her heart is stirred by this disaster to her husband, the most active person she's ever known absolutely helpless, so now that has seized her. She can't have two things in her mind at once—that's where her troubles come from—she cares for you. You'll always be something to her that no one else can ever be, and oh! it's so much better, so much, much better, than if you'd gone off, made a mess of it all, spoilt all your beautiful ideas of one another."

The thrill in her voice made him, even though he was intensely concerned with his own wrongs and losses, consider her. What Lizzie Rand was this? It flung him back, almost against his will, as though he hated to throw over all the ideas he had formed of her, to that first meeting when they had stood at the window and looked out on the grey square and he had called it the Pool. Then he had suspected her of emotion and sentiment; it was afterwards, when he had made her his wise Counsellor and common-sense Adviser, that he had thought of her as unemotional.

He felt now that he had been treating her rather badly. He stopped abruptly and looked down at her; there was something in her earnest gaze at him, something rather nervous and hesitating that did not belong at all to the efficient Miss Rand.

"It is good of you, Miss Rand, to have come and given me this note. I'm finding it all rather difficult at the moment, as I'm sure you'll understand. I'd better go off somewhere by myself a bit, I think, but it was good of you." He broke off and stared desolately about him. He was not very far from tears, she thought.

She too remembered their first meeting. She had found him melodramatic then, a little insincere—Now she knew that she had been wrong. He was sincere as a child is sincere; the world was utterly black, was transcendently bright as it was for a child.

She understood him so well—so much better than Rachel. She knew that neither he nor Rachel would ever have had the wisdom to endure that romantic impatience that was in both of them—"They would have been fighting in a week—But I—should know how to deal with him——"

The green park and the brooding sky seemed to join in her tenderness—She had never loved him so surely, so unselfishly as she loved him now.

"Tell me," he said gruffly. "I wrote to her ... did she tell you anything about that?"

"Yes," Lizzie answered—"I don't know what might have happened if he hadn't had the accident.... But as it is, I know she's glad you wrote—She likes to look back on it, but it's on something that died—gone altogether. And it's much, much better so."

"To you," he said, "it may be so."

"Only because through these weeks I've got to know her so well. She's strange—unlike any other woman I've known. Her great charm is that she's so unattainable. Men will always love her for that and sometimes she may think she loves them in return, but no man will ever call the real woman out of her. If she were to have a child, perhaps that would ... but we—all of us— you, I, Dr. Christopher, her husband—all of us who love her will always love her without quite knowing why and without, in the end, her belonging to any one of us.

"I've grown to love her during these last weeks and I've thought it was because I was sorry for her and admired her pluck—but it isn't that really— It's simply because—well, because—there's something wonderful in her that isn't for any of us."

"Well, you've been very kind, Miss Rand, I shan't forget it. You've said just the thing to put it all straight and clear. I wouldn't do anything now to disturb her or hurt her husband, poor devil ... it must be hell for him ... and it don't anyway matter much what happens to me—it never has done.

"You've been a brick. If you really care to bother about a rotten waster like myself I'll be proud.... Good-bye and thank you— —"

He took her hand and shook it and then was gone, striding off, furiously, towards the trees.

She walked slowly back to Saxton Square.

CHAPTER II
THE DUCHESS MOVES
"Fear of the loss of power has more to do with disasters in the history of
nations than any other motive."

James Anthony Froude.

I

Trouble invaded the strongholds of 104 Portland Place that winter: The
Duchess was not so well ... no evasions, whether above or below stairs,
could conceal the harsh truth. The Duchess was not so well....

To the bewildered mind of Lady Adela the horrid succession of disasters
that the winter had provided no other years could equal. It had all begun,
she often fancied, from the day of Rachel's coming out, from the ball, or
even, although for this she could not find a real excuse, from that visit to the
Bond Street Picture Gallery. It was on that afternoon, Lady Adela well
remembered, that there had first come to her those strange, treacherous
thoughts about her mother that had, afterwards, as they had grown stronger
and more formidable, changed life for her. Yes, it had seemed that, with
Rachel's appearance before the world, disaster to the Beamister house had
appeared also. Her mother's illness, the War, perpetual rumours of Rachel's
unsatisfactory marriage, the uncomfortable presence of Frank Breton, the
horrible disaster to poor Roddy—how they trooped before Lady Adela's
eyes! Finally, more terrible than all of them, was the complete destruction of
the old fiction, the old terror, the old submission. Lady Adela did not now
dare to look into her mind because of the horrible things that she found
there.

Roddy's accident had had the most terrible effect upon the Duchess. Only
Christopher could really tell how Her Grace had taken it, but throughout the
house, it was understood that the effect of it had been serious. "Wouldn't
give her long now," said Mr. Norris. "What with this War and what not she
was goin' as it was, and now Sir Roderick, as was always, as you might say,
her pet, having this awful disaster—no, I don't give her long."

Adela of course saw nothing of her mother's feelings; she never had been
allowed to see anything of them and she was not allowed now.

The old lady was outwardly as she had ever been, although she spoke less
and, if you watched her, you could see sometimes that her hands were
shaking. She used paint for her cheeks and she rouged her lips. Her love of
fantastic things had grown very much, and, on the little table behind her

chair, there was a row of strange china animals and some Indian dolls with wooden limbs that jangled when you touched them.

But Adela was no longer afraid of her mother. Stimulate it as she would, force upon herself her sensations of the days when she had been afraid, as she did, still the terror would not now confront her. There had been a dreadful scene when the Duchess had been told that her daughter was acting on the same committee as Mrs. Bronson, the dazzling American ... a terrible scene ... but Adela had come through it without a tremor—it had not affected her at all. "It isn't that I've changed much either. I'm just as nervous of other things—I'm just the same coward...."

Perhaps it was, a little, that the war had altered one's values—So many Beaminster necessities were not quite so necessary—

Certainly John felt the same, and the one consolation to Adela, through all this horrible time, was that she had grown nearer to John than she had ever been to anyone—John and she had been attacked by the Real World, both of them at the same moment, and they did find comfort, at this terrifying crisis, in being together.

But all Adela's energy was directed towards concealing from her mother that there was any change at all—"She must think that things are just the same, exactly the same. She mustn't ever know that ... well, that ..."

She could not put it into words. Her Grace's illness was never alluded to by any member of the household.

There came word, at the beginning of March, that Roddy had been moved up to London, that Rachel had taken a little house in York Terrace overlooking Regent's Park, that Roddy was wonderfully cheerful, suffered pain at times, but was, on the whole marvellous—

Two or three days after this news when Christopher arrived at 104 on his usual morning visit Lord John met him in the hall.

"I say, come in here a minute," he said, leading the way into his own little smoking-room—Lord John was fatter, scarcely now as rubicund, as shining as he had been—as neat and clean as ever, but there were lines on his forehead, and in his eye, that glance of surprise that had always been there had advanced into one of alarm—

"What the devil is life going to do, what horrible trick is it up to next?" he seemed to say—

"Look here, Christopher," he brought out, when the door was closed. "There's the devil and all to pay. My mother declares this morning that she's going to pay a visit to Roddy!"

"Well?" Christopher seemed amused.

"But ... Good heavens!" John was aghast—"She hasn't stirred out of her room for thirty years! She ... she ... it'll kill her!"

"Oh! no, it won't—" Christopher answered, "not if she really means to do it. Of course she can't walk much—she won't have to—We can get her downstairs, and Roddy's room in York Terrace is on the ground floor—We'll have to see she doesn't catch cold—She'll have to choose a warm day."

"She says she's going this afternoon!" said Lord John, still overwhelmed by this amazing development.

"Well, to-day won't do any harm— —"

"Are you sure?"

"Quite sure. The danger with your mother has always been to stop her inclinations. Indulge 'em all the time if you can, let her say what she wishes, do what she wishes. If you were to carry her out of doors against her will, why it would do a great deal of harm indeed—but if she wants to go she'll see that she's up to it. It may be the best thing for her. She could have gone out heaps of times in the last thirty years if she'd wished to!"

Lord John rubbed his forehead—

"It's a great relief to hear you say that, Christopher. I didn't know how we were going to get out of it. She was so determined this morning— —"

He broke off—"You're sure it won't do any harm?" he said again.

"I'm sure," said Christopher.

"There's something," Lord John went on again, "dreadfully on my mother's mind—She seems to feel that, in some way or other, she was responsible for his accident. I can't get at the bottom of it all and of course she won't tell me—she never tells me things. Perhaps you can get at it. I saw Rachel yesterday."

"Yes?"

"She's very fair about it all. Must be having a very hard time. She was glad to see me, I think, but—" he added a little wistfully—"I've never been anything to her since her marriage.

"She just seemed not to want me after that, and I'd been a good deal to her before. When one's getting old, Christopher, we old bachelors, we begin to notice that nobody wants us very much."

Christopher looked at him—Yes, John Beaminster had changed in the last year. Had he himself, he wondered, also changed?

"Yes," he said, smiling. "But I've been an old bachelor, Beaminster, for years and years and I see no likelihood of your ever being one. You get younger with every year, I believe."

"This accident to Roddy," John said slowly, as though he were thinking it all out, "has upset us all. It seems so terrible, happening to him ... much worse for him ... and then Rachel—But look here, I know you've got to go up to my mother, I won't keep you a minute—But there's a thing I've got to talk to you about—It's been on my conscience now for ages.... I've not known what to do ... at last I've made up my mind."

John Beaminster had made up his mind to do something that he hated! To Christopher perhaps more than to anyone else in the world this was a revelation of the most vital, the most moving interest—He had known John for so long, seen him struggling behind screens and curtains, hugging to himself the happy knowledge that to the very end he would be able to keep life from getting at him, and now behold! Life had got at him, wag clutching him by the throat.

"It's about Frank"—at last he desperately brought out "I've made up my mind. I must go and see him—now, perhaps whilst mother is—is still suffering from the effects of Roddy's accident it wouldn't be wise perhaps to have him here actually in the house—But something must be done.... Adela agrees."

Adela agrees! Well, if the old woman upstairs.... Christopher was moved, as he had lately been often moved, by a swift stirring of pathos.

"You see, this War has upset us all so, has made one feel differently — And then he really does seem to have changed, been as quiet as anything all this time, and I hear that he's working at something sensible down in the City. I must go and see him — —"

Then they hadn't heard, Christopher knew, of any rumours about Rachel and Francis.

Perhaps there were no rumours, perhaps only in the mind of the old lady.... But then let John say a word to her about this visit to Breton and out she would come with it all.

"Yes, Beaminster," Christopher said. "Of course I'm delighted. It's just what I hoped would happen, but perhaps, as your mother has been rather upset lately it would be just as well to say nothing to her...."

"Quite so...." John looked away, out of the window — Poor John!

Christopher held out his hand, and John took it and for a moment they stood there, then Christopher went upstairs.

II

Dorchester no longer asserted that her mistress was "better than she had ever been" — Since that terrible morning when Dr. Christopher had broken the news of Sir Roderick's accident Dorchester had made no pretence about anything. This was the time that must, she had always known, one day arrive, but what she had not known was that it would be quite like this.

She was a woman of some imagination; moreover, were there one person in the world who touched her heart, then was it her mistress; she had penetrated, she thought, some of the strange secrets and fantasies of that old woman's soul, and it seemed that now, in these later days, she was at last in touch with every motive and grim artifice that her mistress adopted —

But no — since that terrible day at the beginning of the year Dorchester had lost touch, was left, bewildered, at a loss, as though she were suddenly in the service of some stranger.

She had known that nothing more terrible could happen to her mistress than this — When she heard it she said to herself, "This will kill her — bound to —" She had known too that her mistress would not flinch, outwardly, and that to the ordinary observer there would be no sign, but the thing for which she had not been prepared was this silence, a silence so profound and yet so eloquent that one could obtain from it no clue, could discern no visible wound, but daily, almost hourly, as she sat there, change was at work ... she was dying before their eyes—

What Dorchester did not know was that the Duchess had been aware, for a long time, that this was to occur, if not exactly this, why, then, something like it.

All through that autumn she had sat there waiting—the War, the rebellion of her children—it only needed that disaster should overtake Roddy and the circle was complete.

She did not doubt that it was because he had married Rachel that this had happened to him, and she might have prevented his marriage to Rachel had she wished.

The girl had now for her sitting there in her room the fatal inevitability of some hostile spirit. She saw all her past years as a duel with this girl, the one soul in rebellion against hers. Rachel had taken everything from her; she had first stirred Adela and John into rebellion, she had encouraged Francis Breton, she had destroyed Roddy ... she rose, before the old woman's eyes, black, titanic, sweeping, with great dark wings, across the horizon.

The Duchess did not in so many words state that Rachel had flung her husband from his horse and then watched whilst his body was dragged along the stones, but, in some way, the girl had plotted it.

The old woman had indeed during these last months suffered from visions. There were days when her brain was as clear as it had ever been and on these days she thought more of Roddy than of Rachel, ached to be with him, longed to comfort him and make life bearable for him, cursed whatever fate it was that had ordained that upon him of all people such a burden should have fallen. Then there were other days when the old china dragons seemed more real than Dorchester, when shapes and sizes altered in an instant, when the cushion at her feet was swollen like a mountain, when she seemed floating through space, looking down upon houses, cities, mountains, when only like a jangling chain upon which everything hung, ran her hatred of her granddaughter.

On such a day if Rachel had come to her and she had been alone with her, she would have wished the dragons to devour her, would have urged the silver Indian snake on the little black table to have strangled her. On such a day she would sit hour after hour and wonder what she could do to her granddaughter....

It was upon one of her clear days that it flashed upon her that she would go and see Roddy. Beyond the actual excitement of visiting Roddy there was the determination to show the world what she still could do. Doubtless they were saying out there that she was bedridden now, ill, helpless, dying even ... well, she would show them.

For thirty years she had not been outside her door—now, because she wished it, she would go.

She said nothing to Adela about this—she saw Adela now as seldom as possible. She told John on the morning of the day itself—on that same morning she told Christopher.

She told him sitting in her chair, with her cheeks painted and her white fingers covered with rings—

"I'm going to pay a visit—this afternoon, Christopher." She had expected opposition—she was a little disappointed when he said—

"Yes, so I've already heard this morning. I think it's an excellent thing—the day's warm. You'll have to be carried downstairs, you know——"

"You and Norris can do that. I won't have anyone else."

"Very well, I shall have to come with you——"

"Yes—You can talk to my granddaughter."

"It's thirty years...."

"Yes—The last time was Old Judy Bonnings's reception. They're all dead—all of 'em—D'you remember, Dorchester?"

"Yes—Your Grace—Very well."

Dorchester expressed no surprise—Anything was better than that silence of the last months. Moreover she had trusted Christopher. She had often been amazed at the knowledge that he showed of her mistress's temperament, would allow her temper, her imperious self-will indulgence one day and on another would control them absolutely. He knew what he was doing....

The picture that she presented, however, when helped downstairs by the pontifical Norris and Christopher! the house, with the decorous watchfulness of some large, solemn, and immensely authoritative policeman, surveying her descent, her own little bird-like face, showing nothing but a fine assumption of her splendid appearance before the public, after thirty years, she thus, once again, was saluted by Portland Place! Black furs of Lady Adela's surrounded, enfolded her, and from out of them her eyes haughtily but triumphantly surveyed a crossing-sweeper, two small children with their nurse, a messenger boy, and Roller the coachman. To Roller this must have been the dramatic moment of a somewhat undramatic career, but stout and imperial upon his box his body was held, rigid, motionless, and his large stupid eyes gazed in front of him at the trees and the light cloud-flecked March sky, and moved neither to the right nor to the left.

She was placed in the carriage—Christopher got in beside her and they moved off. He was interested to see the effect that this breaking into the world would have upon her. He felt himself a little in the position of showman and was glad that he had a spring afternoon of gleaming sunshine and a suggestion of budding trees and shrubs in the Portland Crescent garden to provide for her. They were held up by traffic as they crossed the Marylebone Road; drays, hansoms, bicycles passed—there was a stir of voices and wheels, somewhere in the park a band was playing.

He looked at her and saw that she paid no heed, but sat back in the dim shadow, her eyes, he thought, closed. She was, at that instant, more remote from him and all that he represented than she had ever been—Curiously he was moved, just then, by a consciousness of her personality that exceeded anything that he had ever felt in her before.

"Yes, she must have been tremendous," he thought. And then he wondered of what she was thinking, so quiet, and yet, from her very silence, sinister, and then—how could he have not considered this before? What was she going to say to Roddy?

At this, the dark carriage was suddenly, for him, as flashing with life and circumstance as though it had been the florid circle of some popular music-hall—What would she say to Roddy?

He knew her for the most selfish of all possible old women: unselfish only perhaps if Roddy were concerned, but there also, if some question of her power moved her, ruthless. He had traced the windings of her queer intertwisted brain with some accuracy—He knew also that the coloured unreal state that her closed, fantastic life (resembling, you might say, life inside a Chinese puzzle) had brought upon her led her now to see Rachel as arch-antagonist in every step and movement of her day.

She would not wish to make Roddy unhappy, she might persuade herself that to hint to him of Rachel's infidelity would be to put him on his guard—she might say that it was not fair that Rachel should not be pulled up....

Christopher himself could not tell how far this affair with Breton had gone....

During that short time it seemed to him that a crisis, that had been building up around him, here, there, for months, for years perhaps, had leapt upon him and that in some way he must deal with it.

Even whilst he struggled with the thoughts that were sweeping upon him now from every side, they were at the house—As he stepped out of the carriage he felt that he was before a locked door, that the safety of many persons depended upon his opening it, that he could not find the key.

"Lady Seddon was out. Sir Roderick was alone——" The Duchess was half assisted, half carried into the house.

III

The Duchess's feelings were indeed confused as she was helped into Roddy's room, placed in a large easy chair opposite to him and at last left alone with him.

Enough of itself to disturb her was the fact that now for the first time for thirty years she was able to examine some room different from her own—A large, high white-walled room with wide windows that displayed the park, sporting prints on the walls, antlers over the fireplace, a piano in one corner, a large bowl of primroses on the piano, some boxing-gloves and two old swords over the door, a wooden case with thin rosewood drawers and "Birds' Eggs" in gold letters upon it, a round table near the sofa upon which Roddy was lying and on the table a photograph of Rachel—

All these things her sharp old eyes noticed before she allowed them to settle upon Roddy—

His quiet, almost humorous "Well, Duchess," set, quite concisely, the note for this conversation. Not for either of them was it to betray any consciousness that this meeting of theirs was in any way out of the ordinary.

The Duchess of Wrexe

Formerly it had been the ebullient, vigorous Roddy who had brought his vigour to renew her fierce old age; now that old age must be brought to him—

The Beaminsters did not show surprise at anything at all; had she come from her grave to visit him he would have greeted her with his quiet "Well, Duchess"—his life was broken in pieces, but she was not to offer any comment on that either.

She was exhausted even by that little drive, and that little passage from door to door, so she just lay back in her chair for a little while and looked at him.

His body was covered with a rug; his hands, still brown and large and clumsy, were folded on his lap; he was wonderfully tidy, brushed and cleaned, it seemed to her, as though he were always expecting a doctor or a visitor or were performed upon by some valet or other, simply, poor dear, that the time might be filled. His cheeks were paler of course and his face thinner, but it was in his eyes—his large, simple, singularly ungrown-up eyes she had always considered them—that the great change lay—

They smiled across at her with the same genial good temper that they had always presented to her. But indeed she could never call them "ungrown-up" again. Roddy Seddon had grown up indeed since she had seen him last; she knew now, as she faced the experience and, above all, the strength that those eyes now presented for her, that she had a new spirit to encounter.

Yes—he "had had a horrible time," but she was wise enough, at that instant, to realise that the "horrible time" had drawn character out of him that she, at least, had never, for an instant, suspected.

The old woman was moved so that she would have liked to have tottered to his sofa, to have caught his hands in her old dry ones, to have kissed him, to have smoothed his hair—but she sat quietly in her chair, recovered her breath and, grimly, almost saturninely, smiled at him.

"Well, Roddy," she said, "how are you?"

"I'm quite splendid. Play patience like a professor, can knit five mufflers in a week and am learning two foreign languages—But indeed how rippin' to see you here. I've spent a lot o' time on this old sofa wonderin' how you and I were goin' to see one another."

301

"Have you?" She was pleased at that—"Well, you see, I have managed it and quite easily too, not so bad after thirty years. My good Roddy, you of all people to tumble off a horse! What were you about?"

"Oh! it was simple enough." Roddy's eyes worked swiftly to the park and then back again. "I was worried, you see—my thoughts were wandering, and the old mare just tripped into a hole, pitched and flung me—I fell on a heap o' stones, they knocked the sense out of me, the horse was frightened and went dashin' along with me tangled up in her. All came of my thoughts wanderin'—But you know, Duchess, I've had heaps of accidents, heaps and heaps, every kind of thing has happened to me, but it's never been serious— always the most wonderful luck. Well, for once it left me."

"Poor old Roddy."

"Yes, it was 'poor old Roddy,' I can tell you, for the first six weeks—thought I simply couldn't stand it, had serious thoughts of kickin' out altogether, seemed to me everythin' had gone ... it's wonderful, though, the way you pick up. And then everyone's been so tremendous, and as for Rachel!"

He heaved a great sigh—Her eyes half closed, then she looked very carefully at the photograph on the little round table. "That's a good photograph of her you've got."

"Yes—it's my favourite. But you, Duchess, tell me about yourself. You must be in magnificent form to have planned this great adventure."

She told him about herself—only a little, all very carefully chosen—She was fancying, as she sat there, that she was again playing the great diplomatist before the world.

This expedition had greatly excited her, it had fired her blood, and just now she felt that she was equal to taking up her old life of thirty years ago, playing once more a tremendous part, beating Mrs. Bronson and others of her kind straight off the field.

She had a great plan now of coming often to see Roddy and of gaining a very great influence over him; she did not say to herself in so many words that she could not bear to think of him lying there helpless and therefore completely in Rachel's power, but that is what in reality stirred her.

Roddy's helplessness—the sight and sound of it—drove higher that flame that had burnt now for so long before the altar at which Rachel was, one day, to be sacrificed. "She may come and go as she pleases. He lies here—He can do nothing. He can know nothing of her movements—He's in her hands—after what I know...."

What did she know? The acquaintanceship of Breton's man-servant and Dorchester had produced the fact of Rachel's visit, of letters—but wasn't that all? Amongst the strange mingled visions that now crossed and recrossed her brain it were hard to say what were real and what phantasmal. But granted that the two of them had come together at all, why then it was plain enough to anyone who knew them that only one result was possible—Poor Roddy ... her poor Roddy!

But she did not know even now that she intended to tell him anything; her sense of the pain that that revelation would give to him held her, but as the minutes passed her delight at being back once more in this gay, bustling world (yes, she liked its new invigorating noises) the sense of power that she had, and youth, and strength, spun her brain to finest cobwebs of entanglements.

She was glad to be with her Roddy again, it was only fair that, helpless as he was, there should still be someone to guard and protect him ... to protect him, yes!

Her eyes flashed at the photograph.

But for a long time they talked in precisely their old fashion. The War, friends and enemies, victories and defeats, marriages and deaths; Roddy seemed, for a time, the old Roddy.

And then gradually through it all there pushed towards her the consciousness that he was doing it now to please her; more than that, again and again she was aware that some bitter jest, some sharp distraction, some fierce criticism had been turned by him deftly aside—simply rejected with a deftness and a strength that the old Roddy could never have summoned.

Here again then—and it stabbed her there in the midst of her new pride and confidence—was a reminder that her power, her sovereignty had vanished! Was Roddy also to be beyond her influence, Roddy whom she had had at her feet since he was a boy of sixteen?

The photograph smiled across at her—She bent forward, her hand raised a little as though to lend emphasis to her words—"And then you know, Roddy, I'm still troubled with my abominable relation——"

"What! Breton? Why, how's he been behaving?" Roddy's voice was scornful.

"Oh! he's not done anything that I know of—But he's always there—so tiresome to have him so close, and John and Adela have grown so peculiar lately that there's no knowing—They may ask him in to tea one day——"

"Oh no, they won't," said Roddy. "He must be the most awful outsider."

"I wanted to speak about him to you because I thought you might give a word of warning to Rachel——"

"To Rachel?" Roddy's voice was amazed.

"Yes—She's become such a friend of his! Surely you know? That's what makes it so difficult for me—When one's own granddaughter——"

"Rachel! A friend of Breton's! But I didn't know she'd ever spoken to him— Look here, Duchess, you must explain——"

"I thought you must have known. I've often wished to speak to you about it, only Rachel is so difficult and I didn't want to worry you, and it seems especially hard just now——"

"But it doesn't worry me—not a bit. Only tell me—How do you mean that she's a friend of his?"

"Only that she goes to see him, writes to him——"

"Goes to see him——"

"Oh yes—is in complete sympathy——"

"Are you sure?"

"Absolutely. You must ask her."

"I will of course——"

He lay back on his sofa. For a little time there was silence between them. She was filled now with wild regrets. She wished that she had said nothing. His face was hard and old—She wished ... she scarcely knew what she wished; she only knew that suddenly she was tired and would like to go home.

A bell was rung and Christopher was sent for. She would like to have kissed Roddy, but only wagged her bony finger at him —

"Now be a good patient boy and I'll soon come again."

IV

Meanwhile, five minutes before this, Rachel had come in. She was told of the visits, and going swiftly to the little drawing-room upstairs had found Christopher.

She flung her arms around him and kissed him.

"Oh, dear Dr. Chris!"

But he stopped her.

"Quick, Rachel. I may only have a minute.... I've got to speak to you."

Instantly she drew back, her grave eyes watching him and her hands, as of old, nervously moving against her dress.

"What is it?"

"It's just this. The Duchess may ring at any moment — she's been with him a long while. Look here, Rachel, she knows about Breton — that you've been to see him, that you've written to him — —"

"She told you?"

"Yes — long ago — But never mind that now, although I'd have spoken to you of it before if you'd let me — But the only thing that matters is that I believe — I can't of course be sure — but I believe that she's come now to tell Roddy."

Rachel drew a long breath. "Oh!" she said and, stiffly standing there, showed in her eyes the pitch of feeling to which now her grandmother had brought her.

Christopher went on urgently — "I've been praying for you to come in. I hoped you'd have come half an hour ago. There's no time now, but — it's simply this, Rachel dear — tell Roddy everything — —"

She broke in passionately. "You know it's all right, Dr. Chris—you've trusted me?"

"Absolutely," he said gravely. "But it simply is that Roddy mustn't be there imagining things, waiting, wondering.... Perhaps he won't ask you—Perhaps he will—But, anyway, tell him—tell him at once everything...."

The bell rang, he went across to her, kissed her, and then went downstairs.

She stood there waiting, without moving except to strip off, very slowly, her black gloves. Her eyes were fixed upon the door.

She heard the door downstairs open, the stumbling steps; once she caught the Duchess's voice and at that she drew in her breath. Then the hall door closed, but, for a long time afterwards, she stood there without moving.

CHAPTER III
RODDY MOVES

"... But the Red Dwarf, although as malevolent as possible, found that his ill-temper had no effect against true love, which always won in the end, even with quite stupid people."

Grimm's Fairy Tales.

I

It would have been quite impossible for Roddy to have given any clear description of his experiences since the event of his accident. There, surely, like a gleaming sword, that cut his life into two pieces, the fact itself was visible enough, and there floated before him, again and again, the casual canter, the especial view that was before him just then, a view of undulating Downs, somewhere to his left white chalk hollows in grey hills and to his right a blue strip of sea, the wonder that was in his mind about Rachel, his thoughts chasing back over all the incidents of their life together, then suddenly the jerk, his consciousness of falling with the ground rising in a high wall to oppose him, and then darkness.

After that there was nightmare in which pain and Rachel, Rachel and pain, mingled and parted, were confused and then separate, and with them danced shapes and figures, sometimes in a turmoil that was horrible, sometimes in silence that was the most terrible of all. Clear after that first period of misty confusion was the day when he was told his fate.

He had come out from the heart of the more terrible pain—No longer had he to lie, knowing that soon, after another minute's peace, agony would rise before him like a creature with a wet pale malignant face, and then after looking upon him for a moment, would bend down and, with its horrible damp fingers, would twist and turn his bones one against another until the supreme moment came when nothing mattered and no agony, however bad, could touch his indifferent soul.

He was now simply weak, weak, weak—nothing mattered. In his dream he fancied that someone had said that he would never rise from his back again. For days after that it lingered far away from his actual consciousness. Really it had not mattered; something, this dream, that concerned him, but what could concern him except that people should keep quiet and not fuss?

For instance he loved to have Rachel with him, he was miserable were she not there, but at the same time he was conscious that she did fuss, was not quite like Miss Rand.

But of this thing that he had heard he thought nothing. "There's something that I ought to think about. I don't know what it is—One day when I'm stronger I'll look into it."

There came a day when he was stronger, a day, late in January, of a pale wintry sun and watery gleams. They had placed his bed so that he could see his beloved Downs and the little road that ran from their foot out into the village.

On this morning he was wonderfully better—he had slept well, breezes and pleasant scents came through the open window, geese were cackling, a donkey's braying made him laugh "Silly old donkey," he said aloud to no one in particular. Then he was aware of Jacob, sitting bunched into a heap in the middle of the floor, his brown eyes peering anxiously through his hair. At every sound his ears would rise for a moment, but his eyes were fixed upon Roddy.

The dog had been in Roddy's room a good deal during these last weeks, had been wrenched away from it. Roddy found that he was touched by this devotion; Jacob apparently cared more for him than did the other dogs— "Not a bad old thing—Often these mongrels are more human—But, Lord! he is a sight!"

The nurse was sitting sewing by the window. Roddy lay, happily, thinking that now at last that jolly bad pain really did seem to have been left behind. He was immensely, wonderfully better; it would not be long, surely, before he was quite fit again, before he....

Then down it swung, swung like an iron door shutting all the world away from him, inexorable—"Always on your back ... never get up again!"

His hand gripped the bed-clothes.

"Nurse."

"Yes?"

"Tell me—am I dreaming or did someone say something the other day about—about my never being able, well, to toddle again, you know?"

"I'm afraid——"

"Thanks."

He closed his eyes and then summoned all the grit and determination that there was in him to face this fact. He could not face it. It was as though he were struggling up the side of a high slippery rock—up he would struggle, up and up, now he was at the top, down he would slip again—it could not, oh! it could not be true!

It was true. As the days passed grimly in silence, he accepted it. It had always been his creed that in this world there was no place for the maimed and the halt. He was sorry for them, of course, but it was better that they should go; they only occupied room that was intended for lustier creatures.

Well, now he was himself of the halt and maimed—that was ironical, wasn't it? Indeed he would much rather that he had pegged out altogether—better for everybody—but, as things were, he would square things out and see what he could make of it all. Then he saw as, every day, he grew stronger, that he had no resources; everything in his other life, as he now had come to think of it, had depended upon his physical strength, every pleasure, every desire, every ambition had had to do with his body—everything except Rachel.

In his other life half his happiness arose simply from the sense of his physical movement, his consciousness that, as the rivers flowed and the winds blew and the sun blazed, so did he also live and have his being—And with all this, most intimately was his house mingled. That grey building and he grew and moved and developed together; life could never be very terrible for him so long as he had his place to come back to, his place to care for, his fields and his gardens, his horses and his dogs to look after. Now he could do nothing more for it—perhaps one day he would be wheeled about its courts and paths, but oh! with what pitying eyes would it look down upon him, how sorrowfully his gryphons would greet him, with what memories they would confront him!

He could not bear now to look out upon the Downs on the little village path—His bed was moved. A day arrived when he felt that it was all, really, more than he could endure. He was in wild, furious rebellion, surly, sometimes in raging tempers, sometimes sulking from day to day. He cursed all the world. Even Christopher could do nothing with him—

Then upon this there followed a period of silence. He lay there and beyond "Yes" and "No" would answer no one. His eyes stared at the wall. Christopher feared at this time for his sanity.

Suddenly the silence was broken. He must go to London because he could not endure the memories that this place thronged upon him—At the beginning of March he was moved to the house in York Terrace.

II

The little house by the park helped him to construct his new life. The normality that there was in Roddy, the same balance of common sense, fostered his recovery. He was not going to die—Life would be an infernal trouble were he always to be in rebellion against it—he must simply make the best of the conditions. And then, after all, he had Rachel. Rachel had been a heroine during this time, and to his love for her he now clung, passionately, tenaciously, the one thing left to him out of his great catastrophe.

She seemed, during these months, to have thought for nothing else in all the world. She was not so useful in a sick room as Miss Rand—Miss Rand was wonderful—but there were certain moments when she would bend down and kiss him or would look at him or would take his hand, when he wondered whether love for him had not crept into her heart after all.

Funny when he had gone out for his ride on that eventful morning expecting that he had offended her for ever! Well, if his accident had won Rachel for him, it had been worth while!

But there were other days when he knew for a certainty that it was not so, knew that it was pity that moved her; affection too perhaps, but nothing more than affection....

Nevertheless he hoped that this might be the beginning of something else; he would lie for hours looking out at the park and creating visions.

He made now something tolerable of his life. People showed a wonderful kindness and there was always someone to entertain him, some new present that someone had sent him; people could not be kind enough. He was grateful for all of this, but he spent many, many hours in thinking. He found that he had never thought before; he found that he would have gone to his grave without thinking had not the great catastrophe occurred. He thought of a great many things, but especially of what other people's lives were like. There were, he supposed, a great number of people who had had misfortunes as overwhelming at his—How had they behaved? And what, after all, were all the other people, in all their different circumstances, doing?

Before this it had only occurred to him to be interested in the people who were leading lives like his, now he wondered about everybody.

Little things became of the greatest importance. Every day he read the paper with absorbed care from the first line to the last. The arrangement of the room interested him and he would give its details, minutely, his consideration.

He was greatly interested in gossip and he would chatter, happily, all the afternoon did someone come and visit him. To everyone it was an amazing thing that he should take it all so easily. No one had ever given Roddy credit for the strength of character that was in him and they did not perhaps recognize that his earlier impatient condemnation of other people—"Why the devil don't the feller stand up to it like a man?"—made him now conscious that he was himself at last faced with a similar test to which he himself must stand up.

But, beyond question, he could not have held the position as he did had it not been for Rachel; he seemed to see that here was a chance of seizing her and making her really his own, a chance that would never be his again. He was making an appeal to her—she was closer to him, he thought, with every day.

So his natural humour and spirits returned—At present life was tolerable; he suffered very little pain and he was aware that a number of people to whom he had never meant anything whatever now cared for him very much indeed.

He was ashamed when he heard of the men who were dying and suffering for their country—"He would have had to have gone to Africa," he told himself, "if he'd not had his accident. Then enteric or a bullet and good-bye to Rachel altogether!"

III

He had often, during those long hours, thought of the Duchess. He had, always, in his heart, considered her affection for him strange; he knew that it was difficult for her to be patient with fools and he knew that his own intellectual gifts were on no very high level. He based her friendship for him on the naive transparency with which he displayed his frankly pagan indulgences. His love for Rachel and this accident had changed all that. He was still pagan enough at heart, but there were other things in his world. Principally it occurred to him now that one couldn't judge about the way things looked to other people, and the Duchess, of course, always did judge; if they didn't look her way, why then wipe them out!

He had, in fact, much less now to say to the Duchess; he was afraid that he would no longer agree with her about things — "Of course she knows the world and is a damn clever woman, but she's jolly well too hard on people who aren't quite her style — She'd put my back up, I believe, if she talked." He had, indeed, always been uncomfortable at the old lady's approaches to sentiment. She was never sentimental with other people — He hated sentiment in anyone except, of course, Rachel and she never was sentimental.

He looked out now upon the road that ran through the park beyond his window, watched the nursemaids and the children, the old gentlemen, the girls, the smart women and the pale young men with books and the smart young men with shiny hats, and he wondered about them all.

Sometimes when the grass, was very green, when high white clouds piled one upon another hung above the pond whose corner he could just see, thoughts of his little grey house, his gardens, the Downs, his horses and dogs would come to him —

"Come out! Come out!" a sparrow would dance on his window ledge —

"Damn you, I can't!" he would cry and then his eyes would fly to Rachel's photograph — "If I get her it will be worth it, won't it, Jacob, my son?"

He talked continually to Jacob and found great comfort in the stolid assurance with which the dog would wag his stump of a tail — "He's more than human, that dog," he would tell Rachel; "funny how I never used to see anything in him."

Of course there were many days when life was utterly impossible; then he would snap at everyone, lie scowling at the park, curse his impotence, his miserable degraded infirmities. "Curse it, to die in a ditch like this — to be broken up, to be smashed...."

His majestic butler — now the tenderest and most devoted of attendants — stood these evil days with great equanimity.

"Bless you, of course he's bound to be wild now and again — wonder is it don't happen more often — It does him good to curse a bit."

So things were with him until the day of the Duchess's visit. His surprise at seeing her was confused with an assurance that "she had come for something." After her departure what she had come for was plain enough to see.

He had not taken her words about Breton at first with any credulity. His principal emotion at the time had been anger with the old woman, a great desire that she should go before he should forget himself and be disgraced by showing temper to anyone so old and feeble—But when she had gone, he found that peace had left him now once and for all.

He knew that the Duchess hated Rachel and he was ready to allow for the bias and exaggeration that spite would lend, but, when that was taken away, much remained.

Rachel knew Breton, that was certain; she had never told him. Breton's name had occurred sometimes in conversation and she had always spoken of him as though he were a complete stranger. Rachel knew Breton and she had never told him....

He might tell himself that she had not told him because she knew that he would instantly stop the acquaintance—It was, of course, simply a friendship that had sprung up because Rachel was sorry for his ostracism. Roddy thought that that was just like Rachel, part of her warm-hearted interest in anyone who seemed to be unfairly treated—yet—she had never told him.

Then, lying there all alone with no one in whom he could confide, there sprang before him suspicions. If she had known this scoundrel of a cousin of hers, if she had been so careful to keep from her husband all cognizance of her friendship, did not that very silence and deceit imply more than friendship? Was Breton the kind of man to abstain from snatching every advantage that was open to him? Did not this explain Rachel's avoidance of Roddy during the last year, her moods of restraint, repentance, her sudden silences?

Then upon this came the thought, how much of all this did the world know? Perhaps it was true once again that the husband was the last to be informed, perhaps during the last year all London Society had mocked at Roddy's blindness.

The Duchess, he might be sure, had not spared her tongue—The Duchess ... he cursed her as he lay there and then wondered whether he should not rather thank her for opening his eyes, then cursed himself for daring to allow such suspicions of Rachel to gain their hold upon him.

In Roddy there was, strong beyond almost any other principle, a sturdy hereditary pride. He was proud of his stock, proud of his ancestors and all their doings, worthy and unworthy, proud of his own pluck and standing — "Different from all these half-baked fellers with only their own grandmothers to go back to." It had been this arrogance, with other things somewhat closely allied, that had endeared him to the Duchess. Now it was that same pride that suffered most terribly. Here was some disaster hanging over his head that threatened most nearly the honour of his family — Let Breton touch that....

He was alone on that evening after the Duchess's visit; Rachel had gone out to a party; she went, he had noticed, reluctantly, protested again and again that she wished she could stay with him, seemed to hang about him as though she would speak to him, looked, oh! too adorably, too adorably beautiful!

Whilst she was with him he saw behind her the dark shadow of Breton, that fellow kicked out of the country for cheating at cards or something as bad, disowned by his family, and she, she, Rachel so proudly apart, could have gone to him — He was glad when, at last, she had left him.

Then, lying there, he endured three of the most awful hours of agony that he was ever, in, all his life, to know. Nothing that had come to him through his accident was so bad as this. At one moment it was fury — wild, raging, unreasoning fury — that wished that Rachel and Breton and the Duchess, all of them together might suffer the torments of hell — And then swiftly following it came his love of Rachel, nearer now to burning heights, so that he swore that, whatever she had done, he did not care, he would forgive her everything, but all that mattered was that she should be spared, that her honour should be vindicated. Then, more quietly, he reflected that he was uncertain of everything as yet, he had only that malicious old woman's word, and until he had something more solid than that he must trust Rachel.

Oh! if only she would, of her own accord, speak! If she would only sit there by his sofa and, with her hand in his, tell him, quite simply, in what exactly her friendship with Breton consisted — Ah! then how he would forgive her! How together they would be revenged upon the Duchess!

If she did not speak he did not know what he would do. That old woman's mouth must be stopped; he must find out exactly how far the danger had spread—he must deal with Breton—Now indeed he cursed so that he should be tied to this sofa; there had swept down upon him the hardest trial of his life.

Rachel returned from her party—she sat by his sofa and he lay there looking at her.

Had it been a nice party? Not very—One of those war parties that everyone had now. That silly Lady Meikleham recited "The Absent-minded Beggar," and they had that French tenor from Covent Garden to sing patriotic songs, and of course they got money out of everybody.

There'd been nothing for supper—She'd seen nobody amusing—

She broke out: "Roddy dear, what have you been doing with yourself? You look as white and tired as anything—Has that pain in your back——?"

"No, dear,—thank you."

"I wish I hadn't gone, and the dinner at Lady Massiter's was so stupid—Monty Carfax whom I loathe and Lord Massiter so dull and stupid—says he's coming to see you to-morrow afternoon."

"Well, he can, I'm at anybody's mercy!"

She got up, stood over him for a moment looking so tall and slender, so dark with diamonds in her black hair, so lovely to-night!

She looked down upon him, then suddenly bent and kissed him.

"Roddy——"

"What is it, dear?" He caught her hand so fiercely that she cried:

"Roddy dear, I——"

"Yes."

"Oh, nothing, only you look so tired, I wish I could take some of the pain——"

"There isn't any, dear, I'm wonderfully lucky."

Peters came in to take him to bed.

She kissed him again and left him.

"Looking done up to-night, sir," said Peters.

"I am," said Roddy.

CHAPTER IV
MARCH 13th: BRETON'S TIGER

"If I'd had the power not to be born, I would certainly not have accepted existence upon conditions that are such a mockery. But I still have the power to die, though the days I give back are numbered. It's no great power, it's no great mutiny."—Dostoevsky.

I

Christopher's knowledge of Rachel, long and intimate though it had been, had never made him sure of her. In his relations with his fellow-men he proceeded on the broad lines that best suited, he felt, any investigation of his own character. Broad lines, however, did not catch that subtle spirit that was Rachel; he had been baffled again and again by some fierceness or sudden wildness in her, and had often been held from approaching her lest by something too impetuous or ill-considered he should drive her from him altogether. He had been aware that, since her marriage, she had been gradually slipping from him, and this had made him, during the last year, the more careful how he approached her. He loved her the more in that something that was part of her was strange and mysterious to him; the idealist and the poet concealed in him behind his frank worldliness cherished her aloofness. She was precious to him because nothing else in this life had quite her unexpected beauty.

Since that afternoon when the Duchess had paid her visit to Roddy he wished many times that he were a cleverer man. He felt that something must instantly be done, but he felt, too, that one false step on his part would plunge them all into the most tragical catastrophe.

He was baffled by his own ignorance as to the real truth; neither Breton nor Rachel had taken him into their confidence. He could not say how any of them could be expected to act, and yet he knew that something must be done at once. He saw Rachel through it all, like a strange dark flower, mysterious, shining, with her colour, beyond his grasp, but so beautiful, so poignant! She had never appealed to him as now, in the heart of some danger that he could not define she eluded him and yet demanded his help.

After much puzzled thinking he decided that it must be Breton whom he had best approach, and so he wrote and asked him to come and dine quietly with him in Harley Street on the evening of March 13th. Breton accepted if he might be released at nine-thirty, as he had then another appointment.

"Can't stand a whole evening," thought Christopher, "thinks I want to bully him. Well, perhaps I do!"

He was detained to a late hour on that afternoon by a patient in Halkin Street and it was after seven when he started home, driving through Piccadilly and Bond Street.

It had been an afternoon of intense closeness, and now as evening came down upon the town the thick curtain of grey that had been hanging all day overhead seemed, with a clanking and jolting, one might imagine, so heavy and brazen was its aspect, to fall lower above the dim grey streets. The lights were out, swinging pale and distended down the length of Piccadilly, and already the carriages were pressing in a long row towards the restaurants; boys were crying the latest editions with the war news and upon all those ears their cries now fell drearily, monotonously, for so long had the town been filled with details of escape, folly, death, ignominy, that it was tired and weary of any voice or cry that concerned itself with War....

Christopher, waiting impatiently for his carriage to move on, thought of Brun; this oppressive, stifling evening seemed to call, in some manner too subtle for Christopher's powers of expression, the houses, the streets, the lamps, the very railings into some life of their own. Under the iron sky that surely with every minute dropped lower upon the oppressed town the clubs opposite the Green Park raised their hooded eyes and stirred ever so little above the people, and the twisted chimneys watched and whispered, as the trail of carriages wound, drearily, into the misty distance. Christopher was not an imaginative man, but he thought that he had never known London so evilly perceptive.

It grew hotter and hotter, but with a heat that made the body perspire and yet left it cold. A dim yellow colour, that seemed to herald a fog that had not made up its mind whether it would appear or no, hung at street corners. Figures seemed furtive in the half-light and, instinctively, voices were lowered as though some sudden sound would explode the air like a match in a gas-filled room. A bell began to ring and startled everyone....

"There'll be an awful thunderstorm soon," thought Christopher. "I've never known things so heavy. Everyone's nerves will be on the stretch to-night. Why, one might fancy anything." His own brain would not work. He had just left a case that had needed all his sharpest attention, but he had found that it was only with the utmost difficulty that he could keep his mind alert, and now when he wanted to think about Breton he was continually arrested by some sense of apprehension, so that he had to stop himself from crying out to his driver, "Look out! Take care! There's someone there."

When he got to his house he found that his forehead was covered with perspiration and that he could scarcely breathe. Meanwhile he had decided nothing as to the course he would pursue with Breton. When he had dressed and come down he found that Breton was waiting for him.

"How ill he looks!" was Christopher's first thought. Perhaps Breton also was oppressed by the weather and indeed in the house, although the windows were open, it was stifling enough.

"No, the man's in pieces." Christopher's look was sharp. He had never seen Breton, who was naturally neat and a little vain about his appearance, so dishevelled. His beard was untrimmed, his eyes bloodshot, his hair unbrushed, his face white and drawn and his mouth seemed, in that light, to be trembling.

"Good heavens, man," said Christopher, "what have you been doing to yourself?"

Breton smiled feebly—"Oh, nothing. Don't badger me—I can't stand it."

"Badger you? Who's going to badger you? only——" Christopher broke off, looked at him a moment, then put his hand on the other's shoulder.

"Look here, old man, why have you left me alone all these weeks?"

"Haven't felt like seeing anybody."

"Well, you might have felt like seeing me. I've missed you. I haven't got so many friends that I can spare, so easily, my best one."

"Oh, rot, Chris," Breton said almost angrily. "You know it's only the kind of interest you've got in all lame dogs that ties you to me at all."

"You're an ungrateful sort of fellow, Frank. But no matter—I'm fond of you in spite of your ingratitude. Come in to dinner and see whether you can eat anything on this stifling night." It was stifling, but oppressive with something more than the mere physical discomfort of it. It was a night that worked havoc with the nerves, so that Christopher, who had naturally a vast deal of common sense, found himself glancing round his shoulder, irritated at the least noise that his servant made, expecting always to hear a knock on the door.

Breton contributed very little to the conversation during dinner. He ate almost nothing, drank only water, looked about him restlessly, muttered something about its being strangely close for March, crumbled up his bread into little heaps.

When they were back in Christopher's smoking-room Breton collapsed into a deep chair, lay there, staring desperately about him, then, with a jerk, pulled himself up and began to stride the room, swinging his arm, then pulling at his beard, crying out at last, "My God! it's stifling. Christopher—I must go out. I can't stand this. It's beyond my bearing."

Christopher made him sit down again and then, feeling that he could not more surely hold the man than by plunging at once into what was, in all probability, the heart of his trouble, said:

"Look here, Frank, I said I wouldn't badger you and I won't, but there's something about which I must speak to you. You must tell me the truth. There's more involved than just ourselves."

Breton seemed instantly aware of Christopher's meaning. He sat up. "I knew," he said, "that I was in for a lecture. Well, it can't make any difference."

"No," Christopher answered brusquely. "Whether it makes any difference to you or no you've got to listen, Frank. It's simply this. I happened to hear, a good time ago, that you had met Rachel. I knew that she had been to your rooms. I knew that you had corresponded. I should dismiss that man-servant of yours, Frank."

Breton muttered something.

"You might have told me yourself, Frank. You might, both of you, have told me. But never mind—it's all too late for that now. The point is that it was your grandmother that told me."

"My God!" Breton cried. "She knows? She knew.... But there was nothing to know. There was nothing anyone mightn't have known. If anyone dares to breathe a syllable against one of the purest, noblest ..."

"Yes, yes. I know all that," Christopher answered. "But the thing is simply this. I don't know—she doesn't know exactly what the truth is between you and Rachel. All that she does know is that Rachel went to see you and wrote to you. Now Roddy Seddon isn't—or wasn't aware that his wife had ever

met you. He holds the more or less traditional family point of view about
you. I believe that, two or three days ago, the Duchess told him about
Rachel's visits. I am not sure of this. I hope that by now Rachel herself has
told her husband. But of that also I'm not sure. All I know is that it's our
duty—your duty and my duty to save Rachel all the unhappiness we can,
and still more to save Roddy. Remember the position he's in."

Breton sprang to his feet. "Look here, Chris, I should have told you of all this
long ago. I didn't know that you had heard. I wish to God I had spoken to
you. But as Heaven is my witness, Rachel is a saint. I'm a miserable cur—a
misery to myself and a misery to everyone else. But she——"

"You've been fools, the couple of you," he answered sternly. "It's no use
cursing now. I won't go and urge Rachel to tell Roddy—she must do that of
her own free will—All our hands are tied. It depends upon the steps that
Roddy takes, and after all the old lady may never have told him. But I've
warned you, Frank. It's up to you to do the right thing."

"What do you want me to do?" asked Breton.

"I don't know what you can do. You must see for yourself—only, Frank,"
here Christopher's voice became softer, "by all our old friendship and by any
affection that you may have left for me, I do conjure you to play fair by
Rachel and her husband. Rachel is very, very young. Roddy is helpless——"

"That's enough," Breton cried. "My God, Christopher, of you could realize
the weeks I've been having you wouldn't think, perhaps, so badly of me. It's
been more, I swear, than any mortal flesh can endure. I'm driven, driven—
I'm at the end.... But she's safe from me, safe now and safe forever. And that
now that old woman should step in—now."

Christopher came and again put his arm on Breton's shoulder and held him
up, it might seem, with more than physical strength.

His affection for Breton was an affection sprung from his very knowledge of
the man's weaknesses. He had in him that British quality of ruthless
condemnation for the sinner whom he did not know and sentimental
weakness for the sinner whom he did. He had seen Francis Breton through a
thousand scrapes, he would see him, doubtless, through a thousand more.

"We'll say no more now, old boy—You look done up—I won't worry you,
but if you want me here I am and I promise not to lecture. Only you owe me
some confidence, you do indeed."

Breton got up and stood there, with his hand pressed to his forehead. "What you've told me," he said. "I must do something ... something ... it's all been my fault. If they should touch her——"

Then, turning to Christopher, he said: "You are the only friend I've got, and I know it. I do value it—only lately I've been going to bits again. If it weren't for you and little Miss Rand I swear I'd have gone altogether. You are a brick, Christopher. Another day I'll come to you and tell you everything. To-night I'm simply past talking."

A servant came in and gave Christopher a note. It was from Lord John saying that he was anxious about his mother and asking the doctor whether he could possibly come round and see her.

Breton then said that he must go. He went, promising that he would soon come again. When he had left the house Christopher stood, perplexed, wondering whether he should have left him alone. Then he put on his hat and coat and set off for 104 Portland Place.

II

Breton had, indeed, no destination. He had been frightened of a whole evening with Christopher.

He was frightened of everything, of everybody—above all, of himself. He found himself, with a sense of surprise, as though he were the helpless actor in some bad dream, standing in Oxford Circus. Surely it was a dream.

The sky, grey and lowering, was yet tinged with a smoky red. He had an overpowering sense of the minuteness of humanity, so that the crowds crossing and recrossing the Circus seemed like tiny animals crawling over the surface of a pond from which the water had been drained.

His old fancy of the waterways came back to him and now he thought that Oxford Circus, often a maelstrom of tossing, whirling humanity, had run dry and lay stagnant, filled with dying life, beneath the red-tinged sky.

Ever lower and lower that sky seemed to fall. Theatres, restaurants on that evening were almost deserted. People stood about in groups, saying that soon the thunder would be upon them, wondering at this weather in March, watching, with curious eyes, the sky.

Breton was near madness that evening. He was near madness to this extent, that he was not certain of reality. Were those lamp-posts real? What was the meaning of those strange high buildings in whose heart there burnt so sinister a light? He watched them expecting that at any moment these would burst into flame and with a screaming rattling flare go tossing to the sky.

Near him a girl said, "All right—of course it ain't of no moment what I might happen to pre-fere—Oh, no!"

A mild young man answered her: "Well, if yer want ter go to the Oxford why not say so? That's what I say. Why not say so 'stead of 'angin' about — —"

"Oh! 'angin' about! Say that again and off I go. 'Angin' about! I'd like to know — —"

"I didn't say anythink about your 'angin' about. Yer catch a feller up so quickly, Bertha. What I mean to say — —"

"Oh! yer and yer meanin's. Don't know what yer do mean, if the truth were known. 'Ere's a pleasant way of spendin' an evenin' — —"

Breton regarded them with curiosity. Were they real? Did they feel the strange oppression of this lowering sky as strongly as he did? Were they uncertain as to whether these buildings were alive or no? Perhaps they could tell him whether those omnibuses that came lumbering so heavily up Regent Street were safe and secure.

Oddly enough, although he tried, he could not remember exactly what it was that Christopher had told him. Something, of course, to do with his grandmother. Everything was to do with her.... She was the one who was driving him to destruction. Always she was stepping forward, sending him down when he was climbing up, at last, to safety, always it was she who stood behind him, on the watch lest some happiness or success should come his way.

He felt as though he would like to go and force his way into 104 Portland Place and face the woman and tell her what she had done to him. Yes, that would be a fine thing—to see all those Beaminster relations gathering round, protesting, frightened.

And then it occurred to him that he really did not know the way to Portland Place. Things were so strange to-night. He knew that it was close at hand, but he was afraid that he would never find it. He was really afraid that he would never find it.

Some man jostled into him, apologized and moved away. The contact cleared his brain, asserted the reality of the buildings, the crowds, the cabs and carriages. He pulled himself together and began slowly to walk down Oxford Street in the direction of Tottenham Court Road.

He remembered very clearly and distinctly what it was that Christopher had told him. Rachel was in danger because her husband had heard of her friendship with him, Breton....

It would not have been Francis Breton if he had not taken this piece of news and looked at it in its most sensational colours. He had, through all these last weeks, been striving to accustom himself to the agony of enduring life without her. He dimly perceived that it was the emptiness of life rather than any actual loss of any particular person that was so terrible to him. He had still, very fine and beautiful, his memory of the day when she had come to him in his rooms, and had that day been followed by a secret relationship between them and many hours spent together, then his passion would have been very genuine and moving.

But, after all, she had flashed into his life, and then flashed out of it again, and, so swiftly with him did moods follow one upon another, and ideals and ambitions and despairs and glories jostle together in his brain, that she might have remained, very happily raised to a fine altar in his temple, very distantly recognized as a beautiful episode now closed and contemplated only from a worshipping distance, had any other figure or incident definitely occupied his attention.

But no figure, no incident had arrived. He had had, during all these weeks, no drama into which he might fling his fine feelings, his great ambitions, his glorious sacrifices. Of genuine sincerity were these moods of his—he had never stood sufficiently beyond himself to arrive at any definite insincerity about any of his movements or impulses—but of all things in the world he could not endure that his life should be empty, and empty now it had been for, as it seemed to his swift impatience, a long, long time.

Christopher's news did touch him very deeply. He would instantly have sacrificed his life, his honour, anything at all, for Rachel, and the fact that he would enjoy the drama of that sacrifice did not rob it of any atom of its sincerity.

But the pity of it was that he really did not see what he could do. Had he been able, here and now, to rush into the Portland Place house and seize his grandmother by the throat and shake her, or had it been possible to appear before Roddy Seddon, to declare himself the only culprit, to proclaim that he was ready for any condemnation, any punishment, then, in spite of all his unhappiness, he would be now a happy man, but, alas, the only possible action was to pause, to see what happened, to wait—and waiting it was that sent him mad.

One action indeed was possible and that was that he should put a close to his wretched existence. On this close and sterile night such an action did not appear at all absurd. It had fine elements about it, it would deal a sure blow at his grandmother and all that family who had treated him so basely. What a headline for the papers! "Suicide of member of one of England's noblest families!" Rachel should be, no longer, annoyed with his unfortunate presence: he would make it, of course, quite obvious that she had had nothing to do with his sad end.

He looked about him, with an air of fine melancholy, at the passers-by. Little they knew of the terrible tragedy that was even now preparing in their midst!

He felt almost happy again as he turned this solution over and over again. Some people would be sorry—Christopher, Lizzie Rand, and Rachel: above all, it must be heavy upon the consciences of the Duchess and her wretched children. They had driven him to his death and must bear the blame to the grave and beyond.

Very faintly the rolling of thunder could be heard as the storm approached the town.

He was standing outside the Oxford Music Hall, and he thought that he would go inside for a little time that he might avoid the rain ... and then upon that followed the reflection that it did not matter whether he was wet or no—he would soon be dead.

Faintly behind these gloomy resolves some voice seemed to tell him that if he could only pass safely through this night fortune would again be kind to him. "Wait," something told him. "Be patient for once in your life".... But no, to wait any more was impossible. Some fine action, some splendid defiance or heroic defence, here and now ... otherwise he would show the world that he had courage, at least, to die. Most of his impetuous follies had their origin in his conviction that the eyes of the world were always upon him.

He paid his money and walked into the circle promenade. Behind him was a bar at which several stout gentlemen and ladies were happily conversational. In front of him a crowd of men and women leaned forward over the back of the circle and listened to the entertainment.

On the stage, in a circle of brilliant light, a thin man with a melancholy face, a top hat and pepper-and-salt trousers was singing—

"Straike me pink and straike me blue,
Straike me purple and crimson too
I'll be there,
Lottie dear,
Down by the old Canteen."
"Now," said the gentleman, "once more. Let's 'ave it—all together."

There was a moment's pause, then the orchestra began very softly and, in a kind of ecstasy the crowd sang—

"Straike me pink and straike me blue,
Straike me purple and crimson too," etc.
Breton sat down on a little velvet seat near the bar and gloomily looked about him. Did they only realize, these people, the tragedy that was so close to them, then would they very swiftly cease their silly singing. The place was hot, infernally hot. It glowed with light, it crackled with noise, it was possessed with a glaring unreality. It occurred to him that to make a leap upon the railing at the back of the circle, to stand for one instant balanced there before the frightened people, then to plunge, down, down, into the stalls—that would be a striking finish! How they would all scream, and run and scatter! ... yes ...

Against the clinking and chatter of the bar he would hear the voice of the funny man: "And so I says to 'er, 'Maria, if you're tryin' to prove to me that it's two in the mornin', then I says what I want to know is oo's been 'elpin' yer to stay awake all this time? That's what....'"

It was then that, in spite of himself, he was drawn from his moody thoughts by the eyes of the girl standing near the bar against the wall. She was a small, timid, rather pale girl in a huge black hat. She wore a long trailing purple dress and soiled white gloves, and was looking, just now, unhappy and frightened.

He had noticed her because of the contrast that her white face and small body made with her grand untidy clothes, but, looking at her more closely, he saw something about her that stirred all his sympathy and protection.

Like most Englishmen he was at heart an eager sentimentalist and he was, just now, in a mood that responded instantly to anyone in distress.

He forgot for the moment his desperate plans of self-destruction. A fat red-faced man came from the bar towards her, with two drinks; he was himself very unsteady and uncertain in his movements and his smile was both vacuous and full of purpose. He lurched towards her, put his hand upon her shoulder to steady himself, then, as one of the glasses spilled, cursed.

She refused the drink, but he continued to press it upon her. His fat hand wandered about her neck, stroked her chin, and he was leaning now so that his face almost touched hers.

Breton heard him say—

"Well, if you won't drink—damme—come along, my dear—let's be goin'."
She shook her head, her eyes growing larger and larger.

"Nonshensh," he said. "Darn nonshensh." She glanced about her desperately, but no one, save Breton, was watching them. She caught his eyes, pitifully, eagerly.

The man put his arm about her and tried to draw her from the wall.

"Come," he said. "We'll go home."

She drew away. He pulled at her hand. "Damn the O——Place. Wash the matter? You got to come."

Then he seized her by the arm, and, still lurching from side to side, began to move away.

"No, no," she whispered, obviously terrified of a scene, but using all her strength to resist. Her eyes again met Breton's.

"That lady," he said, advancing to the stout gentleman, "is a friend of mine."

The man looked at him with an expression astonished, simply and rather puzzled.

"Wash—wash...?" he said.

"You'll be so good as to leave that lady alone."

"Well, I'm b— —well damned. Oh! gosh." The stout gentleman contemplated him with furious amazement.

"'Oo the b— —'ell I'd like to know? Get out or I'll kick yer out."

The quarrel had by now gathered its crowd.

The stout gentleman, lurching forward, aimed a blow at Breton which missed him.

"Let her alone, do you hear?" cried Breton.

The stout gentleman, amazed, apparently, at a world that defied all the probabilities, turned, caught the girl by the body and, dragging her with him, pushed past his opponent.

Breton seized him by the waist, turned him round so that, with a little puzzled gasp, he half fell, half sat upon the cushioned seat against the wall.

Then Breton offered the girl his arm and walked away with her, conscious that an attendant had arrived rather late upon the scene and was now abusing the stout gentleman, whilst a sympathetic little crowd listened and advised.

He walked down the stairs with the girl. "That was decent of you," she said. "Most awfully— —"

Beyond the doors the world was a hissing, spurting deluge of rain.

A cab was called and she climbed into it.

"What about coming back?" she said. He shook his head.

"Not to-night. You have a good rest. That's what you want."

"Well, I am done. Meet 'nother night p'raps— —"

"I hope so," he said politely. He raised his hat and the cab splashed away.

328

"Another cab, sir?" said the commissionaire.

"No, thanks," said Breton, and plunged out into the rain. The air was fresh and cool. Streams of water danced and spurted on the gleaming pavements.

Breton walked along. The little adventure had swept completely from his mind his earlier desperate decisions.

There were still things for him to do! Poor little girl ... he was glad that he had been there! What a fool he had been all these weeks, sitting there, letting himself go to pieces because the world had gone badly! What sort of a creature was he? Well, he was some good yet. Just one twist of the hand and that man had gone down ... Yes, she was grateful.... Her eyes had shone.

And what of the candles, his business? Why had he allowed that to drop when he had made, already, so good a start? He would be in the City early to-morrow. Business was humming just now.

And Rachel? Rachel!

Let him be content to have her as his ideal, his fine beacon to light him on, to hold him to his work and do the best that was in him!

After all, things were for the best. They would always have their fine memories, one of the other. Nothing to spoil that idyll.

He arrived, soaked to the very skin, at his door. "Funny," he thought, "how that thunder depresses one. I've been moody for weeks. Air's ever so much clearer now. God, didn't that old beast tumble? — Poor little girl — she was grateful though!"

Then as he opened the door, he remembered what Christopher had, that evening, told him.

"To-morrow," he said to himself, in a fine glow of hope and confidence, "to-morrow I'll get to work and soon stop that wicked old woman's mouth. Rachel — God bless her — I'll show her what I'm like...."

He climbed the dark stairs as though he were storming a town.

CHAPTER V
MARCH 13th: RACHEL'S HEART
"When God smote His hands together, and struck out the soul at a spark,
Into the organized glory of things, from drops of the dark, —
Say, didst thou shine, didst thou burn, didst thou honour the power in the
form,
As the star does at night, or the fire-fly, or even the little ground-worm?
'I have sinned,' she said."
Elizabeth Barrett Browning.

I

Meanwhile Rachel had not spoken to Roddy. Bad though the months had
been since that terrible afternoon at Seddon these days that followed the
Duchess's visit were the worst that she had ever known.

During the weeks that immediately followed Roddy's accident she was
allowed no line for thought. She discovered—and she never forgot the
sharpness of the discovery—that she was the poorest of nurses. Everything
that she did was clumsily and slowly done; she watched Lizzie Rand with
admiration and wonder. Dimly through the absorption that held her,
thoughts of Francis Breton pierced, but always to be instantly dismissed.

Before her was simply the amazing, incredible fact that Roddy, the most
active, the most vigorous of human beings, would never stand upon his feet
again. She could see nothing but Roddy, and no service, no sacrifice, was too
stern or too difficult. Meanwhile subtly, almost unconsciously, she was
influenced by Lizzie Rand. It was not strange to her that Lizzie should have
changed so swiftly from hatred to friendship and affection. Rachel was
passionate enough herself to understand that a woman will go, instantly, to
the person who needs her most, even though she has hated that same person
five minutes before. No, the thing that was wonderful to her was that Lizzie
Rand should combine such feeling with such discipline.

To watch her as she moved about Roddy's rooms was to deny to her the
possibility of emotion, of anything that could disturb that efficiency. And yet
Rachel knew ... she had seen depths of feeling in Lizzie that made her own
desires and regrets small and puny things.

But it did not need Lizzie's power to abase Rachel before Roddy. It would
have been enough for her to have remembered what her thoughts and
intentions had been on that day to have brought her on her knees to beg his
pardon, but when she saw the fashion in which he bore his sentence, his
endurance, his stubborn will beating down any temptation to despair, she

recognized that it was very little of Roddy that she had known before this crisis.

Then as the weeks passed and the world settled into this new shape and form, thoughts of Francis Breton returned to her. She had written to him soon after the accident, but that was for herself, that she might clear her mind of anything except her husband, rather than for Breton. She had considered him whilst she wrote that letter, had seen him as someone in her old, old life, someone who had stirred her then but possessed now no power to move her. She wanted him to be happy, but wished never to see him again; once, long ago, there had been a scene in a room and she had been carried up to strange and dangerous heights and the world had tossed and stormed about her—but oh! how long ago that was! How younger she had been then!

But, as the weeks passed, that scene drew closer to her and life crept back into its heart. Sometimes, when Roddy was sleeping and she was sitting there beside him, and, about her, the house slumbered and the very birds were still, her heart would beat, beat thickly, her cheeks would flush, and she would remember that, had it not been for a horse that stumbled, she might be now far away, leading a life that might be tragedy, but that was, at any rate, Life!

She would beat the thought down—she would tell herself what, now, from this distance, she knew to be true, that she would not have been happy had she gone with Breton. She remembered that even at that supreme moment in Breton's rooms when he had kissed her for the first time her swift thought had been "Poor Roddy!" She knew, with an older wisdom than she had possessed two months ago, that Breton on his side would not have held her any more than Roddy, in his so different fashion, could hold her now. Was she to be always thus, wanting something that was not hers?

During the weeks that had immediately followed the accident she had thought that, at last, love for Roddy had really come to her. Then, as the days threaded their way, she knew that it was not so. He was more to her, much more to her, helpless and courageous, than he could ever have been under the old conditions.

But it was not passion—it was care, affection, even love; she loved him, yes, but she was not in love with him. He held all of her save that one part that Breton alone, of all human beings, had called out of her.

But she had learnt discipline during these weeks—down, down she drove rebellion, memory. She was Roddy's—she had dedicated her life to his happiness.

Then they came to London, Lizzie returned to her mother and to Lady Adela, and Rachel was alone. Life was again very difficult for her. Roddy was wonderfully cheerful, but Rachel found that she could not do very much for him. He liked to have her there, but she knew that many of his friends who could tell him the town gossip, the latest from clubs, the hunting and racing chatter entertained him more than she did. She had not, since her marriage, made many friends and she knew that almost everyone who came to their little house came for Roddy's sake rather than for hers. She did not mind that—she was glad that he was happy ... but she wished that he needed her a little more. Roddy urged her to drive, to see people, to dine and go to the theatre. She went because she saw that it disturbed him if he felt that she stayed indoors for his sake, but she did not enjoy her gaiety. When she was out she wished to hurry back to him and then, when she was with him again, she often wondered whether her presence made him any happier. Through all his intercourse with her she discerned a wistful restraint as though he would like to ask her for something that he had not got and yet was afraid. When she felt this in him she redoubled her affection towards him, but she thought that he noticed this and knew her effort.

Her thoughts went often now to Francis Breton, not as to anyone whom she would ever see again—but she hoped that he was happy, wondered whether there was anyone to look after him, wished that he had some friend so that she might know that he was safe. Her pride did not allow her to speak to Lizzie Rand about him; they had had one talk when Lizzie had taken her letter, but that was all.

Then, as February drew to a close, she was unwell; that was so unusual for her that she might have been disturbed had it been anything more material than headaches, strange fits of indifference to everything and a general failure of energy. She thought that she was indoors too much and was now in the air as often as her duties to Roddy allowed her.

But the indifference persisted. Her feelings for Roddy were an odd confusion; there were times, when she was away from him, and the thought of him made her heart beat—"This is love—at last." There were times again when, as she sat beside him, she could have beaten her hands against the walls for very boredom and for his impenetrable taciturnity as he read The Times from the Births and Marriages on the front page to the advertisements on the last and flung her details—"London Scottish won their game at

Richmond—That Fettes man got over three times," or "I wouldn't give a button for that horse of old Tranty Stummits they're all so gone on. You mark my words...." "I'd like to see that new piece of Edwardes'"—"They've got a girl in it who dances on her nose—jolly pretty she is, too, so Massiter says. He's been five times and there's a song about moonlight or some old rot that they say is spiffin'——" How to adjust this horrible stupidity with the courage, the humour, the affection, even the poetry that she found in him at other times?

There were days when she cared for him with a new thrilling emotion, something that had in it a quality of curiosity as though he were coming before her as someone unknown and unexpected. There were other days when she wondered how he could have remained, through all the crisis, so precisely the same Roddy.

Meanwhile between all these uncertainties she lost touch with herself. It was as though her soul flew, like some bird in a strange country, from point to point, restless, unsatisfied....

II

Then those few hurried words with Christopher on the afternoon of the Duchess's visit flung, at an instant, her whole life into crisis. Even as the words left him she knew that it was up to this that all her days had been leading, that at last she was, in very truth, face to face with her grandmother, that the battle between the two of them had commenced.

She knew, in those few minutes whilst she stood there, motionless, in that room, other things. She knew—and this was the first sharp conviction that struck her heart—that, at all costs, whatever else might come to her, she must not now lose Roddy's love. Strangely, as she stood there facing her danger, some warm glow heightened her colour as she felt from this what Roddy really meant to her. She thought then of Francis Breton, of his danger if her family understood how implicated he was with her. It was true that she had, not very long ago, contemplated running away with him, and surely nothing could have implicated him more than that, but now that he should suffer and yet not have her, secured, as his reward for his suffering— that, at all pain to herself, she must prevent.

Her first impulse after Christopher had left her was to go down instantly to Roddy and confess everything. Then she paused.

Perhaps, after all, her grandmother had not spoken? In that case how cruel to make Roddy miserable with something that was dead and already

333

remote. In her heart too was terror lest she should precipitate Breton into some peril. On every side it seemed to her better that she should wait and discover, perhaps through Christopher, perhaps by her own intelligence, what exactly had occurred.

Four days afterwards, on the afternoon of that day that brought Breton to dine with Christopher, she had not yet spoken. She had taken no steps at all; despising herself, afraid for Breton, feeling at one instant that Roddy knew everything, at another that he knew nothing, ill with this same lassitude that had hung about her now for so many weeks, determining at one moment that she would confront her grandmother, at another that she would go instantly and confess to Roddy.

Yet Rachel hesitated and did nothing.

On this close and heavy afternoon Rachel sat up in her little drawing-room, wondering whether she would wait there for possible callers, or go down to Roddy, who was being entertained at the moment by Lord Massiter, or, complete confession of surrender to nerves and general catastrophe, go up to her bedroom, pull down the blinds and lie there, hunting sleep.

The day was intolerably heavy. The windows of the little room had all been flung open and, through the park, figures wearily dragged themselves and the waters of the lake lay as though they had fallen, because of this leaden heaviness, from the grey sky.

She sat there, listening for every sound, starting at every opening or closing of a door, thinking that were Lord Massiter not there she would go down now and tell everything to Roddy, yet knowing in her heart that if Peters were to come now and tell her that his master was alone she would not move.

Peters did come, but it was to tell her that Lord John would like to see her. Uncle John! She scarcely knew whether she hailed him as a relief or no.

"Oh! ask him to come up, Peters, at once. Bring tea here. Lord Massiter will have his downstairs, I expect."

Had her grandmother told Uncle John anything? Was his visit in connection with anything that he had heard? Of all the changes that her marriage had brought her, that she should have slipped away from Uncle John was one of the saddest. She loved him as dearly as ever, but restraint had been there between them, struggle against it though they might. He was, like Roddy, so ineloquent that anything like a situation was real agony to him; he could never explain his feelings about anything and he would eagerly agree with you that it was a great pity that he had any. What had made this trouble between them? Rachel only knew that now there were so many things in her life which Uncle John could not understand. At her heart her love for him was as clear and simple as it had ever been.

But oh! Uncle John was glad to see her! His picture of her, as she sat there, her cheeks flushed, in a rose-coloured dress, with the room as soft and delicate as a shell around her, filled him with delight: changes had come to him even since their last meeting. The lines in his forehead seemed to her a little deeper, his eyes were anxious and his smile less sure and genial. He wore a beautiful white waistcoat and sat there, with his chest out, his white hair rising into a crest, looking exactly like a pouter pigeon.

"Dear Uncle John! I'm so glad!"

"Well, my dear, I was just passing. Been to some woman who's got a party in Harley House. War party, of course, there were characters of the names of different generals and if you won you paid a guinea to the War Fund—quite a reversal of the ordinary proceedings. I'm sure, my dear, I don't know why I went. Well, it was so close that I felt I couldn't walk back, even to 104, without a cup of tea from you. How's Roddy?"

"All right. Lord Massiter's been down there chatting to him ever since three o'clock. Would you like us to go down and have our tea with them, or shall we stay cosily up here by ourselves?"

"Why, stay up here of course! You're not looking very well, my dear. You've not been the thing lately, have you? This business with Roddy?..." (he took her hand and held it)—"Don't you think it would be a good thing if you went away for a week or two and had a change?"

"No, Uncle John dear, thank you. I am tired and I will go away later on, but just now it would only make me anxious and I should worry about Roddy."

Tea was brought. She looked at Uncle John and thought that he had heard nothing. His guileless eyes smiled back at her; all that she could discern in him was apprehension lest he should say something to displease her, to make her angry. Bless his heart, he need not be afraid of that now!

As she gave him his sugar she felt that some of the old intimate relationship between them was creeping back.

"Of course you heard of grandmother's wonderful visit to us the other day," Rachel said. "Wasn't it amazing? and Christopher says that she was none the worse—rather the better."

"Amazing," said Uncle John very solemnly. "Perfectly astonishing. Your grandmother, Rachel, is an astounding woman. Just when we were all of us thinking that she was really not quite so well, quite so fit as she used to be, she comes along and does something that she hasn't done for thirty years. I confess I was nervous when I first heard of it, but Christopher reassured me—said it would do her no harm, and it hasn't."

"It shows what her affection for Roddy is," Rachel said slowly.

"And for you, dear," Uncle John said timidly. "I know that you haven't— well, haven't—that is, weren't always very friendly, but I hope that now you've come to understand her a little more. She's a difficult woman. She wouldn't be so splendid if she weren't so difficult."

He saw those hard lines that he knew of old strike into Rachel's face. He shrank back himself, afraid that he had, by one ruthless sentence, lost all the happy intimacy that had returned to them.

She had risen and walked to the window. "Dear Uncle John," she said, "I know you'd like us to be friends, bless you. But you may as well give that idea up, once and for ever. Grandmother and I—the old and the new generation, you know. There's never been anything but war and never will be. Besides, she's never forgiven me for marrying Roddy, although she arranged it all."

"Oh! my dear!" said Uncle John.

"No, it is so. I shouldn't be astonished," she continued bitterly, "if I were to hear that she thinks that I flung Roddy from his horse and trampled on him. It would be quite likely."

Then, suddenly, she came back from the window to the sofa where Uncle John, looking greatly distressed, was sitting. She leaned down, put her arms round his neck and her cheek next to his.

"Uncle John dear. Don't you worry about grandmother and me. That's an old, old story and it can't alter. The case of us two, you and me, is much more important. I've been a beast, for a long time, Uncle John. We've got away from one another somehow and it's all been my fault. I've been a prig and all sorts of horrid things, and I've let things come between us. Nothing shall ever come between us again—never."

He kissed her and his fat body thrilled with happiness. Amongst all the distressing things that this last year had brought him, nothing had been more distressing than his separation from Rachel; now the old Rachel had come back to him again.

They sat on the sofa there and he talked of a number of things in his old happy, disconnected way. Some of her apprehension lifted from Rachel, she forgot the closeness of the day and sat there, happier than she had been for many weeks. Six o'clock struck and he got up to go.

"Taking your aunt out to dinner. You going anywhere to-night, my dear?"

"Yes. It's such a nuisance, but Roddy insists on my going. I'd so much rather stay with him. It's only a silly little dinner at Lady Carloes'. She's asked a harpist in afterwards! Fancy, harpist!"

But Uncle John liked Lady Carloes. She was an old friend of his. "Don't laugh at Lady Carloes, dear. She's a kind creature, and been a friend of the family's for ever so long—a devoted friend."

He stopped suddenly. "By the way, something I meant to have told you." He dropped his voice. "You needn't say anything about it and I don't want to worry your grandmother. I'm afraid she wouldn't like it. But the black sheep is to be restored to the fold."

"The black sheep?" said Rachel, wondering.

"Yes," said Uncle John. "Your Cousin Frank Breton, my dear. Your Uncle Vincent and your aunt and I thought that he'd behaved so well, been so quiet and steady all this time, that really something ought to be done about him. It's been on my conscience, I can assure you, for a long time past. Well, I've written to him. I'm going to see him. Of course it's better to be quiet about it whilst your grandmother feels as she does—but in time——"

Rachel's voice was sharp and rather harsh as she said, "Dear Uncle John, that is kind of you. I'm so glad. Poor Cousin Frank! I always felt it unfair."

John looked at her with one of his supplicating, "Please-don't-be-hard-on-me" glances.

337

Rachel really was strange. She seemed to dislike the idea of Breton's redemption. He had thought that she would have been delighted.

She kissed him. "Nothing's ever to come between us again," she whispered. He pressed her hand.

"I must just look in upon Roddy," he said, and they went down together.

III

The thought that instantly occurred to her was that she must not allow Uncle John to talk to Roddy about Breton. She saw some innocent word falling, like a match into a haystack, and starting immediately the most horrible blaze.

There were other thoughts behind that—thought of her grandmother's actions when she heard of this, thoughts of Roddy's probable decision about it, thoughts that she, Rachel, might prove to be the one person in the world who had helped to drive Breton out, thoughts intolerable were they, for a moment, indulged—but now, as she walked, laughing, downstairs, with Uncle John, her one urgent resolve was to prevent an immediate scene.

She need not have feared. Massiter, stout, red-faced, hearty and stupid, held the stage. He had been holding it since three o'clock and Roddy's white face showed fatigue, his eyes were half closed and, although he smiled, his mind, distressed and exhausted, was far away.

Rachel's glance at him told her that his visitor had been too much for him. When she saw Roddy like this she longed to have him alone, away from all the world, to love him and care for him; although, in hard fact, when he was worn out, Peters was of more value than she. She looked at him now, loved him and was also afraid; she hated Lord Massiter, at this moment, and hoped that he would go.

He talked in his cheerful voice, as though he were addressing an assembly in the open air. He spoke of the hunting (pretty rotten), of the musical comedies (absolutely rotten), of our tactics in South Africa (rotten of course beyond all words), and of farming on his land in the country (unspeakably rotten), and was cheerful about all these things. He knew that he had been self-sacrificing and had spent a whole afternoon in cheering up "that poor devil, Seddon. Got to lie on his back all his life, poor chap. Active beggar he was too."

338

He overwhelmed Lord John, whom he liked but scorned. "Never takes any decent exercise, John Beaminster. Always about with a parcel of women." Finally he departed, carrying with him a faint scent of soap and tobacco, swearing that it was the closest night he'd ever known and wiping his red forehead with the air of one who rules this country and is going very shortly to enjoy an excellent meal.

Soon Uncle John also departed.

Roddy, alone with Rachel, faintly smiled and then closed his eyes again.

"Better go and dress, dear. It's gone half-past six."

"What on earth did he stay all that time for, roaring like a bull?" she cried indignantly. "Tired you out. Roddy, dear, I don't think I'll go out to dinner. I'll send a wire to Lady Carloes."

"No, you must," he said firmly. "It's too late to disappoint her."

"It's such an appalling night. I'm not feeling awfully well. I don't think I could stand one of her dinners. There'll be old Lord Crewner, old Mrs. Brunning and young somebody or other for me, and I believe Uncle Richard. I simply couldn't stand it."

"Aren't you well?" He looked up at her sharply.

"Not very." Their eyes met; she turned hers away. She was desperately near to tears, near to flinging herself down at his side and hiding her head and telling him all. "Wait—wait—perhaps he knows nothing ..."

Still looking away from him she said, "Oh yes! I must go, of course. It's only this thunder that one feels."

She bent down, hurriedly, and kissed him. They said good night to one another and she left the room.

Later, in the carriage, she saw his white face and was miserable. She thought of Breton and that made her miserable too. To everyone she seemed to bring unhappiness. The stifling evening held a hand at her throat; the carriage moved languidly along—on every side of her she saw people listlessly moving as though controlled by an enchantment. She really was ill. "If I don't look out," she thought, "I shall be hysterical to-night. I shall just have to hold on and keep quiet. I've never felt like this before. Fancy being hysterical before Uncle Richard. How surprised he'd be and how he'd disapprove!"

In Lady Carloes' small and stuffy drawing-room bony Mrs. Brunning and Lord Crewner were being polite to one another. One would suppose that it had been Lady Carloes' intention to gather together into a confined space as many of her grandmother's possessions as possible. Her grandmother had known Sir Walter Scott and had Lord Wellington to tea and spent several days in the country with Joanna Baillie. The little room had an old faded wall-paper covered thickly with prints, miniatures and fading water-colours. On the many little tables were scattered old keepsakes, "bijouterie" of every kind, dragon china, coloured stones and even an ebony box with sea-shells. There were cabinets and glass cases, several chattering clocks, nodding mandarins and shepherdesses on the mantelpiece, a faded illustrated edition of Sir Walter's poems and, finally, three cats with large blue bows and tinkling bells. All these things added, immensely, to Rachel's distress; on such an evening this jumble of small objects rose, like the sound of the sea, and threatened to throttle her. A fire was burning and only the upper part of one window was open. Rachel felt that she was in real peril of fainting; that she had never done, but to-night she had the sensation that at any moment the floor with its old faded carpet would rise slanting before her and pitch her into the street. Lady Carloes, more hunched together than usual, her voice thick and husky and her dress of blue satin, hurried in. Uncle Richard, untouched by the closeness of the evening, clean and starched and dignified, made his majestic entry; a young man from the Embassy, so beautifully dressed that he appeared to have spent his days in the effort to make his personality of less importance than his studs and his waistcoat buttons, apologized from behind his shining collar for being the last of the party. They all went down to dinner.

Rachel felt, as the young man led her downstairs, that at last she knew what Panic was. Panic was the state of standing, surrounded by ordinary everyday things and people, waiting for the bolt to fall, the enemy to advance, danger to spring, but seeing, in actual vision, nothing to justify terror. She had reached to-night the climax of months of alarm, and, during these past days, unbroken suspense. She was at the end of endurance....

How was she ever to compass this horrible meal? The young man was finding her difficult. She was aware that Uncle Richard watched her and was expecting her to sustain the family ease and dignity. They were at a little round table, so that he was able to hear all the conversation.

"Yes," she said desperately. "I quite agree with you. The lack of enterprise at Covent Garden is shameful. We want more competition...."

"So I said to her, 'My good woman, if you really imagine that I'm taken in by your pretending that that's Dresden'..."

"Herr Becknet is coming in afterwards," old Lady Carloes said. "You'll like him, my dear. He plays the harp too wonderfully. I've asked a few friends to come in. Of course the drawing-room isn't very large, but I hope——"

The room was swimming before Rachel. A stuffed bird in a glass case sailed across the table towards her and the fireplace tottered and staggered. She was just able to gasp: "Lady Carloes—please—it's this heat or something——"

There were cries of agitation. The young man gave her his arm into the passage, she was surrounded by anxious servants; someone fanned her, she drank water and was conscious of Lady Carloes' blue satin and Uncle Richard's shirt-front.

She knew now what she wanted; she pulled herself together and absolutely refused Uncle Richard's escort.

"No, I shall be quite all right—really. No, Uncle Richard, I won't hear of it. It was silly of me to come out really. I've been feeling this thundery weather all day. No, Lady Carloes, thank you, I'll just go straight back and go to bed. I won't hear of anyone coming with me, thanks. No, really I am so sorry, Lady Carloes. I shall be all right in the morning. Yes, if you'd call a cab, please. No, Uncle Richard, I'd rather not."

She was better. She knew what she wanted. At last the cab was there, but it was not "York Terrace" that she had commanded, but "24 Saxton Square."

It was Lizzie whom she needed.

IV

It was a long drive to Saxton Square. She was better now, but still strangely unwell, and to open both the windows was of no use: not a breath stirred, the trees, dark and sombre, were of iron, the lamps gave no radiance and the sky was black.

She was terribly frightened, frightened because here in the dark of her carriage, thoughts of Breton attacked her as they had never done before. She hid her face in her burning hands; her body was shivering. Breton was before her as he had been in his room. She felt his hands about her, his breath on her cheek, his mouth was pressed against hers, her fingers knew again the stuff of his coat and the back of her hand had touched his neck....

And yet, it was at this moment, with those very memories crowding about her, that she knew definitely and with absolute assurance, that it was Roddy, and Roddy only in all the world, whom she now loved.

Her passion for Breton had been a passion of rebellion, of discontent—a moment perhaps in her education that carried her from one stage to another.

She loved Roddy. She could not trace the steps by which her love had grown, but affection had first been changed into something stronger on that day when he had been carried back into his house from whose gates he had passed, that morning, so strong and sure. Pity had been the beginning of it, admiration of his courage had continued it, this moment of this stormy night had struck it into flame—

And now, perhaps, in another day or so, she would learn that he had done with her for ever.

She sat there, huddled, trembling, her eyes burning, her throat dry.

Oh! why wouldn't the carriage go faster! If only this storm would come and that terrible sky would break! She knew that Mrs. Rand and Daisy were away in the country and Lizzie went out very seldom. She would find her. She must find her. She shuddered to think what she might do were Lizzie not at home.

They were there. Yes, Miss Rand was at home: Rachel went in.

Lizzie was sitting quietly by the open window, reading. She looked up and saw Rachel in a dress of black and gold, her face very pale, as she stood there in the doorway.

"Lizzie dear—Lizzie." Rachel flung off her cloak, stood for a moment motionless, then without another word, huddled up on to the sofa and, her face buried in her arm, began to cry. Lizzie came across to her, took her hand, and sat there without speaking.

After a long time she said, "Rachel dear. What is it?"

Rachel clung to her, holding her fiercely. At last, looking up but away from Lizzie, she said, "Oh! if you hadn't been here. I don't know —I simply don't know what—I think it's this night. This awful night. It's so close and the storm is so long coming."

"Has anything particular happened?"

"Yes. The Duchess has told Roddy about—about Francis—or I think she has. Roddy's said nothing to me, but I ought to speak to him, to tell him.... I've put it off."

Lizzie said softly. "You must tell him, Rachel. You know that you must. It's the only thing. I thought it would come to that sooner or later."

"But it's more than that. I'm not well. I don't know what it is, but I've never felt like it before, and it makes me more frightened than I've ever been. To-night I've been more frightened."

But Lizzie was thinking.

"Has your grandmother told many people?"

"I don't know. I know nothing; that's what makes it so hard. It's all had a climax to-night. There was an awful dinner at old Lady Carloes' and it was so hot and stuffy that I nearly fainted. I had to leave. And then, coming here ..."

Rachel began to tremble again and, creeping close to Lizzie, she held her tighter.

"Lizzie ... in the cab coming here ... Francis ... I had such thoughts. I couldn't have believed...."

Lizzie's eyes gazed out into the square, far away —not like a Pool to-night, Mr. Breton. All hard and cruel and even the Nymph has no softness.

She kissed Rachel. "It's the night, dear. When the weather's like this it affects one. London's awful to-night. There'll be such a storm soon."

"But it's worse, Lizzie. I seem to-night to have seen myself as I am —more clearly than before. My priggishness—talking so much about Truth and then—the things I do. Roddy, Francis, all the same. I've treated them all badly. I've been true to no one. I'm no good...."

"Promise me, dear, that you'll tell him—your husband—everything—to-morrow. Promise me."

"But Lizzie, perhaps——"

"No—no—no. Everything. To-morrow."

"He'll hate me. He'll——"

"No matter. You must. To-morrow."

Rachel was silent. Then she looked into Lizzie's face. "Yes," she said, "I will."

Then, with a little sigh, she fainted.

V

When she rose to a realization of life again she was lying upon Lizzie's bed and the storm had broken over the house. Lizzie was holding her hand; the thunder roared. Coming with stealthy steps closer and closer, sometimes to creep stealthily away again, sometimes to break, with crashing splendour, upon their very heads.

The lightning flung Lizzie's bedroom into pale brilliance and was gone; Life leapt into vision, then surrendered to the candle flare, then leapt again.

Rachel smiled faintly. She felt around her and about her a great peace. She knew that all her terror had departed; her one thought now was to return to Roddy and tell him everything.

She sat up. "How silly of me to faint. It's a thing I've never done in my life. How did you get me here?"

"The maid and I carried you in. It's better for you in here."

"I think I'll go now, Lizzie dear."

"Wait a little while."

They stayed in silence. Then they heard the rain that lashed the windows.

"Isn't the rain terrific?... Oh! Lizzie, it's all gone, all the terror, all that awful fright." She added solemnly, "I don't believe I'll ever feel like that again. It'll never come back—I'm sure of it."

Rachel sat silently for a moment, then turned and buried her head in Lizzie's dress.

"Lizzie dear, I've been so frightened—of something else."

"Of what?"

"I'm going to have a child. I've known it for some time. At first I wasn't sure. Then I knew. I was frightened and miserable. Then, as with every day I seemed to grow fonder and fonder of Roddy I became glad about it. Then very happy——"

"Oh, Rachel dear, I'm so glad!"

"Yes. But now, with this, about Roddy it's all dreadful again. If he should turn on me now just when I've begun to care."

She sat up in bed, her eyes staring, her hands clutching the clothes.

"Lizzie, if it should come right!—if it should! Just think what a child would mean for him; he's so brave, lying there all day, making himself amused and interested. I watch him often and wonder where all that courage comes from. I couldn't have done it.... But now, if the child's a boy, he'll be able to put all his old strength and keenness into him—and the Place! Think what it will mean to him to have that!"

"And for you?" asked Lizzie.

"I believe it's what I've wanted. Oh! if only things are all right with Roddy, then I can start again and have some decent pride about it all. I've made such a mess of things so far."

They talked for a little. Then Rachel got up and dressed.

"I'm all right now. Everything seems to have cleared. I'll tell Roddy everything to-morrow, Lizzie dear."

"Come and see me as soon as ever you can, won't you?"

"I will."

Rachel said good night. She held Lizzie's shoulders.

"Lizzie, you're wonderful. Don't think I don't know how wonderful you are. I'll never forget what you've been to-night. And if it's all right to-morrow. Oh! I am going to be happy."

"That's all right," said Lizzie. "Don't go and get frightened again."

"I'll never be so frightened as I was to-night—never."

"I'm afraid you've got dreadfully wet," she said to the cabman.

"It don't matter, mum—but it does come down."

Lizzie stood in the doorway and waved her hand.

The rain slashed the panes and whipped the shining deserted streets. Very far away the faint whisper of thunder bade the town farewell.

CHAPTER VI
MARCH 13th: RODDY TALKS TO THE DEVIL AND THE DUCHESS DENIES GOD

"Que désirez-vous savoir plus précisément?'
Mais le porte-drapeau répondit:
'Non, pas maintenant ... apres ...'"
A l'Extrême Limite.
Artzybachev.

I

That afternoon had been a difficult one for Roddy. He felt, lying so eternally on his back, the vagaries of the English weather. There were days when the wind was in the park, when sunshine flashed and flung shadows, when the water of the pond glittered and every duck and baby thrilled with life. Then it was very hard to lie still, and memories of days—riding days and swimming days and hunting days—would persecute him. But there were dark wet hours when his room seemed warm and cosy—then he was happy.

On a day of thunder, like this afternoon, his one desire was to get out; never had he felt the bars of his cage so sharply, with so intense an irritation as on to-day.

Massiter broke the chain of his thoughts and he was glad. Four days now and Rachel had said nothing; many times he had thought that she was going to speak, but the moments had passed. He had not slept for two nights— over and over he turned the question as to what he was to do.

Had he been up and about, some solution would have naturally come, he thought, but, lying here, thinking so interminably with one's body tied to one like a stone, nothing seemed clear or easy.

This was the worst day in the world to make thinking simple. The leaden sky pressed one down and held one's brain.

"I'm goin' to have a jolly bad evenin'," said Roddy, "I know I am."

Massiter was a relief; there was no need to talk whilst Massiter was there and his fat cheerful body restored one's balance. The same, sensible world that had once been Roddy's own and had, of late, slipped away from him, was restored when Massiter was there. Nevertheless one hour of Massiter was enough. Roddy could detect in Massiter's attitude that pity moved him to additional cheerfulness, and this was irritating; then Massiter's clumsy efforts to avoid topics that might be especially tactless—that also was tiresome.

347

Roddy was glad when Rachel and John Beaminster came down and relieved him, and then the moment arrived when he thought again that Rachel was going to speak, and perhaps if he had made a movement of affection he would have caught her, but always when some expression of feeling was especially demanded of him did he feel the least able to produce it.

The whole relationship between them depended on such slender incidents; one word from anybody and there would be no more confusion or doubt; the situation had the maddening tip-toe indecision of a dream.

"I'm going to have a bad time to-night," he thought. "It's no use giving in to the thing." He faced it deliberately; if only he could think clearly, but the damned weather.... Well, he and Jacob must face the night as best they could.

The dog lay flat near the window, moving restlessly under the close air, but pricking his ears at every movement that Roddy made, ready to come to him at any instant.

"That old dog cares for me more than anyone else does—and I only appreciated him after I was laid up—Rummy thing!" Roddy was conscious that high above him, somewhere near the ceiling, hovered a Creature, born of this damnable evening, and that did he allow himself to relax for a moment, down that hovering Creature would come. Very faintly, as it were from a great distance, he could catch its whisper in his ear. "What's the good of this?... What's the good of this? What did you always say? What would you have said about anyone placed as you are now? Better for him to get out."

"Damn you, shut up...."

He was in great physical pain, the pain that always came to him when he was tired out, but that was nothing to the mental torture. Twisted figures—Rachel, Breton, himself, the Duchess—passed before him, mingling, separating, sometimes coming to him as though they were there with him in the room. He had not, even on the day that had told him that he would never get up again, felt so near to utter defeat as he was now. He had been proud of himself, proud of his resistance to what, with another man, might have appeared utter catastrophe, proud of his dogged determination. "To have the devil beat...." To-night this same devil was going to be too much for him, did he not fight his very hardest, and the cruelty of it was that this weather took all one's vitality out of one, drained one dry, left one a rag.

"Curse you, get out," he muttered, clenching his teeth, then whistled and brought Jacob instantly to his side. The dog jumped on to the long sofa, taking care not to touch his master's legs. Then he moved up into the hollow of Roddy's arm and lay there warm against Roddy's side.

"What's the use?" The Creature was close to him, his breath warm and damp like the night air. "She doesn't care for you. You can see that she doesn't. She's been in love with her cousin for ever so long, only you didn't know. Wouldn't she have told you that she was a friend of his if there had been nothing more than that in it? What a fool you are—lying here all broken up, simply in the way of her happiness, no good to yourself or anyone else."

"I wish the thunder would come and smash you up...." Then, more desperately, "What if that's right? if I were to clear out...."

"After all," said the Creature, "you've never before seen yourself as you really are. You thought that you were all right because you could use your legs and arms. Now you know what you are—You're nothing—only something that many people must trouble to keep alive—useless—useless! Why not?"

Yes, Roddy did see himself to-night, sternly; as in the old days he might have looked upon someone and judged him unfit, so now he would confront himself. "It's quite true. You've got nothing—nothing to show, you've no intellect, you're selfish, you despise all kinds of people for all kinds of reasons. You've stood a little pain—so can any man. You'd better get out—no one will know."

"Yes," said the Creature, very close to him now. "You can do it so easily. That morphia that you've had once or twice—an overdose. No one would suppose.... She would never know, and you'd be rid for ever of all this wrong and you'd free so many people from so much trouble."

"Jacob, my son," he whispered, "do you hear what they're saying?"

He went right down, down to the depths of a pit that closed about his head, filled his eyes with darkness, was suffocating.

"Yes, he's beaten," he heard them say. "We've succeeded at last. We've succeeded...."

But they had not.

With an effort of will that was beyond any power that he had believed himself to possess, he pulled himself up.

"There's one thing you've forgotten." He gasped as he came struggling up.

He took the Creature in his hands, wrung its neck and flung it out of the window.

"There's one thing you've forgotten. There's my love for her. That's strong enough for anything. That's reason enough for living even though she doesn't want it. I'll beat you all with that ... go back to hell, the lot of you."

II

"I must never let it happen like that again. What a state this weather can get one into...."

But he had come back to his senses. His brain was clear; he could think now. The great point was that it was of no use to think of himself in this affair. "Rachel, Rachel's the only thing that matters."

Then upon that came the decision. "That old woman's got to pay for it. She's been wantin' to give Rachel a bad time. She's tried to. Her mouth's got to be stopped however old and ill she is!"

He was fiercely, furiously indignant with her—vanished, it appeared, all his affection, the sentiment of years. "I've got to defend Rachel from her, no knowin' whom she's been tellin'." Roddy still found it impossible to admit more than one idea at a time, and the idea now was that "he must stop the old lady dead."

His brain came round now to Breton, and halted there. What kind of fellow, after all, was he? What, after all, did Roddy know about him that he could so easily condemn him?

To-night, fresh from the battle with the Creature, Roddy's view of the world was painted with new colours. The man had been condemned for things that his father had done, and one recognized, here in London, how difficult it was for a fellow to climb up once he had been pushed down.

Was the man in love with Rachel? Well, Roddy did not know that he could blame him for that? ... difficult enough, surely, for anyone not to be. But was he? What, after all, was he like?

350

Then swiftly the answer came to him. See the man.... Talk to him ... know him. He stared at the idea, felt already new energy in his bones and a surging victory over the lethargy of this awful evening at the suggestion of some definite action.

But see him, yes, and see him here and see him soon. His impatience leapt now hotly upon him; he pulled Jacob's ears. "That's the ticket, old boy, ain't it? See what kind of a ruffian this is! My word, but wouldn't the old lady hate it if she knew?"

But, and at this the room flared with the thrill of it, why not have her here to meet him? Confront her with him.

He was cool now. Here was matter that needed careful handling. Still as vigorous now as in his most active days was his impatience. Was something in the way, cobwebs, barriers, obstacles of any sort? Brush them aside, beat them down!

Here was a plan. Here, too, most happily at hand, was the Duchess's punishment.

All these years had the old lady been refusing to set eyes upon her grandson, therefore, how dramatic would it be were she confronted with him unexpectedly. Out of the heart of that meeting would come most assuredly the truth about Rachel.

There, in a flash, solid, substantial, beautifully compact, magnificently splendid his plan lay before him. He would have them there. Rachel, the Duchess, this Breton, all of them there before him. They should come ignorant, unprepared, Breton first, then Rachel, then the Duchess.

Having them there he would quite simply say that someone had been pouring into his ears a story of friendship to which he might take objection.

He would then, very quietly.... But here he paused. Oh! he knew what he would do. He smiled at the thought of the success of his plan.

When he had made his little speech to them all there would never again be any danger of scandal. The old lady would never again have any single word to say.

The thought that Rachel might be angry at his deceptive plot did not disturb him. When she had heard his little speech she would not say that—and here, suddenly, he knew how deeply, in his heart, he trusted her.

But what if, after all, it should be a lie on the old lady's part? Was he not doing wrong to take things so far without a question to anyone else, Christopher or Lizzie Rand?

But this was Roddy. Here both his pride and his impatience were concerned. He did not wish that the business should pass beyond its present bounds. He could not go from person to person asking them whether they trusted his wife. And then he could not wait. Here was a plan that killed the danger at one blow, something direct, open, with sharply defined issues. Oh! Rachel should see how he loved her!

"All these days," he said to Jacob, "I've been worryin' about her, but I knew—yes, I knew—that she was comin' to me all right." He thought of a day long before and of Miss Nita Raseley and of a meeting in the garden. "I'll show her that I can forgive, too, if it's necessary. Not because I care so little, but, by God, because I care so much. No," he thought, shaking his head over it, "she doesn't love me, not yet. But she's beginnin' to belong to me. She's coming."

There was also the thought that the Duchess was an old, sick woman and that the scene might be too much for her strength. "Not she," he grimly decided, "that's the kind of thing she lives on. Anyway, I owe her one. Didn't do her any harm comin' to me the other day, won't do her any harm now. I know her."

His scheme must be carried out at once. He felt that he could not wait a moment. He would have liked to have had them all there, before him, to-night.

"Why, by this time to-morrow, old boy, it will all be straight. Thank God, my brain cleared, in spite of this damn weather."

He rang the bell and Peters, large, solemn, but bending a loving eye upon his master, appeared.

"Writing things, Peters."

He wrote swiftly two notes.

"Very close to-night, sir."

"Yes, Peters, very."

"You're looking better, sir ... less tired. Your dinner will be up in a quarter of an hour. Nice omelette, nice little bird, nice fruit salad, sardines on toast."

"Thank you, Peters, I'm hungry as—as anything."

"Very glad to hear it, sir."

"I want these two notes sent by hand instantly, do you see?"

"Yes, Sir Rod'rick."

"At once."

"Yes, Sir Rod'rick."

Roddy lay back and surveyed the black sky.

"Nasty storm comin' up—look here, Peters, give me that bird book over there. That big one. Thanks."

Peters retired.

III

Meanwhile Her Grace had found this close evening very trying. That visit to Roddy had not harmed her physically, but had made her restless. The very fact that it had not hurt her, urged her to have more of such evenings. Having shown them once what she could do she would like to show them all again, and yet with this new energy was also lethargy so that she sat, thinking about her adventures, but felt that it would be difficult to move.

Then this thundery afternoon really did drag the strength from her. She allowed her fire to fall into a few golden coals, she allowed Dorchester to move her from her high-back chair on to a sofa that was near the wide window, now flung open. She could see roofs, chimneys, towers of churches, all dingy grey beneath the leaden sky.

She lay there, a book on her lap, but not reading; she was thinking of Roddy. For perhaps the very first time in all her life she regretted something that she had done. Nobody but Roddy could have called this regret out of her and now, she would confess it to no living soul, but she lay there, thinking about

353

it, remembering every movement and gesture of his, seeing always that, at the end, he had wanted her to go, had, as her sharp old eyes had seen, hurried her away.

There had been so splendid a chance, she had shown her love for him so magnificently that he could not but have been touched and moved had she only left Rachel alone. Ah! that girl! again, again.... The Duchess looked at the plain roofs that lay dry and sterile beneath the torrid sky and wished, not by any means for the first time, that she had left that marriage with Roddy alone.

Roddy would have married some other girl, Nita Raseley or such, and he would have been mine ... mine!

Hard and utterly selfish in all her ordinary dealings with a world that she professed to despise but really adored, her love for Roddy was a little golden link to a thousand softnesses and, as she termed them, weak indulgences. Why had she loved him so? She was like the grim pirate of some conventional fiction. See him on his dark vessel surveying with cold and cruel eye the beautiful captives provided by the stricken ship, on every side of him! See him select, for the very flavour that the contrast gave him, some ordinary slave from the crowd to whom he shows weak indulgence! So much blacker, he feels, does this kindness make his infamies.

But the Duchess's career as the dark pirate of her period was swiftly vanishing; the black hulk of her vessel remained, but upon its boards only the little slave was to be seen, and even he, with furtive eye, sought his way of escape.

Yes, on this torrid evening every soul in that vast city, surely, felt that he was alone, abandoned, in a desert of a world. But the fear that she was losing even Roddy brought the Duchess very close to panic. She had not grasped before how resolutely she had been using him to bolster up life for her, how important his friendly existence was for her.

Since his marriage that friendliness had grown, with every hour, weaker. Something she must do now to repair her error of the other day; she was even ready to pretend affection for her granddaughter if that would bring Roddy back to her.

She watched the sky and longed for the threatened storm to break; her bones were indeed old and feeble to-day, to move at all was an effort and, with it all, there was a sense of apprehension as though she were some terrified bird conscious of the hawk's approach, she who had, until now, been herself the hawk. She remembered the day when she had realized more poignantly than ever before, that the hour must come—and indeed was not far away—when she would inevitably meet death. She had loathed that realization, attempted to defy it, been defeated by it. Now on this evening, she suspected again the invasion of that same power. But to-night there was no resistance in her, she lay there, whitely submitting to the tyranny of any enemy. She could scarcely breathe; London, like a scaly dragon, flung its hot breath upon her and withered her defiance. She would have moved away from the window had not those grey roofs held her, by their ugly indifference, with a terrible fascination. "I'm going—I'm going—and they don't care. Just like that—just like that—long after I'm gone."

The evening slipped away and Dorchester, coming to her, thought that she was sleeping; she did not disturb her, but ordered her evening meal to be kept until she should wake.

The Duchess did sleep. She awoke to find, in the sky above the now vanishing roofs, a golden glow and in the room behind her the shaded lamps, the fire burning, and her table spread.

But she had had a horrible dream; she struggled to recall it and, even as she struggled, trembling seized her body as the vague horror that it had left behind it still thrilled and troubled her.

She could recollect nothing of her dream except this, that she had died, and that being dead, she was immediately aware that God awaited her. She could remember her frantic effort to reassert all those earthly convictions that had been based on the definite creed that the Duchess existed but not God. She had still with her the sensation of hurry and dismay, the dismal knowledge that she had only a moment with which to break down the discoveries of a lifetime and place new ones in her stead.

She had, above all, the horrible knowledge that her punishment was settled, that at last she was in the hands of a power stronger than herself and that nothing, nothing, nothing could help her.

She was frightened, but she knew not by what or by whom. She tried to tell herself that she had been dreaming, that this breathless evening was responsible, that she would be all right very soon. But she was seized by that terrible vague uncertainty that had been with her so much lately, uncertainty as to what was real and what was not. She looked at the French novel lying upon her lap; that was real, she supposed, and yet as she touched its pages her fingers seemed to seize upon nothing, only air between them.

The fits of trembling shook her from head to foot and yet she could scarcely breathe, so close and heavy was the night.

"That was only a dream—only a dream. Suppose it should be true though. What if I were to die—to-night?"

Dorchester came to her and was alarmed.

"Dinner is ready, Your Grace."

Her mistress did not answer, but lay there, looking through the open window and shivering.

"Your Grace will catch cold by that open window. I had better close it."

"It's stifling—stifling."

"Will you have dinner now?"

"No—no. Why do you worry me? I can eat nothing."

Dorchester was seriously alarmed; an evening like this might very easily.... She determined to send word round to Dr. Christopher.

She went away, gave directions about the dinner, saw that her mistress's bedroom was warm and comfortable.

She came back. The Duchess was sitting up, colour in her cheeks and her eyes sparkling. On her lap lay a note.

"I've had a dream, Dorchester—a horrid dream. I was disturbed for a moment. I think I will eat something after all."

"The way she goes up and down!" thought Dorchester. "Must say I don't like the look of her—not knowing her own mind, so unlike her—Who's the letter from, I wonder?"

It was the letter, plainly, that had done it. Sitting up and enjoying her soup, forgetting that black sky and the Dragon's scaly menace, the Duchess knew that that dream—that dream about God—had been as silly, as futile as dreams always are.

The note, brought to her by Norris and lying now beside her plate, had told her so. The note of course had been from Roddy. It said:

"Dear Duchess,

I don't want to ask anything impossible of you, but, encouraged by your coming to me the other day and hearing that you took no harm from your expedition, I am wondering whether to-morrow afternoon about five you could come again and have tea with me. There is something about which you can help me—only you in all the world. If I don't hear from you I will conclude that you can come—five o'clock.

Your affectionate friend,

Roddy."

That letter showed the perfection of his tactful understanding....

No absurd talk about her age, her feebleness, the weather, but simply it was taken for granted that of course she would be there. Well, of course, she would be there—nothing should stop her. She was aware that Christopher, hearing that to-night she had not been so well, would certainly forbid her to move. He should, therefore, know nothing about it, nothing at all. His visit would be paid in the morning—she would have the afternoon to herself—Norris and Dorchester should help her to the carriage.

Christopher expected, on his arrival, to find her in a very bad way, exhausted by the closeness of the evening: it was possible that he might have to remain all night. He found her in bed, a lace cap on her head, a crimson dressing-gown about her shoulders, and all her rings glittering upon her fingers. An old-fashioned massive silver candlestick with six branches illuminated the lacquer bed, the black Indian chairs, the fantastic wall-paper. The windows were closed and the dry heat of the room was appalling.

She was in her mildest, most amiable mood, had enjoyed an excellent dinner, laughed her cracked, discordant laugh, was delighted to see him.

"Sit down, there, close to me. Have some coffee."

"No, thank you."

357

"Dorchester can bring it in a minute."

"No, really, thank you."

"Who sent for you?"

"Lord John."

"Yes, I thought so. Pretty state of things with them all hanging round like this waiting for me to die—never felt better in my life."

"So I see—delighted. I'll go."

"Not a bit of it. Stay and talk. I feel like telling someone what I think of things, although you've heard it all often enough before. But the truth is, Christopher, I did have a nasty dream—a very nasty dream—and the nastiest part of it was that I couldn't remember it when I woke up.

"But it's the weather—I was frightened for a minute although I wouldn't have anyone else know."

"But you had a good dinner."

"Splendid dinner, thank you."

She lay back in bed and looked at him; delightful to think that she would play a little game with him to-morrow; he would in all probability be angry when he knew—that would be very amusing; delightful, too, to think that, just when she was afraid that she had seriously alienated Roddy away from her, he should write and say that he needed her. She would go to-morrow and would be exceedingly pleasant to him and would reassure him about Rachel....

Yes, she had seldom felt so genial. She told Christopher stories of men and women whom she had known, wicked stories, gay stories, cruel stories, and her eyes twinkled and her fingers sparkled and her old withered face poked out above the dressing-gown, with the white hair, fine and proud beneath the lace cap.

Once she said to him: "You think all this queer, don't you?" waving her hand at the bed, the chairs, the paper. "This colour and the odds and ends and the rest."

"It's part of you," he said; "I shouldn't know you without them."

"I love them," she breathed. "I love them. Oh! if I'd had my way I'd have been born when one could have piled up and splashed it about and had it everywhere—jewels, clothes, processions—Ah! that's why I hate this generation that's coming; the generation that you believe in so devoutly, it's so ugly. It wears ugly things, it likes ugly people, it believes in talking about ugly morals and making ugly laws...." Then she laughed—"It's funny, isn't it? I had to use the age I was born into, I cut my cloth to it, but what a figure I'd have made in any century before the nineteenth. All the old times were best. You could command and see that you were obeyed.... None of your Individualism then, Christopher."

She was silent for a time and he said nothing. He was thinking about Breton, wondering where he was, feeling that he should not have let him go. She said suddenly:

"Christopher, do you think there's a God?"

"I know there is."

"Well, I know there isn't—so there we are. One of us will find that we've made a mistake in a few years' time."

He said nothing. At last she began again:

"You're sure of it?"

"Quite sure."

"So like you—and you get a deal of comfort from it, no doubt. But what kind of a God, Christopher?"

"A just God—a loving God."

"How any doctor can say that truthfully! The pain, the crime you must have seen——"

"Exactly. I've known, I suppose, of as much misery, as much agony, much wickedness as most men in a lifetime. I've never had a case under my notice that hasn't shown the necessity for pain, the necessity for struggle, for defeat, for disaster. If this life were all, still I should have had proof enough that a loving God was moving in the world."

She lay back, smiling at him.

"You're a sentimentalist of course. I've heard you talk before. You're wrong, Christopher, badly wrong. I shall prove it before you will."

"Well," he said, smiling back at her, "we'll see."

"Oh, yes, you're a sentimentalist of the very worst—I don't know that I like you the less for it. I'm an old pagan and it's served me all my life. Ah! there's the thunder!"

She sat up in bed, her cap pushed back, her skinny arms stretched out in a kind of ecstasy. "There! That's it! That's the kind of thing I like! There's your God for you, Christopher."

A flash of lightning flung the room into unreality.

"I'd hoped for one more good storm before I went. I've been waiting all day for this."

He never forgot the strange figure that she made; she displayed the excitement of a child presented with a sudden unexpected gift.

He himself had known many storms, but, perhaps because she now made so strange a central figure of this one, this always remained with him as the worst of his life. He had never heard such thunder and, as each crash fell upon them, he felt that she rose to it and exulted in it as though she were a swimmer meeting great ocean rollers.

There was at last a peal that broke upon them as though it had tumbled the whole house about their ears. Deafened by it he looked about him as though he had expected to find everything in the room shattered.

"That was the best," she cried to him.

At last she lay back tired, and he bade her good night.

She held his hand for a moment. "I regret nothing," she said, "nothing at all. I've had a good time."

But, after he had left her, the sound of the rain had some personal fury about it that made her uneasy.

She called to Dorchester. "I think I'd like you to sleep here to-night, Dorchester. I may need you."

"Very well, Your Grace."

"After all," she thought as, the candles blown out, she lay and listened to the rain, "that dream may come back...."

CHAPTER VII
CHAMBER MUSIC—A TRIO

"A place may abound in its own sense, as the phrase is, without bristling in the least."—The American Scene.

Henry James.

I

The storm savagely retreating left blue skies, spring, and the greenest grass the parks had ever displayed, behind it. Roddy, lying before his window, watched the pond, gleaming like blue grass but crisped by the breeze into a thousand ripples. Two babies ran, tumbled, screamed and shouted, and all the many-coloured ducks, the ducks with red bills, the ducks with draggled feathers, the ducks in grey and brown, chattered beneath the sun.

By midday a note had arrived from Breton saying that he would be with Roddy at half-past four; there was no word from the Duchess. He knew therefore that his plan had prospered. But, with those morning reflections that freeze so remorselessly the hot decisions of the night before, he was afraid of what he had done; he was afraid of Rachel.

He was afraid of Rachel because he recognized, now that he was on the brink of this plunge, how much deeper and more dangerous it might be for him than he had thought. During these last months he had been slowly capturing Rachel; that capture was the one ambition and desire of his life.

But in the very intensity and ardour of his desire he had learnt more surely than ever the strange contradictions that made her character. His accident had increased his own age and so emphasized her youth; she was ever so young, ever so impulsive; her seriousness was the seriousness of some very youthful spirit, who, guessing at the terrific difficulty of life, feels that the only way to surmount it is to close eyes blindly and leap over the whole of it at once. This was what he knew in his heart—although he would never have put it into words—as her adorable priggishness.

She had found her solution and everything must fit into it, but, since she had finally resolved it, nothing would fit into it at all—and there was the whole of Rachel's young history!

To Roddy one thing manifest was that a very tiny blunder might shatter the bond that was forming between them, and it was eloquent of a great deal that, whereas before in the Nita Raseley episode, it had been Rachel who feared the one false step, it was now Roddy. What it came to was that, in spite of everything, he was still unable to prophesy about her. She was still unrealized, almost untouched by him, that was partly why he loved her so.

Roddy's brain had been alive last night and ready to grapple with anything; to-day he felt stupid and confused. "We're in for a jolly good row," he thought, "far as I can see. There's no avoidin' it. Anyway, some clearin' up will come out of all of it."

So intent was he upon Rachel that he scarcely considered the Duchess. He had not very much imagination about people and made the English mistake of believing that everyone else saw life as he did. He had, for that very reason, never believed very seriously in the Duchess's passion for himself; he liked her indeed for her hardness and resented any appearance of the gentler motions—"She'll like tellin' us all what she thinks of it"—placed her in the afternoon's battle. He might have taken it all, had he chosen, as the most curious circumstance, that he should be "arranging things"—eloquent of the changed order of his life and of the new man that he was becoming.

He lay there all the morning, nervous and restless—Rachel had looked in for a moment and had told him that she was going to see Christopher, that she might not return to luncheon. He had fancied that, in those few moments, he had divined in her some especial thrill—"We're all going to be tuned up this afternoon."

If he found—and this was the question that he asked himself most urgently—that Rachel really had, in the competent interpretation of the term, "deserted" him for Breton, what would be his sensations? Being an Englishman he would, of course, horsewhip the fellow, divorce Rachel and lead a misanthropic but sensual existence for the rest of his days. But here the wild strain in Roddy counted. That is exactly what Roddy would not do. What was law for the man must be law also for the woman.

He had, on an earlier day, told her that were he to present her with a thousand infidelities, yet he would love her best and most truly, and therefore she must forgive him. Well, that should be true too for her.... Any episode with Breton seemed only an incident in the pursuit of her that Roddy had commenced on that day that he had married her.

And yet was not this readiness on his part to forgive her sprung from his conviction that she would have told him had she had so much to confess to him? Let her relations with Breton remain uncertain and shifting, then she might have found justification for her silence; let them once have found so definite a climax and she must have spoken—Roddy had indeed advanced in his knowledge both of her and himself since two years ago.

By the early afternoon he was in a pitiable state. Should he send notes to the Duchess and Breton telling them both that he was too unwell, too cross, too sleepy, too "anything" to see them? Should he retire to bed and leave Peters to make his excuses? Should he disappear and tell Rachel to deal with them? What a scene there'd be between the three of them!

His illness had made a difference to his nerve, lying there on one's back took the grit away, gave one too much time to think, showed one such momentous issues.

On the events of this afternoon might hang all his life and all Rachel's!

His capture of her was indeed now to be put to the test!...

II

Rachel came into his room at four o'clock. She carried a great bunch of violets and a paper parcel.

She smiled across the room at him; a cap of white fur on her head, and the hand with the violets held also a large white muff.

"Roddy—I'm coming to have tea with you—alone. You'll be out to everyone, won't you? But first, see what I've brought you."

She was dreadfully excited, he thought, as though she knew already the kind of thing that awaited her. Her smile was nervous, and that trembling of her upper lip, as though she would, perhaps, cry and perhaps would laugh but really was not sure, always told him when she was afraid.

"See what I've brought you!" She put the violets down upon the table beside him—"Now! Look!" She undid the paper and held up to his gaze a deep, gleaming silver lustre bowl, a beautiful bowl because of its instant friendliness and richness and completeness—"I found it!" she said, "staring at me out of a shop window, demanding to be bought. I thought you'd like it."

She put it on his table, found water and filled it, then arranged the violets in it.

"Oh! my dear! it's beautiful!" he said, and then, with his eyes fixed upon her face, watched her arrange the flowers. But he brought out at last, "I'm afraid I can't promise to be alone for tea."

"Oh!" she stepped back from the flowers and looked at him. They faced one another, the silver bowl between them. She stood, as she always did, when she had something difficult to face, her long hands straight at her side, her hands slowly closing and unclosing, her eyes fixed upon some far distance.

"Roddy, please!" she said, "I do want to be alone with you this afternoon. I have a special, very special reason. I want to talk."

"You see——" he said.

"No," she cried impatiently. "We must have this afternoon to ourselves. Tell Peters that you're too ill, too tired, anything. I'm sure, after all that storm last night, it would be perfectly natural if you were. Now, please, Roddy."

"I'm awfully sorry, Rachel dear. If I'd only known. If you'd only told me last night."

"I didn't know myself last night. How could I? But now—it's most awfully important, Roddy. I've—I've something to tell you."

His heart beat thickly, his eyes shone.

"Well, they won't stay long, I dare say."

"Who are they?"

"Oh! nobody—special. Friends——"

"Then if they aren't special put them off. Roddy dear, I beg you——"

"No, Rachel, I can't——"

"Well—you might——" For a moment it seemed that she would be angry. Then suddenly she smiled, shrugged her shoulders—at last, moved across and touched the violets; then, with a little gesture, bent down and kissed him.

"Well, my dear, of course you will have your way. But am I to be allowed to come or are these mysterious friends of yours too private—too secret?"

"Not a bit of it. I want you to come."

"I'll go and take my things off. I hope they'll come soon; I'm dying for tea, I've had such a tiring day, and last night — —"

"How was last night? You haven't had time to tell me."

She was by the door, but she turned and faced him. "Oh! I was so silly. The weather upset me and I went and fainted at Lady Carloes'."

"Fainted!" His voice was instantly sharp with anxiety.

"Yes — in the middle of dinner. Such a scene and Uncle Richard thought I let down the family dreadfully."

"I hope you went straight to bed — Ah! that was why you saw Christopher this morning!"

"Yes, that was why! No, I didn't come straight back last night — I went round to Lizzie's — I was frightened and felt that I couldn't come back all alone."

They were both of them instantly aware that someone else lived at 24 Saxton Square beside Miss Rand. There was a sharp little pause, during which they both of them heard their hearts say: "Oh! I hope you aren't going to let that little thing matter!"

Then Roddy said — "Well, dear. I'm jolly glad you did go to Lizzie. I hate your fainting like that. What did Christopher say this morning?"

"Oh! nothing — I'll tell you later."

She was gone.

When she returned Peters was bringing in the tea and they could exchange no word. The spring was beginning, already the evenings were longer and a pale glow, orange-coloured, lingered in the sky and lit the green of the park with dim radiance. Within the room the fire crackled, the silver shone, the lustre bowl was glowing —

Rachel went across to the table, then staring out at the evening light said, "Roddy, who are your visitors?"

Peters answered her question by opening the door and announcing—

"Mr. Breton, my lady."

III

She took it with a composure that was simply panic frozen into stillness. She saw him come, straight from the square immobility of Peters, out to meet her, noticed that he looked "most horribly ill" and that his eyes cowered, as it were, behind their lashes, as though they feared a blow—she saw him catch the picture of her, hold her for an instant whilst his cheeks flooded with colour, then all expression left him; he walked towards her as though the real Francis Breton, after that first glance had turned and left the room, and only the lifeless husk of him remained.

For herself, after the word from Peters, her mind had flown to Roddy. He knew everything—there could no longer be doubt of that—but oh! how she turned furiously now upon the indecision that had allowed to surrender her courage and her self-respect! With that she wondered what it was that her grandmother had told him. Perhaps he believed worse than the truth. Perhaps he thought that nothing too bad....

And what, after all, did he intend to do? This meeting had sprung from some arranged plan and he had, doubtless, now, some end in view. Had he meditated some vengeance upon Breton? At all costs, he must be protected.

Meanwhile Breton had, apparently, taken it for granted that she had known about his coming.

"How do you do, Lady Seddon?" he said, shaking her hand.

"You don't know my husband," she said quietly. "Roddy, this is Mr. Breton."

Breton went over to the sofa and the two men shook hands.

"How do you do?" Roddy said, smiling. "My word, the feller does look ill!" was Roddy's thought. He did not know what type of man he had expected to see, but it was not, most certainly, this nervous rather pathetic figure with the pointed beard, the white cheeks, the blue eyes, the armless sleeve, that uncertain movement that invited your consideration and seemed to say, "I've had a bad time—not altogether my fault. I'm trying now to do my best. Do help me."

"Just the sort of feller women would be sorry for," Roddy thought. But he was rather happily conscious that, although he was lying there helpless on his back, he was on the whole in better trim than his visitor.

Breton, before he sat down, turning to Roddy, said, "I was very nearly wiring to you my excuses, Sir Roderick. I've been most awfully unwell lately and all that thunder yesterday laid me up. I got sunstroke once in Africa and I've always had to be careful since."

"Jolly good of you to come," said Roddy. "Sorry it was such short notice. But I can never tell, you know, quite how I'll be from day to day."

Breton sat down and the two men looked at one another. To Breton, whose imagination led him to live in an alternation of consternation and anticipation, the whole affair was utterly bewildering. He had reached his rooms, on the night before, soaked to the skin, and had found Roddy's note waiting for him. It had seemed to him then as though it were, in all probability, some trick of the devil's, but he had of course accepted it as he accepted all challenges.

He had supposed that he would be confronted by a raging, tempestuous husband. He would welcome anything that would bring him again into contact with Rachel and he always enjoyed a scene. But he had never, for an instant, imagined that Rachel would be present. The sight of her took all calmer deliberation away from him because he wished so eagerly to speak to her and to hear her voice.

They were sitting with the table between them and they were both of them conscious first of Roddy, lying so still and watching them from his sofa, and then of the last time that they had met and of that last kiss they had taken. But Rachel, with strange relief and also with yet stranger disappointment, was realizing that Breton's presence gave her no spark, no tiniest flame of passion. She was sorry for him, she wished most urgently that no harm should come to him, she would, here at this moment, protect him with her life, with her honour, with anything that he might demand of her, but her emotion, every vital burning part of it, was given to her retention of Roddy.

She might have felt anger because she had, as it were, been entrapped, she might have felt terror of the possible results to herself ... she felt nothing except that she must not lose Roddy.

"I know now," she said, perhaps to herself, "I know at last what it is that I have wanted. And, knowing this, if, just grasping it, I should lose it!"

"Tea, Mr. Breton—sugar? Milk? Would you take my husband's cup to him? Thank you so much. Yes, he has sugar——"

"I was so sorry," Breton said, "to hear of your accident. You must have had a bad time."

"Yes," said Roddy, laughing. "It was rotten! But what one loses one way one gains in another, I find. People are much pleasanter than they used to be."

Roddy, as he looked at them both, had something of the feeling that a schoolboy might be expected to have did he suddenly find that some trick that he had planned was having a really great success.

He was strangely relieved at Breton's appearance, he was more sure than ever of his retention of Rachel, he had, most delightfully up his sleeve, the imminent appearance of the Duchess. As he looked at his wife he could see that she was appealing to him not to make it too hard for both of them. He could, now he had seen Breton, flatter himself with something of the same superiority that Rachel had once shown on beholding Nita Raseley.

Breton, as the moments passed, felt firmer ground beneath his feet. Rachel, wondering how she could contrive their meeting, had chosen this, the boldest way, had begged her husband to invite him, planned to make him a friend of the house. And yet with all this new confidence, he felt too that there was something that he missed in Rachel, some response to his thrill, he could see that she was ill at ease and was relying on him perhaps, "to carry it off."

So he carried it off, talked and laughed about his experiences, the countries that he had seen, things that he had done, and, as always when he was striving to make the best impression, made the worst, letting that note of exaggeration, of something theatrical that was dangerously near to a pose, creep into his voice and his attitude.

Rachel and Roddy said very little. He stopped, felt that he had been speaking too much, and, sensitive always to an atmosphere that was not kindly to him, cursed himself for a fool and wished that he had never spoken at all.

There was a little pause, then Roddy said, "That's very interesting. I've never been to South America, but I hear it's going to be the place soon. Everyone's

as rich as Cr[oe]sus out there, I believe. Another cup, Rachel dear, please—
Oh! thank you, Mr. Breton."

Breton brought the cup to Rachel and then stood there, with his back to
Roddy, his eyes upon Rachel's face, trying to tell her what he was feeling.
Quietly Roddy's voice came to them both.

"There is one little thing—one reason why I wanted you to come this
afternoon, Mr. Breton."

Rachel got up, her eyes fixed intently upon Roddy's face. "No, Rachel, don't
go. It concerns us all three." Roddy laughed. "I don't want any of us to take it
very seriously. It is entirely between ourselves. I do hope," he went on more
gravely, "that I haven't been takin' any liberty in arrangin' things like this,
but it seemed to me the only way—just to stop, you know, the thing once
and for all."

Breton had left the table and was standing in the middle of the room. A
thousand wild thoughts had come to him. This was a trap—a trap that
Rachel....

The room whirled about him—he put his hand on to the back of a chair to
steady himself, then turned to Rachel, seeking her with his eyes.

He saw instantly in her white face and eyes, that never left, for an instant,
her husband, that there was nothing here of which she had had any
foreknowledge.

"It's only," said Roddy, "that somebody came to me, a few days ago, and told
me that you, Mr. Breton, and my wife were on friendlier terms than I—well,
than I would, if I had known, have cared for——"

Breton started forward. "I——" he began.

"No, please," said Roddy. "It isn't anythin' that I myself have taken, don't
you know, for a second, seriously. I have only arranged that we three should
come like this because—for all our sakes—if people are sayin' those things it
ought to be stopped. It's hard for me, you see, bein' like this to know quite
how to stop it, so I thought we'd just meet and talk it over."

Roddy drew a deep breath. He hated explaining things, he disliked intensely
having to say much about anything. He looked round at Rachel with a
reassuring smile to tell her that she need not really be alarmed.

She had left the table and stood facing both the men. Full at her heart, was a deep, glad relief that, at last, at last, the moment had come when she could tell everything, when she might face Roddy with all concealment cleared, when she might, above all, meet her grandmother's definite challenge and withstand it.

But, indeed, she was to meet it, more immediately and more dramatically than she had expected. Even as she prepared to speak, she caught, beyond the door, strange shuffling sounds.

The door, rather clumsily, as though handled with muffled fingers, slowly opened.

Framed in it, leaning partly upon Peters, and partly upon a footman, staring at the room and its occupants from beneath the sinister covering of a black high-peaked bonnet, was the Duchess.

The old lady caught, for a second, the vision of her grandchildren, beat down from her face the effect that their presence had upon her, then moved slowly, between her supporters, towards the nearest chair.

CHAPTER VIII
A QUARTETTE

"Her dignity consisted, I do believe, in her recognition, always sure and prompt, of the dramatic moment."—Henry Galleon.

I

Rachel came forward: Roddy from his sofa said something.

She was, it seemed, unconscious of them all, fixing her eyes upon a large black-leather arm-chair, settling slowly down into it, dismissing Peters and the footman with "Thank you—That is very kind": then, at last leaning her hands upon her ebony cane, raised her eyes and smiled grimly, almost triumphantly, at Roddy.

He had been aware, at that first glimpse of her in the doorway, that he was ashamed of himself. He should not have done it.

She was older, feebler, more of a victim than he had ever conceived her possibly to be, and in some way the situation that awaited her changed her entirely from the old tyrant who had sat there talking to him only a week ago into someone who demanded of one's chivalry, of one's courtesy, protection.

Roddy had also caught the light of fierce recognition that had leapt up into Breton's face as he had realized who it was that stood before him. Breton must have many old scores to pay.... Roddy was suddenly frightened of the emotions, the fierce resentments, the angry rebellions that he had brought so lightly into collision.

But the smile that the Duchess flung to him had in it no fear. It said to him: "Oh, young man, this is your little plot, is it? Oh, Roddy, my friend, how young you are and how little you know me if you think that I am in the least embarrassed by this little gathering. I'm glad that you've given me a chance of showing what I can do."

She dominated the room; she was, from the minute of her appearance, mistress of the situation. They realized her power as they had never realized it before.

Sitting there, leaning forward upon her cane, she remarkably resembled Yale Ross's portrait. She was even wearing the green jade pendant, and her black dress, her bonnet, her fine white wrists, a gold chain with its jangling cluster of things—a gold pencil, a card case, a netted purse—these flung into fine relief the sharp white face lit now with an amused, an ironic vitality.

She was old, she was ill, she was being trodden down by generations hungrier than any that she had ever known, but she was as indomitable as she had ever been.

She looked about the room; her glance passed, without any flash of recognition, without sign or signal that she had realized his presence, over the fierce figure of her grandson.

"Well, my dear," she said to Rachel, "I'm sure this is all very pleasant and most unexpected. Let's have some tea."

"I'm afraid," said Rachel, "that it's been standing some time. Let me ring for some fresh."

"No—I like it strong. It used always to be strong when I was younger. This new generation likes things weak, I believe."

Rachel, looking at her grandmother, felt nothing of Roddy's compunction. She did not, even now, grasp entirely Roddy's intention; she had no sure conviction of the climax that he intended; but she did know that here, at last, was her chance; she should lift, once and for all, out from all the lies and confusion that had shrouded them, her attempts at courage and honesty, attempts that had wretchedly, most forlornly failed.

Breton should know, Roddy should know, the Duchess should know, and she herself should never again go back.

Breton did not move from the corner where he was sitting; he waited there, his hand pressing hard upon his knee.

Roddy said, "Most awfully good of you, Duchess, to come out again. I wouldn't have dared to ask you to come if Christopher hadn't said that last time did you no harm."

"Only for you, Roddy," she answered him almost gaily, "and Rachel of course. To-day's a nice day. All that thunder has cleared the air."

What her voice must have seemed to Francis Breton, coming back to him again after so vast a distance, bringing to him a thousand memories, scenes and faces that had been buried, a whole world of regrets, and disappointments.

Rachel gave her her tea; brought a little table to her side.

"Thank you, my dear. How are you, Rachel? You're not looking very well. Richard, who came in to see me this morning, told me that you were ill at dinner last night. He seemed quite anxious."

"It was nothing, thank you, grandmamma. That thunder always upsets me. I was sorry to interfere with Lady Carloes' dinner-party."

"Not much of a party from what Richard told me. And she had in a harpist afterwards. Why a harpist? Poor Aggie Carloes! Always done the wrong thing ever since she was a child. Yes, her little drawing-room's so stuffy, they tell me—must have been intolerable last night."

It was for all three of them a quite unbearable situation. Roddy had never, even when he was a boy of sixteen, been afraid of her; now at last he understood what the power was that had kept her family at her feet for so many years, indeed, he seemed now to perceive in all of them—in Breton, in Rachel, as well as in the Duchess—a strain of some almost hysterical passion, that, held in check though it was, for the moment, promised to flare into the frankest melodrama at the slightest pretext.

Anything better than this pause; he plunged.

"You won't forgive me, Duchess," he said abruptly. "I believe I've done a pretty rotten thing. I didn't intend it that way. I only meant just to clear everything up and make it all straight for everybody, but if I've been unpardonable just say so and give it me hot."

He paused and cleared his throat. "I wonder if you'd mind, Rachel," said the Duchess, "passing me that little stool that I see over there—that little brown stool. Just put it under my feet, will you? Thank you."

Roddy desperately proceeded.

"It's only this. You said the last time you came that you had heard—that you knew—that you were afraid that Rachel and your grandson, Mr. Breton, were—had been—seein' too much of one another. You just put it to me, you know—Well," he went on, trying to make his voice cheerful and ordinary and failing completely, "lyin' on one's back one gets thinkin' and broodin', specially a feller who hasn't been used to it, like me. I got worried—not because I didn't trust Rachel—and Mr. Breton, of course, all the way, because I do; but simply that, you know, it's rotten for a feller to be lyin' helpless on his back, thinkin' that people are talkin' about his wife—you know how malicious people are, Duchess—and I thought it jolly well must be stopped, don't you know, and I wanted it stopped quick and straight and clean, and I didn't see how it was goin' to be stopped unless I'd got us all friendly together here and just squashed it, all of us. And so—well, to speak—well, here we are.... And," he concluded, trying to smile upon everyone present, "I do hope it's all right. It didn't seem then a poor sort of thing to do, but somehow gettin' you all here as a surprise...." He broke off, made noises in his throat, and felt that the room was of a burning heat.

He remembered, vaguely, that he had designed this meeting as a punishment to the old lady; he had only succeeded, however, in revealing his own cowardice; the first glimpse of her had made a poor creature of him. Oh! how he wished himself now well out of it! And yet, behind that thought was the knowledge of the little speech that he was soon to make and the way that, with it, he would win Rachel and hold her for ever! After all, it came to that, absolutely: Rachel was the only thing in all the world that mattered.

The Duchess flung upon him a kindly satiric glance, then, turning from him, bent her sharp little eyes upon Rachel, leaning forward upon her cane so that it appeared that it was now only with Rachel that she had any concern.

"Had I known that my few careless words!"—She broke off with a little impatient gesture.

"Ah! Rachel, my dear, I'm truly sorry. My stupidity...."

But Rachel, her eyes upon Roddy, had got up, had moved across to Roddy's sofa, and stood there, above him. Her eyes moved, then, slowly to her grandmother.

"There was no need," she said, her voice low and trembling, "for this. If I'd done, as I should, it couldn't have happened. I'm responsible for all of it and only I. Roddy has got you here on false pretences, grandmamma. If you'd rather go now...."

"Thank you," the Duchess said, "I'd much rather stay. It amuses me to see you all together here."

"Then," said Rachel, "I'll say what I ought to have said before. Roddy," turning passionately round to him, "you shall have everything — everything—from the very beginning. Mr. Breton—Francis—will agree that that's what we should have done—long ago."

Breton made a movement as though he would rise, then stayed.

"Aren't we, my dear Rachel," said the Duchess, "making a great deal of a very small affair?"

But Rachel, speaking only to Roddy, sinking her voice and bending a little down to him, began, "Roddy, one thing you've got to know—it's been from the beginning only myself that was to blame. Francis"—she paused, for an instant, over the name—"Francis, please," as he moved again from his corner, "let me tell Roddy...."

She went on then more firmly, turning a little round to her grandmother again: "Roddy, I don't want to defend myself—it's the very last thing I can try to do—I only want to tell you—all three of you—exactly the truth. You know, Roddy, that when I said I'd marry you it wasn't a question of love between us at all. We had that out quite straight from the beginning. I was awfully young: I wanted safety and protection and so I took you. You rather wanted me, and grandmother wanted you to marry me, and so there you were too. Then I met my cousin—I'd heard about him since I'd been a baby and he'd heard about me. We had a lot in common, tastes and dislikes—all kinds of things. We met and he stirred in me all those things that you, Roddy, had never touched. I had found marriage wasn't the freedom I had thought that it would be. I was fond of you, you were fond of me, but there was something always there jogging both of us—just putting us out of patience with one another. Things got worse. You never could explain what you felt. I tried, but the whole trouble wouldn't go into words somehow.

"Francis and I wrote to one another a little and then one day—as grandmamma has so kindly told you—(here her voice was sharp for a moment)—I went to his rooms." Rachel stopped. She was looking straight in front of her, her hands clenched. She seemed to dive deep for courage, to remain for an instant struggling, then to rise with it in her hands. Her voice was strong and unfaltering. "We found that we loved one another. We told each other ... it seemed to Francis then that the only thing was for us to go away together. But I refused. Odd though it may seem, Roddy, I cared for you then more than I'd ever cared for you before, and I think it's gone on since then, getting stronger always. I wouldn't go and I wouldn't see Francis again and we weren't to write again—unless I found that our living together, Roddy—you and I—was hopeless. Then I said I'd go to him."

Her voice sank and faltered—"There did come a day when I thought that— we couldn't get on any longer. You know what finally ... Lizzie Rand found out. She knew that I intended to go away with Francis. She fought to prevent it—she was splendid about it, splendid! We quarrelled, and in the middle of it, came your accident.... I wrote afterwards to Francis and told him that it was all over—absolutely—for ever. Since then—only once...." She broke off, recovered: "Since then there's been nothing—no letter, no meeting—nothing. My whole life now is wrapped up in you, Roddy, and Francis knows that. I've told you the whole truth!" She turned from him, fiercely, round to her grandmother. "I don't know what you told Roddy, what you made him believe—you've wanted, always, to harm me with Roddy if you could. At least, now, you can't tell him more than I've done."

The Duchess stared first at Rachel, then at Roddy. She had behaved from the beginning as though Breton did not exist.

Some of her amiability had left her. Her lips were tightly drawn together as she listened and her rings tapped one against the other.

"This is all rather tiresome," she said sharply. "Very like you, Rachel, to do these things in public. You get that from your mother. But you're strangely lacking in humour. It all comes from my own very unfortunate remark the other day. Not like you, Roddy dear, to arrange this kind of thing. Stupid ... distinctly—I'm sure now, however, that you're satisfied. Rachel's certainly been very frank—and now perhaps we might leave it."

It was then that Francis Breton came forward into the middle of the room, his face grey with anger, something suddenly unrestrained and savage in his eyes so that the room was filled with a wind of angry agitation.

He stood in front of his grandmother, but turned his head, sharply, now and again, round to Roddy. So agitated was he that his words came in little gasps, flung out, in little bundles together, and strangely accented as though he were speaking in a language that was strange to him.

The sarcastic smile came back into the old lady's eyes and she leaned forward on her stick again, looking up into his eyes.

"I didn't know—I didn't know—that we were going to meet like this. You didn't know either or you wouldn't have come, but I've been waiting for years for this. It's been nice for me, hasn't it, to sit by whilst you've done everything to make things wretched for me, to ruin me, to push me back to where...."

Roddy's voice interrupted.

"Mr. Breton, I think you forget — — "

Instantly Breton stopped. He forced control upon his voice, he stammered, "I'm ashamed — I oughtn't to have — But sitting there — not being allowed to speak — you must excuse me — — "

He turned round to Roddy. "You must think me the most complete blackguard. It's only a climax to everything that's happened since I came back. I don't want to defend myself, but it isn't — it isn't all so simple as just talking about it makes it look. You're the kind of man to whom everything's just black or white — you do it or you don't — but I — I've never found that. I've been in things without knowing I've been in them. I've done things that would have turned out straight for any other fellow, but they've always been crooked for me. Something always blinds me just when I need to see straightest. That's no excuse, but it's an awful handicap.

"I won't hide or pretend about it. Why should I? I loved Rachel. We've only met so little — really only that once in my rooms — that you can't grudge us that. We had things — heaps of things — in common long before we knew one another. It wasn't like any ordinary two people meeting, and I knew so well that she could make all the difference to my life that I took the chance of knowing her even though she wasn't ever going to belong to me. I don't think I ever really believed that I'd be the man. I know now that she's yours altogether and you ought to have her — now that I've seen you I know that. And last night when I faced the fact that I'd have to go all my life without her I realized what she told me long ago, that it was much better just to have my idea of her and not to have had my regret about having spoiled anything for her. I've no confidence in myself, you see. If I thought I were the kind of man just to carry her off and make her happy for ever and ever, then I suppose I'd have been bolder about her long ago, but I know, even if she didn't belong to you at all, that I should be afraid that I'd spoil her life just as I've always spoiled my own.

"I expect this is all very confused. It's all so difficult and you don't want long explanations, but I'm only trying to say that you needn't ever have any fear again that I'm going to step in or try to have any part in her. We've got our things together that nobody can take from us. We've seen each other so little that most people would say it wasn't much to give up. But things don't happen only when you're together...." He stopped suddenly, seemed to stand there confused, turned and flung a fierce, defiant look at his grandmother—exactly the glance that an angry small boy flings at someone in authority who has seen fit to punish him—then went back to his corner and stood there in the shadow, watching them all.

Even as he finished speaking he had realized finally that his relationship with Rachel was over, closed, done for. He had known it on that afternoon in the park—He had realized it perhaps again in the heart of the storm last night, but now, when he had seen the soul pierce, through Rachel's eyes, to her husband, he knew that Roddy, one way or another, had at last won her.

Moreover, to anyone as impressionable as Breton, Roddy's helplessness, his humour, his bravery had, on the score of Roddy alone, settled the matter. Breton had his fierce moments, his high inspirations, his noble resolves!... Now, as he looked this last time upon Rachel, his was no mean spirit.

Rachel drew a sharp breath and looked at Roddy with wide eyes, flooded with fear. He had heard now everything that they had to say; although she had watched him so closely she could not say what he would do. As she saw the two men there before her she felt that she knew Francis Breton exactly, that she could tell what he would say, how he would see things, what would anger him or surprise him.

But about Roddy she was always uncertain: she was only now, very slowly, beginning to know him, but she was sure that if Roddy were to beat her she would care for him the more, but if Francis Breton were to beat her she would leave him for ever.

A flush meanwhile was rising over Roddy's neck, up into his face, to the very roots of his hair.

"It's rather beastly," he said, speaking very slowly and trying to choose his words, "all this talkin'. I might have known, if I'd been able to think about it, what it would be like, but there, I never did. I had a kind of idea that we'd all get it over sort of in five minutes and then have tea, don't you know, and all go away comfortably. I don't feel now that you've rightly got all that everybody thinks about it. It was very decent of you, Mr. Breton, to say exactly—so plainly, you know—how you felt. But I don't want to talk a lot— I can't you know, anyhow.

"It's only this. I wanted the Duchess to hear me say, amongst ourselves, that I know all about it, that we all know all about it and that there isn't anything for anyone to talk about because there isn't anything in it, and if I hear of anyone sayin' a word they've just got to reckon with me. Rachel and I know one another and, Mr. Breton, I hope you'll go on bein' a friend of ours and come and see us often. Of course you and Rachel have a lot in common and it's only natural you should have.

"Now Duchess, you can just tell anyone who's talkin' that Mr. Breton is welcome here just as often as he pleases and he's a friend of mine and my wife's—and they can jolly well shut their mouths. Thank God, all that's over."

II

But he was very swiftly to realize that it was not all over. Sharply, quivering through the air like an arrow from a bow, came the Duchess's words.

"Good God, Roddy, are you completely insane?"

She was twisted, distorted with anger, she seemed to take her rage and fling it about her so that the chairs, the tables, Roddy's innocent little sporting sketches and even the case of birds' eggs were saturated with it.

The gleaming park, the peaceful evening sky, the sharp curve of an apricot-tinted moon, these things were blotted out and the noises of the town deadened by this indignant fury. Rachel had known it in other days, to Breton it evoked long-distant nursery hours, to Roddy it was something utterly new and unsuspected. For the first time in his life he caught a shadow of the terror that had darkened Rachel's young days.

To the Duchess it was simply that she now clearly discovered that she was the victim of an elaborate plot. The three of them! Oh! she saw it all! and Roddy, Roddy—who had been the one living soul to whom her hard independence had made concession! This came, the definite climax to the year's accumulations, the final decision flung at her, before she died, by those two—Rachel and Breton—from whom, of all living souls, she could endure it least.

With her rage rose her fighting spirit. She would show them, these young fools, the kind of woman that an earlier and a finer generation than theirs could produce!

They had more there before them than one old woman, sick and ailing, and they should see it.

Her voice shook a little, but she gave no other sign, after that first challenge: her little eyes flamed from the mask of her face like candles behind holes in a screen.

"This is your sense of fun, Roddy, I suppose," she said. "You always were lacking in that. I've told you so before. As you asked me here I suppose you're ready for my opinion. You shall have it. I'll only ask you to cast your eye over any friend of ours: see what you would say if this—this idiotic folly committed by someone else had come to your ears. I suppose you'd arranged this, the three of you. Well, you shall know what I think. Your tenderness to Rachel is magnificent—she has obviously reckoned on it, knew that her frankness would serve her well enough. You've already been more patient with her than men would have been in my day. I only hope that your patience may not be too severely tried....

"As for my grandson, to whom you have so tenderly entrusted Rachel, your acquaintance with him is quite recent, is it not? I am sure that if you were to enquire of any man at one of your clubs he would give you quite excellent reasons for my grandson's long unhappy absence from his relations and his country. At any rate you don't know him as well as I do. I could tell you, if you asked me, that it is a long time now since any decent man or woman has sought his society. Do you suppose that his family have not the best of reasons for trying to forget his existence—an attempt that he makes unpleasantly difficult?

"Have you heard nothing, Roddy? Do you really want a man who has been kicked out of society for the most excellent reasons, who has disgraced his name as no member of his family has ever disgraced it before him, for your wife's lover? If she must have one...."

Rachel, trembling, had come forward, Roddy had cried out, but quietly, stronger than either of them, Breton had faced her. She had not, throughout the afternoon, looked at him nor spoken one word to him. Now, her anger carrying her beyond all physical control, she was compelled to meet his gaze.

He stood very quietly beside her chair, looking at the three of them. "My grandmother is wrong," he said, "I am not quite as deserted as she thinks. Just before I came here this afternoon Uncle John called upon me. I had half an hour's very pleasant talk with him: he told me that, although his mother had not altered her opinion of me, Uncle Vincent and Aunt Adela and himself considered that I had earned"—he smiled a little—"forgiveness. He hoped that I would understand that—while my grandmother was alive—I could not be invited to 104 Portland Place, but that he thought that I would like to know that they had realized my—well, improvement, and that he hoped that we would be friends. I said that I should be delighted."

The Duchess spoke to him then, her voice shaking so that it was difficult to catch her words.

"John—came—said that—to you?"

"Yes. It was a curious coincidence that to-day——"

Her eyes had dropped. She murmured to herself:

"John ... John ... Adela ... behind my back ... Adela ... Vincent——"

They were all silent. She sat there, her head down, leaning on her hands, brooding. Her anger seemed to have departed, her fire, her fury had fled: she was a very old woman—and the room was suddenly chilly. Before her were Rachel and Breton: they faced the ancient enemy. But as Rachel stood there, realizing that there had flashed between them the climax of all their lives together, yes, and a climax of forces greater and more powerful than anything that their own small histories could contain, she had no sense of drama nor of revenge nor of any triumphant victory. A little while before she had been almost insane with anger.... Now something had occurred. Rachel only knew that the three of them—Roddy, Francis and herself—were young and immensely vigorous, with all life before them; but that one day they would be old, as this old woman, and would be deserted and sick and past anyone's need of them.

"Oh! I wish we hadn't! I wish we hadn't!" she thought.

In that moment's silence they all might have heard the sound of the soft, sharp click—the click that marked the supreme moment of their relationship to the situation that had, for all of them, been so long developing—

Breton surrendered Rachel, Roddy received her, and, beyond them all, the Duchess definitely abandoned her world.

For them all, grouped there so closely together, the heart of their relations the one to the other had been revealed to them.

382

Other dramas, other comedies, other tragedies—This had claimed its moment and had passed....

After the silence the Duchess said, "My family—I no longer...." She stopped, collected, with all her will, her words, then in a low voice said, looking at Breton, "I owe you, I suppose—an apology. I owe that perhaps to you all. My children are wiser in their own generation. I no longer understand—the way things go—all too confused for my poor intelligence." She pulled herself together as an old ship rights itself after a roller's stinging blow. "This has lasted long enough.... We've all talked—My family are—wiser—it seems."

But she could not go on. "Please, Roddy," she said at length, "I think it's time—if you'd ring."

"I'm sorry——" he said and then stopped.

Soon Peters and a footman appeared. She leaned heavily upon them and, staring before her at the door, slowly went out.

CHAPTER IX
RACHEL AND RODDY
"Tell me, Praise, and tell me, Love,
What you both are thinking of?
O, we think, said Love, said Praise,
Now of children and their ways."
William Brighty Rand.

I

Breton had gone; the room was empty.

Rachel came and, kneeling on the floor, hid her face in Roddy's coat. He put his hands about hers.

His only desire now was that there should be peaceful silence. His hatred for scenes had always been with him an instinct, natural, alert, untiring, so that he would undertake many labours, forgo many pleasant prizes, if only emotional crises might be avoided.

This afternoon had showered upon him a relentless succession of reverberating displays, he had perceived one human being after another reveal quite nakedly their tumultuous feelings. It was, for him, precisely as though the Duchess, Rachel, Breton had stripped there before him and expected him to display no astonishment at their so doing—that he should have been the author of the business made it no better; he reflected that he had even looked forward with excitement to the affair. "If I had only known how beastly...."

He was ashamed—ashamed of his own action in provoking these things, ashamed of his own lack of understanding, ashamed to have watched the sharpened tempers of his friends.

He would never, Heaven help him, take part in any such scene again!

But out of it all one good thing had come—he had got Rachel! As she had looked across the room, meeting his eyes, he had known that at last his long pursuit of her was at an end....

It never occurred to him that most husbands, after such a declaration as Rachel had just made, would have stormed, reproached, ridden, for a long time to come, the high horse of conscious superior virtue.

It did not seem odd to him that at the very moment of Rachel's confession he should feel more sure of her than he had ever been before. At last the Nita

Raseley debt was paid off. At last he knew, beyond question, that Rachel loved him. Best of all, perhaps, he had seen Breton and felt his own superiority.

That being so, he wanted no words about the matter. He would like to lie there on his sofa, with her hands enclosed in his and nothing said between either of them—very pleasant and quiet there in the dusk. He hoped that he would never again have to explain anything or speak to anyone about his feelings—no, not even to Rachel.

Then he discovered that she was sobbing as she knelt there, and his face crimsoned with confusion and alarm. Rachel, the proudest woman he had ever known, kneeling to him, crying!

He tried to lift her, pressing her hands.

"Rachel dear ... Rachel."—Her words came between her sobs.

"I should have told you ... long ago ... I tried to—I did indeed ... but it was because I was frightened ... because I ... Oh! Roddy! you'll never trust me again!"

He was burning hot with the confusion of it: he was almost angry both with himself and her.

"Please, Rachel ... please ... don't ... it's all over, dear. There's nothing the matter."

"It's fine of you ... to take it like that ... But you'll never forgive me, really, you can't—It isn't possible. This very afternoon ... I was going to tell you—if all this ... hadn't happened. You'll be different now—you must be ... just when I want you so much."

He glanced in despair about the room. He looked at the sporting prints and the case of birds' eggs and at last at Rachel's photograph. How proud and splendid she was there! This dreadful abasement!

He stroked her hair.

"See here, old girl—we've had a rotten afternoon, haven't we? Awfully rotten—never remember to have spent a worse. All my fault, too—poor old Duchess!... but look here, it's all right now. I understand everythin' and—and—dash it all—do stop cryin', Rachel, old girl."

"It's been bad enough," she said, her voice steadier now, "the way I've been to you all this time, but I thought—at least—I was honest—I've tried—I've made a miserable failure—But, Roddy, you need—never—never—be afraid of anything again—I'm yours altogether, Roddy, to do anything with...."

"All about Francis—I was mad somehow—It was grandmamma—feeling she had driven me into marrying you. And then Nita ... and then I didn't know you a bit—all there was in you—but now," and she raised her eyes and looked at him, "I love you with all my heart and soul and strength."

He bent down his head and rather clumsily kissed her.

"You know, Rachel, I was a bit frightened myself this afternoon—thought you might be angry because I took you by surprise. You bet, if I'd known what it was going to be like ... Well, thank the Lord, it's done, and we'll never have another like it—I'll see to that. Scenes are rotten things, aren't they?—I always loathed 'em even when I was tiny—so did the governor.... If he had me up for lickin' all he ever said was, 'Down with your bags!' That was all there was about it."

She leant her cheek against his.

"You've forgiven me all, everything—absolutely?" she asked.

"There isn't any forgiveness in it," he answered. "It's all the other way, if it's anythin'.... You see, I've been thinkin' a lot while I was lyin' here. When there was that business over Nita I said you should always be free just as I told you I ought to be. Well, since—since I got that old tumble—I haven't any right to hold you at all. I'm just an old log here, no good, anyway, and only a nuisance. And if I thought I was keepin' you tied I'd be miserable. You see, I know you're fond of me now. I've got that.... Don't let's talk any more about it. You've got me and I've got you—and we aren't afraid of any old woman in the world."

He held her closely to him, his arms strong about her.

"There's something else to tell you."

"Something else?"

"Yes. We're going to have a child, you and I, Roddy. And now that you've forgiven me it's all right—but that's partly what's made me afraid all these last weeks. As it is, you've got me, got me, got me, safe for ever and ever!"

"Well, I'm damned!" said Roddy.

She could feel his hand trembling upon hers.

"Oh," she whispered, "I was frightened this afternoon—terrified. I thought you'd never see me again."

Roddy was turning things over in his mind.

"A kid ... my word. Just the thing. A boy ... it'll be jolly for the Place and I can teach him a lot. It'll be somethin' to go back to the house for. Gosh! There's news!"

His eyes wandered round the room.

"Good thing I kept all those eggs—nearly broke 'em up too. They're a jolly fine collection. I'd have prized 'em like anything if they'd come to me when I was small." He caught her hand so fiercely that she gave a little cry.

"What a day! We'll have to see about the shootin' down at Seddon again, old girl ... Lord, what an afternoon!"

CHAPTER X
LIZZIE BECOMES MISS RAND AGAIN

"So she put the handkerchief, and the pin, and the lock of hair back into the box, turned the key, and went resolutely about her everyday duties again."—Mrs. Ewing.

I

Lizzie was waiting for Lady Adela. She had finished her work for the day, had come from her own room to Lady Adela's and now stood at one of the high windows looking down upon the April sunshine that coloured the dignities of Portland Place.

The room was spacious and lofty, but curiously uncomfortable and lifeless. High book-cases with glass shutters revealed rows of "Cornhill" and "Blackwood" volumes, a long rather low table covered with a green cloth held a silver inkstand, a blotting-pad, pens and a calendar. There were stiff mahogany chairs ranged against the wall and old prints of Beaminster House (white-pillared, spacious with sloping lawns) and Eton College chapel faced the windows.

This was where Lady Adela spent several hours of every morning and she had never attempted to "do" anything with it. A large marble clock on the mantelpiece ticked out its sublime indifference to time and change. "We're the same, thank God," it said, "as we've always been."

Lady Adela had told Lizzie that she would come in from a drive at quarter to four and she would like then to speak to her.

Lizzie's eyes were fixed upon Portland Place, deserted for the moment and catching in its shining surface some hint of the blue sky above it. There was a great deal just then to occupy her thoughts. Ten days ago, in the middle of a little dinner-party that Lady Adela was giving, upstairs the Duchess had had a stroke. Lizzie had, of course, not been there, but, coming next morning she had been told of it. Her Grace was soon well again, no unhappy effects could be discovered, she had not, herself, been apparently disturbed by it, but it had rung, like a warning bell, through the house. "The beginning of the end.... We've been watching, we've been waiting—soon these walls will be ours again," said the portraits of those stiff and superior Beaminsters.

News ran through the Beaminster camp—"The Duchess has had a stroke.... The Duchess has had a stroke."

But, for many weeks now, Lizzie had been aware that some crisis had found its hour. Rachel and her husband, Lady Adela and Lord John, even the Duke and Lord Richard had been involved. It was not her business to ask questions, but every morning that saw her sitting down to her day's work saw her also wondering whether it would be her last in that house....

Lady Adela, however sharply she may have changed in herself, had never permitted her relationship to Lizzie to be drawn any closer. When Lizzie had returned from that terrible Christmas at Seddon, Lady Adela had asked her no questions, had shown no sign of human anxiety or tenderness. She had never, during all the years that Lizzie had been with her, expressed gratitude or satisfaction. She had, on the other hand, never bullied nor lost her temper with her. She had separated herself from all expression or human emotion. And yet Lizzie liked her. She would miss her when their association ended: yes, she would miss her, and the house and the whole Beaminster interest when the end came.

She wondered, as she stood at the window, whether that old woman upstairs were suffering, what her struggle against extinction was costing her, how urgently she was protesting against the passing of time and the death of her generation. Flying galleons of silver clouds caught the sun and Portland Place passed into shadow; the bell of the Round Church began to ring. "Poor old thing," thought Lizzie; she would not have considered her thus, a year ago.

Lady Adela came in; she reminded Lizzie of Mrs. Noah in her stiff wooden hat, her stiff wooden clothes, her anxiety to prevent any mobility that might give her away. She looked, as she always did, carefully about the room, at the "Cornhills" and "Blackwoods," at the marble clock, at the prints of Beaminster House and Eton College Chapel, a little as though she would ascertain that no enemy, no robber, no brigand, no outlaw, was concealed about the premises, a little as though she would say—"Well, these things are all right anyway, nothing wrong here."

"I'm sorry, Miss Rand," she said. "I hope that I haven't kept you."

"No, thank you, Lady Adela, I have only just finished."

Lady Adela sat down; they discussed correspondence, trivial things that were, Lizzie knew, placed as a barrier against something that frightened her.

At length it came.

"Miss Rand, I wonder whether—the fact is, my mother has just decided that she wishes to be moved to Beaminster House. I must of course go with her. I hope that this will not inconvenience you. You can, if you prefer not to leave your mother, come down every day by train; it only takes an hour. Just as you please...."

Lizzie's heart was strangely, poignantly stirred. The moment had come then; the house was to be deserted. This could only mean the end. She herself would never return here, her little room, the large solemn house, that walk from Saxton Square, the Round Church, the Queen's Hall, Regent's Park....

But she gave no sign.

Gravely she replied: "I think I'd better come down with you, Lady Adela, if you don't mind. My mother has my sister. Perhaps I might come up for the week-ends."

"Yes. That would be quite easy. The other places, you know, are let, but Beaminster has always been kept. The Duke has been there a good deal. It reminds me ... I was there for some years as a girl."

Lizzie realized that Lady Adela was very near to tears; she had never before seen her, in any way, moved. She was distressed and uncomfortable. It was as though Lady Adela were, suddenly, after all these years, about to be driven from a position that had seemed, in its day, impregnable.

"Oh! don't, please don't, now!" was Lizzie's silent cry. "It will spoil it all—all these years."

Lady Adela didn't. Her voice became dry and hard, her eyes without expression.

"We shall go down, I expect, on Monday if Dr. Christopher thinks that a good day."

"I hope that the Duchess——"

"My mother's very well to-day—quite her old self. I have just been up with her. It is odd, but for thirty years she has never expressed any interest in Beaminster. Now she is impatient to be there."

"One often, I think, has a sudden longing for places."

"Yes. I shall be glad myself to be there again."

"This house?"

"Oh! we shall shut it up—for the time Lord John will come down to Beaminster with us. I have spoken to Norris, but to-morrow morning, if you don't mind, we will go through things."

"Certainly."

"The house has not been shut for a great number of years—a very great number. During the last thirty years through the hottest weather my mother was here.

"It will seem strange ..." Her voice trembled.

"Is there anything more this afternoon?" Lizzie turned to the door.

"No, I think not. Except—perhaps ..." Lady Adela was in great agitation. Her eyes sought Lizzie, beseeching her help.

"Miss Rand—I think it only right to say. I'm afraid one cannot—in the nature of things—it's impossible, I fear, to expect—my mother to live very much longer." Her voice caught in a dry strangled cough. "Dr. Christopher has warned us. After my mother's death my life, of course, will be very different. I shall live very quietly—a good deal in the country and abroad, I expect.

"I shall not, of course, have a secretary."

"I quite understand," said Lizzie quietly.

"I want you to know, Miss Rand," Lady Adela continued, "that although during all these years I have seemed very unappreciative.... It is not my way—I find it difficult to express—But I have, nevertheless, been very conscious—we have all been—of the things that you have done for me, indeed for the whole house. You have been admirable; quite admirable."

"I have been very happy here," said Lizzie.

"I am very glad of that. I must have seemed often very blind to all that you were doing. But I should like you to know that it is more—it is more—than simply your duty to the house—it is the many things that you have done

391

personally for me. You have not yourself been, I dare say, aware of the effect that your company has had upon me. It has been very great."

Lizzie smiled. "I've loved the house and the work. It has meant a very important part of my life. I shall never forget it."

Their embarrassment was terrible. After a moment of struggle Lady Adela's voice was hard and unconcerned again. "You know, Miss Rand, that—when the time comes for this change—anything that I, or any of us, can do ... I do not know what your own plans may be, but you need have no fear, I think."

"Thank you very much, Lady Adela. That is very kind."

There was a little pause—then they said good night.

As Lizzie went down the great staircase, on every side of her, the stones of the house were whispering, "You're all going—you're all going—you're all going."

Her heart was very sad.

II

As she passed the Regent Street Post Office Francis Breton came out of it. They had not met often lately, but she was conscious that ever since that interview in Regent's Park, they had been very good friends. Her absorption with Rachel and affairs in the Portland Place house had assisted her own resolution and she had thought that she could meet him now without a tremor. Nevertheless the tremor came as she caught sight of him there and, for a moment, the traffic and the shouting died away and there was a great stillness.

He was very glad to see her. He stood on the post office steps looking richer and smarter than she had ever known him. He wore a dark blue suit and a black tie and a bowler hat—all ordinary garments enough—but they surrounded him with an air of prosperity that had not been his before. He seemed to her to gleam and glitter and shine with confidence and assurance. One hurried glimpse she had had of him some weeks before, miserable, unkempt, almost furtive. She was glad for his sake that all was well with him, but he needed her more when he was unhappy....

But he was delighted. "Miss Rand. That's splendid! Are you going back to Saxton Square now? The very thing! I've been wanting badly to see you!" It was always, she thought, in little hurried and occasional walks that they exchanged their confidences. There was not much to show for all the elaborate palace that she had once been building—snatches of conversation, clutches at words and movements, even eloquent interpretation of silences—well, she was wiser than all that now!

But, when they started off together, she found that she was caught up instantly into that fine assumption of intimacy that was one of his most alluring qualities. Radiant though he was he still needed her; he was more eager to talk to her than to anyone else even though he had forgotten her very existence until he saw her standing there.

"I am glad to see you. I should have come down and tried to find you, anyway, in a day or two. I've been through a rotten time—really rotten—and one doesn't want to see anyone—even one's best friends—in that sort of condition, does one?"

"That's just the time your real friends—if they're worth anything—want to see you. If they can be of any use——"

"But you'd been such a tremendous help to me. I was ashamed to come to you any more. Besides, you'd showed me, in a way, that I ought to get through on my own without asking help from anyone. You'd taught me that I did try."

She saw that he was shining with the glory of one who had come, rather mightily, unaided through times of stress. A pleasant self-congratulatory pathos stirred behind his words. "It was a bad time—but it's all right now. And I expect it was good for me," was really what he said.

"I do want to tell you," he went on eagerly, "about Rachel. It's all been so strange—wonderful in a way. After that talk I had with you in the park I was absolutely broken up. Oh! but done for! I simply went under. I tried to go back to some of that old set I've told you about before, but the awful thing was that Rachel wouldn't let me. Thinking of her, wanting her when all those other women were about. It simply wasn't possible...

"It got worse and worse. I thought I'd go off my head. Then—do you remember that awful thunderstorm we had?"

"Yes," said Lizzie, "I remember it very well."

"That night was a kind of climax. I'd dined with Christopher, then got wandering about—it was horribly close and heavy—got into some music

393

hall. I suppose I'd been drinking—anyway, I had suddenly a kind of vision, there in the music hall. I thought Rachel was dead, that I'd lost her altogether. And then—it's all so hard to explain—but when I came to myself I seemed to understand that the only way I could keep her was by giving her up.... I've got it all muddled, but that was what it came to."

"You were quite right," said Lizzie.

"Well, then—what do you think happened? The very next day my uncle, John Beaminster, came to see me—yes, came himself. Talked and was most pleasant and wanted to be friends. At the same time—now just listen to this—came a note from Seddon asking me to go and see him. I went, found Rachel there. Apparently my delightful grandmother had been telling him stories about Rachel and me, and he wanted to put things straight. As though this weren't enough, right upon us, without a word of warning, dropped my grandmother herself!"

He stopped that he might convey fully to Lizzie the drama of the occasion.

There was, in his words, just that touch of absurdity and exaggeration that she had noticed at her very first meeting with him. He was always too passionately anxious to thrill his audience!

"There was a scene! You can imagine it! We all tried to behave at first, although of course it was immensely difficult. I don't think Seddon had in the least realized the kind of thing it would be. Then she—the old tyrant— could contain herself no longer and burst out concerning me, the blackguard I was and the rest of it. She was furious, you see, at Seddon taking my friendship with Rachel so quietly. He was splendid about it!

"Well, when she burst out about all the family cutting me and everybody casting me out, the opportunity was too good. I couldn't help it. I had to tell her that Uncle John had been round that very afternoon to see me and that the family was holding out its arms."

"What happened?" said Lizzie, as he paused.

"She collapsed—altogether, completely. She never said another word—she just went."

"You shouldn't have done it!" Lizzie cried, turning almost furiously upon him. "Oh! it was cruel—she was so old and all of you so young and strong."

"Yes!" he answered her—"But think of the years that I've waited—the times she's given me, the suffering——"

"No," interrupted Lizzie, quiet again now. "If you're weak enough to be pushed down by anybody like that, then you're weak enough to sink by your own fault, whether there's anyone there or no. She's been hard in her time, I dare say, but everything's left her now and she's ill and lonely. It was wrong of all of you. I shouldn't have thought Sir Roderick——"

"He only wanted things to be straightened out," Breton said eagerly. "He didn't intend to have a scene. But I expect you're right, Miss Rand, as you always are. I've been a brute, the most howling cad. But there's one thing—I don't think it's hurt my grandmother. She likes those scenes, and she's been none the worse since."

"She's been much worse," said Lizzie gravely. "She's dying—She's going down to Beaminster on Monday."

He stopped. "Oh! but I'm sorry ... That's dreadful ... I'd no idea. I'm always responsible——"

He had sunk to such depths that she was compelled to raise him.

"I don't think you need be disturbed, Mr. Breton. Something of the sort would have been certain to happen very soon. She would have found out in any case ... and there were other things, I know. Rachel——"

"Ah!" he broke in, eager again and almost cheerful. "That was the wonderful thing. When I saw her there first with Seddon—I'd met him before, you know—I felt angry and impatient. I wanted to carry her off—away from everybody. And then, when Seddon began to speak I lost all sense of Rachel's belonging to me. She seemed older, ever so far away from him, and he was so fine, so splendid about it all that I felt—I felt—well, that I'd do anything in the world for both of them—but never anything that could separate them or make him unhappy."

"You can't separate them now," said Lizzie, "nobody can."

"No. It was just finished—our episode together that wasn't really an episode at all if you consider the little that we saw one another.... Besides, I've never got near Rachel, and I felt in some way that the nearer I got to her the farther away she was. Why, the only time that I kissed her she was the farthest away of all!"

They were walking up the grey, peaceful square.

"You don't mind my telling you all this, do you, Miss Rand? You've seen it all from the beginning. But I'm odd in a way....

"Uncle John coming to me, Seddon being friendly to me, the family taking me back ... that seems to have made all the difference to me. Although I'd never confess it, even to myself, I know that if Rachel and I had gone off together I'd never have happy. You see, we're both alike that way. We're restless, one half of us, but oh! we're Beaminster the other, and even Rachel, who's been fighting the family all her days, has one part of her that's happy to be married to Seddon and to be quiet and proper and English. That's why neither I nor Seddon ever could hold her—because to be with me she'd have had to give up the other. If she had a child, that might——"

"She's going to have a child!" said Lizzie.

He stopped and stared at her.

"Miss Rand!... Is that certain?"

"Quite."

"Ah, well, Seddon's got her all right. They'll be happy as anything." He sighed. "You know, Miss Rand, Rachel and I have been fighting the old lady, and we seem to have won ... but I'm not sure whether, after all, she hasn't!"

On the step he paused.

"I'm sticking to Candles, I've got work. I'm recognized again. I've got that little bit of Rachel that she gave me and that nobody else can have, and—I've got you for a friend—Not so bad after all!"

He laughed, opened the door for her, and then as they stood in the dark little hall he said:

"All along you've been such a friend for me. I want someone like you— someone strong and sensible, without my rotten sentiment and impulses. We'll always be friends, won't we?"

He held her hand.

"Always," she said, smiling at him.

But, perhaps, to both of them there came, just then, sighing through the dark still hall, a breath, a whisper, of that hour when life had been at its intensest, that hour when Breton had held Rachel in his arms, that hour when Lizzie had dressed, with trembling hands, for the theatre....

For Breton his place once again in the world, for Lizzie work and peace of heart, but once on a day life had flamed before both of them and they would never forget—

"Well, good night, Mr. Breton."

"Good night, Miss Rand."

When he had gone, she stood in the hall a moment.

Their little dialogue had closed, with the sound of a closing door, a stage in her life. She would never be the same as she had been before that episode. It had shown her that she was as romantic as the rest of the world. It had made her kinder, tenderer, wiser. And now once again she was independent— once again her soul was her own. She could be, once more, his friend, seeing him with all his faults, his impetuosities, his weak impulses.

Her place was there for her to fill. It was not the place that she would once have chosen. But she had regained her soul, had once more control of her spirit. She was free.

There stretched before her a world of work, of thrilling and ever-changing interest. There were Rachel and Rachel's baby....

"You seem in very good spirits, Lizzie," said Mrs. Rand as she came in. "I'm sure I'm very glad because it's too tiresome. Here's Daisy gone off...."

III

Afterwards she said to her mother:

"I'm going down to Beaminster on Monday. I'm afraid I shall be away some time."

"Oh! Lizzie!" said Mrs. Rand reproachfully. "Well, now—That is a pity. Why must you?"

"The Duchess is going and Lady Adela must go with her and I must go with Lady Adela."

"Dear, dear. Whatever shall we do, Daisy and I? Daisy gets idler every day. It's always clothes with her now.... I suppose we shall manage."

"I shall come up for week-ends."

"What a way you speak of it! Of course you don't care! If you went away for years you wouldn't miss us, I dare say. I can't think why it is, Lizzie, that you're always so hard. Daisy and I have got plenty of feeling and emotion and your father, poor man, had more than he could manage. But I'm sure more's better than none at all, where feelings are concerned."

"I suppose," said Lizzie, speaking to more than her mother, "that if everyone had so much feeling there'd be nobody to give the advice. Feelings don't suit everybody."

"You're a strange girl," said Mrs. Rand, "and you're like no one in our family. All your aunts and uncles are kind and friendly. I don't suggest that you don't do your best, Lizzie. You do, I'm sure—and nobody could deny that you've got a head for figures and running a house. But a little heart...."

"I've come to the conclusion I'm better without any," Lizzie laughed. "I expect I'm more like you and Daisy, mother, than you know——"

"Well, you're a strange girl," said Mrs. Rand again, "and I never understand half you say."

Lizzie came to her and kissed her.

"You always miss me, you know, mother, when I'm away, in spite of my hard heart."

"Well, that's true," said Mrs. Rand, looking at her daughter with wide and rather tearful eyes. "But I'm sure I don't know why I do."

CHAPTER XI
THE LAST VIEW FROM HIGH WINDOWS

"Not without fortitude I wait ...
... I, in this house so rifted, marr'd,
So ill to live in, hard to leave;
I, so star-weary, over-warr'd,
That have no joy in this your day."
Francis Thompson.

I

Rachel, on the morning of April 28th, received this letter from Lady Adela:

"Beaminster House,

April 27th.

My dear Rachel,

Mother suddenly last night expressed an urgent wish to see you. She has not been at all well during the last few days and Dr. Christopher, who has been here since last Saturday, says that if you can come down and see her he thinks that it would be a comfort to her. She is sleeping very badly, but is wonderfully tranquil and seems to like to be here again.

If you can come down to-morrow afternoon I will send to meet the 5.32 at Ryston. That is quicker than going round to Munckston. If I don't hear I conclude that you are coming by that train.

My love to Roddy.

Your affectionate aunt,

Adela Beaminster."

Rachel showed the letter to Roddy.

"I'm so glad," she said, "I've been hoping that she'd send for me. I've felt, ever since that day, that I should never be easy again if I hadn't the chance to tell her that I see now that I—that we—were wrong."

"She's never answered my letter," said Roddy. "Perhaps she wasn't well enough to write. Yes, I'm glad you're going, Rachel."

She was moved by many emotions, the old lady dying, the house in whose shadow she had spent so many of her timid, angry, adventurous young years, the thrill that the thought of her child gave her now at every vision of the world, the knowledge that in Roddy she, at last, had someone in her life to whom, after every absence, however short, she was eager to return—these things shone with new, wonderful lights around her journey.

The April evenings were lengthening and the dusks were warm and scented. The little station lay peacefully in the heart of green fields; across the sky, washed clean of every colour, a dark train of birds slowly, lazily took their flight, trees were dim with edges sharp against the sky-line, a dog barking in the distance gave rhythm to the stillness. Rachel, driving through the falling dark, felt, as she had felt it when she was a small child, the august colour and space and dignity of the first vision of the great house, white as a ghost now under the first stars, speaking to her with the old voice, fountains that splashed in gardens, the river that ran at the end of the sloping lawns, the chiming clock that rang out the hour as she drove up to the door.

Aunt Adela, Uncle John, Dr. Chris, Lizzie, they were all there, and their presences made less chill the dominating reason for their assembly.

Over all the house the shadow fell. The wide, high rooms, the long picture gallery, the comfortless grandeur of a house that had not found, for some years, many human creatures to lighten it, these echoed and flung forwards and backwards the note of suspense, of pause, of impending crisis.

But Rachel spent one of the happiest evenings of her life with Uncle John and Christopher. She knew that Uncle John had had a short but terrible interview with her grandmother, that he had been charged with treachery and dishonour and every traitorous wickedness.

A week ago, when he had told her this, he had been the picture of despair and shame. "I hadn't meant her to know. She wasn't to come into it at all. And then that she should meet him at Roddy's on that very afternoon.... There's nothing bad enough for me." But he had added with a strange note of defiance so unlike the old Uncle John: "I had felt it my duty, Rachel ... to speak to Francis. I had felt it the right thing to do. I had felt it very strongly."

Then he had been overwhelmed, now he was once more at peace, and tranquil.

"It's all right," he told Rachel. "I've been forgiven. I think she's forgiven all of us.

"She wouldn't listen when I wanted to tell her how sorry I was. She seems now not to care."

"She's never forgiven anyone anything before," said

Rachel.

"Hush, my dear, I don't think you ought to say that. We've never understood her, any of us. She's always been beyond us. You'll realize to-morrow, Rachel, how wonderful, how wonderful she is!"

But he was very happy. He had his old Rachel back, the old Rachel whom he had expected never to see again. She sat between him and Christopher, at dinner, no longer fierce and ironical, with sudden silences and swift angers, but affectionate, sympathetic, happy.

"Mother will see you to-morrow," Adela told her. "She's glad that you've come. The morning's rather a bad time for her. Could you stay for the whole day?"

"Of course," Rachel said.

At the end of the evening she went up to Lizzie's room; when midnight rang from the tower they parted, but first, Rachel said:

"Lizzie, I wonder whether you realize what you've been—to all of us—to me of course ... but to the others—to the whole family."

"Oh! Nonsense!"

"Roddy was speaking about it yesterday. He said that you were the most wonderful person in all the world for making all the difference without saying or doing anything—by just being there."

"Oh, Roddy thinks everybody——"

"But this is what I'm coming to. You can't yourself know how much difference you make to everyone. But there's just this.... Roddy feels and I feel that when—He—comes (of course it'll be a boy) we'd rather have you for his friend than anyone in the whole world. You will—you will be, won't you?"

"My dear—I should think so. I'll whack him and bath him and snub him and teach him his letters—anything you like." Then she added, rather gravely:

"There's one thing, Rachel, I've wanted to say for some time. I want you to know definitely, that all wounds are closed now, everything's healed—about Mr. Breton, I mean. I was afraid that you might think I still cared.... That's all ended, closed up, that little episode.

"You needn't be afraid, Rachel. I'm happier, I'm freer than I've ever been in my life.... Good night, my dear. Your friendship is more to me than any number of heart-burnings.... I was always meant to be independent, you know...."

II

It was very strange to Rachel, who had been, on so many, many evenings, to that other room, to pause now outside this new door, to knock with the house solemn and still around her, to hear Dorchester's voice, then, with the old hesitation and—yes—with some of the old fear, to enter.

She had considered what she would say. Coming down in the train she had turned it over and over—her apology, her submission, her cry: "See, I'm different—utterly different from the Rachel whom you knew.... I was a prig of the very worst. I deserved everything you thought of me. Just say you forgive me even though you can't like me." This was the kind of thing that, in the train, had seemed possible enough; now, with the opening of the door and that sharp recurrence of the old thrill, she was not at all sure that she wanted to be submissive and affectionate. "I don't feel fond of her—nothing could make me—there are too many things...."

Space and silence saluted Rachel. Two great mirrors ran from floor to ceiling, high windows flooded the room with light and everything seemed to be intended only for such a situation as this—the very house, the grounds, the colour of the day had arranged themselves, in their purity and air and silence, about the central figure. The Duchess lay in a long low chair before the window; she was wrapped in white shawls and thick rugs covered her body; Dorchester, the same stern, unbending Dorchester, said gravely to Rachel, "Good afternoon, my lady. I hope that you are well," then moved into another room.

The Duchess had not stirred at the sound of the closing doors, nor at Dorchester's voice, nor at Rachel's approach. She was gazing out, beyond the windows, to the expanse of sunlit country, fields that sloped towards the river, an orchard, white with blossom, running down the hill, its colour, dazzling, almost visibly trembling against the sky.

Rachel had only seen her in the Portland Place rooms, with the china dragons, the gold ornaments, the red lacquer bed, the blazing wall-paper. It had seemed then that she must have those things around her, that she needed the colour and extravagance to support her flaming passion for life, so curbed and shackled by disease.

Their absence made her older, feebler, more human, but also grander and more impressive. Rachel had always feared her, but despised herself for her fear; now she was in the presence of something that made her proud to be afraid.

She thought that she might be asleep, so she moved, very quietly, a chair forward near the window and, sitting down, waited. The only sound in all the world was the steady splash—splash—splash of the fountain below, the only movement the stealthy creeping of the long shadows, flung by white boulder clouds, across the shining fields.

Suddenly, without turning her head, the Duchess spoke.

"Very good of you, Rachel. I hoped that you would come."

Her voice was weak, her words indistinct as though she were speaking through muffled shawls, but, nevertheless, behind them the presence of the old dominating will was to be discerned, but now it was a will quiescent, struggling no longer for power.

"I would have come before if you had sent for me. I'm so glad that you did."

"I can't talk for very long, my dear, and I don't suppose that you want to spend hours in my company any more than you've ever done. No, you needn't protest. We're neither of us here for compliments.... But there's something that I must say to you. Christopher allows me half an hour."

"I hope you're better—that being here has done you good."

"Better? Nonsense. I don't want to be better. That's all over and done with. I had another stroke three days ago and the next one will finish me. So don't pretend. You used to be honest enough. I've asked you to come because I want to speak to you about Roddy."

"He wrote," Rachel said.

"Yes. I got his letter. I couldn't reply. I can't write myself and I won't have anyone else do it for me. Besides, there was nothing to write about. He said he was sorry about that little conversation we all had together the other day."

"And I—" Rachel began eagerly, "I was so sorry. I've been longing to tell you—it was all wrong, but Roddy has no imagination. He didn't realize in the least— —"

"Ah, my dear. I expect I know Roddy a great deal better than you do. He'll do the same sort of thing to you, one day. He's got the devil in him and will always have it, however much you coddle him or let him lie there thinking over his sins. Do you suppose I'd have been so fond of Roddy all these years if I hadn't known him capable of such little revenges? I liked it. There was no need to write to me and he knew it—but I'm afraid you influence him a good deal."

Rachel coloured. "I hope— —"

"Oh yes, you do, and that's exactly why I wanted to see you."

She turned then and, very carefully, very slowly, her eyes searched Rachel's face.

"I let him marry you, you know. I thought it would be good for you. If I'd guessed the effect that you'd have had upon him I'd have prevented it."

Rachel's anger was rising.

"What effect?"

"He's begun to worry about other people—a fatal thing with a man like Roddy who was meant to do things, not think about them. But, anyway, that's all too late now.... Waste of time discussing it.... What I wanted you for is this— —"

Her eyes left Rachel's face and returned to the window.

"You're the one person now that influences him and you will always be so. I can see ahead well enough. Poor Roddy ... and he might have been a fine man. All the same, I admire him for it; there are things about you I could have liked if I'd wanted to find them, but we've been fighting from the beginning until now—when it's the end ..." She caught her breath, stayed for an instant struggling for words, then went on:

"We can call a truce now. We don't like one another, but just at the moment you're moved a little because I'm feeble and shall be dead in a fortnight. That disturbs you.... It needn't. Some months ago a moment did come when I realized that I should die soon. I hated it—I fought and struggled with all my might ... but now that it has come it doesn't matter. Nothing matters. I regret nothing. I've had my time. I hate the new generation, the manly woman and the soft man with all this sentimental nonsense about caring for other people. Think of yourself, fight for yourself, keep up your pride— that's the only way the world's ever been run. You're a sentimentalist and you're making one of Roddy.... Nonsense it all is.... But all this isn't what I really wanted to say." She turned back and her eyes, as again they held Rachel, were softer.

"Roddy's been my only weakness. I've loved that boy and he's far too good and fine for a wobbler like yourself. That's why I hated it the other day. I couldn't bear that he should see me beaten by the pair of you, both of you thinking yourself so noble with your fine confessions—not that I believe a word that you said—but it was clever of you. You are clever and know how to manage men.

"Yes, that hurt me, but afterwards I loved him all the better, I believe. I'd rather he hadn't written me that soppy letter, but that was your doing, of course.... But listen. After I'm gone, I want Roddy to think of me kindly. He's going to think very much what you make him. It's in your hands. You, when you've got past this sentimental moment, will hate the memory of me. It's natural that you should and I'm sure I don't mind. But I want you to leave Roddy alone. If he likes to think of me kindly, let him. Don't blacken his mind to me. I wish to feel—my only weakness I do believe—that Roddy will be fond of my memory. That rests with you."

She stopped with a little final movement of her head as though, having said what had been in her mind for a long while, she was finished, absolutely, with it all, and wanted no word more with any human being.

Rachel answered quietly: "You've said some rather hard things. You mustn't feel that I'd ever try to make Roddy think badly of you. That's not fair.... I'm not very proud of myself, but you don't understand me. You've always been determined not to—and perhaps, in the same way, I've not understood you. We're different generations, that's what it really is.

"But over Roddy we can meet. I didn't love him when I married him, but I do now, and we're going to have a child.... That will make us both very happy, I expect. You love Roddy and I love him. You needn't be afraid that I'll harm his memory of you."

Her voice was trembling and she was very near to tears. She would have liked to have said something that would have offered some terms of peace between them, something upon which, afterwards, she might look back with comfort. For her that hostility seemed, in the face of death, so small and poor a thing.

But no words would come.

Her grandmother, in a voice that was very weak, said:

"Thank you, Rachel; that's a great relief to me. That's good of you ... and now, my dear, I think Christopher would say that I'd talked enough. Good night."

Rachel knew that this was their last meeting, that here was the absolute conclusion of all the years of warfare that there had been between them.

There was nothing to say.... She bent down and kissed the dry cheek, waited for an instant, but there was no movement.

"Good night, grandmamma," she said. "I hope that you'll be better to-morrow," then softly stole away.

III

The Duchess lay very still, watching the shadows as they crept across the fields. They were evening shadows now, for the sky, pink like the inside of a shell, had no clouds upon its surface.

She would not get up again; this evening should be the last to see her gaze upon the world. It was too fatiguing and all energy had flowed from her, leaving her without desire, without passion, without regret, without fear. Very dreamily and at a great distance figures and scenes from her past life hovered, halted, and passed. But she was not interested, she had forgotten their purpose and meaning, she did not want to think any more.

The splashing of the fountain was phantasmal and very far away.

The long black shadow crept up the field. She watched it. At the top of the red ridge of field, against the sky-line, very sharp and clear, was a gate, golden now in the sun. When the shadow caught it she would go to bed ... and she would never get up again.

She waited lazily, indifferently. The gate was caught; the last gleams of the sun had left the orchard and the evening star glittered in a sky very faintly green.

She touched a bell at her side and Dorchester appeared.

"I'll go to bed, Dorchester."

"Very well, Your Grace."

"I shan't get up again. Too much trouble." She turned away from the window and closed her eyes.

CHAPTER XII
RACHEL, RODDY, LORD JOHN, CHRISTOPHER
"'Everybody came in to dinner in the best of spirits.... Everything was
discussed.'"—Inheritance.

I

The Duchess of Wrexe died on the morning of May 2nd at a quarter-past
three o'clock. The evening papers of that day and the morning papers of the
next had long columns concerning her, and these were picturesque and
almost romantic. She appealed as a figure veiled but significant, hidden but
the landmark of a period—"Nothing was more remarkable than the
influence that she exercised over English Society during the thirty years that
she was completely hidden from it"—or again, "Although disease compelled
her, for thirty years, to retire from the world, her influence during that
period increased rather than diminished."

It must be confessed, however, that London Society was not moved to its
foundations by the news of her death. People said, "Oh! that old woman;
gone at last, I see. She's been dying for years, hasn't she? Quite a power in
her day ..." Or, "Oh, the Duchess of Wrexe is dead, I see. I must write to
Addie Beaminster. Don't expect the family will miss her much—awful old
tyrant, I believe ..." or "I say, see Johnnie Beaminster's old lady's gone? She
kept the whip-hand of him in his time.... Damned glad he'll be, I bet."

Two years earlier and it would not have been thus, but now there was the
War (daily the relief of Mafeking was frantically anticipated) and fine regal
majesty, sitting dignified in a solemn room, irritated the world by its
quiescence.

"What we're needing now is for everyone to get a move on. No use sitting
around." A few carefully selected American phrases can very swiftly kill a
great deal of dignity and tradition.

In the Beaminster camp itself there was an unexpressed disappointment.
They had grown accustomed to thinking of her as a fine figure, sitting there
where, rather fortunately, they were not compelled to visit her, but where,
nevertheless, she had a grand effect. They had known, for a long time now,
that she was not so well, but they had expected, in a vague way, that she
would go on living for ever. They had been making, during the last two
years, a succession of enforced compromises and now the crisis of her death
showed them how far they had gone without knowing it.

408

"Things will never be the same as they were...." And in their hearts they said, "We're getting old—we aren't wanted as we once were."

Meanwhile there was a fine funeral down at Beaminster. The Queen was represented, the Prime Minister, the Leader of the Opposition, all the heads of all the old families in England, artists and one or two very distinguished actor-managers (who looked far more sumptuous than anyone else present).... Everyone was there.

Christopher detected Mrs. Bronson and wondered what the Duchess would think of it if she knew: Brun, also, although Christopher did not see him, flashed upon them from the Continent, was present, neat and solemn and immensely observant. It was all admirable and worthy of the best English traditions.

"She was a fine figure," said the Prime Minister, who had known her and disliked her intensely. "We shall never see her like again," but his sigh was nearer relief than regret.

II

Christopher, three days after the funeral, went to have tea with Roddy and Rachel. He was a man of great physical strength and had never had "nerves" in his life, but he was feeling, just now, tired out. He had not realized, in the least, during all these years, the part that that old woman played in his life, and he found that his whole scheme of things was now disorganized and without vitality. It was vitality that she had given him, a tiresome, troublesome, irritating vitality perhaps, but, nevertheless a fire, an energy, a driving curiosity.

He would capture it again, his eagerness to investigate, to assist, to prophesy, but it would never any more be quite the same energy—everyone with whom she had had anything to do would find life now a little different....

Some weeks before her death Roddy had sent for him. "I'm awfully upset, Christopher," he said and then he had told him about the scene in his rooms and had begged to know the truth. "I hear she's much worse—she's had a stroke—I wrote to her and she hasn't answered me. Christopher, tell me truthfully, was it her comin' to me that day and all the kick-up and everythin' that made her so much worse?"

Christopher had reassured him—"Quite honestly, if she'd asked my leave to let her go out that afternoon I'd not have granted it. But as it turned out she wasn't a bit the worse. I saw her directly afterwards—she told me all about it. She was rather grimly pleased. Mind you, it marked, I think, a kind of crisis. As she put it to me she saw that afternoon that the whole scheme of things had gone out of her hands and that the new generation didn't want her—But I think she was glad to have it settled for her, she was tired of it all, her struggle to keep it had been much earlier.

"She just wasn't going to bother any more and she might have gone on in that sort of way for years."

But although he had thus reassured Roddy he was not, in his heart, so certain. He seemed to see a long chain of events (he dated his own observation of them from the time of Rachel's coming out), that had led both Rachel and the Duchess to the climax of their actual challenge one to another. It was not that that meeting in Roddy's house had been of itself so important, it was rather that the fates had selected it as a definite culmination of the struggle. That meeting stood for a sharp visualization of much more than the personal conflict.

She had been glad to go, he did not in any way see her death as a tragedy, but her departure had marked the opening of a new period, a new personal history for the remaining characters, ultimately perhaps a new social epoch for everybody—

Meanwhile he was happy about Roddy and Rachel for the first time since their marriage and, as he was a man who lived in the lives of his friends, their happiness meant his own.

He found Lord John with Roddy, Rachel was with Aunt Adela, but "would be back for tea." Lord John, rather solemn and awkward in black clothes, was demanding comfort and assistance from his friends. His trouble was that he did not miss his mother as fundamentally as he desired, and that, at the same time, life was now most terribly different. His brothers, Vincent and Richard, had instantly after the funeral adapted themselves, with gravity and assurance, to the new conditions.

Lord John had never adapted himself to anything, but had fitted his stout body into the soft places that life had offered to him and had been placidly grateful for their softness. Only once had he shown energy of his own initiative and that had been in the matter of his nephew Francis, and of that now he did not dare to think.

He could never, so long as he lived, forget the slightest detail of that horrible quarter of an hour with his mother when she discovered his iniquity—and yet, even now, he felt, obscurely but obstinately, that he had done right. Nevertheless he would never again take life into his own hands: upon that he was absolutely resolved. What he needed now was reassurance from his friends. He had always before found that life arranged itself about him in a comfortable way and he confidently expected that it would do so now, but meanwhile he must have kind looks and words from somebody. He was a man who hailed with joy the opportunity of bestowing affection upon a friend who was not likely, at a later time, to rebuff him. He had never been quite sure of Rachel—she was so strange and uncertain—but upon Roddy, helpless, good-natured, and a man of his own world, he felt that he could rely. He spent therefore many hours at Roddy's side, rather silent, smiling a great deal, playing chess with him, sticking little flags on the War Map.

At times, as he sat there, he would think of his mother, of the Portland Place house shortly to be sold, of a world altered and alarming, and then he would wonder how long the time would be before he might again take up his old habits, his old houses, his old comforts, and then his fat cheerful face would gather wrinkles upon its surface. "It's after a thing like this that a feller gets old—Richard and Adela and I—We'll have to make up our minds to it."

Christopher found them busied with the map, discussing the probable hour of Mafeking's relief. Lord John looked at Christopher a little anxiously, perhaps he was going to be down upon him! But Christopher was a very quiet and genial Christopher. He sank down into a chair with a sigh of comfort, waved his hand to them.

"Don't you mind me. I'm tired to death. Was up all last night with a case——"

"You see," said Roddy, "there's Ramathlabama. Well—Plumer lost a lot o' men there and they say his crowd have had fever too and there ain't much to hope for there—now Roberts——"

But Lord John's attention was distracted. He wished to be quite sure that Christopher did not regard him with severity.

"You look fagged out, Christopher."

"I am!" said Christopher, smiling.

"I'm feeling a bit done up, too. Think I'll take Adela abroad somewhere for a little."

"I should," said Christopher. "Excellent thing for both of you."

"Now where do you suggest?"

"Oh, anywhere different from London. Go on a cruise——"

"Adela's a bad sailor—wretched. I'm not very good myself."

They discussed places. Christopher was more than friendly. There had been occasions when he had been the stern family physician and had treated Lord John with some severity. Now there was implied a new comradeship as though they had passed through perils together and would have always between them in the future a strong bond of friendship.

John felt that the atmosphere at this moment was so friendly and comforting that he would not risk the disturbance of it.

He got up.

"Think I'll be going on, Roddy. Don't like leaving Adela alone. Rachel will be on her way here now, so I'll be getting back."

He was staying with Adela at a quiet little hotel in Dover Street.

"Well, good-bye for the moment, Christopher. Adela'd be very glad if you'd come in and see her. Come and have lunch with us to-morrow."

"Thanks, I will."

He stood, for a moment, looking out upon the park, warm and comfortable under the sun. He thought of Rachel. He had regained the old Rachel the other night at Beaminster—dear Rachel!

Rachel, Roddy, Christopher—how nice they all were! There was, he felt, a new feeling of security amongst them all. Yes, he really did believe that life, now, was going to be very comfortable and safe and easy....

"So long, Roddy."

He beamed happily upon them and went.

Jacob, the dog, came in from his afternoon walk, very grave, paying no attention to Christopher, but going at once and lying, full length, near Roddy's sofa, his head between his paws, his eyes fixed upon his master.

"What's happened to all your other dogs?" asked Christopher. "They must be missing you very badly."

"Oh, they're down at Seddon, got a jolly good man there whom I can trust—don't think they miss me. This beggar would though. Funny thing, Christopher—when I was goin' about and all the rest of it I thought nothin' of this dog, couldn't see why Rachel made such a fuss of it—now—why I don't know how I'd ever get on without it, so understandin' and quiet with it all too. Nothin' like a trouble of some sort for showin' who's worth what, whether they're dogs or people...."

"I hope the funeral did Rachel no harm," Christopher said.

"Not a bit of it. She'd had a last interview with the old lady and knew, after that, she'd never see her again. In a way she hasn't felt it, but in a way too I believe she'd like to have all the old time over again and see whether she couldn't manage it better ... she said to me she'd never understood the old woman until that last talk with her, not that there was much love lost between 'em even then. Was Breton there?"

"No—He scarcely could go, in the circumstances."

"Funny feller, Breton. What puzzles me is what did he go and give up Rachel so easily for? I couldn't tell you why, but that day he came here I was as sure as I was lyin' here that whatever there was between them was finished. I wouldn't have said what I did, seemed to take it so quietly, if I hadn't seen in a minute it was all over."

"Ah, you don't know Francis," said Christopher. "It's all romantic impulses that set him going—Rachel romantic impulse on one side, getting back to the family romantic impulse on the other. He knew if he went off with her that getting back to the family would be over for ever as far as he was concerned. He knew that he'd never cease to regret it.... John Beaminster coming to him gave him what he'd been waiting for, longing for. He seized it——"

"Yes, but it was more than that," said Roddy slowly. "It all lies with Rachel. He never got close to her any more than I've done. I know now that she's fond of me, but it's by the child I'll hold her and by my helplessness, nothin' else. And she'll have her wild moments when myself and everythin' about me will seem simply impossible, just as if she'd gone off with Breton she'd have had her comfortable domestic sort of longin's and hated him and everythin' about him. I believe Breton knew—just as I knew—that never tryin' to hold her was the way to keep her, and he'd have had to have her if he'd gone off with her....

"Anyway, Rachel wouldn't be so adorable if there wasn't a lot of her that no one man could master. But I've been given all the tricks in the game by bein' laid up like this—just when I thought I'd lost all worth havin' in life and never a chance of a kid again!... Funny thing, Life!

"But she's mine! Christopher, and no one can take her. Breton's got his idea of her; there is a bit of her that he stirred that I never could touch, but it don't matter—she's the most wonderful creature on this earth and I'm the luckiest beggar."

"She'll be quieter," said Christopher, "now that the Duchess is gone. They were always conscious of one another...."

"And now there'll be the kid instead. If he's a boy I swear he shall be the best rider, the best sportsman in this bloomin' old world—not that I'd mind a girl, either. I'd like to have a girl—just the time for a woman nowadays. Whichever way it is I'll be contented. Not, you know," he added hastily, "that I'm going to be a sort o' blessed angel with domestic bliss and never wantin' to get off this old sofa and the rest—not a bit of it—it's damned tryin' and I curse hours together often enough. Peters has the benefit of it. I wasn't born an angel and I shan't die one...."

"Nobody wants you to," said Christopher.

"Well, you needn't worry. But it's funny how I get talkin' nowadays—never used to say a word—now I gas away.... Well, cheers for the new generation, cheers for young Roddy Secundus.... Long life to him!"

"There's one thing," said Christopher, looking at him. "Whatever inspired you, that day you had the scene here, to behave to Frank Breton as you did? To give them both carte blanche—it wouldn't be the way of most husbands confronted with such a question—it was the only way for Rachel ... but how did you know her well enough? You'll forgive my saying so, your method as a rule is to drive straight in, let fly all round, and then count the bits."

"If you love anybody," said Roddy, with confusion and hesitation, "as much as I love Rachel you become wonderfully understandin'.... Look here," he broke off, "don't let's talk any more rot. Just drop all jaw about feelin's and such. There's been an awful lot of it lately."

He would say no more; they got the war map and, very happily for the next quarter of an hour, moved flags up and down its surface.

Then came Rachel and, after her, tea. They were a quiet but very happy company during the next half-hour.

"How's Aunt Adela?" asked Roddy.

"Very well, considering," said Rachel. "Of course she's confused and lost her bearings rather. She misses the Portland Place house more than anything, I think—she was there so long. But Uncle Vincent was right; it would have been very bad for her if she'd stayed in it.... She's quiet and depending a lot upon Lizzie——"

When tea was ended Rachel said, "Dr. Chris, I've got something to say to you. I'm going to tear you away from Roddy for five minutes if you'll come upstairs."

"Well, that's a nice sort of thing——" protested Roddy.

"I won't keep him." She took him up to the little drawing-room and as they sat there by the window together he thought of that day when he had told her the Duchess was downstairs with Roddy. They had all travelled a long way since then.

"There's a favour I want you to grant me."

"Anything in the world."

"It's about Francis—" She gave him the name with a little hesitation and with an air of restraint as though about the very whisper penalties could linger.

"You're the best friend that he's got—the best friend any man could have—and I want you to care for him, to look after him, to watch over him. I know," she went on hurriedly, "that you always have done that, but I want you to feel now that you're doing it a little for my sake as well as your own. I want you to be the one link that I've still got with him."

"But Roddy asked him— —" began Christopher.

"Oh yes! I know—Roddy was splendid. But of course that can't be. We can't meet, at any rate for years. Besides, that time is so utterly done with. There's only Roddy now for me in all the world. But I know, better, I expect, than you think, how weak Francis is, how much he depends upon what the people whom he cares for say to him—and so I want you— —"

"But of course," Christopher said. "He knows that he can count on me whatever happens—he's always known that."

He stopped and waited for her to continue; he saw that she had more to say.

"It's so strange," she said, staring, her eyes deep and black seeing into sacred places that were known only to her, "how grandmother's death has cleared, amazingly, the air. The motive for almost everything has gone. I didn't see— I hadn't the least idea—how all my thoughts and actions and wishes and impulses came from my sense of opposition to her. Francis saw that— knowing that we both hated her—and that was why I was so difficult with Roddy, because I thought that grandmother had arranged the marriage and had him under her thumb—I had no idea of the kind of person Roddy was."

"Nor had I—nor had anyone," said Christopher.

"That whole affair with Francis was in idea—always—more than in fact. I knew, and I believe that he knew, that it was simply a piece of wild rebellion on my part; and on his—well, he's like that, romantic, rebellious, responding in a minute to everything, but wanting, really, all the time to be safe and proper. That day we met in his rooms, we both knew, at heart, that something was missing—something one had to have if one was going to break away altogether. He was always a rebel by force of circumstances, never by real inclination."

She put her hand on Christopher's knee and drew very close to him. "Chris dear, I'm terrified now when I think of how near I was to absolute, complete disaster. If it hadn't been for Roddy's accident and for Lizzie ... Lizzie's been to all of us everything in the world.

"Do you remember once telling me about Mr. Brun's Tiger? I've often thought of it since and it seems to me now that to all of us—for Roddy and Francis and Lizzie and me—the moment of our consciousness came. Ever since that day when they carried Roddy back to Seddon each one of us has had to wait, just holding ourselves in.... But, you know, Dr. Chris, that's the secret of the whole matter. It wasn't I, or Breton, or even Lizzie or Roddy that defeated grandmother—it was simply Real Life. First the War, then Roddy's accident—Roddy's accident most of all. We had, all five of us, been leading sham lives, then suddenly God, Fate, Providence, what you will, steps in, jerks us all back, takes away from all of us what we thought we wanted most, puts us in line with the real thing—our Tiger, if you like. Grandmother simply couldn't stand it. Lizzie and Roddy are real—half of Breton and me, and most of grandmother unreal—Well, Lizzie and Roddy have just put things straight quietly.... Grandmother's generation saw things 'through a glass darkly'—They're gone. It's all going to be 'face to face' now."

Christopher looked at her, smiling. She was so young, so adorably young with her seriousness.

She broke in—"What rot I'm talking! It only comes to this, that I wish now, like anything, that I'd been nicer to grandmamma. One sees things always too late.... I'd like to have another try, to begin with grandmamma again, to be more tolerant, to hate her less. But I expect in the end it would be the same. She'd have had me tied up, without a will of my own, without a word to say!... that was her idea of controlling us all. It's over, it's done with—no one, I expect, will have her kind of power again.... But she was fine! I only see now how fine she was!

"No one, I expect, will have her kind of power again...."

Now she stood away from Christopher, looking at him and also beyond him, as though she were finally, once and for all, surveying, cataloguing that same power—

"She wasn't terrible, she wasn't fine, she wasn't really anything except a kind of peg for all sorts of traditions to hang on to. In herself she was just a plucky, theatrical, obstinate old woman. It was simply the idea of her that frightened us all. I remember the first time that I saw Yale Ross's picture of her—He'd caught all the ceremony and the terror. It was then that I had the first faint suspicion that she didn't, in herself, live up to the picture in the least.

"I suppose," she went on, coming up closer to him, "that that's why no one will ever be like her again—because no one will ever be taken in so completely by shams again, never by the empty shell of anything. But that's just how she influenced us—all of us. Myself, you, Lizzie, Roddy, Francis ... we were all mixed up in it—

417

"And then the first moment that we really came into contact with her she wasn't anything—wasn't simply there. Do you know, Dr. Chris, seeing her now, just an old sick woman, conscious that everyone was escaping her, I almost love her!... I do indeed!"

She sprang up and stood before him and laughed, crying—

"I'm grown up, Dr. Chris, I'm grown up! It's taken a time, but it's happened at last! Meanwhile I shall be the most perfect wife, the most perfect mother, and when the Tiger is restive there'll be the youngest Seddon to put it all into. Oh! What a child that child will be! Roddy and his impatience, me and my tempers——"

She laughed and for an instant her old fierce defiance was there then, as though some spirit had flashed, before his eyes, through the window into space and freedom it was gone. She herself proclaimed its dismissal.

"It's gone—it's all gone—Dr. Chris. I'm the happiest woman in England!"

But even as she spoke her eyes were wistful; half-seen, half-recalled, eloquent with a colour, a flame that was too fierce for her present world, hung before her the memory of a moment when, in a darkened room, she had caught a letter to her lips, had sunk upon her knees before a passion whose face she had scarcely seen but whose voice she had heard and still now, in her new life, remembered. She had had her moment ... the last strains of its dying music were still in her ears. She caught her breath, then, turning, dismissed it; and, standing back from Christopher, gave him her last word—

"But look after Francis. Be with him as much as you can.... He needs all that you can spare—He's got to be—he's simply got to be—the success of the family!"

CHAPTER XIII
EPILOGUE—PROLOGUE
"Third Apparition—A Child Crowned ..."

Macbeth.

I

Late on the evening of May 17th Christopher heard of the relief of Mafeking. It was too advanced an hour, he understood, for the town to display its triumph that evening. Let Christopher wait.

The following night Brun, whom he had not seen for many months, appeared. The clocks had struck nine and Christopher was finishing his dinner, when the little man, shining and dapper, pleased and impersonal, was shown in.

"Hullo!" cried Christopher; "thought you were abroad somewhere."

"I saw you at the Duchess's funeral. Of course I was there. What do you suppose? Meanwhile come out now and see your fine people make manifestations."

"Is there a noise?"

"A noise! Mon Dieu! But come and look!"

They went out together. Harley Street was silent and deserted and above it a night sky, scattered with stars, was serenely still. But, beyond the further roofs and chimneys, golden light hovered and a confused murmur, like the buzzing of bees, hummed upon space.

Through Oxford Street a great crowd of people was passing, but it was a crowd hurrying to find some other crowd. Oxford Street was plainly not the meeting-place. There was a good deal of shouting and singing; young men, five abreast, passed, girls with "ticklers" and whistles screamed and laughed and sang; merry bells were ringing, lights flared in the windows and now and again a rocket with a whiz and a shriek flashed into the sky and broke with a little angry splutter into coloured stars.

They crossed into Bond Street, down which other people were hurrying; sometimes a roaring echo of a multitude of discordant voices would be carried to them and then would be hidden again as though some huge door in front of them were swinging to and fro.

At the end of Bond Street, suddenly, as they might turn the corner of some sea road and, instantly, be confronted with the crash of a plunging surf, they met the crowd.

"Look out!" cried Brun, clutching hold of Christopher's arm. "We don't want to get drawn into this!"

Although they had apparently been walking quietly down Bond Street with no crowd about them, they now were pursued, upon all sides, by people. They raised themselves on to a doorstep, hanging there, bending their feet forward, and feeling that if the crowd in front of them were for a moment to give way down they would go!

Meanwhile, along Piccadilly, towards the clubs and Hyde Park Corner, a thick mass of human beings was pressing. This gathering seemed, of itself, to lack all human quality.

A face, a voice, a hand, a cry — — these things might now and again, as fish flash in a stream, detach themselves; sometimes a light from a flaring window or an illumination would fling into pale, unreal relief a bundle of faces that represented, at that instant, a piece of human history, but sank instantly back again into chaos.

One might fancy that this was no crowd of human beings, but some new, unknown creature, dragging its coils from the sluggish bed of some hidden river, stamping to destruction as it went.

Then as though one were watching a show, with a click, the human element was back again. There two girls, their hats pushed aside, their hair half uncoiled, their cheeks flushed, their eyes partly bold and partly frightened, were screaming:

"Oo're yer 'itting? Don't again then. Good old England! Gawd save — — "

It was not on the whole a crowd stirred only by national joy and pride. It may, in its units, when it first left its many homes, have announced its intention of giving "a jolly 'ooray" for our splendid country and our Beloved Queen, but, once in a position from which there was no returning, once in the hands of a force that was stronger than any felt before, it had forgotten the country and its defeats and successes. Only two courses open. Either admit fear, feel that the breath of you is slowly but quite surely in process of being crushed out of you, feel that your arms and legs are being torn from you, that your ribs are being smashed into powder and that your heart is being pressed as flat as a pancake, let then panic overwhelm you, fight and scream to get out and away from it, see yourself finally falling, trampled, kicked, your face squashed to pulp, your eyes torn out, your breath strangled in your body ... so much for Fear. Or, on the other hand arouse Frenzy!

Be above and beyond your body, scream and shout, rattle rattles and blow whistles, trample upon everything that is near you, smack faces with your hand, pull off clothing and scatter hats and bonnets, scream aloud, no matter what it is that you are screaming, let your voice exclaim that at length, at length, you, a miserable clerk on nothing a week, in the City, are, for the first time in your existence, the Captain of your soul, the ruthless master of a wretched, law-making tyrannous world.... So much for Frenzy!

Either way, be it Frenzy or Fear, the Country has not much to say to it at all. With every moment it seems that from the Circus more bodies, more arms and legs are being pressed and crushed and packed; with every moment the clanging of the bells is louder, the fire in the sky higher and wilder, the singing, the screaming, the oaths and the curses are nearer, the defiance that loss of individuality gives.

"Let's get back," said Brun. He turned, but, at that moment, someone from behind him cried, "Oo are yer shoving there?" He was pushed, with Christopher, half falling, half clutching at arms and shoulders, forward into the street.

They righted themselves, Brun fastened upon Christopher's arm, shouting into his ear, "We'd better go along with the crowd for a bit. We'll get a chance of cutting up Half Moon Street. Can't do anything else."

They were pressed forward. Now, received into the bosom of the crowd, they were conscious both of the human element and of the stronger composite spirit that was mightier than anything human, a creation of the City against whose walls they were now so riotously shouting.

Next to Christopher was a young man in evening dress; his hat had disappeared, his collar was torn, sweat was pouring down his forehead and at the top of his voice he screamed again and again:

"Good old England! Good old England! Good old Bobs! Good old Bobs!" Squeezed up against Christopher's arm was a stout body that looked as though it had once belonged to some elderly gentleman who liked white waistcoats and brass buttons. From somewhere, in obvious connection with these buttons, came a weak, breathless voice: "You'll excuse me hanging on so, sir. It's familiar—not my way—but this crowd ..."

A girl, with crimson face, leant against Christopher, put her arm round his neck, tickled his face with a feather; she screamed with laughter: "Oo-ray! Oo-ray—Oo-bloody-ray!"

"Look out, you swine!" somebody shouted.

"And 'e shouted out, did Bobs
Come along, you stinking nobs,
We will show you—"
Around them, above them, below them there tossed a whirlpool of noise, something outside and beyond the immediate sounds that they were making. Bells, voices, shouts that seemed to have no human origin, the very walls and stones of the City crying aloud.

Then, opposite the entrance to Half Moon Street another crowd seemed to meet them. There was pause. "Get out of it!" "Go the other way." "Damn yer eyes, step off it." "Go back, carn't yer?"

It was then that for the briefest moment and for the first time in his life Christopher was afraid. Someone was pressing into his back until surely it would break, some other was leaning, and driving his chest in, driving it so that the breath flooded his face, his eyes, his nose. Colours rose and fell; someone's evil breath burnt upon his cheeks. Light flashed before him in broad, steady flares.

"Brun, Brun," he cried.

"All right," a voice from many miles away answered him.

He was seized with the determination to survive. They thought that they could "down" him, but they should see that they were mistaken; his rage rising, he was no longer Dr. Christopher of Harley Street, but something savage, lawless beyond even his own control. He drove with his arms; curses met him and someone drove back into him and a ridiculous face with staring eyes that stupidly pleaded and a nose that was white and trembling and a mouth that dribbled at the corners came up against his.

"Keep back, can't you?" someone shouted.

"Brun, Brun," he called again, and then was conscious that bodies were giving way before him. His hand met a stomach covered with cloth and little hard buttons, and then coming against a woman's arm soft and warm, Christopher had instantly gained possession of his soul once more.

"Hope I didn't hurt you," he heard himself saying, then, some barrier of legs and bodies yielding, found that he was flung out, away, stumbling, in spite of himself, on to his knee.

He caught someone by the arm, and it was Brun.

"Good Lord!" said Christopher.

"It's all right," answered Brun. "We're in Half Moon Street. We're out of it."

II

Somewhere in the peaceful retirement behind the clubs they surveyed one another and then laughed. Brun—the dapper perfect Brun—had a bleeding cheek, a torn waistcoat, and a large and very unbecoming tear in his trousers. He was half angry and half amused—finally a survey of Christopher, with mud on his nose and his collar hanging from one button and revealing a fat red neck, restored his good temper.

"You'd better come back with me," said Christopher, "and be cleaned up."

They went back to Harley Street and half an hour later were sitting quietly in easy chairs, with the house as though it were made of cotton-wool, so silent and hidden was it, about them.

Both men were excited; Christopher had been changed by the events of the last few weeks, and Brun, if he had not been so personally involved, had seen enough to excite his most eager curiosity and speculation.

Brun's sharp little eyes, flashing across the tip of his cigar, sought Christopher's large comfortable face, fell from there over his large comfortable body, down at last to his large comfortable boots.

"Well ... First time I've seen a Continental crowd in England."

"Continental?"

"Always your Englishman, however excited and of whatever rank, knows there are things a gentleman doesn't do. Those people to-night had not that knowledge. Very interesting," he added.

Christopher peacefully smoked, his body well spread out in the chair, his broad rather clumsy-looking fingers clutching devotedly at his pipe.

"So you were at the funeral the other day?"

"I was. I expect I mourned her more sincerely than any of you. I'd never seen her, but she meant a lot to me—as a symbol. And I like symbols better than human beings."

He pulled his body together with a little jerk and leaned forward: "Christopher, do you remember, a long while ago, going into a gallery in Bond Street and meeting Lady Adela Beaminster there and Lady Seddon? It was just after Ross's portrait was first shown."

"I remember," said Christopher, nodding his head. "You were there."

"I was. I was there with Arkwright the African explorer man. I only mention the day because Arkwright was interested in Lady Seddon, wanted to know all about her, and I talked a bit, I remember. My point to him was that there was a situation between that girl and her grandmother that would be worth anybody's watching. I followed it myself for a while and then I lost it. But you're a friend of the family—tell me, Christopher, what happened between those two."

"Nothing," Christopher said, laughing.

"Oh, nonsense," Brun answered. "They were all in it. Something went on. Then Seddon had that accident ... Breton was in it."

But Christopher only smiled.

"Well, if you won't—n'importe—I have my own idea of it all. That girl was a fine girl, and the old woman was fine too—

"But how they must have hated one another!"

He chuckled; then sitting back in his chair, his little eyes on the ceiling, he said almost to himself—"Once, years ago, when I was very, very young and romantic—almost—just for a year or two I loved your Shelley. He was everything—I could quote him by the page.... He's gone from me now, or most of him has, but there was one line that seemed to me then the most romantic thing I had ever read and has remained with me always. It went— 'And we'll have fires out of the Grand Duke's wood'—It's in the letter to Maria Gisborne, I think—I've quite forgotten what the context is now—it's all pretty trivial and unimportant, but those were the days when I made pictures—I saw it! Lord, Christopher, how it comes back! The wood, very thick, very large, very black, no sun—very still, and the great house behind it, huge and white, with long gardens and green lawns and peacocks, and the Grand Duke, with his powdered wig, and diamond-buckled shoes, his gorgeous suit, his jewelled sword, his snuff and his wine, his silly little dried-up yellow face.

"Then the rabble—dirty, smelling, ill-conditioned fellows—breaking through the silence, tearing up the Wood, knocking down the palace, hanging the Grand Duke from a tree, last of all, setting the whole thing into the most splendid blaze!... Oh! of course that wasn't Shelley's context—his was all about boiling a kettle or something—but that's the way I saw it—just like that." Nothing stirred Brun like the sound of his own voice and now he was getting very excited indeed and was waving his hands.

"Yes," said Christopher placidly. "Very dramatic. What does it all mean?"

"Well, this. It seems to me that that's just what's been happening over here. Your Duchess is dead and instead there is to-night's crowd. The Grand Duke is gone and all that was his—now for the fires!"

Christopher, filling his pipe, paused, and then, his voice grave and serious: "Romantics aside, Brun, for a minute. Do you remember your Tiger idea you delivered to me once? I've often thought of it since. You said then that the reason why the Duchess and her times—the Grand Duke and his wood— had got to go was because their policy had been to give the Tigers of the world no liberty—to pretend indeed that they weren't there, and that now the time had come when every man should declare his Tiger, should give it liberty and, whether he restrained it or no, acknowledge its existence.... Well, now—what I want to know is this. What to your thinking is going to come of it all? I'm old-fashioned. I like the old settled laws and customs and the rest of it, and yet I'm not afraid of this new Individualism; but what I expect and what you expect to come of it all are sure to be mightily different things."

"They are," said Brun, laughing. "You see, Christopher, as I've often said to you before, you're a sentimentalist—people matter to you; you're concerned in their individual good or bad luck. Now none of that is worth anything to me. I observe from the outside—always. What I want to see is less muddle, more brain, less waste of time, more progress. I believe the loosing of the Tiger is going to bring that about. That's why I welcome it—I don't care one little damn about your individual—let him be sacrificed every time for the general wisdom. Your Duchess, she was good for her age. Now she is against progress. She vanishes. That crowd of to-night has swept her away.... There'll be a chaos here for a time—people like the Ruddards will mix things up; a woman like Mrs. Strode will destroy as many good people as she can. But the time will come; out of that crowd that we got into to-night a world, ruled by brain, by common sense, by understanding, not by sentiment and confusion, will arise.... May I not be with the good God!"

"'Sentiment and confusion,'" said Christopher, smiling. "That's me, I suppose."

"Well, you are sentimental," said Brun. "You're stuffed with it."

"Do you yourself ..." asked Christopher, "is there no one—no one in the world—who matters to you?"

"Nobody," said Brun. "No one in the world. I think I like you better than anybody; you're the honestest man I know and yet one of the most wrong-headed. Yes, I like you very much; but it would not be true to say that it would leave any great blank in my life if you were to die. Women! Yes, there have been women! But—thank the good God! for the moment only. The Heart—no—The Brain—yes——"

"Well, then," said Christopher, "that's all clear enough. It isn't very wonderful that we differ. People are to me everything. Love the only power in the world to make change, to work miracles; I don't mean only sensual love, or even sexual love, but simply the love of one human being for another, the love that leads to thinking more of your neighbour than yourself—self-denial.

"Self-denial; the only curb for your Tiger, Brun. I've been watching it in a piece of private history, all this last year and a half. There might have been the most horrible mess; self-denial saved it all the time. You'll say that all this is so vague and loose that it's worth nothing."

"Not at all," said Brun politely. "Go ahead."

"Well, then, the reason why I, old-fashioned and Philistine as I am, hail the passing of the Grand Duke with joy—and I cared for the old woman, mind you—is just this. I see some chance at last for the plain man—not the clever man, or the especially spiritual man or the wealthy man—but simply the ordinary man. When I say Brotherhood I don't mean anything to do with associations or meetings or rules—Simply that I believe in an age when a man's neighbour will matter to a man more than himself, when it won't be priggish or weak to help someone in worse plight than yourself, when it will simply be the obvious thing ... when, above all, there'll be no jealousy, no getting in a man's way because he does better than you, no knocking a man down because he sees the world—this world and the next—differently. That's my Individualism, my Rising City, and if you had watched the lives of a few friends of mine during the last year or two as I've watched them you'd know that 'Love thy neighbour as thyself' is the fire that's going to burn all the Grand-Ducal woods in the world in time."

Brun laughed. "You'll be taken in horribly one of these days, Christopher."

"You speak as though I were a chicken," Christopher broke out indignantly. "Man alive, haven't I lived all these years? Haven't I seen the poorest and rottenest and feeblest side of human nature time and time again? But this I know: That it's losing the thing you prize most that pays, it's the pursuit, the self-denial, the forgetting of self that scores in the material, practical world as well as the spiritual, heavenly one. That's where the Millennium's coming from. Brains as well perhaps, but souls first."

"We'll see," said Brun. "A bit of both, I dare say. Anyhow, it's the next generation that's going to be interesting. All kinds of people free who've never been free before, all sorts of creeds and doctrines smashed that seemed like Eternity. The old woods flaming already. Après la Duchesse!... But as for your Love, your Brotherhood, Christopher, I've a shrewd suspicion that human nature will change very little. Unselfishness? Very fine to talk about—but who's going to practise it? Every man for his own hand, now as ever."

"We'll see," answered Christopher. "I'm not clever at putting things into words. If I were to go along to the man in the street and say, 'Look here, I've made a discovery—I've got something that's going to make everything straight in the world,' and he were to say, 'What's that?' and then I were to answer, 'Self-denial. Unselfishness—Love of your neighbour,' he would, of course, instantly remind me that Someone greater than myself had made the same remark a few thousand years ago. He'd be right.... There's nothing new in it. But it's coming new to the world just because the laws and conventions that covered it are breaking. The Tiger in Every Man and Self-denial to curb it ... That's my prophecy, Brun."

Brun gave himself a whisky-and-soda. "No idea you were such a talker, Christopher.... But I'm right all the same."

He held up his glass.

"Here's to the Tiger in the next generation." He drank, then held it up again. "And here," he cried, "to the memory of the last Great lady in England!"

III

When Brim had gone it seemed that he had left that last toast of his in the air behind him.

Christopher was haunted by the thought of the Duchess, he felt her with him in the room; she stirred him to restlessness so that at last, desperately, he took his hat and went out.

His steps took him, round the corner, to Portland Place; here all was very quiet, a few cabs in the middle of the street, a few lights in the windows, the silver field of stars, in the distance the sky golden, fired now and again into life as a rocket rose shielding beneath its glow all that stirring multitude. Sounds rose—a cry, a shout, singing—then died down again.

He was outside No. 104. He thought that he would ring and see whether Mrs. Newton were in; perhaps she had gone to bed, it was after eleven, but, if she were there, he would take one last look at the Portrait before it was packed up and sent down to Beaminster.

Mrs. Newton unbolted the door and smiled when she saw him—"I was just going to bed—There's only myself and Louisa here—and the watchman."

"I won't keep you, Mrs. Newton," he said. "The fancy just took me to look at some of the pictures once more before they're packed up. Lady Seddon told me that a good many of them were to be packed up to-morrow; they won't look quite the same at Beaminster."

"No, that they won't, sir," said Mrs. Newton. "I shall miss the old house. Just to think of the years; and now, all of us scattered!"

She lit a lamp for him and he went up the stone staircase, found the long drawing-room, and there, on the farther wall, the Portrait.

428

The furniture, shrouded in brown holland, waited like ghostly watchers on every side of him. The huge house, always a place of strange silences and vast disturbances, multiplied now in its long mirrors and its air of cold suspense as though it were waiting for something to happen, showed its recognition of death and death's consequences.

But the Portrait was alive! As he held the lamp up to it the face leapt into agitation, the eyes were bent once again sharply upon him, the mouth curved to speak, the black silk rustled against the chair.

A host of memories crowded the room, he was filled with a regret more poignant than anything that he had felt since her death.

"She was fine! I miss her more than I had any notion that I would! She stirred one up, she made one alive!"

He put the lamp upon the floor and sat down for a minute amongst the shrouded furniture.

His mind passed from Brun's generalizations to the little bundle of people whom he knew—Rachel, Francis, Roddy, Lizzie Rand. To all of them the Tiger's moment had come; and out of it all, out of the stress and suffering and struggle, Rachel's child was to be born—instead of the Duchess the new generation. Instead of this old house, the hooded furniture, the anger at all freedom of thought, the jealousy of all enterprise, the slander and the malice, an age of a universal Brotherhood, of unselfishness, restraint, charity, tolerance ...

Perhaps after all, he was an old, sentimental fool. There had always been those at every birth and every death who had had their dreams of new human nature, new worlds, new virtues and moralities....

He looked his last at the Portrait—

"I'm nearly as old as you. I shall go soon. But I miss you ... you'd be yourself surprised if you knew how much!"

He took up the lamp and left her.... He said good night to Mrs. Newton and closed the door behind him.

Standing on the steps of the house he looked about him. Portland Place was like a broad river running silently into the dark trees at the end of it. There was a great rest and quiet here.

Southwards the sky flamed, the noise of a great multitude of people came muffled across space with the rhythm in it of a beating song. Rockets slashed the sky, broke into golden stars; the bells from all the churches in the town clashed and, from some great distance, guns solemnly booming rolled through the air.

Christopher, standing there, smiled as he thought of Brun's little picture.

Brun springing up, of course, at the right moment, to point his moral. Brun, who appeared, like some Jack-in-the-box, in city after city, with his conclusion, his prophecy, neat and prepared.

"And we'll have fires out of the Grand Duke's Wood..."

There was the Wood, there the mob, there the Grand Duke, dead and buried—

Christopher shrugged his shoulders; whatever Brun might say human beings were more than summaries, prophecies, conclusions.

As he looked towards the trees and felt a little breeze caress his face with, he could swear, some salt of the sea, he thought of the human beings who were his friends—Rachel, Roddy, Lizzie, Francis.

And then it seemed to him that, out of the trees, down the shining surface of Portland Place, a figure came towards him—the figure of Rachel's child.

Milton Keynes UK
Ingram Content Group UK Ltd.
UKHW032138041224
452010UK00002B/320